"An action-packed tale of classic good versus evil from the depths of human despair and heights of God's grace. Filled with romance, betrayal, love, loss and ultimate triumph."
— Tosca Lee, *New York Times* bestselling author of *Legend of Sheba*

"With crisp writing, relentless action, and breathless stakes, Amy Brock McNew's *Rebirth* will grab readers from the first page and keep them riveted until the last. Liz Brantley is sure to claim a spot on the list of favorite kick-butt heroines right alongside Black Widow and Buffy the Vampire Slayer. Fans of gritty urban fantasy won't want to miss this ride!"
— Evangeline Denmark, author of *Curio*

"Amy is a terrifically capable novelist. Her prose is a joy to read. And this character and story world are brilliant fun."
— Jeff Gerke, author of *The Irresistible Novel*

"*Rebirth* is a thrilling story, complete with love, loss, danger, and hope. The tension between Liz and Ryland is palpable, and the twists keep you guessing until the very end. This book will keep you on the edge of your seat and strengthen your faith, all in one whirlwind adventure."
— Avily Jerome, editor of *Havok Magazine*

"*Rebirth* has the sweet and spicy that romance readers love, with the action and intensity of spiritual warfare—but it is ultimately the story of a flawed heroine struggling to hold on to her faith and find her self-worth through the eyes of Christ that will touch this book's audience."
— Kat Heckenbach, author of *Finding Angel*

"An intriguing debut from a fresh new voice that merges the spiritual and the supernatural, creating an inventive Christian Fantasy in the style of Peretti and Myers. Plus, there's a bossy angel and a kick-butt heroine with a sword, folks!"
—Rachel A. Marks, author of *Darkness Brutal*

"*Rebirth* is a heart-wrenching, intensely spiritual novel. It definitely lives up to Amy's promise of guts on the page—she is refreshingly raw and honest with her story."
—H. A. Titus, author of *Forged Steel*

"Amy Brock McNew's writing style is engaging, honest, and unique. It feeds the part of me that loves fantastical stories, plus it adds a healthy dose of truth. I'd recommend her stories to anyone who enjoys gritty spec fic."
—Ben Wolf, award-winning author of *Blood for Blood*

"*Rebirth* was an action-packed story all the way to the end. I thoroughly enjoyed it."
—Sarah Armstrong-Garner, author of *Sinking*

"*Rebirth* cuts deep to the heart. It plunges you into a heart-wrenching story and makes you feel the intensity and agony the characters feel. Amy Brock McNew's descriptive wording leaves you breathless. Beauty at every turn of the page. The passion is prevalent throughout every scene, and the romantic elements warm your soul and make you long for more."
—Deanna Fugett, author of *Ending Fear*

Rebirth:

The Reluctant Warrior Chronicles

Coming Soon:

Reconciliation
Book Two of the Reluctant Warrior Chronicles

Resistance
A Reluctant Warrior Novella

Rebirth:
The Reluctant Warrior Chronicles

Amy Brock McNew

Love2ReadLove2Write Publishing, LLC
Indianapolis, Indiana

© 2016 Amy Brock McNew

Published by Love2ReadLove2Write Publishing, LLC
Indianapolis, Indiana
www.love2readlove2writepublishing.com

All rights reserved. No part of this publication may be reproduced, stored in a retrieval system, or transmitted in any form or by any means—for example, electronic, photocopy, recording—without the prior written permission of the publisher. The only exception is brief quotations in printed reviews.

Library of Congress Cataloging-in-Publication Data is on file at the Library of Congress, Washington, DC.

ISBN: 1-943788-06-5
ISBN-13: 978-1-943788-06-4
Library of Congress Control Number: 2016935229

Scripture taken from the New King James Version. Copyright © 1982 by Thomas Nelson, Inc. Used by permission. All rights reserved.

This is a work of fiction. Names, characters, incidents, and dialogues are products of the author's imagination and are not to be construed as real. Any resemblance to actual events or persons, living or dead, is entirely coincidental.

Cover Design by Sara Helwe (www.sara-helwe.com)
"Girl with Katana" Stock—vwalakte / DepositPhotos.com
Male Stock Model—Jason Aaron Baca, photography by Portia Shao

*To my Grandma,
Elizabeth Coffey*

She was a feisty, fearless, and loving woman who taught me that true strength isn't always physical.

I
By Your Side

Liz Brantley crash landed into hard-packed earth.

Air left her body in a sharp *whoosh*. Gravel bit the skin on her hands and forearms as she tried to roll herself out of the way of an oncoming blade. The demon's sword scraped the rocks where she'd been. She had the fleeting thought it was a good thing they were at a deserted gas station in the middle of nowhere.

Liz's strength dwindled. She dug deep and made it to her feet. Wobbling, she edged away from her repulsive opponent. The monster sported a malicious grin as it lumbered toward her. This one wouldn't stay down. It kept bouncing back like one of those punching clown toys.

For the umpteenth time, she wished she weren't facing the enemy alone. But now wasn't the time to think about that.

Liz drew on every reserve she had. She shifted to the left and slashed her dagger through the demon's flank. Without stopping, she spun and landed a vicious sidekick to its knee, buckling the leg. The small victory revived the flagging fighter. Her yell rang across the lot as she charged.

She slashed into gray flesh with a flurry of strikes. The demon's blade caught her twice, opening the skin on her back and arm. Blood flowed, and with it, her strength. Adrenaline flooded her veins, her body fighting to compensate. Soon, the creature lay at her feet. Though she had no idea how.

Liz braced her hands on her knees and sucked breath into her burning lungs. As she recovered, a black mist rose from below to envelop the fallen attacker. It soon dissipated, devouring the demon without leaving a trace.

At least they cleaned up after themselves.

She wiped her knife on the leg of her jeans and grimaced as the black ooze smeared. An explosion of heat blasted through her. Liz gritted her teeth. Yet again, she bore the remnants of battle. Why did this keep happening to her? Every fight more brutal than the last. Every enemy more difficult to defeat.

Dad called her abilities a gift. If that were the case, she'd rather return it.

If those angels would help instead of just watching... Bitterness tasted sour in her bloody mouth. It mixed with a fresh dose of heartache and abandonment.

Liz shoved the dagger into its sheath under her pant leg. She struggled to her beat-up Jeep, each step feeling as though she were dragging her feet through wet cement. Twenty-three years old, and the last six had been an endless war of fruitless battles. She'd passed done a few miles back. Drawing a dusty arm across her dripping brow, she sagged against the vehicle's door.

The rumble of an engine and a distinctive *pop* snagged her attention. Liz fought to lift her head as an elderly man eased his car into the lot. The rubber of a flat tire slapped the pavement. She watched as the man climbed out and hobbled his way to the offending tire. He kicked at it before opening his trunk.

As he struggled to drag out the spare, Liz spared a fleeting thought to helping him. But she hadn't slept, today's fight was the third in only two days, and there wasn't a part of her that wasn't either aching or bleeding.

The man turned to her, eyes pleading. "Miss, would you be so kind to give me a hand? I'm not as spry as I used to be." Apparently, his vision wasn't the best. He didn't seem to notice her wounds.

Two brawny angels flanked the man. Liz held back a snort. They'd probably end up helping him with his pathetic tire. An old man stuck in the middle of nowhere obviously ranked higher than a woman fighting for her life against demons.

Liz gave what she hoped was a sympathetic smile. "Sorry. I'm pretty beat up, and I gotta get home."

The man's shoulders sagged, and confusion swept his face. Liz couldn't bring herself to care.

She didn't even have a heart anymore. Not since three years ago, when she'd hightailed it out of town like a coward in the night. Leaving behind her family and everything she knew. Including the only man she'd ever truly loved.

Liz sighed and reached for the door handle. She froze. A breeze rose from nothing, brushing her skin like cool, green leaves. Electricity charged the atmosphere. She glanced at the trio surrounding the decrepit car. The angels were indeed helping the man, even though he didn't realize it. They still hadn't looked her way.

The fire of recognition zipped down her spine. A benevolent presence she'd sensed before wafted over her shoulder and wrapped around her like a warm blanket. The rustle of wings filled the air. The tips of pristine feathers danced in her peripheral vision.

He'd never shown himself. Never said a word. Even so, she had to admit it was kind of comforting having him with her. One whisper of his presence sent peaceful echoes throughout her soul. If he'd done more than let her know he was there and watching her fight, she might actually welcome his visits.

As it was, his showing up more frequently wasn't sitting well. It felt like an omen. Something was coming. Liz sensed it down to her toes. It was part of the reason she was heading home. To see if she could find some answers where all of this had started.

Her pulse filled her ears as the angel glided closer. She tried to turn to see his face, but her body wouldn't obey her commands. Liz opened her mouth to speak. No sound emerged.

Feathers brushed her back as he bent to her ear. "There is a time and a purpose for everything under the sun. Your gift is your purpose, and now is the time. Follow where the Most High leads."

As suddenly as he'd arrived, he was gone.

Liz's bones vibrated from the current that remained in the air after his departure. She stifled a scream as rage boiled and bubbled in her gut. Part of her had dared to hope the change she'd sensed meant the angels would start helping.

Boy, had she been wrong.

Liz jerked open the door, desperate to get away from the uneasy feeling the angel had left behind. She didn't have the time or patience to figure out riddles from a supernatural spectator who liked to watch her bleed.

She yanked a first aid kit out from under the seat. Liz wrapped the gash on her arm, noticing for the first time how deep it was. Still, it should be closed by the time she got to her destination. The cut on her back wasn't as bad. It stung like the dickens, though.

The fast healing included with her "gift" was definitely a perk, as were sharper senses and an extra dose of strength. Add in her naturally athletic build, and she could do more, handle more, than most men. Those advantages had been helpful in more than battles. Like when it came to the things she'd had to do to keep a roof over her head and food in her belly. Things she'd rather forget.

Sometimes, being a freak came in handy.

Liz shoved the box back under the seat.

You don't have to live this way.

"Whatever," Liz retorted, wishing she could silence the Voice that plagued her.

She swallowed the nausea churning in her gut. The Voice from above continually tried to offer hope, but she'd given that up a while ago.

She yanked a wrinkled tank top from her bag. After checking to make sure the old man wasn't looking her way, Liz fisted the hem of her ruined shirt. Stinging pain had her wincing as she peeled it from her skin where the blood had dried. She wiped the grime from her face with it and tossed it onto the passenger floorboard before carefully tugging the clean shirt over her head.

Every centimeter of her five-foot-nine-inch frame felt like a swing twisted too tight and let loose to spin. The jerky feeling blended her insides until she was sure she'd lose the potato chips she'd eaten for lunch.

Liz retightened her rust-colored ponytail, letting out a grunt as the movement riled her wounds. She found an ibuprofen in the glove box and swallowed it with a drink of flat Cherry Coke, then maneuvered onto the highway.

It was time to head into the lion's den.

Liz drew in a deep whiff of the humid country air. The drive to her Arkansas hometown nestled in the Ozark foothills had done nothing to calm her. The pines, the river water, and the aromas coming from the industrial bakery downtown weren't working their magic.

She turned down a road she could drive with her eyes closed. The road to her parents' house. Liz had never planned on coming back. Now here she was, crawling home three years later, broken and pathetic. Out of money and out of options.

Fire crept into Liz's blood at the thought of everything her most recent ex, Alex, had taken from her. The memory of him set off tremors in her muscles. Her windpipe tightened. She did the breathing exercises she'd learned off a website to find her calm. Alex was another reason she was headed home. It was one place he had no reach, no power.

Liz had always missed this place. She hadn't wanted to leave but thought at the time she had no other choice, not if she wanted to keep her loved ones safe and away from the danger that threatened her every day. Now something had changed within her. The need to go back had planted in her head and heart, refusing to be uprooted. She couldn't explain it. Like nearly everything else in her life. So, too tired to fight it, and, needing a refuge, Liz gave in.

She tried to grab on to a happy thought as she took in the beautiful countryside. It was a futile effort. She wondered if anyone would be happy to see her. Her parents would be, most likely, but she doubted others would be so thrilled. Especially Ryland Vaughn, the only man who had ever truly loved her. The one who knew all of her secrets and had still wanted her. The only man who'd done everything in his power to help her. The man she'd tried to replace with Alex.

Liz floated back to the present as she passed a small grocery store. A cluster of demons loitered around the front entrance, and a few angels were sprinkled throughout the lot. Each shadowed an unaware human. Most people went through their lives never knowing what was beside them, behind them, or leading their way.

Liz envied their ignorant bliss. Her abilities couldn't be shut off. She couldn't avoid the demons who seemed to be on a mission to destroy her. God had given her this curse, then Heaven had abandoned her. In return, she'd tried to get as far away from Him as possible.

Liz pushed the thought away as she wound down a long driveway and came to a stop in front of her childhood home. Mom stood from the rocker she'd occupied on the porch as Liz climbed out of the Jeep. The woman launched her small frame at Liz, and Liz caught her, her stomach dropping. A whirling dervish of emotion clogged her throat.

After a fierce hug, Mom leaned back and shoved her thick, mahogany hair out of her beaming face. "You're home! Finally, God's answered our prayers!" She clasped Liz to her again, squeezing as if she never planned on letting go.

Liz croaked out a response. "It's good to see you, Mom."

"Liz Whiz."

Dad's mellow baritone floated across the yard, a slight hitch betraying the depth of his emotion. Liz smiled at the nickname she hadn't heard in years. He'd given it to her when she was six or seven, declaring she was a little miss know-it-all, but smart as a whip to back it up.

His towering height made him intimidating to some. Not Liz. He wasn't "Pastor Brantley" with her. He was Dad. The tender-hearted giant she'd always adored. He took the porch steps two at a time and wrapped her in a bear hug.

Dad kissed the top of her head. "I'm so glad you're back."

Liz disengaged herself and took a good look at him. His strawberry-blond hair was now salted with flecks of gray. New wrinkles creased his face, and his eyes had lost some of their sparkle.

Because of me. A lump rose in her throat. "Hey, Dad."

Liz fidgeted. She climbed the porch steps and leaned against the rail, eying her boots. After a few moments of silence, she scanned the yard. Several angels ringed the perimeter. When she raised her head, Liz caught the knowing look that passed between Dad and Mom. Liz's eyes narrowed. Okay. Shouldn't they be preaching at her? Yelling? Something other than looking like two kids who were planning a fantastic prank?

"I'll go finish supper." Mom kissed Liz's cheek and bounced inside.

Dad settled on the porch swing. "So, rough morning?" He pointed at her jeans.

Liz tore her gaze from the angels scattered around the yard and glanced at the stained denim. Strange, Dad didn't appear surprised about her disheveled state. Or the tar-like substance smeared on her pants.

"Yeah."

While he and Mom knew what she could see, they didn't know about the constant battles. She wasn't about to offer the information.

Dad jerked his chin toward the yard. "How many are out there?"

His question threw Liz off balance. She had to get used to being around people who knew about her abilities again. "Eight." She rubbed her tired eyes.

"God's hand of protection. How exciting for you to be able to see it for yourself." Dad pushed the swing back and forth as though all were right with the world. He smiled and let his eyes rove over the area where the angels stood, almost as if he could sense them.

"Yeah. Blessing. More like a curse."

He shot her a reproving look. He sighed, then raised one eyebrow, watching her intently. "Ryland left town a couple of years ago. He checks in every other week or so. Seems to be doin' good with his computer business, though I don't really understand what he does."

Liz's chest clenched. What would possess him to bring up Ryland? She'd rather talk about the angels. "Good for him."

Mom poked her head out the front door. "All right, y'all, get in here. It's ready."

Liz leaped toward the door. Dad chuckled behind her. Mom's cooking and an escape from talking about Ryland? She was all over it.

Some things hadn't changed.

After supper, Mom shooed Liz out of the kitchen. "You go get settled." She took the towel and plate from Liz's hands. "It's been a while since I've had to clean up after you. I've missed it." Mom flashed her a brilliant smile.

Liz kissed Mom's cheek and headed outside to unload her stuff. Dad met her at the Jeep. Without saying a word, he grabbed a threadbare suitcase, the one he and Mom had bought for the trip to college she'd never made. He wedged another hand under a small box and tucked it to his side before striding into the house. Liz followed with her own armful, which sadly, between that and what Dad carried, was all she owned.

Dad set down his cargo beside her old bed. "Why don't you unpack later? You should go out and get some fresh air." He tugged her ponytail. "It'll be good for you, traipsing around in the woods again."

"That's actually a decent idea."

"I've been known to have those."

Liz smiled as she watched him slide into his chair and pick up his newspaper. He and Mom exchanged another odd look, and she couldn't help feeling they were up to something.

Liz slipped out the back door. She didn't have the energy for a run yet, but a walk sounded good. She breathed deep as she strolled down the trail that led deep into the forest. The aromas of rich earth, limestone, and pine soothed her. She'd missed those comforting aromas while living in Dallas.

Liz walked to her favorite spot by the crystal-clear creek and plopped down on a fallen log. The peace and quiet gave her time to think, which only brought up memories she'd rather forget. She couldn't seem to outrun the darkness inside. Even in the place that had always been her sanctuary.

Liz pulled her knees in tight. She wanted to punch something until her knuckles bled and the hurt leached out. Instead, she rested her head on her knees and tried to shut off the horror reel playing in her mind. To bring quiet to the raging storm. She swallowed against the lump in her throat and rubbed the gathering tears away with the back of her hand.

Serenity. Peace. A little bit of normal. That's all she wanted.

A harsh whisper in her mind said she'd never have any of those things.

The angel had not left her after relaying his message. He had simply veiled himself from her sight. His heart wept as he thought of what she had suffered and what lay ahead. Elizabeth's life was about to change. For better or for worse, for good or for evil.

Only she could decide.

Still cloaked from her view and her senses, the angel cradled the woman in his wings as her heartbreak spilled onto the ground. He loved her as a father would. The guardian would do everything in his power to see she was protected and taught well. He had watched over her for so long. Dispatching many demons before they could reach her.

Cheering her on when she bravely fought those allowed through the protective wall around her.

Yes, she was strong enough to face what lay ahead. She just did not know it yet. The choices she would make in the coming weeks would determine the course of the rest of her life. He could only lead her toward the right path and pray she chose to walk it.

"Please, Elizabeth," he whispered to her. "You are so close to your salvation. Do not plunge further into the darkness."

II
Desperate

Liz's skin prickled. He was watching her again.

She glanced over her shoulder as she stood in the checkout line at the supermarket, half-expecting him to be there. The angel who had spoken to her two weeks ago rarely left her side. Yet he hadn't spoken or shown himself again. His silent observation made her uncomfortable, but also soothed her in an odd way.

Liz shifted the basket filled with items Mom had requested and took a gander around the store. There were only a few angels present. No demons. For once, she was able to pull her shoulders out of her ears. The angels may not jump in to help, but at least they didn't attack. As she relaxed, a display of home decorations caught her eye. In particular, a small blue plaque. She stepped out of line to get a better look.

To everything there is a season, a time for every purpose under Heaven.

The words etched into the distressed wood plucked a chord. Liz had forced the angel's words from her mind. But as she read the verse, his little speech came rushing back.

Your gift is your purpose, and now is the time. Follow where the Most High leads.

Liz had run so far from God, to even think He had a plan for her seemed ludicrous. Or was it?

She returned to the checkout, plaque in hand.

Heading out the door with her bags, she stopped to pull on her sunglasses against the August sun. They slipped on her sweaty nose. She definitely hadn't missed the humidity.

Liz marched toward her vehicle. A semi-truck's brakes ground nearby. The sound raked across Liz's nerves like cheese across a grater. She skidded to a halt, teeth clenched. A cloud of diesel exhaust assaulted her nose. Liz closed her eyes, forcing away the nightmare the sound and smell of the big rig had dragged into daylight. The reminders of a past that had nearly killed her.

She held her breath until the truck disappeared down the highway.

Back in the Jeep, her heart wouldn't still. It whipped her blood into a frenzy. Liz swallowed hard and did her breathing exercises. That nightmare was over. She was back home. Safe. Alex couldn't touch her anymore.

Liz shifted into reverse and glanced at the rearview mirror. What she saw sent her jumping so high, she hit her head on the roll bar and slammed her knees into the steering wheel. The whipping in her blood returned to a fevered pitch.

A man stood behind her vehicle.

Piercing blue eyes fixated on her with single-minded focus. He stood inhumanly tall. A perfect face capped with white-blond hair took her measure. Liz stared, mesmerized. A tingle crawled over her skin. Recognition? No, not possible. She'd never seen him before. When she swiveled around to get a better look, he was gone.

She shook her head to clear it and started the engine. Liz chanced another look back. Nothing. As she backed out of the space, a whisper in her thoughts told her it wasn't the last time she'd see the platinum mystery man with the magnetic eyes.

Liz deposited the bus tub beside the dishwasher, then rubbed her neck as she ambled out to the dining room. The diner was a ghost town. *Ah, the Monday night rush.*

Hank, a member of Dad's church, had offered her the job, and she'd gladly accepted. Waiting tables was one of the few things, besides fighting, she was good at. Liz grabbed a broom and headed to a booth, pulling the table out to sweep under it.

She wished the time would go by faster. She'd worked a double today, and the early shift had been crazy. Not to mention, with all the people came a steady stream of demons and angels. That was the only thing about this job Liz didn't like. But she had to make money. To do that, she had to be around people. Thankfully none of the demons she had seen today had been in the mood to throw down.

Liz's nerves were shot, she was exhausted, and all she wanted to do was go home, get in her sweats, and bake a bunch of chocolate chip cookies. Baking cookies calmed her. This was one of those days she'd probably eat half of them before they made it to the oven.

The door chimed, and Liz jumped. An elderly woman entered, flanked by two of the brawniest angels Liz had ever seen. The woman smiled at Liz as she moved toward the front counter. The angels followed. They each gave Liz a cursory glance.

Liz ignored the guardians. "Hi. Have a seat anywhere, and I'll be right with you."

Liz couldn't help but smile. Love and kindness radiated from the woman. Liz had gotten used to getting whiffs of what people were feeling. It had started a couple of years ago and had gotten more intense as time passed. Liz chalked it up as one more oddball trait to add to her resumé.

"Thank you, but I called in an order." The woman's blue eyes twinkled. She tilted her head, inspecting Liz. "You're Pastor Brantley's daughter, aren't you?"

"Yes, ma'am." Liz peered through the window into the kitchen. Hank was boxing up the food, so she grabbed a bag and put in the side items the woman would need as well as a set of plastic silverware.

"I bet they're glad to have you home." The lady settled herself on a bar stool. Her bodyguards remained standing. "I'm Ruby Dixon."

"I'm Liz. Nice to meet you."

Hank rang the bell for Liz to pick up the food. As Liz moved to the pass-through, the heads of the two angels snapped up. They gave a single nod smacking of deference. Liz's brow furrowed, and she swiveled to see what had captured their attention. Her stomach slid upward.

It was the blond-haired watcher from the parking lot.

He sat at a table by the far window, his gaze locked on to her, his head cocked to the side. Amusement swam in pools of crystal blue. Liz stood with her mouth hanging open and her eyes as big as the sweet potato pies in the cooler.

"Are you okay, dear?" Ruby asked.

"Yeah. I'm fine." Liz tore her eyes away from the man. "Be right back with your supper."

Liz backed her way toward the pickup window, unwilling to let the blond man out of her sight. Halfway there, she tripped over a mat. With burning cheeks, she righted herself and snatched the to-go box from the warmer, then shoved it into the bag.

"Here you go." Liz handed the bag to Ruby, who dug in her purse. Liz held up a hand to stop her. "It's on me."

"Oh, I can't let you do that." Ruby shook her head and clicked her tongue.

"Really, it's my pleasure." Liz grinned. It felt good to do something nice for the woman. That was a feeling Liz hadn't experienced in a while. She dug for the small wad of bills in her apron and shoved some into the cash drawer.

Liz glanced at the table by the window. The man had vanished. She craned her head to see outside. No sign of him. What was he, a stalker who wanted her to know he was there? She didn't need any more weirdness in her life, and she had the feeling this guy would bring exactly that.

Ruby thanked her, snapping Liz out of her thoughts. The smiling woman stuffed a tip into the jar by the register. She surprised Liz by moving to the end of the counter and pulling her into a warm hug. "This is your time. God has big plans for you!" Ruby marched out of the diner, her heavenly companions hemming her in.

Liz stared, mouth wide open for the second time in the past few minutes. *Enough already. Time for what?* Her permanently short-fused temper flared to life.

She peeked into the kitchen. "Hank, I'm taking a break."

Hank's head didn't even pop up. "Okie doke."

Liz flew out the back screen door, letting it slam behind her. She plunked down on the picnic table under a large shade tree.

Clouds covered the moon, the only light wrestling its way out of the dingy fixture above the door. Liz leaned back and closed her eyes. The sticky evening breeze bathed her skin. Crickets started their serenade, and she soaked in the song. She stretched her neck side to side, trying to stave off a headache. The last thing she needed was another migraine. Typically, all it took was a few minutes, some controlled breathing, and usually something to hit, and she could calm herself. After a few more deep breaths, she pushed off the table.

A sound to her right caused her nerves to spring back to life. A raccoon was probably in the trash again. She grabbed a stick to scare it off. A moving shadow caught her eye, and her blood froze in her veins.

Definitely not a raccoon.

Then she saw it—the silhouette of a man standing by the dumpster. Liz gripped the stick tighter. Her entire body went on alert, adrenaline surging and muscles bunching. Crap. The one night she didn't have her knife. She usually kept it on her. Demons didn't keep a schedule, and she never knew when she'd need it.

Like now.

Liz shook out her shoulders and widened her stance. She could handle this guy. As he moved toward her, her certainty faded. *He's freaking huge!* Larger than most demons she'd faced. A swear erupted under her breath. Liz backed in the direction of the door. The shadow man matched her steps. Her mind scrambled to identify avenues of escape.

Too far from the building. He could catch her first.

Hank was probably doing count in the cooler now, so he couldn't hear if she hollered.

Liz decided to give this guy her best ferocious glare and hope he'd decide she wasn't worth the trouble. If not, she'd fight like a rabid bobcat. She found herself being thankful for her curse for once.

She slid her foot back and dropped into a fighting stance while he stood still and watchful. Like a sentinel guarding the gates. The standoff went on for several minutes. Why wasn't he making a move? Liz cocked her head to the side to examine him more closely.

The moon appeared and lit the night. By its glow, she could make out his hands clasped in front of him and a smile on his face. Not a drop of tension stiffened his body. He moved forward slowly, as if trying not to scare her. Liz drew in a sharp breath and staggered as he walked out of the shadows.

The mystery blond.

He loomed over her. His electric-blue eyes glowed in the dark, sapphire orbs ablaze. Expansive shoulders topped impressive arms. He had the rugged look of a warrior, yet features so pristine they were elegant. A peculiar aura encircled him, majestic and out of place in the rural setting.

Fear tickled Liz's senses, and the fleeting thought she had no control over the situation gave it solid purchase. Yet she was captivated.

"Who are you?" Liz couldn't keep the wonder out of her words.

"I am Arie-Chayal." His voice was oddly familiar.

The back of her neck prickled. "What do you want?"

"I am here for you."

Those five words snapped her chin lower and her shoulders back. Liz's grip tensed on her paltry weapon. "What's that supposed to mean?" She edged toward the door.

"You need not fear me." He followed her retreat. "I have been sent by the Master. It is time." He spread his arms and gave a small bow. "I am your guardian and teacher."

The branch fell from her hand to the pine needles below. Liz's head roared, and her stomach churned. It was him. The angel. That softening spot in her heart grew. Teacher? There was something she was supposed to learn to do? The thought simultaneously terrified and thrilled her. Yet her shield of cynicism refused to be laid down.

Liz put her hands on her hips. "Wait. All these years. Now all of a sudden, it's time. Time for what?" She glared at him. "Have I suffered enough and now I'm worthy?"

Heat boiled in her belly. God and His merry band of angels had hung her out to dry for years. Now, out of nowhere, an angel stood in front of her, saying he was her guardian. Where was he when she'd needed him? Where was God?

The blue of Arie-Chayal's eyes slid from flame to ice, and his easy stance disappeared as he stiffened. Liz went back on guard. The sprout of fear within her punched through and shadowed her anger. He opened his mouth, but before he could say anything, the back door opened.

"Liz? You okay?" Hank's round head peered around the door. He didn't acknowledge her visitor.

Liz swallowed hard. "Yeah, sorry. I thought there was a coon in the trash."

"All right. Come on in, and we'll close up." He disappeared back into the kitchen.

When she turned around, the angel was gone. "Arie-Chayal?" No answer. Liz waited a bit, then went inside.

Hopefully, he'd be back. At least this time he'd given her a bit more information. The answers she craved were possibly within reach. God had sent her an angel. Maybe He did care. A hesitant smile crossed her lips.

A smile born of hope once abandoned.

The demon Markus seethed as he watched Arie-Chayal converse with Elizabeth. Thankfully the angel hadn't detected Markus or, if he had, hadn't bothered to confront him. As much as Markus thrived on a good row, tonight he desired information more.

This was a pivotal meeting. It meant the other side was moving forward. It was the first contact of this type Heaven had made with the woman, and Markus needed to observe how the little warrior reacted.

He'd put too much time in to her these past few years and couldn't have his effort wasted. If Heaven was stepping up its game, so must he. He wouldn't let this one get away. Judging by this interaction, it seemed she still had plenty of rage and doubt controlling her. That he could use.

Markus watched Elizabeth until she went back into the diner. Then he took flight, plans swirling in his mind for the chaos he was about to rain down on her.

Oh, this was going to be more fun than he'd had in centuries.

III
Make a Move

Nothing. Five days of nothing.

Liz tried to ignore Arie-Chayal's continued silence and focus on getting ready for church. She absently flipped through her makeup case. Her desire for answers commandeered her brain. A fire had been lit, and only the explanations she sought could extinguish it.

The angel hadn't answered, even when she'd begged. Still, she couldn't stop herself from trying again. "I know you're there, Arie-Chayal. I can sense you, you know." She swiped gloss over her lips and waited. "Fine." Liz shrugged, feigning indifference.

She tossed the gloss onto her dresser. Liz twisted her curls into a semblance of order and checked her reflection. It'd do. Grabbing her purse and keys, she flew out the door.

She sneaked in as the music minister, Dylan Skaggs, strummed out a song on his guitar. Liz waved at his wife, Shelley, who she knew from school. They'd spent a little time together since Liz had been back, and, to Liz's surprise, it was comfortable. Friendship, especially with other women, was a foreign concept to Liz.

Liz squirmed in her seat all the way through Dad's sermon. She crossed and uncrossed her legs. She dug in her purse for a mint.

The buried desire for redemption scratched for the surface. Liz picked at her nails, blinking away tears. She never cried, and she certainly wasn't going to start in public.

Liz felt like a cartoon with an angel on one shoulder and a devil on the other. The Voice cranked up the volume, promising grace and forgiveness. The other side whispered in her ear as well. *You're beyond help. You might as well embrace living in the shadows.*

Dad gave the altar call. Moisture beaded on Liz's forehead. The battle between the two factions revved up. One saying, *Run to the altar*, the other screaming, *Run for the door*. Liz was so stinking tired of being ripped apart.

The Voice butted in. *Let me hold you together.*

Several people made their move down the aisle.

I can't. She'd hurt too many people. Done too many unforgivable things. She'd never be able to make it right.

Liz breathed a sigh of relief when service ended. She worked her way through the crowd toward Shelley. She needed to talk to someone else to drown out the voices in her head.

In her rush, she ran smack into a man exiting a few rows ahead of her. Her eyes traveled up, finally meeting his. *Wow. Hello, beautiful.* She'd never thought of a guy as beautiful before. Wavy, coal-black hair brushed his collar. Chocolate eyes swam with mystery. They complemented an olive complexion, making him look Mediterranean and exotic. Yeah, "beautiful" fit.

He flashed her a devastating smile. His body brushed her arm and hip as he passed. The contact sent chills skittering up her back and fire sparking across her skin. She stared as he ducked out the door. She'd avoided men at all costs since Alex, but this one captivated her. Liz stood there in a daze until a thin, tan arm draped over her shoulders.

"Hi, Liz!" Shelley was on the perky side. Blonde and slim, Liz wanted to hate her, but she had a sweetness about her that rivaled sugar. How could you hate that?

"Hi. Who was that?" Liz pointed out the door where the guy had disappeared.

"Oh, Blake? He's in town for business. Seems like a good guy."

Liz nodded, his image stuck in her head.

Mom jolted her out of her daydream. "You were late."

"Sorry." Liz wrinkled her nose.

Mom nodded and focused on Shelley. "Y'all are still coming for dinner, right?"

"Oh, definitely."

Two hours later, they'd polished off Mom's chicken and dumplings and had cleaned up the kitchen.

Shelley grabbed Liz by the hand. "Let's go for a walk."

"Okay."

Liz was sure Shelley wanted to talk. While she wasn't looking forward to hearing the same sermon again, she knew Shelley only kept going on about it because she cared about Liz. Liz hoped she could redirect the conversation. As it turned out, she didn't have to worry. They walked mostly in silence, Shelley only commenting on the beauty around them and how glad she was to have Liz back.

When they stopped by the creek, Shelley squeezed her friend's hand. "Can I pray for you?" She tugged Liz to sit on a huge rock.

That was it? Shelley just wanted to pray for her? She was so sincere, Liz didn't have the heart to turn her down. "I guess. Sure."

The prayer was beautiful, and after Shelley said amen, Liz smiled. "Thanks, Shelley. I—" The words died on her tongue. An unwelcome prickle raised the hairs on the back of her neck, and alarm shot through her like a jolt from a Taser.

Something watched them. Something evil.

Liz sprang to her feet and whirled around, looking for the source.

"What's wrong?" Shelley stood behind her, a hand on Liz's arm.

"I thought I heard something." She scanned the woods. "Probably just a deer." Liz forced a smile.

Liz's smile died as evil collided with her. The sensation felt like cement blocks landing on her chest. It emanated from a single source. One more powerful than any she'd come across yet. A malevolent whisper rode the breeze. Liz couldn't make it out. But the voice—had she heard it before?

"Let's head back to the house," Liz suggested. "Dylan's probably ready for his Sunday nap." She tried to joke to ease the tension.

A protective urge welled inside of her. She had to keep Shelley safe. Liz should've known this would happen. She should have stayed gone. If only she'd ignored the urge to come home. Ignored the Voice that guided her in the direction of home, this wouldn't be happening.

"Yeah. He's likely asleep on your mom's couch." Shelley laughed.

As they started down the trail, a figure bathed in shadow darted between the trees ahead. Liz glanced at Shelley to make sure she hadn't seen.

The woman chattered away. "He gets cranky when he doesn't get his Sunday nap. Like an old man. I keep telling him he's only twenty-five and shouldn't be so set in his ways."

The women cleared the woods, and Liz chanced another look back. An ominous figure stood in the path they'd traveled. The sight before her drank the rage right out of her and sucked the strength from her legs.

Magnificent black wings unfurled from its back. Burnished bronze armor encapsulated its body. Well-defined muscles rippled beneath leathered, charred skin. Terrifying power exuded from the creature. What demanded her attention, though, were the eyes. Red and shimmering, they impaled her. They called to her without words. Malevolence rolled off the demon, and even the accompanying darkness beckoned her forward. It was terrible and beautiful, a shadow of its former celestial self.

Liz's heart hammered, trying to spring free. Her body trembled. The demon's voice pierced her consciousness.

Come to me.

The truth pummeled her. She knew where she'd heard this voice before. It had whispered to her while awake and had screamed at her in her fitful sleep.

Ice careened through her veins, ripping the vessels along the way. Before, she'd thought the voice was her own subconscious, reminding her she wasn't good enough. That there was evil inside of her. But it'd been him all along.

What terrified her more was that his pull was so seductive. She fought her own body to keep from running to him, despite the knowledge he was the enemy and would likely relish the idea of ripping her apart.

Elizabeth, come to me. His beguiling tone lanced her brain. *Don't resist.*

"Liz?" A frown creased Shelley's brow. "You okay?"

Liz ignored her. The demon's words echoed in her head. A fierce urge to meet the challenge she saw in his eyes rumbled through her system. She took one step forward, and an invisible hand clamped on to her shoulder. Arie-Chayal. The restraining touch jerked her back to her senses.

Liz answered Shelley. "Fine." Liz forced another smile and headed for the house, tossing a glance over her shoulder. The demon filled the path, so still, even the air around him held its breath.

He was waiting for her.

Liz had always tried to avoid the demons. Any confrontation came out of necessity. And she'd never before felt a lure from one of them. Yet, here she was, wanting nothing more than to go marching after the most ferocious demon she'd ever seen.

She must have a death wish.

Liz hustled Shelley into the house. Once Shelley and Dylan had gone, Liz stood on the porch and eyed the trail.

The demon remained in the same spot, his eyes taunting her. The angel's guiding hand wasn't going to dissuade her this time. Her rage at the demon's audacity and the intrigue he held for her overshadowed her fear.

Liz was done. She was sick of being at the mercy of these things. Sick of not having a normal life. Done waiting for Arie-Chayal to show his face and answer her questions. The flames of fury consumed her. Caution disintegrated to ash.

A lazy, victorious smile widened the demon's lips.

Liz leaped off the porch and forged straight toward him. Every instinct of self-preservation, every bit of common sense, fell under the haze engulfing her.

Warnings from an unseen force peeled out. Invisible hands reached for her.

"Elizabeth, stop. Do not do this. Please, turn back now."

She ignored them. Heaven wasn't making a move, so she would. Things were going to change. Today. Half of her hoped the demon would put her out of her misery. Anything was better than the suspended animation she lived in.

Even death.

IV
Rebirthing

Markus laughed as Liz stomped toward him. "That's it. Come to me. To where you belong."

Rage billowed around her in the form of an opaque cloud. He inhaled, indulging in the dark aroma. Markus had seen this cloud over her many times. He was more than happy to use it for his own purposes, to feed it until it devoured her.

He had never let her feel the full impact of his power before. He'd always kept a portion cloaked during his visits to her. This time, he wanted her to know who he was. To experience the power she could have. To feel the darkness they had in common. To know she could never defeat it, only succumb to it.

"You have no place here, demon!" a voice boomed behind Markus.

"Arie-Chayal." Markus twisted his sword in his clawed hand. "I'd hoped you'd miss the party. But I should've known. You've always been a pain in my—"

"Remove yourself! I command you on the authority of the Holy One." The angel emphasized the order by drawing his own sword.

Markus shrank back from the radiance emanating off his opponent. He had no choice in this moment. His time would come, though. He'd be allowed access to tempt her soon enough. For now, he'd acquiesce. As much as it galled him to do so.

"You won't always be able to keep her from me. She is mine, *brother*," Markus taunted as he vanished, leaving a foul, sulfuric stench in his wake.

Another mammoth form, bathed in brilliant light, materialized on the path, and Liz ground to a halt. Her mind shuddered to a stop a second behind her body, and she stood in silent awe. After what appeared to be a heated argument, the demon evaporated.

It took her a few seconds to recognize the remaining being as Arie-Chayal. His skin glowed, opalescent. In contrast to the demon's charred feathers, Arie-Chayal's wings exhibited a luminous white, edged with bluish flame. His cerulean eyes shimmered. Brilliant silver armor encased his torso. Liz couldn't bear the brightness and looked away.

"What, pray tell, were you thinking?" His stern voice broke her trance.

"I-I'm...well, I was—" Reeling from the vision before her and feeling foolish, Liz hesitated. Stubbornness won, and she lifted her chin. "I wanted answers." She winced at the whiny sound in her voice. No way was she telling him she'd been unable to resist the demon's pull.

"Answers?" He grunted. "The tongues of devils spew lies. He would have toyed with you, then killed you." The angel's eyes narrowed. Concern swirled with righteous anger and wafted in her direction.

The light around Arie-Chayal dimmed, and Liz met his blazing stare. "I'm sorry."

"Markus is the commander of one of Lucifer's greatest legions. One of the most ferocious beings in existence." He paced, his face contorted. "And you, rushing in without a thought!" Arie-Chayal shook his head and raised his eyes to Heaven before commanding her gaze again. "You are undisciplined, impulsive, and utterly at the mercy of your emotions." He stalked toward her.

Liz stumbled backward. Her pulse skipped a beat as the words "avenging angel" crossed her mind. Yet when he took her by the shoulders, gentleness resided in his touch.

Liz's brain snapped to attention. "I'm sorry. It was stupid. I just want it all to stop."

Arie-Chayal lifted her face with a tender hand. "Elizabeth, there is no end to this. Not for you, not in this life. They will continue to come because you were born to fight them."

Liz stared. "What?" Her throat constricted.

"The Father has imbued a number of humans throughout history with talents, gifts. These gifts carry grave responsibility. They are to be used in battling the darkness that plagues the earth. You are one of that select number."

Liz dropped to her knees as the implications of his words snuffed out her strength. She wasn't sure she wanted those answers now.

She looked up at Arie-Chayal. Pity swam in his eyes. He wanted to spare her. Liz's blood heated to boiling. If he wanted to spare her so badly, why didn't he? She didn't need or want his pity. What she needed was help. A way out of this.

"I don't want this! I didn't ask to be a freak!" Her voice rose as she did. She glared at the angel and shook her head violently. "No way. Let someone else do it. I'm out." Liz spun back to the trail.

Arie-Chayal grabbed her arm and whirled her around. The ground shook beneath them. A sudden wind teased her curls.

His voice took on an arctic edge. "No one else can fulfill your calling. God decides your purpose and designs you to accomplish it. If you choose to deny that call, the consequences, though of your own making, will be dire." His tone softened a bit. "As you have already experienced."

Terror exploded in Liz's gut. "I can't do this." The admission slipped from her lips. She wasn't strong enough. And man, was she screwed up. God couldn't possibly want her. "This is a mistake."

"It is no mistake. And no, you cannot do this on your own. The Master will equip and empower you." Arie-Chayal's hold on her arm loosened. "You will do more than you could ever imagine. But first, you must give yourself over to Him. You must accept your calling."

Liz closed her eyes. She wanted to believe. Wanted to be better, to be more. Suddenly, a picture came into focus, like shards of shattered glass, heated and melding back together. She saw a bridge across a bottomless chasm. It was the chasm she'd created between herself and the One who waited on the other side. Liz looked across the expanse. He extended His hand, love and pleading in His gaze.

Was it really possible God still wanted her? Had a calling just for her? She was damaged. Broken into so many pieces, even God couldn't put her back together. Now this angel challenged those beliefs. Would God bother to send Arie-Chayal if she really were too far gone?

The answers stared her down as the figure across the abyss continued to reach for her. Then the vision faded.

Her eyes snapped open.

"This can't be real." Sure, her life was chock-full of weird. She'd never had a vision before, though. Was that even what it was?

"Yes, I promise it is real." Arie-Chayal's hand slid to her shoulder. "Accept Him, and He will accept you. Just as you are."

Could she change? Liz had felt it happening to some extent already. Her heart softening. She wanted out of the abyss threatening to swallow her whole. To extract the darkness coating her soul. To be rid of whatever had drawn her to the demon.

So she latched on to the hope being offered.

She had nothing to lose.

Peace swirled around her, imploring her for entrance. The air crackled. Angels appeared and circled Liz and Arie-Chayal, forming a wall of protection. Liz didn't want to fight it any longer. If healing were truly being offered, she wanted it.

Liz Brantley finally gave up control.

Liz's knees hit the dirt again, all of that pain spilling onto the pine needles beneath her. "I can't do this anymore. I can't live like this. I need help. Please!"

Liz relinquished the madness and agony that had twisted her into something unrecognizable. Her words jumbled. She wasn't sure what came out of her mouth. It didn't matter. All that mattered was she let it go. Bonds fell from her heart, chains snapping with an audible pop. Light speared the darkness inside, slicing it to ribbons.

It was a strange sensation, being reborn. Empty, yet full. Broken, yet healed. She gave herself over to it. Let it wash away the blackness. Those tiny pieces that made up her fragmented heart and soul fused into a cohesive whole. A patchwork, for sure, but the fissure lines would diminish.

Her healing had begun.

She had no idea how long she'd been there, but Liz finally rose from her altar on the forest floor and gazed into the shining face of her guardian. He gathered her into his arms. A song of praise exploded from his lips and those of the other angels surrounding them. Shock rippled through Liz's body. His embrace and the song were peculiar, yet comforting, so she relaxed in the warmth. Iridescent tears of joy landed on her cheek from Arie-Chayal's eyes and mingled with her own.

Liz knew, with a surety born of surrender, she could face what lay ahead. A new vigor fizzed and popped within her. Light and hope. There was still work to be done inside, and she was still scared. But now she knew she wasn't alone. Never had been.

Arie-Chayal brushed her face with his velvety wing. "Do not fear, young one. The Lord of Hosts holds you in His hands. He will fight for you." He stepped back. "It is time to receive your anointing."

Liz cocked her head as he produced what appeared to be an ancient horn from under his armor. He twisted off the cap. A substance that looked like golden honey poured into his hand. Oil. An actual anointing. Nervous energy curled in her stomach. Arie-Chayal put his hand on her forehead, saying something in a language she didn't understand.

A bolt of invisible lightning zapped her between the eyes.

Sparks shot out in every direction, emanating from her fingertips.

Liz was carried upward on the embers. Her body tingled as if electricity had been injected into her. Power coursed through her veins. The liquid fire seared every vessel along its path. She floated on the swell. That familiar Voice whispered to her.

"I love you, My precious daughter. My warrior. Welcome home."

The One she'd abandoned now cradled her in gentle arms. Suspended mid-air, Liz basked in the sensations swirling within her. Then the power began to ebb, and the sparks, diminish. Her feet touched solid ground. A twinge of sadness seeped through her. She could've stayed in that embrace forever.

Arie-Chayal stood next to her, his smile a shining beacon. Liz's head spun, and she reached for him as she pitched forward. Her knees buckled. The angel held her close, never letting her fall.

"Sit for a moment." He maneuvered her to a fallen log.

"That was amazing! Like it was a part of me. The power, I mean." She struggled to catch her breath, the surge still rippling in her blood.

"It is a part of you now. He has given you something few experience."

Her head felt impossibly heavy. It was all she could do to stay upright. This whole day had been more than she could process in her current state.

The angel must have sensed her fatigue. "Go home. Rest. Spend time in prayer and remain vigilant. Our enemy will not be pleased with what has happened here."

She was too drained to worry about what he meant. He moved to leave, but Liz caught his elbow. A thought pierced the fogginess in her brain. "Hey, what do I call you?"

He crinkled his brow. "My name is Arie-Chayal."

"I know, but that's kind of a mouthful." Liz saw his head tilt and one eyebrow raise. "Am I supposed to address you a certain way? I mean, you are my guardian or…whatever."

He shook his head, not comprehending, and she let out an exasperated sigh. Apparently, she'd have to instruct her teacher on a few things.

"Can I just call you Arie?"

He stared for a moment, then nodded once. "That would be acceptable." The next second, he was gone.

Markus stood a good distance away, forced there by the small army of those he once called brothers. His thoughts oozed venom as he looked from the guards to Elizabeth. He turned to the hunched imp at his side.

"Tell the master we're moving forward. She has returned to Him." He spat the words. "For now."

The imp disappeared, and Markus returned to watching Elizabeth. Disgust curled his lip. He was surprised she'd succumbed to Arie's influence this quickly. She'd been so consumed with anger and fear, Markus had thought it inevitable she would come to his side. He should've tried harder to keep her from making it home. Neutralizing her was critical. It had to be done before she realized the power she could wield and the role she was destined to play. A different approach was in order, and he already had a plan in motion.

He always had a backup.

His second-in-command, Kade, stood at his right. "What now? Slit her throat and be done? We were to bring her over or kill her. Looks like it has been decided."

Markus exhaled forcefully. Kade was a deadly warrior. However, he'd never been adept at strategy. He was a "kill first and never ask questions" type. It made him a deadly assassin.

"No. If we move in for the kill now, we'll have heavenly warriors all over us."

"You backing down?" Challenge dripped from Kade's words.

Markus scowled. "There are rules of engagement. I'll have my chance, and she'll be dealt with." He needed to get Kade reassigned. The damned warmonger had been after Markus's position for eons. "I may yet be able to turn her." Markus wasn't about to reveal his plans to Kade.

He thought again of how he'd be allowed to try to persuade her. A predatory smile creased his face. Free will. It was a beautiful thing. As his target walked into the house, Markus headed for the underworld while Kade snarled at his heels.

V
Like a Machine

If Liz thought she had extra juice before, it paled in comparison to the mojo crackling along her muscles and pumping through her blood now.

When she lifted the five-gallon bucket, water sloshed out, and the whole thing nearly went flying through the air. It seemed weightless. Liz glanced around the diner to be sure no one had seen her little display of strength. A grin tickled her lips. This would sure make cleaning easier.

The power sizzled, boosting her like a supercharged engine. Every sense she owned was more acute. Everything was more brilliant. Richer, deeper. She even healed faster than before. She'd made that discovery when she was slicing lemons the other night and filleted her finger.

Yet a hint of fear knocked around in the back of her brain. What if it was too much to handle? Plus, she still didn't think she deserved it.

Liz's mind wandered as she cleaned. She hadn't seen Arie since their encounter in the woods last Sunday. But she wasn't worried. This time she knew to be patient, and he would appear when he was ready. Or ordered to. Or however that worked. It didn't stop her from fretting. Liz scrubbed the bar with a vengeance. What was next? What was she supposed to do until Arie showed up? She hadn't even seen any demons lately, so there'd been no opportunity to try out what she'd been given.

"Liz?" Hank poked his head out the kitchen door.

Liz jumped. "Yeah?"

"You're gonna scrub that counter down to the wood, girl. Why don't you move on to the trash?" He laughed and ducked back into his haven.

Liz stared at the shiny surface. She tossed the sponge into the bucket next to her and moved to gather the trash.

It made her nervous the demons hadn't attacked. Which sounded strange, but she could sense them lurking, watching. Her sense that trouble was brewing intensified. She could practically smell it in the air.

Liz headed out the back door, bag in hand. *If Arie would just show up and—* Her thoughts screeched to a halt when she collided with a mountain of a man. Instinctively, she swiped at him with a trash bag. He snatched her arm mid-air. The bag tumbled to the ground. In a crazy fast move, he twisted the arm behind her and shoved her against the porch railing. Her breath gushed out with an *oomph*.

"Never lower your guard, young one."

Liz wiggled out of his loose hold. Heat seeped into her cheeks. She picked up the bag and stomped around Arie.

Well. Embarrassing much?

The fact she hadn't sensed her own guardian was humiliating. She was usually more aware, but all the waiting and her heightened senses had spawned psychotic lightning bugs in her stomach. Who could blame her for being off her game?

"Do you always appear out of nowhere and scare the crap out of people?" she snapped while she tossed the trash into the dumpster and let the lid slam shut.

Arie said nothing. His eyes twinkled in the sunshine, and the side of his mouth twitched. He was laughing at her discomfort.

Liz quelled the urge to smack the grin from his lips. "I don't like people sneaking up on me." Her voice came out harsher than she intended.

Arie's smile fled on its own. "The wrath of man does not produce the righteousness of God."

"I wanted to slap you and didn't. That's progress for me." She flashed a contrite smile in answer to his glower. "I'm sorry, I didn't mean to be disrespectful." *Change the subject.* "What's up?" At his raised eyebrow, she explained. "Why are you here?"

Add slang to the list of things to teach him.

"Your training will begin in the morning."

She waited for him to continue. He stared.

They stood in silence until exasperation pushed her to break the stalemate. "What time?"

"Oh yes, time. Humans are so constrained by time." Arie's brow crinkled. "First light." At her blank look, he corrected himself. "Six o'clock." The words sounded foreign coming from him.

Liz waited for more and was again awarded with silence. This was like pulling teeth. She sighed. "Where am I supposed to be at six?"

"I will give you instructions in the morning."

"Are you gonna meet me—" Before she could finish, he dematerialized right before her eyes. Lovely. Hopefully Mr. Cryptic was more talkative when he was teaching, or this was gonna be a nightmare. She let out another sigh and walked back inside. At least now she had some direction. Of a sort.

Ready or not, her new life was about to begin.

The next morning, Liz dragged herself outside as the sun crawled over the hills. She grunted, then squinted against the brightness. She pulled on her shades and grunted again. After climbing into the Jeep, she headed west, figuring that was as good a route as any. Liz drove slowly and kept watch for Arie or any sign leading her to her destination. She reached for her coffee and guzzled as if she were dying of thirst.

After a while, she wondered if maybe she'd chosen the wrong road.

She couldn't think of any place out here where they could train. A few houses, several barns, and an abandoned repair shop that used to cater to semis. The sight of the garage peeking through the trees made her skin feel like ants were crawling all over it. *Nope. Not going there.*

She was about to give up and turn around when Arie appeared in the passenger seat. Liz yelped and swerved into the other lane. She jerked the wheel and corrected their course, her heart threatening to crack ribs.

"Are you crazy?" She shot him an aggravated look. *Well, I'm awake now!*

"I said I would give you instructions." He remained irritatingly calm.

"You can't pop out of thin air. Especially while I'm driving!" Hadn't they had this discussion already?

"I apologize if you were startled. You will become accustomed to my appearance. Turn left at the next opportunity."

Liz clenched her hands on the wheel. Her pulse began to slow, and her anger cooled as she controlled her breathing. *In for five, out for five.* Better. She chewed her lip. Well, now that he was here and she had a destination, she might as well take the time to get a question or two answered.

She took another calming breath before jumping in. "So, if you're an angel, why do you look like a human sometimes? I mean, a huge one, but still, human." Liz glanced at him.

Arie tilted his head. "We can assume a mortal form when necessary to deal with humans. Most people cannot comprehend the sight of us in our heavenly glory. Demons can take an earthly form as well. They do so frequently to tempt humans."

"Wow. Okay." Liz chewed on the inside of her cheek. "Do you have the same power when you're in human form?"

"Our power is repressed when we pour ourselves into the mortal vessel we have been given. It cannot contain all we receive from the Father."

"Oh, so you don't possess people like demons?" Her stomach

soured. "Wait, is that how demons get their bodies?"

"Not necessarily. Demons can possess those who provide a gateway. However, they can also take forms like ours, as unique as each human is." Arie pointed to a dirt road coming up. "There."

Liz opened her mouth to ask another question, but he shook his head. Clammed up.

Apparently question and answer time was over.

It was more of a trail than a road. Weeds grew in the tracks, and little gravel remained. They bounced around for a couple of minutes until they came to a field with an old barn at the center. Arie held up his hand for her to stop.

Liz gave the barn a once-over. The gray wood cracked, and the paint peeled. The awning over the loft hung at a funny angle, and the whole thing sported a side lean. She hesitated to park near it. It looked as if it could come tumbling down at any time. She chose a spot a good distance away and killed the engine.

Overgrown brush reached her knees, and wildflowers clustered among the weeds. She would definitely have to check for ticks when she got home. Liz scanned the area and saw a huge pond off to the right. As she and Arie approached the double doors, Liz noticed they looked surprisingly solid. Arie pushed them open with a loud creak.

Liz peeked in, not confident the aging timbers wouldn't land on her head. "Who owns this place?"

"A family who has granted permission for its use."

She opened her mouth, but Arie gave her another one of his looks. This one said, *Don't ask any more questions.* Liz snapped her lips shut.

Liz followed him in and wrinkled her nose when she caught a whiff of the air. Musty and acrid—the odor of rotting hay. Once her eyes had adjusted to the dark, she saw scattered lumber lying around. Ancient tools hung from huge beams. Those beams ran floor to ceiling. The main area was empty and spacious. To each side, the ceiling sloped low. The right held stables, and the left boasted old farm implements, worktables, and two rough-hewn benches.

Arie opened the pair of doors at the back of the barn. Light poured inside. "Come," he ordered. "Let us begin."

Liz joined him in the center of the barn. "What do we start with?" The possibility of sparring with an angel sent a jolt of excitement through her. Man, she was weird.

"With prayer, of course."

"Oh."

Arie prayed quietly. Liz said a prayer of her own but couldn't shake the ghosts of the past that shadowed her. She still didn't know why she'd been chosen. God needed a real warrior, not her. How could she ever be what He expected?

"For the Lord your God will hold your right hand. He will help you." Arie smiled. Could angels read minds?

Her fear slid into the background, replaced with calm. Arie lifted his face, and a song erupted from him. She listened in wonder. He lit up with pure bliss. It rolled off him and suffused the barn.

Arie finished as abruptly as he had begun. He raised an eyebrow at what she was sure was confusion on her face. "The angels praise Him at all times. It is our focus and joy." The next second he was back to business. "Now. I need to fully assess your capabilities."

Without warning, Arie threw a lightning-fast backfist. She ducked to the side and raised her forearm to block. The punch grazed her head with enough force to smart.

"Excellent." Arie stepped back. "Quick reflexes and good instincts."

Liz rubbed her bruised head.

Arie dropped into a fighting stance. "Take your position."

Liz sucked in a deep breath. It was gonna be a long day.

"Faster!"

Liz braced her hands on her knees and gulped in air. *Sir, yes, sir!* Arie reminded her of an overbearing drill sergeant from the movies.

They'd been at it for hours, and she'd barely been allowed to catch her breath. *He's trying to kill me.* Her lungs burned, and her legs quivered. Arie tossed a water bottle at her. She caught it and emptied it before standing back up.

He took position in front of her. "Now, once more. And faster! The enemy will not stand and wait for you to strike. Like this." Arie threw a perfect three-hundred-sixty-degree roundhouse with unnatural speed.

His foot stopped a hair's width from her—she'd barely seen it move. At his nod, she slid her foot back. Liz threw a high side kick at his head. He deflected with ease.

"Too slow. Again!"

Right now, he was her least favorite being in the universe. Sweat dripped between her shoulder blades, and she shrugged to unstick her shirt. Liz marshaled all the strength she had, stilled her quivering legs, and skewered Arie with her gaze. With a quickness she didn't know she possessed, she pulled her right leg up and across, bringing a vicious axe kick down—straight toward Arie's head. It grazed his chin past his block.

She smiled. *Nice.*

"Sufficient." Arie straightened. "That is all for today." Without another word, he closed the back doors and strode to the front of the barn.

Liz's jaw dropped. "Sufficient? I've never thrown a kick that fast in my life!"

"We will meet here again in the morning."

"Wait, how am I supposed to do this again in the morning? I'm human! I can't go like this every day."

Arie stopped and pivoted. "Much is expected because much has been given. You have to stretch beyond what you believe your limits to be." His eyes softened. "Otherwise you cannot hope to defeat the evil that is coming."

His eyes held foreboding that sent a chill over her skin, raising the hairs with goosebumps. She almost asked what was coming, then decided she didn't really want to know.

Liz swallowed hard. "What if I'm not ready?"

"You will be. That is why I am here." Arie placed a tender kiss on her forehead. The move thoroughly surprised her. It was the same way her dad kissed her. "Go. Rest."

Was he right? Would she be ready for whatever was coming?

VI
Welcome to the Freak Show

"Oh yeah. That's the stuff."

Liz eased into the tub with a groan. Four days of intense training were swallowed up by the hot water and Epsom salts. She closed her eyes. She wasn't crazy about her new regimen, but at least it was getting easier. Even so, she was glad Arie had given her a couple of days off.

It felt like she'd just drifted off when Mom knocked on the door. "Liz?"

She jerked back to consciousness. "Yeah?"

"Hurry on out. You have company."

Since when did she get company? Liz climbed from the now-tepid water, her body mostly soothed. She yanked on some shorts and a tank top and sauntered into the living room. Shelley and Dylan were waiting for her.

"Hey, girlie!" Shelley's smile lit up the room. "A bunch of us are heading to the lake, so we stopped by to pick you up." She laced her arm through Liz's.

Liz sighed. Crowds meant people. People meant supernatural company. And she would have to pretend, playing at normal no matter what went on around her.

Mom nudged her elbow. "I think it'd be good for you, honey. Get out and have some fun. You've been working an awful lot lately." She eyed Liz knowingly.

Liz knew Mom had seen her drag her sweaty butt back into the house every day, clean up, and head to work until late. Still, Liz had said nothing to her parents about her new occupation as soldier. Guilt warmed her cheeks. Some things her parents were better off not knowing.

Lying in the sun did sound great, though. Liz shrugged. "Okay. Why not?"

Mom's face lit up. "Good! You girls go get Liz's things together." She pointed at Dylan. "You come help me make some sandwiches."

A grin split Dylan's face. "Do you have any of your ham salad?"

"Always." Mom winked at him, and he grinned harder. He followed her to the kitchen like a hungry puppy at suppertime.

Shelley made a face. "You'd think I never feed the man!"

Liz laughed and headed for her room. She pulled her swimsuit out of a drawer and ran to the bathroom, suddenly full of energy. "Can you find my bag in the closet?" She tossed the question over her shoulder to Shelley.

When the girls emerged, Dylan met them in the living room, a large picnic basket in his hand. Liz looked from his cargo to Mom and raised an eyebrow.

Mom put her hands on her hips. "You can't be out there all afternoon with nothing to eat."

"Thanks, Mom." The woman clearly felt it was her mission to feed everyone this side of the Mississippi.

Shelley and Dylan echoed her sentiment. Shelley smacked Dylan's hand when he tried to sneak a sandwich.

Mom laughed. "You're welcome. Now you kids git!" She shooed them out.

Within minutes, they were on their way. They drove to the same cove where they used to hang out in high school. As they pulled up, Liz's gaze fell on several imps around the edges of the group of young people who had gathered. The imps looked more nervous than anything. Several angels were scattered among the humans. Some standing guard between their charges and the imps. Some observing the beachgoer's activities with curiosity and confusion displayed on their faces.

Maybe this wouldn't be as bad as she'd thought.

Liz relaxed and inhaled the scents of pine and lake water. She set her mind to enjoying this precious free time. She half-expected Arie to show up and say he'd changed his mind. Then drag her back to the barn and put her through her paces again to toughen her up for battle.

As they staked out their spot on the shore, Liz saw the hot guy from church climb out of a pricey-looking sports car. What did Shelley say his name was? Blake. Her hands got clammy. He smiled. Liz's answering one wobbled.

A faint whisper in her mind said he could be trouble all spread on a cracker. She disregarded the warning and chalked it up to nerves. Her rocky past made her jumpy. That was all. There was no reason not to get to know this new guy. She desperately wanted a little slice of normal. Preferably the delectable slice currently marching toward her.

Liz swallowed her nerves and wiped her hands on her shorts. "Hi. Blake, right?"

She extended her hand, and his long fingers wrapped around hers. Again she found her heart blocking her airway. The combination of fire and ice that swelled in her the last time they'd touched erupted again.

Shelley chose that moment to interrupt them. "Glad you could make it! You're just in time to eat. Pull up a patch."

Blake dropped his bag and settled beside Liz. Shelley winked behind his back, and Liz rolled her eyes. Lovely. Her friend was now playing matchmaker.

Dylan ran up from the water, which he'd made a mad dash for while the girls set up. "Hey, Blake. Ooh, lunch! Awesome, I'm starved." He shook himself like a dog, flinging water all over Shelley and most of the blanket.

Shelley screamed. "Dylan! For Pete's sake!" She threw a towel at him and laughed. "Dry off, you goofball." She shook her head and started passing out sandwiches.

A still-dripping Dylan snuggled into Shelley, wrapping his arms around her and nuzzling her neck.

She tried to shove him away. "Why did I marry an overgrown child?"

"'Cause you can't resist me!" Dylan grinned innocently. He plopped down, and they started in on their lunch.

Liz tried to quench the envy rolling over her. Would she ever have that? Stupid question. A silent sigh reverberated in her head, along with the thought of Ryland, the one chance at love and happiness she'd thrown away. She glanced over at Blake. He may not be a forever guy, but she could have a little fun. Right? If she could remember what that was like.

Liz sipped her Coke. She should say something smart. Or funny. She could be hilarious when she wanted to be. Liz took a deep breath and a second sip to buy time.

Blake startled her. "So, are you going to introduce yourself or leave me to come up with my own name for you?" His voice was deep and smooth, sending tremors through her—just like his touch. "I could think of a few."

Good Lord. Those chocolate eyes and that velvet voice made her all gooey inside. "Sorry. Elizabeth Brantley. Everyone calls me Liz."

"Nice to meet you. I think I prefer Elizabeth. It suits you. Elegant and intriguing."

Liz stifled a snort. No one had ever accused her little tomboy self of being elegant. "Your call." She took another swig of soda. "Shelley said you were in town for business. What do you do?"

"Mergers and acquisitions. Sounds fancier than it is." He laughed, and she melted a little more. "One company taking over another. I'm here to close a deal."

"Not staying long?" A hint of disappointment swelled in her belly.

"Depends. Could be a few more weeks, could be longer. You never know." Blake popped the rest of his sandwich into his mouth and winked at her.

The dedicated bevy of lightning bugs in her belly went nuts.

When everyone had finished eating, Shelley and Dylan took off for the water. Liz watched as Blake tugged his shirt over his head. She couldn't have looked away from his chiseled abs if the world had exploded. They were truly a thing of beauty. Covered with tanned skin, rippling as he moved. She blushed when he caught her staring.

Blake smiled and reached his hand out to her. "Come on. Let's have some fun."

Her stomach flipped as she took his hand and stood. She shed her tank top and cutoffs and couldn't help but notice he was watching her now. *Ha.* At least she wasn't the only one affected. He led her to the water without another word. The boys took off in a swimming contest, and Liz hung out close to the beach.

Blake slogged over to her when he'd returned victorious. "You can't cool off if you barely get wet. Let's swim out to the island."

"Nope." She shook her head. "I'm good right here. Go ahead if you want."

The second Liz saw the mischievous glint in Blake's eyes, she knew what was coming. She backed toward the shore. He snaked an arm around her waist and scooped her into his arms as if she weighed nothing. Before she could catch a breath, she flew through the air and landed in the water, limbs flailing.

She came up sputtering and laughing. "You're a dead man." Liz jumped at him and reached out, her hand sliding off slick skin covering powerful biceps.

"Too slow, baby. Try again." Blake laughed and swayed back and forth in the water, teasing her.

A few minutes and some sneaky moves later, she managed to get a grip on him and climbed on his back. She laughed. He hollered. She yanked him to the side, sending them both crashing into the wake of a passing speedboat. When they surfaced, he spun her around to face him and pulled her close.

Their eyes met, and Liz choked. His gaze was intense, holding secrets she wanted to explore. His hands settled on her hips in the thigh-deep water. They were cool, but heat filled her at his touch. Excitement quivered throughout her limbs, and her heart pounded erratically. Both of them ignored the yelling and laughing around them.

Blake leaned in. Liz panicked. She smacked his pecs with both hands and wrenched away. "I need a drink, and I wanna work on my tan." She waded to the beach, but not before catching the confusion whispering across his face as he followed her.

She needed to get it together. He seemed like one of the good guys. She shouldn't hold her past against him.

Liz made it to the blanket and reached for a towel. Blake set her insides wobbling. She liked the feeling. Mostly. Though not being in control was something she didn't care for.

Blake toweled off and stretched out beside her. He rolled to his side and dug in the cooler. He handed her a bottle of water and extracted one for himself. Without mentioning what had happened, he talked about the area and how much he liked it. He asked her the occasional general question, and she relaxed almost instantly.

How did he do that? Set her at ease, making her forget her worries? She could easily fall for him. Oh man, she was in trouble.

The hours passed quickly, and gray crept up on the edges of the day. Everyone packed up to leave. Liz felt energized and completely chilled at the same time. She was glad she'd decided to come.

Liz tapped Shelley's arm. "I'm gonna jump off the cliff once before we head out."

"Well, hurry up if you want a ride."

Blake piped up. "I can take you home."

Shelley jumped on the offer for her. "Great! Be careful and have fun." Shelley grabbed their bag and the basket, and Dylan shouldered the cooler. "See you Sunday." She wiggled her eyebrows at Liz and bounded up the trail to the cars.

Liz's stomach took up residence in her mouth.

Alone.

With Blake.

Oh, God.

"Go ahead." Blake tossed his bag back on the ground. "I'll wait here. Hurry before it gets too dark. I don't want you getting hurt." His perfect smile didn't help her present condition.

Liz nodded and started the trek up the hill. A snap sounded behind her. Had Blake decided to follow her? She whirled around. There was nothing—just trees swaying in the wind and an empty trail. A moment later, branches cracked under feet. There was no mistaking the sound. An unwelcome sensation crawled over her skin. *Seriously? Today?* Liz slowly twisted to face what she knew awaited her.

Two demons stood in the path. Their eyes glinted yellow. Their putrid stench filled her nostrils. Grayish-black hide covered their deformed bodies, and torn wings extended from their spines. Both had swords at the ready.

Great. Two for the price of one.

Nervous energy tingled down her limbs. She'd faced two at a time before, but they hadn't been this big. She was even more thankful for her new strength. She instinctively reached for her dagger. Wait. She was in a swimsuit. Her knife was tucked in the bottom of her bag.

Lovely.

The intent in their eyes lanced her with terror. Oh, this could be bad. Nausea overtook her. She breathed deep and gagged on their stink.

Liz forced herself to accept reality and think. She couldn't get around them, and there was no way she could make it to the top of the hill and jump in time. Liz glanced around for anything useful, then reached for the fallen branch at her feet. She grabbed the makeshift weapon and backed up.

The biggest one sprang forward. She sidestepped. Adrenaline surged and shoved fear from her veins. The need to fight devoured her as her brain kicked into battle mode. She brought the stick across the back of the demon's neck as he slid past.

Liz swiveled to see the second demon swing for her head. The blade skimmed her hair as she ducked. She flung herself forward and smashed the end of the branch into his face. They crashed to the ground, her body landing across his, her weapon flying from her hands. The stench of rotten eggs and ages-old decay turned her stomach.

The demon grabbed her shoulders and lifted her for his companion's incoming blade. His claws dug into her skin. Blood trickled down her arms. She could worry about the pain later. She reacted. Liz slammed her palm into her captor's nose, shoving upward. He loosened his hold.

The demon racing to impale her skidded to a stop and jerked his head to the left. Her captor snapped his head in the same direction. She took the opportunity and wrenched herself free. Liz scrambled for the sword her attacker had dropped, then buried it in the demon's side. He let out a howl and convulsed as she twisted. She raised her foot to his midsection for leverage and tugged on the blade. When it released, she fell back, landing on her backside.

Before she could recover, a black, scaly fist bashed her head. The force sent Liz rolling down the embankment and crashing into a tree. Razors tore through her body. Her ears rang. Her vision blurred. The demon slid down after her. She crawled to her feet and swayed. Liz was barely able to lean right as the demon's blade buried into the tree where her head had been.

The movement exacerbated the dizziness, and she lurched forward. No way could she fight like this. She stumbled, clawing back up the hill, scrambling to gain a foothold on the steep incline. Liz slipped on a moss-covered rock, and her knee scraped the surface, tearing a jagged gash. She winced and held back a cry.

Where was Arie? Didn't he say she'd have help now?

Liz crawled through the brush. Something wasn't right. She paused to listen. No leaves crunched. No heavy footsteps lumbered after her. Where did the demon go? She was about to chance a look back when a voice rang out in the forest.

"Elizabeth?"

Blake. Oh, man. He hadn't seen anything, had he? To him, she would've looked like a nut job fighting thin air.

"Are you okay?" He met her at the top as she pulled herself out of the ravine. Not waiting for her answer, Blake yanked off his shirt, ripped it in two, and carefully tied a piece around her gushing knee. "What happened?" Worry and anger ripped into his normally smooth voice.

What could she say? "I fell. It got dark quicker than I thought." At least it wasn't a total lie. Still, Liz felt bad. She'd just met him, and already she was hiding things.

Concern etched into the hard planes of his face, and a hint of it whispered to her senses. "Can you walk?"

"Yeah, I think so."

She glanced over at the dark pile that was the neutralized demon, partially hidden in the waning light. Where had the other gone? As she watched, thick fog encompassed her downed enemy. The ground opened, swallowing its fallen. She slid her gaze to Blake who, thankfully, was busy checking her wounds.

Liz sank against Blake's chest, fatigue swallowing her. He slid his arm around her, anchoring her to him. Liz relaxed a fraction. He felt like safety and strength. She'd missed that.

"Thank you. You didn't have to come after me." She held his gaze and had the strangest sense of falling under a spell. "I don't even know your full name."

Blake rubbed dirt from her uninjured cheek with his thumb. "Blake Ronin. And it was my pleasure." He wove his fingers into the hair at the nape of her neck. "It's a good thing I did. Looks like you took a pretty nasty tumble. I wouldn't want to lose you before we got to know each other."

Liz was metal; Blake a magnet. He leaned down, and she rose to him. Static electricity zapped when their lips met, and she jerked away. He grinned and drew her back in.

A thousand emotions and leftover adrenaline from the fight collided in her brain. His desire danced on her skin. The energy pooled in her belly. Okay, feeling other people's feelings could be a really good thing sometimes.

Blake deepened the kiss, exploring. Liz let him. She hadn't realized how starved she was for a connection, for tenderness. His actions fueled the fire in her blood, and she clung to him as he yanked her hard against him. He brought feelings to the surface she'd kept squashed for so long. And for once, panic wasn't one of them.

Too soon, Blake raised his head with a groan. He loosened his hold and caressed her back. "We should get going."

Liz nodded. *Breathe. Slow down.* They'd spent one afternoon together, and here she stood kissing him like he was hers. He was a stranger. Her cheeks flamed, and she pushed away. A familiar alarm ate at the corners of her brain. She could lose her mind with this man.

That thought scared her more than the demons had.

Liz nodded. "Yeah. I've had enough for one day." She gave a nervous laugh and hobbled down the trail. Though part of her couldn't help but wonder, could she ever get enough of him? But surely it wouldn't take long before he realized she was hiding a huge secret and got fed up. Especially if things like this kept happening.

So much for her slice of normal.

Blake stopped her by tugging her hand. He leaned down, carefully tucked an arm under her knees, and cradled her against his solid torso. She wasn't about to complain.

Liz settled in. "Sorry about this. Welcome to my freak show."

Blake gave her a sharp look. "You are not a freak. You're perfect." He kissed the top of her head as he strode toward his car. "I'm looking forward to whatever happens next. I don't plan on letting you go anytime soon."

His words gave Liz chills. And not all the pleasant kind.

VII
Perfect Storm

Liz barreled down the road to the barn. She didn't care when mud from last night's late rain splashed inside her old Jeep. Yesterday's events had her blood boiling. Arie had a lot to answer for.

The object of her anger waited out front as she pulled up.

Liz started in as soon as she parked. "Do you have any idea what happened yesterday?" She didn't give him a chance to answer as she jumped out. "I was attacked! I coulda died! Where were you?"

Arie stared calmly as if she'd said she was happy it was cooler today. "It was not the first time you have been attacked." He scanned her. "You are still alive."

Thanks for the update, Mr. Obvious.

"That's not the point. I needed you!" Betrayal infused her words.

"I was occupied with other business."

Liz glared.

"I am not omniscient, and you did not ask for help. If you had, it would have been sent." Arie's already stern face grew harder.

"I—well, I was a little busy trying to survive." Heat rushed up her neck.

"Yet again, you let your anger cloud your mind. You cannot let emotion drive you. It is critical. You must think, Elizabeth. Form a plan and use the tools available to you."

Liz swallowed hard and focused on the Jeep's muddy tires. "Sorry."

Arie exhaled, irritation hardening his tone. "You cannot simply say you are sorry every time you make a mistake and think that makes amends. Make the required change."

Liz felt like a two-year-old being smacked on the diaper. "I did kill the first one. The other one disappeared. Luckily before Blake showed up."

Arie cocked his head. "Who is Blake?"

Oh, boy. Should've kept her mouth shut. She didn't need the angel all up in her personal life. "Just a friend. He came looking for me. Thank God he didn't see anything."

He nodded. "By the way, you did not kill the demon. All angels are immortal, even the fallen. When demons are wounded, they retreat to dry places to rejuvenate." He walked toward the barn. "Or are punished for their failure. Angels retreat to Heaven, of course, where we rest and are ministered to."

"Oh. Okay."

"Do not let this man sway your attention. Your mission must come first."

Liz nodded. She saw no point in arguing. She didn't even know how she felt about Blake. But she didn't want to chance Arie telling her she had to let go of her shot at something separate from all of the battles and training. Even if it were short-lived.

Arie extracted a large duffle bag from underneath one of the benches and plopped it onto a worktable. "Shall we begin with weapons?"

Now that, she could handle.

Liz leaned against a beam and massaged her aching arms. Her hands sprouted blisters, and bruises decorated her body. After the round she'd had with the demons the day before, she didn't mind so much. The enemy wasn't going to back off because she was hurt or tired. They'd keep coming until they killed her.

"Remember, watch the hips." Arie reiterated his instructions while he gathered the scattered weapons. "They will tell you where your opponent will move next. Swing from the elbow, not the shoulder. It's faster. And stay light on your feet so you can pivot easily."

Arie retrieved a long, polished cherrywood box from the shelf under the worktable. Liz gasped as he pulled a beautiful sword from the purple velvet. She recognized it as a Katana, a Japanese single-edged blade. Black cording wrapped the grip with silver intricately woven throughout. The silver guard sparkled with delicate carvings. He slid off the sheath, revealing a pristine blade.

"Is this for me?" Liz held her breath.

"Yes." He gently laid the blade across his palms and extended his arms. "Many warriors before you have used it for the Master's glory. May you as well."

She tentatively reached out to claim it, afraid to touch something so exquisite. Liz stepped back and drew the blade from side to side. She looked at Arie and grinned.

"Thank you. I'll take care of it, I promise."

Arie-Chayal's heart swelled as he observed Elizabeth's fascination. He let her enjoy the moment, yet his smile flagged. Happiness would be in short supply in the coming days. She would be tested relentlessly, both in and out of battle. Some lessons would be brutal.

Much of it, he could prepare her for. More would rely upon her faith, her strength of character, and her choices. She had come far in such a short time, but there was still much she struggled with. He had faith she would emerge stronger.

The angel's faith did not stop him from wishing he could fight the battles for her.

Liz raced home to get ready for a lunch date with Blake. Her nerves teetered on a razor's edge. There was a lot she didn't know about him. What she did know drew her like flies to honey. She chose to focus on that and not the odd feeling taking residence in her stomach.

It didn't take Liz long to get ready after a quick shower. She pulled her raging curls into a high ponytail. A little mascara, powder, and lip gloss were all the makeup she wore. Liz examined her dress. It wasn't fancy—a red and white cotton sundress finished off with a pair of flip flops. It complimented her perfectly, draping over her muscular body and giving her feminine curves. She settled her sunglasses on her head and grabbed her bag.

Liz pulled in to the park and spotted Blake at a picnic table along the riverbank. He waved as Liz trotted across the grass. A quick scan told her there was one smallish demon and four angels hanging around. She could deal with that.

She flashed her best smile. "Hi there."

"You're late," Blake chided with a grin. "It's all right, though. I only got here a few minutes before you." He stood and waved his hand at the table. Two brown paper bags and two large Styrofoam cups sat in the center. "Your late lunch is served, m'lady."

Liz laughed as he guided her onto the bench. He placed a light kiss on her cheek before sliding in beside her. Flame and frost crept along her skin again. Her heart raced as he settled next to her, leaving only a fraction of space between them.

She opened one of the bags. "Cheeseburgers and fries. Mmm, my favorite."

"I know." At her raised eyebrow, guilt flushed his face. "I asked

Shelley."

How sweet. His sheepish grin stole a shard of her heart.

They spread out their feast and dug in. Liz told him a little about herself as they ate, giving him the much-abbreviated version. No point scaring him off right away. When she'd finished, she poked his chest. "Your turn."

"What do you want to know?" Tension flooded Blake's body.

Liz wondered about the change but didn't give it much thought. She didn't want to talk about her past either. "Well, where are you from? What do you do for fun? Are you really just in town for business? And what about your family? Do you have brothers or sisters?"

Blake scooted back and flipped his leg over the bench. "You have a lot of questions." He tweaked her nose. "I'm from everywhere. Military brat. My family is spread all over the place. I like driving fast cars, and working out, and hanging out with you. I really am in town for work. Although, now I have a better reason to be here." His gaze zeroed in on her.

Liz bit her lip. There was one more question she needed answered. Make or break time.

"So, I have to ask, do you have a girlfriend?" She flicked a glance at his left hand. "Or a wife stashed somewhere?" Liz tried to laugh and erase some of the bite. It came out as an odd squeak.

Blake's eyes twinkled. "No girlfriend, no wife." Blake grabbed her hand and eased closer. He ran the back of his hand down her cheek. "I've known a lot of women. None like you. There's something about you..." His fingers rested on the back of her neck while his thumb rubbed her jaw.

She swallowed to combat the sudden dryness in her mouth. His reference to "a lot of women" maybe should've given her pause, but all Liz could think about was the warmth that seeped into her skin from his touch. He tugged her close.

Liz's stomach flipped. Panic teased the edges of her mind. She squeezed her eyes shut. There was nothing for her to worry about.

Blake was a good man. He was sweet, acted like he cared about her, and treated her like she was precious.

He reminded her a lot of Ryland. Her eyes shot open. Why did he keep popping into her head? They were over. Done for good. Here, with Blake, she had a chance at a fresh start. He had no idea she was a freak, and she planned on keeping it that way. She had a shot at something amazing here. Liz's nerves settled, and she leaned further into Blake.

Their lips were millimeters apart when the air around them abruptly changed frequency. It crackled with tension of a different variety. Invisible fingers of warmth caressed her spine. Whispers of chaotic emotion and thoughts not her own swirled in her mind. Her heart flew into a frenzy, reaching for him, recognizing the spirit bathing her senses. Her stomach went skydiving.

What in the…? No way.

Liz backed away from Blake. His brow furrowed, and his smile ran away. He jerked his head to the left. A low rumble emerged from his chest, sending a warning flare through her.

She found herself rising to her feet and turning around as though someone or something else controlled her body. Her eyes locked on to the source of the disturbance. Her heart fell into her stomach with such force, it felt like she'd been shot. Liz grabbed the table behind her for support as her knees turned to jelly.

Blake jumped up and put an arm around her shoulders, drawing her to his side. Possessiveness roared through him, jarring her. "Let's go."

Liz wasn't listening. Her world shrank to center on the titan striding confidently toward them. Strength radiated from him in waves, and she was drowning in the current. The nearer he got, the deeper she sank.

His nose was now slightly crooked from being broken. A vicious scar decorated his forehead. Those injuries couldn't diminish his handsomeness, though. His chestnut hair was cut short, almost military style. Tattoos slid from the sleeves of his T-shirt. His chest was thicker, muscles protesting against being confined. Broad shoulders capped massive arms. He stood well over six feet, a commanding presence she couldn't drag her eyes away from.

Liz couldn't ignore the sense of restrained power and the illusion of danger that clung to him. It didn't dull the light shining from within, though. There was so much different about him, but his hazel eyes still sparkled, and an innate goodness still emanated from his pores.

The man focused on Blake. Fire flashed in the newcomer's stare, and his jaw clenched. Every muscle coiled tightly, making him look like he was a snake about to strike. The stiffness vanished when his eyes swiveled back to her. He stopped within arm's reach. A hesitant smile hinted on his full lips.

"Lizzy. It's good to see you." The deep timbre of his smooth voice slid over her skin like a caress. His gaze took her in from head to toe. "You look beautiful."

Liz was swept up in a tornado, emotions and memories swirling, smacking her on their way around. It was impossible to tell where she ended and he began. This was different than anything she'd experienced before. Intense. Terrifying. His heart seemed to beat in her chest, right along with her own. The storm he created threatened to sweep her away.

She managed to force her voice to work.

"Hello, Ryland."

VIII
Chasing Twisters

He was back.

Liz had known there was always a chance Ryland would come home. But she hadn't been ready for this. This new force that was Ryland. Blackness hinted at the edges of her vision. Her hands curled around the edge of the table behind her. The rough wood bit into her palms.

The grating sound of a throat clearing dragged her out of Ryland World.

"Are you going to tell me who this guy is, and what's going on here?" Blake was clearly aggravated he'd been forgotten.

Liz cut through the fog in her brain. "Sorry. This is...Ryland Vaughn." Her eyes didn't leave Ryland's. They couldn't. "Ryland, Blake Ronin."

Blake didn't give Ryland a chance to acknowledge the introduction. "Who is he to you?" His arm tightened possessively around her shoulders.

"Oh. He's, ah, a friend." This wasn't really happening. Right?

Blake spoke through gritted teeth. "Well, nice to meet you, *friend*."

The men shot daggers at each other. Liz looked from one to the other. She put her emotional psychosis on the back burner. There had to be a way to regain control of this mess. She had to distract them before they decided to draw blood. Though she had no idea why Ryland even cared.

Liz coughed and faced Ryland. "When did you get back?" Her voice wavered. She hated that.

"A little while ago. I called the house, and your mom told me you were here." Ryland's eyes never left Blake's. "She didn't mention you were on a date."

Blake's steel gaze didn't falter. "Yes. We are. You're interrupting."

Blake stepped back, hauling Liz with him. She shot him a look. *Seriously?* He squeezed her tighter, his fingers biting into her shoulder. She winced and pulled away from him. What was his deal? Ryland inched forward, eyes snapping and anger singeing the air. Blake backed off a bit. Ryland refused to retreat.

Ryland crossed his arms. The muscles in his forearms twitched. He glanced at Liz. "Can we talk? Alone?"

Liz knew she had to let him have his say. She owed him that much. But Blake didn't deserve to be cast aside like scraps after supper.

Ryland's shoulders tensed. "Liz, it's important."

Blake's face was stone. His hand flexed on her shoulder. He tried to slide her behind him. "She's busy at the moment."

Liz snapped to full attention, perfectly clear and in control. Suddenly she didn't feel as bad for cutting their date short. "I can answer for myself." She moved out of Blake's grip. She could've sworn she saw Ryland's lips twitch. "I need to talk to Ryland, and you need to chill."

Blake's expression softened. He closed the gap between him and Liz and took her hand. His award-winning smile didn't make it to his eyes. "Forgive me? I was looking forward to having you all to myself today, and I got carried away."

Liz relaxed. A little. "It's okay. I'm sorry, too." She eyed Ryland, who looked like he wanted to throw Blake into the river. "But we have, um, unfinished business."

Blake's jaw ticked as he nodded. He brushed his lips over hers, publicly staking claim. Ryland made a noise. Liz sighed. Idiots. Jealous idiots. Even though neither had a right to be.

Blake gripped her waist. "I'll call you tomorrow. Or later tonight?"

"Tomorrow's fine."

A shadow crossed Blake's countenance before he smiled. "Whatever you want, gorgeous. Are you sure you'll be all right?" His gaze bored into Ryland's.

"I'll be fine." *I hope.* Anxiety set in with a vengeance. Would Ryland fly into a rage at her for what she'd done? In the past, she never would've wondered. Now he was different. Harder. Emotions billowed off him that actually scared her.

Blake shot Ryland a final glare and bumped Ryland's shoulder as he walked by. Ryland didn't move an inch. He grinned like he'd won some sort of prize.

Idiots.

Blake climbed into his car and peeled out of the parking lot. Those two were definitely more than friends. The undercurrent between them had sucked all the oxygen from the air.

He slammed his fist on the steering wheel. He'd been making headway with her. Now this Ryland had shown up, drawing her attention and pushing Blake to the side. He downshifted and took the corner wide. A horn blared. Blake swung back into his lane and sped on.

Elizabeth wasn't like other women. There was an intriguing toughness to her. A hint of darkness lurking, lending her a mysterious edge. Not to mention, she was beautiful. She was all kinds of special in one package.

Blake flew across the river's bridge. He cast a glance back over at the park. His blood seethed at the thought of her alone with Ryland. He had to solidify his place in her heart to make sure there wasn't room for Ryland to resume whatever position he'd once held.

There was no way he was losing her.

Liz analyzed her sandals.

The emotional firestorm she'd been bombarded with made her head pound. She rubbed her temples. The last thing she needed right now was one of her headaches.

The sick feeling she got every time she thought about how she'd hurt Ryland soured her stomach. Liz longed to make it right, but fixing it would be like roping a storm. Impossible. There was one route she could travel here. Take her lumps and move on.

Even if he did still have her freakin' heart in his hands.

Ryland broke the silence. "I don't like that guy."

"Really? Gee, I didn't get that." Liz exhaled sharply. "He's a good guy. He helped me out in a bad situation."

Ryland narrowed his eyes. "What kind of bad situation?"

"Doesn't matter." She waved it off. "Why do you care?" What was she doing? She was in the wrong in this situation, not him.

He looked hurt at the bite in her voice and ignored her question. "You guys aren't together, are you?" Ryland looked like he was holding his breath.

"Not really." *Not yet. Maybe not ever.*

His shoulders lowered, and she felt some of the tension melt. "Well, watch yourself." Worry and something else wafted on the breeze. He covered it with a smirk. "I never pegged you for liking the pretty boy type."

Liz sucked her cheek between her teeth before she said something she'd regret. She cleared her throat. "So, you wanted to talk?"

Ryland moved closer, and her stomach constricted. "Can we sit?"

He took her by the elbow and guided her to the table. Heat radiated and sparks flew from his fingers into her bones. She was tempted to look down to see if her heart had melted onto her sandals. Their eyes collided. She thought she heard an explosion.

It doesn't mean anything. Liz tore her gaze away and sat down. She rested her hands on the table and clenched them together. They hadn't stopped shaking. Her stomach flopped around like a fish on the riverbank.

Ryland settled across from her. "I'm not here to light into you."

Crap. He always could read her too well. She feigned ignorance. "What?"

"I'm not mad. It was a long time ago, and you were…in a bad place. Thank God that's changed." His eyes held a slight question as his hand covered hers.

How could he know? They hadn't had any contact in three years. Liz nodded, trying to ignore the way his touch made her feel. "I am sorry, though. I never wanted to hurt you." She switched to a whisper. "I loved you." Okay. She hadn't meant to say that part out loud.

"I know." He stroked her hand with his thumb, each brush adding fuel to the fire. "I was hurt. And really ticked. It took me a while to get my head straight." Ryland's eyes met hers. "Yet, here we are. I'd like to leave it in the past, where it belongs."

Surely it wouldn't be that easy. There was too much between them. She'd broken his heart and handed it back to him in minuscule pieces.

After she'd left, he'd tracked her down and found her in a flea-bag motel. He'd begged her to come home. Even asked her to marry him. Said he could help. Said to trust him. He hadn't explain how, but she'd desperately wanted to believe him. Then a demon had materialized in the corner. The monster had sealed their fate. Liz had sent Ryland home. Alone. It haunted her every day.

Liz let it drop. If he could let the past go, so could she. Right?

Ryland took a deep breath. "I need to tell you something."

Dread dropped back into her gut. Liz tightened her defenses and prepared for the hit. "All right." Her phone rang. She glanced at the screen. "It's work."

She hesitated, and he motioned for her to answer. A few minutes later she hung up. Disappointment swelled inside of her. Or was it relief?

Ryland quirked an eyebrow. "Something wrong?"

"Kind of. Hank needs me to come in for a little while. Julie's sick, and there's no one else."

"It's fine. Go." Ryland squeezed her hand. "Your mom asked me to come to supper anyway. And I'm not going anywhere."

A thrill rumbled through Liz. What did he mean? Was he back for good? She needed to get her head around all of this. Ryland forgave her. And he was here, sitting right in front of her.

Ryland kept a hold of her hand as they got up. He walked her to her Jeep and stood there as she drove away, not saying another word. She couldn't resist a look back. He watched her, a delicious smile creeping across his face.

Things just got way complicated.

Liz stumbled through the motions all afternoon. From the moment she'd laid eyes on him at the park, the box that held everything Ryland, the one she'd kept tightly sealed, had been pried open.

Now there was this new intensity between them. Like all their thoughts and emotions were amplified. She sensed more from him than she had from anyone else. And she felt even more drawn to him than she had before.

Her hands trembled as she wrote the customer's order on her pad. She tripped on her way to the kitchen, almost knocking over a stack of plates. Liz dropped the order off with Hank, ran to the restroom, and splashed water on her face. After a few deep breaths, she headed back out to finish the shift.

Her thoughts never strayed far from Ryland. Part of her hoped he was there to rekindle things. But she knew that was a dream. He'd never want her now anyway.

Then there was Blake. It was easy with him. Fun. With the exception of his abrupt case of possessiveness today. There was no history, no baggage.

Yep. She was smack in the middle of a mess. And she had no idea how to get out of it.

When the evening waitress came in, Liz flew out the door.

Ryland had beaten her to the house. She tossed everyone a quick hello and raced to her room. When she emerged, she'd changed back into the sundress she'd worn earlier. Her mom raised an eyebrow. Liz shrugged. They gathered around the table like they'd all done so many times before she'd left. Liz lifted her chin as Dad spoke.

"Ryland, why don't you pray for us tonight?"

Liz swallowed hard as they linked hands. Ryland's hand gripped hers tight, sending shockwaves up her arm. When he said, "Amen," he gave her hand a squeeze.

Dad started the table talk. "It sure is good to have both of you home. The way it should be." Dad cleared his throat and Mom fought a grin while Liz coughed and Ryland grabbed a biscuit. "What have you been up to?" Dad scooped out some mashed potatoes and passed the bowl to Ryland.

Ryland swallowed the bite in his mouth. "I've been working pretty much nonstop." Ryland gave the basket of biscuits to Liz and grazed her fingers.

"Now, what is it exactly that you do?"

"I do freelance computer work, software design mostly. Occasionally I'll get a contract for working on security issues and such."

Liz laughed silently. *Code for: I do some hacking on the side. At least he's getting paid for it now.*

"Sounds interesting. I may have you take a look at the computer in the church office. I know enough about 'em to do a little research and watch videos. Maybe you could speed it up?"

"I'll give it a shot."

Mom handed Ryland the chicken. "Have you spent any time with your brother?"

Ryland shifted in his seat. The wooden chair squeaked under his large form. "Uh, I haven't seen Nate in a while. I'm sure he's fine, though." He quickly shoved in a mouthful of chicken.

Liz watched him out of the corner of her eye. What was he leaving out? He looked up at her, and she ducked her head, very interested in getting butter on her biscuit.

She stayed quiet through most of the meal. Having Ryland beside her, his knee brushing hers, had her feeling like she sat on a knife blade. An electrified blade. Especially when she caught him watching her.

When they had finished, Mom shooed the men into the living room. Liz knew what was coming. She loaded the dishwasher while Mom rinsed.

Sure enough, Mom started in. "Now, tell me why you were so quiet during supper, and what you're going to do now Ryland is back."

Well. That escalated quickly.

"Mom!" Liz dropped the silverware into the dishwasher. "Just because Ry is in town doesn't mean anything." She slammed a plate between the prongs. "And I was quiet because I didn't have anything to say. You guys were doing a great job of grilling him on your own."

Mom laid a hand on Liz's shoulder. "Honey, it's Ryland. So it means something. From the way he was looking at you, I'd say you're the biggest reason he's home."

Liz sighed. She filled the soap container and flipped the dishwasher shut. She held up a hand when Mom started to speak. "Please drop it, Mom. I've got a full plate right now, okay? I need time to figure everything out, and Ryland is the least of my worries."

Heat crept up her neck from the huge lie she'd just told her mother.

Ryland rescued her by poking his head around the corner. "Are you done in here? I thought we'd take a drive." He smiled, and Liz wondered if he'd heard any of that.

Oh boy. "Yeah. All set."

Mom grinned and winked at Liz. "You kids have fun."

Liz rolled her eyes.

After saying goodbye to an already half-asleep Dad, Ryland

whisked her to his truck. Neither said a word while he drove. He pulled into an overlook with a beautiful view of the valley, and they sat in silence for what seemed like an eternity.

Finally he spoke up. "I meant what I said. I forgave you a long time ago."

"Thank you," she whispered. Liz looked out over the river, not really seeing. She swallowed the lump in her throat. "I need some air." She opened the door.

She walked to the front of the truck and leaned against the hood. The full moon washed a path across the river below, and stars punctuated the blackness above. Liz breathed in the humid air and let it bathe her nerves.

Ryland stood in front of her and propped his boot on the bumper to her left. "Everything okay?"

His deep voice, dominating presence, and wild, outdoorsy smell wrapped around her. He was way too close. She could feel the heat pouring off him.

"Yeah." She drew a design in the dirt with her foot. Liz looked up and flashed him a smile. "Fine."

"What I was trying to say earlier…I wanted to tell you a long time ago." Ryland ran his thumb down the side of her cheek. "I hope you can forgive me."

Liz ignored the pounding in her veins and pushed off the truck. "Forgive you for what?"

He let out a loaded sigh. "First, you have to understand something. I had ord—"

"Ryland, look out!" Pure instinct had her yelling as a black form darted out of the trees.

Ryland grabbed her and ducked in time to miss the demonic blade. Three more demons materialized. Liz jumped forward to meet the attack, but Ryland shoved her out of the path of the next strike. He tackled the demon, and they rolled, a flailing mass in the dirt.

Liz's mouth fell open. Ryland tossed the demon off him, leaped to his feet, and backed up to her side. With one arm, he pulled her behind him as the creature regained its footing. Fury bubbled inside Liz. It gurgled its way up her throat, leaving a bitter aftertaste. Adrenaline and power surged through her, readying her for battle.

Part of her wanted to go after the demon. The other part wanted to start a fight with a human opponent.

Shock kept her from doing either.

What just happened here?

IX
Blow Me Away

"Weapons in the toolbox. Keys in the ignition. Go! I'll hold 'em off." Ryland shoved her in the direction of the truck as he yanked a knife out of a sheath on his hip she hadn't noticed.

Every muscle in Liz's body bunched to spring as she stared at Ryland.

The demons rushed in. Ryland dodged, then kicked the demon holding the blade slicing toward Liz. She arched backward, but it skimmed across her abdomen and left a bright red trail. A burning sensation followed. She hissed and took off after her attacker.

"Liz! Weapons!" Ryland plowed into the demon from the side and knocked the sword from its clawed hand. "Now!"

Liz skidded across the gravel and tripped over her flip flops. Righting herself, she yanked the keys out of the truck. Finding the key that looked like it'd work, she pried the toolbox open and gasped. Every kind of weapon she could think of was tucked in its own spot. She marveled over Ryland's arsenal. Then betrayal overrode wonder as everything he'd kept from her sank in.

Ryland landed at her feet, his arm sporting a vicious gash.

Liz noticed she couldn't feel any emotion from him now. It was as if he'd shut down. Or her little talent was somehow broken. *Whatever. No time to worry about it now.*

She quickly withdrew a long blade and tossed it to him.

He caught it deftly. "Thanks." Ryland sprang to his feet without using his hands. Show off. "Can you fight in that?" He pointed at her shoes and dress.

Righteous indignation stoked the fire burning inside of her. "Watch me."

Liz kicked off her sandals and dove back into the toolbox. Out of the corner of her eye, she saw Ryland shake his head, grin, and dive into the fray. Before Liz could choose her poison, Arie appeared with a shout and burst of light, another angel at his side. Thank God! And right on time. Four more demons had joined the assault.

Liz grabbed two wooden handles with curved blades at their ends. She turned to see a demon making a beeline for her.

She slid to the open driver's door and pulled it toward her. Then shoved it into the oncoming threat. The creature stumbled back. It pivoted and rushed her again. She moved out from behind the door, and a thick, scaly arm snaked around her neck.

Sliding easily into full battle mode, Liz brought the hooked blades she'd chosen wide behind her. She dragged them across the demon's neck, ripping outward. When he released her, she dropped, twisted, and swiped them through his knees. After an ear-piercing scream, he fell. She looked up to see Arie had dispatched the one charging her. She nodded her thanks.

A flash of black to her right. A rush of wind. The glint of moonlight on steel. White hot pain seared her left shoulder. The demon landed, charred wings flapping, a wicked smile creasing its face. A strangled cry escaped Liz's lips. The weapon in her left hand clattered to the gravel, and she followed it. She tucked her throbbing arm to her side and fought tears.

Liz raised her remaining weapon in an effort to block. Every nerve lit on fire as she braced herself. Fear stabbed her skull. She covered with what she hoped was a brave face. No way was she backing down.

A guttural roar shredded the air. A blade sliced through the demon's arm. The limb fell to the ground, still holding its sword. Another swing removed its head.

Ryland reached for her. His eyes blazed with battle rage and darkened with concern. His clothes were covered in black ooze and his arm, drenched in crimson.

He hoisted Liz to her feet. "Are you all right?" He didn't wait for an answer and pulled her against him.

She grimaced from the agony in her shoulder. Ryland leaned back and searched her eyes.

For a moment, it was as if no time had passed. The pain faded. There was only the joy of being back in his arms. Her hiding place. The safest place in the world.

Before she knew what was happening, their lips were fused as though they'd never parted. She melted into his embrace and opened up to him. Giving what she had left. Taking what he offered. Losing herself in him. His lips claimed hers, relished them, said things words couldn't. Leaving no doubt of his intent. No doubt he owned the feelings wrapping around them like silk. Liz sank further into his arms and let herself rest against his granite chest.

She'd relinquished any hope of ever feeling his touch again. And now, here they were.

Ryland drew back, his eyes full, his breath labored. Liz sucked in air.

The stench of sulfur yanked Liz to the present. It rushed in with no mercy. She pushed him and stepped back. The truth was an arrow to her soul. She grabbed her shoulder as a fresh wave of pain blasted her, and not just from the wound. Liz shifted her gaze beyond him, unable to meet his eyes.

The last ten minutes had changed everything. It had all been a dream. Their past, any hope of a future, these few stolen moments. Reality slapped her, leaving a stinging imprint.

The dream was over.

"Are you hurt badly?" Ryland looked her over, pausing at the wicked gouge on her arm and wincing. He carefully pulled away the damaged strap of her sundress.

"I'll be fine." Liz trembled, as much from his closeness as the anger seeping in. She jerked away.

Ryland ignored her little fit and gently moved her hand from her shoulder. He ran his fingers around the edges of the wound. His touch scorched her. "It's already closing."

Liz finally met his gaze.

He gave her a half-smile and removed his hand. The regret she sensed from him turned to bitterness in her mouth. Her eyes narrowed. What did he regret? The kiss or his betrayal?

Ryland reached out to touch her face, then stopped. "I wanted to tell you."

Liz shook her head. He was a warrior. Same as her. Yet he'd never said a word. He'd let her push him away, believing she was alone in this. That she had no choice. The hurt burrowed in. She'd thought she was totally at fault for what had happened between them. And he'd let her think it.

He'd abandoned her.

Before she could respond, Arie drew up at her side.

"The victory is the Lord's!" Arie's voice rang out, followed by a similar exclamation from his companion.

Liz looked the new angel over. He was maybe an inch shorter than Arie and had a shock of red hair. His bright green eyes and pale skin gave him a decidedly Irish appearance. She wondered if he were as humorless and insistent as Arie.

He interrupted her perusal. "I am Chammu'el. Ryland is my charge."

"Nice to meet you." Liz gave Ryland a cursory glance. Heat ignited under her skin. Her voice cut sharp and low. "I need to get home."

Ryland's eyes clouded, and his shoulders sagged. "Of course."

Arie and Chammu'el said their goodbyes and vanished. Liz stomped to the truck, leaving Ryland to follow. He sprinted to her side and slid his arm around her waist. She was hurting, wiped out, and the support would've normally been welcome. But not from him. Not anymore. Liz moved out of his reach.

"Lizzy."

"Don't call me that."

He grabbed her good arm and brought her around gently. "I was trying to tell you before something like this happened. I wanted you to know years ago…" Ryland ran a hand through his hair and blew out a breath. "I wasn't allowed to use this to interfere when you left. I had orders."

Liz jerked her arm out of his grasp and glared. She bit her cheek so hard the taste of copper filled her mouth. If she spoke, she'd regret it. The storm brewing inside had to be contained. *Breathe. In for five, out for five.*

Ryland's eyes delved deep into her, as they always had. "It wasn't my choice. I was told you had to find your own path."

Liz embraced the rage and hurt clawing at her. She didn't want excuses. They were a knife to her heart, and his confession twisted the blade.

Her mind blanked as she squared off with him. Liz reared back and slammed her fist into his jaw. Shock lit his face as he stumbled. Part of her felt remorse for unleashing. The rest of her felt satisfied and avenged.

He deserved it.

Ryland rubbed his face while he worked his jaw. He stayed beyond her reach. Smart man. His look was fierce. A whisper of warning sounded on the breeze. "I'll take you home for now, but we're not done."

His vehemence shocked her, and she fought the sudden need to retreat. Of course, she *had* just punched him. But the Ryland she'd known had never been so forceful. This Ryland was powerful and demanding. There was steel in him. Attraction welled up inside her without her permission.

Man, she needed help.

Harsh truth stemmed the flow of that attraction. How could she want a man who would keep something like this from her, knowing what she was going through? Who all but fed her to the demons? Screw that. Screw him. All of her fury rested in the stare she leveled at him.

"Oh, we are definitely done."

Liz sneaked into the house. Thankfully her parents were in bed, saving her from an explanation. She really needed to get her own place. She crept to her room and extricated herself from her ripped and bloody dress, stifling a cry.

She stepped into the shower. Liz watched the blood color the water and swirl around the drain. Her dreams of Ryland blended with the eddy and disappeared into the ether.

Liz finished her shower, popped some ibuprofen, and slipped into bed. She curled around her pillow and buried her face. Her mind replayed the day. Her heart bled through each scene and seeped onto the pillow. Sobs wracked her battered body.

Things could've been different. She could've stayed. She never would've met Alex.

He asked you to stay, to trust him.

Liz argued with the Voice. *Maybe I could have if he would've trusted me. You should have had faith in him. And Me.*

He proved I couldn't trust him by walking away. He could've saved us. He could've saved me.

The Voice quieted, and Liz was left alone with her thoughts.

When Ryland had kept his secret after she'd opened her heart and soul to him, he'd perpetrated the deepest kind of betrayal.

I never want to see him again, she thought as the nightmares claimed her again.

X
Made of Stone

Man, that woman had a killer right cross.

Ryland rubbed his jaw again, even though the bruise had healed. He should've expected the punch. Liz had always had a hot temper, and he'd been on the receiving end of it before, although, never physically. But Liz's violent outburst wasn't what cut. It was her uncharacteristic silence and the betrayal in her eyes. He would've preferred she scream at him. Or hit him again.

Ryland laced his fingers behind his head and exhaled slowly. He lay in his bed, staring at the ceiling and wishing he'd had the chance to tell her the way he'd planned.

When he'd first caught a glimpse of her again, his heart had rolled over. Their connection was stronger than ever. He knew she had to feel it, too.

He'd come home because he'd been sent. Setting things right and winning her back was a bonus.

But seeing her with another man's hands on her had sent fire coursing through his blood. She was his.

He knew keeping his silence three years ago was right, even though the pain he'd caused her made it feel wrong. It made it even worse seeing and feeling the hardness in Liz's eyes that told him she'd been through hell. She was different. She carried too much weight on her shoulders. An ache throbbed deep inside his chest.

He would make this right. He'd put her gorgeous smile back on her face. He'd break through the wall she'd built and prove himself to her.

He would have to if he had any hope of completing his primary mission here.

Liz needed a distraction. Last night had been crazy—earth-shattering, really—and she needed to stay busy. Keep Ryland off her mind. Arie had said she could take today off, and she was thankful. Most likely, Ryland and his guardian would've shown up for training, and she couldn't face him. Not yet.

She focused her excess energy on finding a place of her own.

Dad had a friend with several rental properties, and he'd given her the number. Liz called the guy and set up a viewing of a small, one-bedroom apartment. As soon as she saw it, she fell in love. Windows everywhere and an open floor plan. Perfect. Plus, it was ready to move into right away. She put down two month's rent and a deposit and walked out with the keys.

Liz smiled as she started the Jeep. It might end up being a good day after all.

She was about to put it in reverse when her phone rang. Blake's name flashed on the screen, and a stray butterfly fluttered in her belly. At least there were some people she could still count on.

"Hey."

"Morning, gorgeous. What are you up to?"

"Just signed the lease on my new place."

"That's great! When do you move?"

"Tonight."

"Ah, well, I was going to ask you to dinner. How about I help you move, and we order in instead?"

Liz hesitated. Nope. She wasn't going to let Ryland's return affect her. "Sounds good. I've got a few things to do first, but I'll give you a call in a couple of hours."

"I look forward to it." He paused. His voice hardened. "How did your conversation go with what's-his-name?"

"Fine," she lied.

Blake didn't probe further, and she was grateful. Liz hung up and headed for the barn. If Arie had given her the day off, maybe he'd done the same for Ryland. She hoped. Besides, it wouldn't take long to pack, and she wanted to practice with her new sword. And she needed to hit something. An hour of running drills and working on the heavy bag she'd set up sounded awesome. She cranked up the stereo and sang at the top of her lungs, losing herself in the music.

As Liz drove into the clearing, her smile faded. Ryland's truck sat out front, and he hung over the side, digging in the toolbox. Her first reaction was to turn around. Instead, she lifted her chin. No man would dictate her life.

Never again.

Ryland straightened and offered a tentative smile when he spotted her. She averted her eyes as she pulled to a stop. A blast of his guilt choked her, and she coughed. *Good. He should be guilty.*

He pulled a bag from his truck and set it on the ground as Liz climbed out of her Jeep. He swallowed loudly before speaking. "I didn't think anyone else would be here today."

Liz gathered her gear and forced herself not to look at Ryland. She strode past him, feigning a confidence she didn't feel. In truth, she was two seconds from turning into a quivering, weepy blob. His nearness wrecked her entire system. Man, she was turning into a cry-baby.

Ryland followed her. "Lizzy. Stop."

"I said not to call me that." She trotted away. "I need to get busy. I have to practice with this new blade."

"You have time to talk." He grabbed for her elbow, but she wrenched away.

"No, I don't."

"Elizabeth Diane, quit acting like a child." Ryland pried her bag out of her hand and tossed it in the dirt. "I swear, woman, you could make a saint cuss up a storm."

"Give. It. Back." Liz whirled to face him and clenched her fists at her sides. *Do not hit him. Again.*

"I need to explain, and you're going to listen. There are some things you need to understand." His commanding tone would've caused anyone else in the world to think twice. Or at least, shut up and listen.

Not Liz. She glared at him, years of rage fueling her.

"Oh, I understand. I told you my secrets, you hid yours." She let out a curt exhale. "I felt so bad for what I did. But it wasn't all on me. You could've saved us. Could've saved me. And you walked away. You knew I was sinking, and you turned your back on me." She squared her shoulders.

Ryland's body went rigid. His eyes flashed. Regret and anger pelted her. A red flush swept across his cheeks, and a muscle ticked in his jaw. She should apologize, and she knew it. But there was no taking it back. She wasn't sure she wanted to.

The misery twisting her gut was awfully lonely.

Liz's words dragged across Ryland's heart like a serrated blade. How could he make her understand? He had to get her to trust him again.

Red-hot rage surged down his spine and infused his limbs, aimed at whoever had killed part of his Lizzy. Someone had cut her deep. Every protective instinct he had roared to life. But he'd have to deal with that another time.

Ryland ran a hand down his face. "I didn't turn my back on you. If I'd told you, it wouldn't have made any difference. As much as I love you, I couldn't have stopped you. No matter what I'd said. And you know it."

Liz's eyes flared when he'd said 'love' in the present tense. He reached for her, and she backed away. *God, please, help her understand. Help me reach her.*

She glared at him. "For years, you watched me run around thinking I was bat-crap crazy or was being punished. That's not love, Ryland." She swiped at her eyes and dropped her gaze.

Her words flayed him.

Ryland watched her heart break and drip down her nose. This was killing him. Without hesitation he reached up and wiped the tears, leaving his hand on her cheek. He wished he could pull the knife out of her heart as easily.

He could see the battle raging in her, could feel it in his bones. The hurricane spinning inside of her shook him to his soul. He wanted to hold her. To erase the hurt he'd caused. To let her know it was his faith and his love for her that drove him.

Ryland could only hope she could feel his heart, see his soul. Hope that doing what he'd been told to do hadn't cost him everything.

The hurt was too much. Too deep. Liz had to forget him. Forget anything they ever could've been. She had a job to do, and she couldn't do it if she was wrapped up in the past. Her feelings for Ryland had to be stuffed back down in their box. She had to do whatever was necessary to get him to back off.

Liz straightened her shoulders, swallowed her tears, and placed her hand over his. His face lit up. It dulled when she dragged his hand away. "I'm sorry. I shouldn't have said that." She meant it. Liz watched his shoulders loosen. "You had your orders. I get it."

Ryland's brow furrowed. Just like yesterday, she felt what he did. His current confusion. Love. Hope. His desperate need for her to understand. But she didn't understand. Her chest grew heavy as her heart turned to stone.

Ryland backed up a step. "So, that's it. You forgive me?" He watched her closely.

Liz forced her face to go blank. She shoved her emotions down. "It's done."

"Not an answer."

"It's all I can give."

She could feel him digging—trying to see into her soul again. Liz could tell by his rigid stance and the vein popping in his neck he didn't believe her. Whatever. His problem. This conversation was over.

Liz snatched her bag and headed for the barn. Time to move on. "Arie says something big is coming. I need to be ready, which means I have to step up my training."

Ryland stared after her. She could feel his eyes on her. The heat rolling off him cooled, and he let out a sigh.

"That's one reason I came back to town." He picked up his own equipment and met her at the door. As he shoved it open, Ryland shifted between watching her and watching the tree line with great interest.

"I can't stay long today. I'm meeting Blake for dinner." Why did she say that? Oh yeah. Her misery screamed for a friend. She kept blabbering. "He's a good guy. He actually helped me out after an attack. Not fighting or anything. But if he hadn't shown up, I'd probably be dead."

Ryland's left eyebrow shot up, and he gritted his teeth. "Interesting." He flashed her a tight smile and opened the door. "I'll have to remember to thank him."

Liz knew thanking Blake was the last thing Ryland intended to do.

Markus watched from deep within the forest. A smirk tugged at his mouth. Not exactly a joyous reunion.

Two of his imps had caught the immediate brunt of Markus's explosion when he'd been informed Ryland and his guardian were in the area. The creatures were currently recovering in the Nevada desert. It would take a few years.

Markus's mind spun, concocting plans to rid himself of two of his most annoying enemies. Chammu'el had been a problem for centuries. And ever since Elizabeth had left him, Ryland had run all over the country, putting some of Markus's best soldiers out of commission.

Ryland was also hunting Kade. Apparently he was still ticked off about that possession in Omaha. Or was it something else? Markus laughed, knowing it had taken Ryland and the preacher two days to force Kade's claws out of the girl. Ryland now sported a nice little scar for his trouble.

Markus didn't really care. He was more concerned about Ryland's return. It threw a wrench in his plan. If Elizabeth and Ryland were joined... Well. He couldn't let that happen. He had to keep Ryland away from her. Whatever it took.

It was time to send a message they couldn't ignore.

XI
Familiar Taste of Poison

"Ow!"

Hot spaghetti sauce splashed on Liz's hand. What had made her think this was a good idea? Cooking wasn't one of her talents. Liz sucked the heated concoction from her hand. At least it tasted good. She slid the garlic bread into the oven and set the table.

The past couple of weeks had been exhausting. Unlike the weeks before, there were constant demon attacks, the ferocity ratcheting up with each one. Arie had doubled training hours. Between practice and work, she hadn't had a lot of free time. What she did have, she'd spent with Blake.

Her main problem, though, was extra training meant she had to spend the majority of her days with Ryland. He was apparently here under orders, so there was no getting out of their joint training sessions. Liz huffed. And he'd made it sound as though he'd come back because of her. Right.

A knock sounded at the door. Liz checked her shirt for splattered sauce and did a sweep of the room, making sure everything was in its place. She opened the door to a grinning Blake, who held a beautiful bouquet of roses.

"They're gorgeous! Thank you." Liz took the vase and waved him in.

"What kind of date would I be if I didn't bring a gift?"

Once she'd set the vase on the table, he pulled her to him and planted a firm, quick kiss on her lips. The sound of a pot boiling over reached her ears, and she slipped out of his grasp.

Liz rescued the pasta and dumped it in the strainer. Blake came up behind her and put his hands on her waist, tugging her back against him. A thrill skittered through her belly. Blake was extremely affectionate, and she'd gradually gotten used to it. The attention was nice.

"The place looks great."

She glanced at her mismatched furniture and eclectic decorations. The couch was fluffy and comfortable, though it'd seen better days. A leather recliner sat next to it, her one splurge. An old bookcase stood beside the TV, and a large wardrobe in the corner served as a weapons cabinet. The huge picture windows in the living room were her favorite part.

Liz let a smile curl her lips. "Thanks. It's not much." She wriggled away from him and set the pot of sauce on a trivet. "But it is pretty great."

Blake helped her put the rest of the meal on the table. He pulled out her chair, seated her, and reached for her plate.

Liz watched with a raised brow. "You're my guest. I'm supposed to serve you." She hadn't been treated like this since… Her smile faded.

She had to stop letting Ryland creep into her thoughts.

Blake winked. "You cooked, so I'll serve."

After filling her plate, he sat and filled his own. As they ate, he regaled her with stories of all the countries he'd visited. She sat in wonder, never having gone anywhere besides Mexico. Liz felt her shoulders loosen and her muscles free themselves from their knots. She lost herself in the moment, reveling in the fact this gorgeous guy was focused solely on her.

When dinner was finished, they moved to the couch to watch a movie. Liz let him choose, and he picked a comedy. Blake put his arm around her shoulders, and she snuggled in to his side. It was blissfully normal.

They laughed and commented on the movie, the easy banter from the table continuing. Liz leaned over the coffee table to get her drink and caught Blake staring. When she recognized the look on his face, something deep within panicked. She said nothing, just took a gulp of soda and sat back.

Blake's hand slid to her neck. He gently pulled her close. "You're beautiful." His voice was liquid chocolate. So smooth.

Their lips met with a spark.

Blake slowly deepened the kiss, gauging her response. Liz had confided in him some of what had happened with Alex. Blake had been furious, wanting to hunt him down. He'd held her and promised he'd never let anyone hurt her again. Now she could feel his restraint. He didn't want to frighten her, and he was careful to let her retain enough control to ease her mind.

She could also feel the craving in his touch. Alarm bells sounded as his hands roamed. One landed on her outer thigh, and the other cradled her lower back. Her body involuntarily curved into his. Both resistance and desire sprang to life in her belly. His kiss intensified as though he were trying to devour her.

And she wanted to let him.

I'm in control. I can stop. But I don't want to. Or do I?

Liz disengaged from his mouth and leaned back. The demand he made was more than she could give. His grip on her tightened. Suddenly, she wasn't sure control was hers.

Run! This isn't you anymore.

She finally made her voice work. "Maybe we shouldn—"

Blake worked his lips along her jaw and down the delicate skin of her neck. Rational thought scampered away. His touch was all. The chill. The heat. The charge lighting her up like a thousand firecrackers detonating.

His eyes darkened, the black swallowing the brown. She could've sworn she actually saw flames in them. Blake gave her a smile filled with intent. Liz sucked in a breath.

She needed to make him leave.

Not because he scared her. Liz had no doubt if she asked him to stop, he would. No, she was scaring herself. A side of her she never wanted to see again stretched awake, demanding to be fed.

Blake kissed her cheek and recaptured her gaze. "Don't be scared. You don't have to hold back with me." He kissed her chin. "Let go. Be who you really are. You're safe here with me."

Liz closed her eyes and wondered how he knew what she was thinking. His lips claimed hers again. Urgent hands caressed her skin, leaving a trail of fire wherever they traveled. Overwhelming need ate away at her self-control.

Blake slowly laid her back on the couch. Liz didn't resist. She couldn't. His weight felt amazing against her. Heat wrapped her in a cocoon. Her bones went soft. His strength surrounded her, cradled her. Safety. Love?

They could be amazing together. Why couldn't she have this?

Blake had power over her, sure. But she'd handed it to him. He held her captive by her consent.

"Blake—"

"Shh. I'll take care of you." He ran his hand down her ribcage. Tucking under the hem of her shirt, he glided his fingers up her side. She shivered.

God, help me. I'm not strong enough.

Blake's lips on her throat sent a wave of delicious sensation cascading over her. It drowned her thoughts. Liz sighed and slipped under the waves. She could stay right here in his arms forever. *Forever. Mmm.* Maybe Blake would end up being "the one" after all. Right now, she didn't care. *This* was what she wanted. What she'd missed.

As Blake continued to shower her with kisses and tender caresses, Liz surrendered, letting the tide sweep her away. Just as she was losing herself, an image of Ryland floated by on the current, filling her mind. With it came the unrelenting truth she didn't want to acknowledge. A bucket of ice water to her overheated brain and body.

Liz flushed with a different kind of heat as guilt warmed her. The truth burrowed, ruthlessly digging in.

She still loved Ryland.

Suddenly, she couldn't escape fast enough. Blake shifted his body, and she took the opportunity to wriggle out from underneath him. He raised himself up and let her go. His frown declared his displeasure.

Liz slid off the couch and ran to the kitchen. She leaned against the counter, her erratic breath and spastic pulse making her dizzy. She wasn't that woman anymore. She was a new person. A warrior. And the only part Ryland played in that equation was coworker.

She could handle this.

Liz reached into the fridge and rooted around for a Coke. Sugar and caffeine. That's what she needed. When she closed the door, she jumped. Blake stood behind her.

"Don't sneak up on me!" she snapped and stomped across the room. "I hate when people do that!"

With two long strides, Blake was in front of her. "I didn't mean to scare you, darling." He brushed his knuckles across her forehead. "I pushed too hard. I'm sorry."

Liz softened a bit. He seemed sincere, even if she couldn't sense much from him, which was weird. "It's okay. It's just, things are different for me. I can't..." Tension strangled her words. "I mean, we're not even in love, Blake. I should've never let—"

"Maybe I am. Or at least getting there." Blake's hands circled her arms. "We're amazing together. You have to see that."

Liz choked on her Coke. A vise closed on her throat. She pushed him away.

"Blake, I care about you, but I don't—" Her words were cut off by a flutter in her chest and prickles on the back of her neck. Someone was coming. Someone not welcome.

That person pounded on her door.

What the heck? Sure, she could feel what others felt. But how in the world did she know it was him on the other side of that door?

Liz rolled her eyes. It was official. She was losing her ever-lovin' mind. She wrenched herself out of Blake's grip.

This wasn't what she'd had in mind when she'd prayed for help. A healthy dose of guilt showered her head again, like Gatorade on a sideline. Why him? And why did she feel guilty? They weren't together. They weren't anything.

Nothing was going as planned. Blake was supposed to be fun, but things had climbed up the serious meter about twenty notches. Then Ryland. The betraying, the lying by omission, the perpetually present thorn buried deep under her skin, refusing to let her dig him out.

Liz stomped across the living room and swung the door open, ready to tear into him. Instead, Ryland bull-rushed her, nearly bowling her over as he enclosed her in his arms.

Everything she'd planned to say flew out of her head and bounced down the hallway.

XII
Heavy Rain

"Thank God you're all right!"

Ryland crushed Liz to him, drinking in the smell of warm vanilla. All day, a bad feeling had him on edge. It had only intensified after what he'd found out a little while ago. But she was safe. In his arms. He could finally breathe.

She struggled out of his hold. "Of course I'm fine. What's your problem? And why are you all dirty and…" Liz eyed at the double blades strapped to his back. "Armed?" She threw a worried glance back toward the kitchen.

"Arie will be here soon. He'll fill you in." Ryland's eyes took her in, and his relief slipped away. "Are you sure you're okay? You look—"

Blake stepped out from behind the door and put his hand on the back of Liz's neck. The move smacked of possession. She flinched at his touch. Ryland ground his teeth. Blake sported a smug grin.

Ryland used every ounce of control not to throttle the man. "What's going on?"

"Nothing. We had dinner." Liz moved out from under Blake's hand.

Ryland took in Liz's flushed face, swollen lips, and tousled hair. A rush of blood swamped his ears and roared in his head. Oh, no she didn't. She wouldn't. Ryland glared at Blake, promising pain.

Do not rip his throat out.

Liz stared at Ryland, defiance lighting her eyes. He reached deeper with all of his senses. He found what he was looking for and relaxed a fraction. Then he analyzed Blake. Frustration wrapped around the man like a blanket. *Shot him down. Good girl.* Still, the fact Blake had had his hands all over Liz swelled a possessive, jealous rage inside Ryland.

He gestured to Blake, eyes never leaving Liz. "We have business, so your friend needs to leave." He didn't even try to hold back the smirk as Blake's eyes narrowed.

Ryland could barely read anything from Blake. That didn't sit well. The only reason he caught the frustration was because it was blatant. And there was something else. Something off. But Ryland couldn't nail it down. Maybe he was just overloaded with whatever was steamrolling off Liz. Either way, he didn't like not having the upper hand.

Liz motioned Ryland in. "Fine. Whatever."

Ryland shouldered Blake to the side as he passed. This time, he caught a whiff of unbridled fury. Good. The guy needed to learn his place.

Ryland stood sentinel in the living room. With arms crossed, he watched Blake follow Liz to the kitchen. When the man put his arms around her, every nerve in Ryland's body rubbed raw. Liz pushed Blake away, and Ryland smiled. There were hushed words, then Blake stalked out of the apartment. Not without giving Ryland a death glare first.

Liz marched to her bedroom and banged the door shut. Best to let her cool off. Otherwise he'd have another war to deal with. He didn't feel like battling on this front tonight. They had enough other issues to deal with.

A shadow cascaded over his mind. Ryland wanted to tell her everything would be all right. He wanted her to know he'd protect her. That they'd fight this together. Yet when she came out of her room, his thoughts veered onto another track.

"You shouldn't be with him."

Liz couldn't look at Ryland right now. She figured changing gave her an excuse to escape. She tugged on a tank top and a pair of cargos and shoved her feet into her boots. After jerking the strings tight, she threw the door open and headed for the table, making sure to keep her eyes focused straight ahead.

Then he just had to go and spout off.

She grabbed a plate from the table and viciously scraped it into the trash. "You have no right to tell me who I should or shouldn't be with." She tossed it on the counter.

"I care about you, Liz. I don't want to see you hurt."

You mean like you hurt me? Liz bit the end of her tongue. She needed to forgive him. Punishing him wasn't fair. Plus, she was punishing herself in the process. They were both to blame in all of this.

Liz sighed and leaned her hip against the counter, the anger draining from her. "I know."

She searched Ryland's face. Several emotions mingled with exhaustion. The fact she felt them so strongly perplexed her. Was it because they'd once been so connected? Or was it the fact she was so confused, she didn't know the difference between his feelings and hers?

Ryland moved toward her, graceful as a panther. He brushed a stray curl from her face. Liz's mouth went dry. Could she muster the strength to get the words out? To forgive him? Doing so would lay her heart bare. It would leave nothing standing between them.

That thought was scarier than facing a hundred demons.

She looked at the floor. "I'm sorry I snapped. I'm not having the best night."

"It's all right. I know better than to rile you up, and I did it anyway." He tweaked her chin.

Liz gave a weak laugh. For a moment, it was like old times. When she glanced at the couch, though, what had happened there earlier smacked her in the face. She'd been seconds away from a choice that would've brought everything she'd rebuilt crashing down. All because she wanted comfort, a gentle touch. A distraction from being so furious at Ryland. She was playing with fire. It wouldn't be long before she ended up a smoldering pile of ash.

She drew in a deep breath. He deserved her forgiveness, and she would give it.

Before she could tell him, Arie, Chammu'el, and three other angels appeared, taking position around the kitchen and living room. Ryland reached for her hand and squeezed. His eyes promised they were far from finished. A shiver zipped down her spine.

Arie surveyed them, a question in his eyes. She nodded, and he turned his attention to the group at his back. "This is Hadriel, Aelaem, and Sidriel."

Liz tilted her head to the side, surveying the new angels. Sidriel stood a few inches taller than Arie, short-cropped dark hair framing his square face and hard jaw. Despite the fact he looked like the ultimate soldier, a twinkle glistened in his eyes.

Hadriel was beautiful. She looked like an elf from myth with her long, almost white-blonde hair, ethereal features, and lithe, graceful stature. Liz didn't get a good look at Aelaem before Arie spoke again.

Arie's face was unreadable. "It seems Markus has been busy."

Fear blossomed in Liz's stomach. The angels were armed, alert, and poised for a fight. The solemn looks on everyone's faces were far from reassuring.

When Liz spoke, her voice shook. "Did something happen?"

"We discovered Markus has several humans under his control. He is looking to gain a hold here, a base from which to branch out. For what, we are not quite certain. Yet. Since the area is plagued with poverty and depression, it is a choice target. And there has been little resistance." Arie pointed at Liz and Ryland. "That is why you have both been led back here now."

Liz swallowed hard. "Are you saying we have to fight other humans? Wouldn't that draw attention, like the cops? And kind of go against our whole purpose?"

"It has to be dealt with delicately. The Father does not wish any to be lost, but man has free will." Arie sighed. "Ideally, we neutralize the demons and break their hold. Then guide the humans toward the Light. Some of them may not wish to be saved. They may attack, and you will have to defend against it." He sent a pointed look in Ryland's direction.

Ryland closed his eyes, and she could feel him erect a barrier, shutting her out of his emotions. Talk about a handy skill.

She tried to focus. Her pulse kicked into high gear as she felt Ryland's warmth hovering at her side. Ryland glanced at Arie, then back to her. Liz looked around the room, taking in the furtive glances. It seemed like no one wanted to look directly at her.

Liz threw out her hands. "Is somebody going to tell me what's going on?"

Ryland cleared his throat and ran his fingers through his hair. Something caught her eye. Nausea claimed her.

"Ryland, what happened tonight?"

Ryland followed her gaze and saw the blood he'd missed under his fingernails in his rush to get here earlier. *Smooth, Ry.* He looked at Arie and Chammu'el and pleaded silently. They nodded, wordlessly commanding him to answer.

"We did some recon tonight, hoping to find out what Markus has planned. We figured he had to have a place here, where he could gather the humans. So we found it." Ryland paused. "I've been hunting Kade, Markus's second-in-command, for a while. When I saw him there, I wanted to move in. Chammu'el said no. Then Kade said some things to the men with him that…didn't sit well. So I rushed in anyway, and three guys jumped me before I got to the door."

Ryland could feel Liz's confusion and fear. He couldn't tell if she was scared *of* him or *for* him. He didn't like that. Her gaze raked him from head to toe. She was probably looking for wounds. She wouldn't find any. The blood wasn't his. Liz stepped away from him.

"Ry, what did you do?" Her voice quaked.

"Just enough to keep them from following me or warning the others right away. They're alive." He dragged his hands down his face. "Chammu'el pulled me back."

"And if he hadn't?" Liz waved her hand. "Never mind. What did this Kade say to push you over the edge?"

Ryland hesitated, and Arie nodded again.

Liz moved back toward him. "I swear, if you don't tell me what's going on..." She closed her eyes and pursed her lips. "Either I'm a part of this, or I'm not. Which is it?" When she opened her eyes, they smoldered.

Ryland didn't want to be the one to do this. He gripped her shoulders, and she tensed. "It was about you."

"Me?"

"Markus is here to kill you. And he's got an army at his disposal to get it done."

Liz had been clocked on the temple and sent reeling. She would've sunk to the floor if Ryland's arms hadn't held her steady.

Liz clung to Ryland and felt Arie's wing at her back. But comfort wasn't what she wanted right now. She wanted to scream. She wanted to hit something.

She needed to run.

Liz pried herself from Ryland's arms and avoided his attempts to stop her. Ignoring the voices calling to her, she flew out the door and onto the porch. Liz ran across the grass until she hit gravel. Thunder rocked the ground, and the bottom fell out of the sky. She fell to her knees and lifted her face as rain soaked her through.

A scream ripped from her throat.

Rain pelted her. Liz blinked away the drops as they mixed with her tears. Heaven was silent. Doubt wrapped its sticky fingers around her.

Liz smacked her hands down in the mud. "God, I can't take any more. Please, you gave me this gift. Help me! You promised you'd fight for me."

Finally, a whisper of assurance blew through her soul. She'd come too far to let this shake her faith. Quiet strength bloomed inside of her. She'd do whatever it took to protect everyone she loved and defeat this demon. That meant doing whatever was necessary, even if it hurt. The Voice was silent again, but she knew what she had to do. Just the thought of it wrung her heart. She would make this stand, and it would cost her dearly.

Liz felt Ryland move in behind her. She imagined a steel gate slamming down in her mind. Maybe that was how he'd blocked her earlier. Worth a try. If he had the same gift, he could feel her too. See the truth. He'd try to stop her.

Ryland crouched beside her. "Come back inside. You're soaked."

"Really? I hadn't noticed." She stood, and he followed suit.

He ignored her sarcasm. "Come on, let's get you dry." He reached for her, and she pushed at him.

"Don't touch me." Each word lanced her heart. Just when she'd started to come to terms with what had happened, to begin to heal, she had to shatter both of their hearts. Again. At least this time, she knew for certain she was doing the right thing.

Times like this, being called to be a warrior royally sucked.

Ryland boxed her between him and the tree at her back. Understanding lit his eyes. "No. You're not doing this." He shook his head. "We'll figure it out and fight this. Together."

"There is no 'we.'"

This new threat was a train headed straight for her. There was no way she was letting him lay himself on the tracks in her place. Liz knew, without a doubt, he would sacrifice himself for her if it came to that. She couldn't allow it. And she couldn't wait to see if the demons would attack everyone else she loved just to get to her. She had to leave, draw the threat away.

It was the only choice that protected those she loved.

Ryland watched Liz duck under his arm and move toward Arie, who'd come out on the porch. He didn't like what he was sensing from her. Or rather, what he wasn't. Either she'd learned to shield overnight, or she was strangely calm. The latter was never good.

She marched up to Arie and spoke heatedly. Her voice rose above the wind. "Please, Arie!"

Arie's words were sharp. "Your desires do not dictate the path of another, and certainly not the Father's will." His voice softened. "Do not give in to pride and think you can win this battle alone." Without another word, he nodded to Ryland and shot upward, the others following.

Ryland moved under the cover of the porch. When he caught Liz's gaze, her eyes were blank and cold.

"Let's go inside and talk about this. Please."

"No. We're done here. You need to leave."

A bolt of guilt shocked the air. Yep. Shields. And they were crumbling.

He inched closer. "You don't mean that."

"Yes, I do. Leave." She reached for the door. "And don't come back."

"Oh, no you don't." He grabbed her shoulders and swung her around. "You can't get rid of me this time. I came back to help you, and that's exactly what I'm going to do."

Liz clamped her jaw. He could feel the turmoil inside of her. She shook him off and edged toward the steps. "This is my choice, Ryland."

Frustration gnawed at his control. "Did you not hear a word Arie said? It's not your decision. This isn't just about you."

"I know that. That's the point."

Ryland stepped forward. "You think I could let you walk away and leave you to face all of this on your own? You really think so little of me?"

The flash of anger across her face was unmistakable. He knew she'd almost said, *You did before.* The fact she'd thought it tore into him.

"I'm doing this because I know you'll jump in front of anything if you think you can save me." His heart melted as tears flooded her eyes. She still cared. "And I'm not alone. Arie and the rest of them have my back." She laid a hand on his arm, then yanked it away. "Go, Ry. Before it's too late."

His anger began to rival his concern. She was the most stubborn woman he'd ever met. Well, he could be just as stubborn. "No." She had to learn she didn't get the final say in everything.

Liz stared at him, wide-eyed, hands on her hips. "What? No marriage proposal to keep me where you want me this time?" She bit her lip. Whatever shield she'd erected tumbled down, and her regret sank its teeth into him.

Still, he couldn't stop the growing rumble deep within. "That's not why I asked you to marry me, and you know it."

He gritted his teeth, and the vein in his throat pulsed. He felt her uncertainty and fear as she stepped back. Ryland never wanted her to be scared of him. But a man could only take so much before his anger yanked at its tether.

He tried to smooth his expression. "I'm not going anywhere." The still-harsh tone of his voice surprised even him.

"Fine."

Liz pivoted and took off in a wild sprint. Ryland barreled after her, but he wasn't quick enough. She slammed the door of the Jeep and locked it. He banged on the door while she rummaged in the glove box, probably for the spare key. She found it and jabbed it into the ignition. Ryland called to her. She turned the stereo up, drowning him out. She threw it into reverse and peeled out of the drive, spewing mud.

He jumped into his truck and sped off after her. His stomach clenched. She must have it floored. It was pouring sheets of rain, and he couldn't see her taillights.

Was she trying to do the demon's job for him?

Liz could barely see the road. She let off the accelerator and eased around the next corner. Lights flashed in her rearview mirror. Shadows darted in and out of her high beams, pulling her attention back to the road. Uneasiness grew in her belly, and a prickle assaulted the back of her neck. Her skin crawled and tightened, stretching her nerves.

The vehicle behind her closed in. She didn't have to wonder whose it was. This new Ryland was like a bulldog with a bone.

Something slammed into the side of the Jeep. She kept control of the vehicle but couldn't unravel the knot winding together in her stomach. The ball of alarm expanded when whatever it was rammed into the vehicle again.

Ryland rounded the curve and saw taillights. Thank God she'd slowed down. He flashed his headlights, trying to get her attention.

He reached for his phone to call her when evil invaded his senses, sitting on his chest. Black forms darted through the air like a swarm of bats. The cloud blasted into the side of the Jeep. She corrected immediately. He prayed as the dark mass increased in thickness and closed around the vehicle.

The cloud lowered and blasted into the driver's side. He watched in helpless horror as Liz lost control and careened off the road.

XIII
Game On

Liz pried her eyes open to a busted windshield and a ferocious ringing in her ears. She clung to the steering wheel, her entire body vibrating. The Jeep had flipped several times, then had come to rest right side up. She'd never been more thankful for seatbelts. Or roll bars.

The door flew open, and Liz jumped, letting out a yelp.

Ryland reached in and took her head between his hands. "Are you hurt?" He looked her over, his fear making her dizzy.

Or was it her fear?

"I'm fine, I think." She reached to remove her seatbelt.

Liz fumbled with the button for a minute before Ryland loosened it and gently lifted her out. He set her on the soggy ground and folded her in his arms.

Hideous screeches and wails emitted from the darkness above them. He pulled her in tight, shielding her body with his. His touch grounded her, stopping the cyclic motion in her skull and bringing her out of her fog from the accident. Good thing, because the cacophony above them intensified.

Arie and Chammu'el dropped out of the sky.

Arie analyzed her from head to toe. "You are well?"

Liz nodded. *Ouch.* "Yes."

They watched the black cloud descend in front of them. Liz shivered. The brutal groundswell of evil paralyzed her. Shadows pressed in. Ghostly, icy fingers seized her, dragging her from Ryland's grasp.

Liz clung to him. Ryland's hold tightened as she felt him push his fear aside. Fierce protectiveness and determination took its place. For the first time, she was glad she knew what he felt. It soothed her. A fact she'd analyze later. As Ryland placed himself between her and the demonic mass, its pull lessened.

Arie and Chammu'el barricaded Liz and Ryland with broad backs and stretched their wings to cover them. She sucked in a breath as the pressure eased. Hadriel, Aelaem, Sidriel, and others appeared around the foursome. Insanely white light radiated from the angels and blasted the darkness, forcing it back.

Arie's eyes glowed. "Find a weapon. Quickly!"

Ryland set Liz aside and climbed into the Jeep. He found her sword wedged under the backseat. After handing it to her, he drew his own blades he hadn't had time to take off.

Liz couldn't suppress a shiver as shapes took form and emerged from the cloud. She counted thirty demons. At least. She glanced at the large group of angels, and warmth flooded her. She let the strength flowing from the angels and Ryland seep into her.

This would be the biggest test she'd faced yet. And on the heels of getting beat up in a wreck. Lovely.

God, I could use some serious juice about now. The prayer hadn't fully formed in her mind when a surge of heat blistered through her limbs. *Thank You.*

Ryland nudged her with his elbow. "You good?"

Liz nodded.

Another presence sucked the oxygen from the air. Her head pounded as the force of it shook her. With renewed power, the darkness pushed inside of her again and clung like ivy on an old building. Her skin crawled as the sensation slithered along her flesh.

Liz looked up at Ryland, trying to keep the panic out of her voice. "He's here."

Ryland stepped closer. Liz peeked around Arie's wing and watched the demons part, wilting and bowing as Markus sauntered past. Another towering demon, wearing an air of authority, followed right behind him. Judging by Ryland's clenched jaw, and the fact his body went rigid as he looked at the demon, she figured this was Kade.

Markus's eyes sought hers. He was fiercer than she remembered. Or the fact she knew she had a bull's-eye on her back made him seem scarier. She lowered her gaze, suddenly afraid of what she might see reflected in those black, flaming pits.

Ryland hauled her behind him, blocking her from Markus. The move sliced her heart and proved she'd made the right choice earlier. He'd put himself between her and danger. Without hesitation.

Liz breathed another prayer, slid out from behind Ryland, and met Markus's razor-sharp stare with one of her own. She was a warrior, a daughter of the King. *Greater is He who is in me…* She pushed back against the vileness emanating from Markus. She tuned out the pounding rain soaking her through and issued a silent challenge.

With a laugh devoid of mirth, Markus released her gaze and waved his hand toward Arie. "Yet again you interrupt me."

Arie answered evenly, "I go where the Lord commands."

"Ah yes, have to protect your pet." Markus tilted his head toward Liz. "Why hide, little girl? Are you frightened?" He speared her soul with his eyes. "If not, you will be."

Kade laughed at his leader's words, turning her stomach.

Arie stepped in front of her. Liz rested her throbbing head against the cool armor on Arie's back. Sandwiched between the angel and Ryland, the struggle eased. Markus had liquefied her with his heated gaze. Her insides solidified again as she absorbed the peace flowing from her guardian.

Arie spread his wings further. "She has no need to fear you or your master. The victory is and always will be the Lord's."

An even more brilliant glow sprang from each angel and impaled the darkness. Some demons cringed and threw up scaly arms to block the light. Others bowed and drew back. Markus took a retreating step, his visible tremble and pained expression revealing agony.

Arie leveled a glare at Markus that would make anyone, or anything, run quivering in fear. "You cannot defeat the Light."

"We will see." Markus let out a piercing howl, ripping the fabric of the quiet night.

In one swift move, the demon unsheathed his sword and swung. Liz heard and felt the dark blade collide with the illuminated length of steel in Arie's hand. The world erupted in malevolent screams and heavenly battle cries. The clanging of metal and the sounds of bodies and armor crashing together filled the air.

Ryland and Liz were left exposed when Arie and Chammu'el were forced from their guard. Ryland nodded at Liz, and they took position back-to-back.

"Like we practiced. Let them come to us. Ready?" Ryland gave her a grin, and she could see the thrill in his eyes. Feel the anticipation of battle. He was born for this. And so was she.

"Ready as I'll ever be." Liz smiled back at him. She couldn't help but get caught up in his enthusiasm.

Despite being sore and shaken, Liz felt a surge of adrenaline and pure power in her veins. Her breathing sped up as the sounds of battle galvanized her. The atmosphere charged, and the desire—the need—to fight filled her.

Movement to her right. A greenish-black demon slinked across the top of her Jeep, murderous intent glistening in its yellow eyes. It pounced. Liz thrust her blade into its belly midair. They tumbled to the ground, the sword buried deep in the demon's center. Liz winced at the impact.

Ryland lifted her off. They both ducked to avoid an incoming strike. Two more demons bore down on them. He yanked her sword from the demon's body and handed it to her. She spun to block the next volley. Ryland tangled with the demon at her back.

She swung for the neck. Her blade lodged in the thick tissue and bone. *Now what?* Liz sawed back and forth. Putting all of her strength behind it, she soon had the disfigured head rolling away.

Well. Not as easy as it looks in the movies.

She had no time to catch her breath. An enormous demon rushed them from the left. Ryland dropped to his knees. He swept outward with both blades, cutting the thing down. He staked the demon to the ground with the knives. Ryland sprang to his feet, eyes blazing.

"Here it comes." He nodded at the line of demons marching their direction.

Liz widened her stance. Two of the demons were distracted by angels, evening their odds. Liz parried the first thrust. The second. She spun. Blocked. Waited for her moment. It wasn't hard. For some reason, none of the demon's attempted strikes were killing blows.

Weird.

When her enemy raised its broadsword above its head, she pulled her katana through the demon's midsection. Thank God the thing didn't have armor. Its eyes opened wide. Arms dropped. She slashed across the throat, dropping it face-first into the mud.

Liz's breath came in gasps, and exhaustion burned in her arms. The cold rain seeped into her bones and chilled her from the inside out.

As she turned to check on Ryland, a rock-hard fist blasted the middle of her back. The impact drove the air from her lungs with a strangled cry. She landed on her stomach in the muck several feet away. Pain detonated in small explosions down the length of her frame.

It took everything she had to roll to the side and avert the steel headed for her. The blade sliced through her shirt, taking a strip of skin with it. She crawled to her feet. Liz grunted with the effort. Stinging agony ripped through her. The demon laughed. It was playing with her. Again, nothing it'd done had been aimed to kill. It made no sense. Wasn't she supposed to be marked for death?

Liz stood on wobbly legs.

The demon advanced. She prayed.

She pulled what was given into her body and let it fuel her. Her mind sharpened. She swung at her attacker's waist. It blocked the attempt, forcing her blade into the ground. Liz flung out her leg in a furious side kick. It drove the demon back and gave her the chance to free her sword from the mud.

A red haze replaced emotion. A guttural yell erupted from her as she rushed forward.

With a speed and power not her own, she whirled and slashed at the demon's neck. The blade found its mark. The monster fell to its knees.

Liz stepped back and slipped in the mud. The demon brought its sword up and caught her left arm, tearing a ragged laceration. She stuffed the scream filling her throat and buried her blade in the demon's gut as deep as she could. Its weapon fell. The creature grabbed the object now embedded in him. It pulled the katana out and yanked it from her hands, tossing it in the mud.

The demon grabbed a fistful of her shirt and jerked her close. Even on its knees, it was as tall as she. Liz tried to wrench free. Gnarled hands dropped her shirt, and claws locked around her hands. Hellish breath assaulted her nostrils. Tar-like ooze exuded from the wound on its neck. It mixed with the rain and covered them both in a sticky mess.

Liz's mind froze. Her muscles refused to move. Her head screamed, her body was on fire, and terror crept up her spine.

The demon rasped. Its eyes had already begun to dull. Liz closed her eyes. Finding what she needed, she inhaled deeply and smiled. When she opened them, she met her enemy's stare with the confidence of a true warrior. Her gaze didn't waver as she wrenched a slippery hand from the demon's grasp and freed her dagger from its sheath. She drove the blade up and into the demon's chin, twisting it.

The creature released her, a look of disbelief on its face. It fell back and landed with a crash of scales and wings. Her own relief and fatigue flooded her. Before she collapsed to the saturated ground, a wall of fury and the overwhelming desire for revenge waylaid her from behind.

Ryland tried to keep track of Liz. They'd been separated after the first wave. Each time he spotted her, another demon rushed him. He sliced and blocked at every turn. Both blades dripped black ooze. He pulled his knives from the creature at his feet and scanned the field.

She had to be wearing down. He spotted her near the fence line. His breath seized when he saw the size of the monster she faced. Ryland picked up speed in her direction. He swung his blades in a frenzy and hacked down any demon in his path.

He spotted Aelaem, who was closer to Liz. "Aelaem!" Ryland pointed at Liz.

The angel yanked his sword from a pile of scales and relieved another demon of its arm. He nodded and pushed through the throng toward Liz. Ryland relaxed as Aelaem reached her. His relief was short-lived. She was on her knees. The demon had her.

"No!"

Ryland sprinted forward. He jerked to a stop as a sharp sting lit up his back. He shook it off and blocked the next blow. A heavy shield slammed into his wounded arm. Fire shot to the tips of his fingers, and black spots floated in his eyes.

He pushed into the creature's midsection. He parried, then tied up the demon's blade with his. Ryland gritted his teeth against the torturous burn in his arm. Twisting his wrists clockwise, he flipped the sword from his opponent's grasp. He quickly drew both blades to center and carved through the demon's uncovered abdomen. His enemy dropped.

Ryland glanced toward Liz again. Aelaem was at her side. His sigh of relief hadn't even left him when a battle cry he recognized erupted to his right. Followed by a wicked, hot slice of steel into his calf. He stumbled, then turned to face Kade.

Ryland sneered. The rest of the battlefield fell away. "'Bout time." He charged, revenge his only thought.

Liz panted as she lay in the muck. She wrapped her fingers around her arm to slow the bleeding. Her eyes widened as she stared at the massive creature crumpled next to her.

I cannot believe I did that.

Someone knelt beside her, and a warm hand grasped her shoulder. Another surge of adrenaline raced through her veins. Liz scooped up her sword and jerked to her knees.

"Friend, it is Aelaem."

The gentle voice calmed her, and she lowered her blade.

His gaze took in the gash on her arm, and his eyes filled with concern. "Here, let me tend your wound." Aelaem reached inside his armor and pulled out a piece of cloth.

Liz watched the angel as he carefully wrapped the white fabric around her filleted arm. For some unknown reason, she felt as familiar with him as she had with Arie. She looked him over, trying to remember if she'd seen him before.

His raven hair fell down his back. Soft, amber eyes exuded peace. The chiseled face bespoke many battles. Still, his beauty was undeniable. Long nose. Solid jaw. He reminded her of a Native American warrior.

Aelaem patted her shoulder. "That should hold for now."

"Thank you."

Liz picked up her sword, and Aelaem helped her to her feet. They surveyed the battlefield. The noise had quieted. It was clear which side had won. Hadriel and Sidriel were among those dispatching the remaining demons. Liz scanned the area again. Dread iced her blood.

"Aelaem, have you seen Ryland or Arie?"

"Arie-Chayal is in pursuit of the enemy. Ryland is—" He turned to look over the field, and his brow furrowed. Aelaem touched her shoulder before taking off.

Liz prayed as she picked her way across the rapidly disappearing carnage. The rain had stopped, but the mud was deep. She slogged through, each step draining her. Her panic grew the longer she searched. She dodged the streaks of light that were injured angels returning heavenward. She waded through the black fog. Would she find Ryland under it? Someone called her name, and she spun.

Aelaem and Chammu'el appeared over the rise. Ryland walked between them, clutching his right arm. Blood seeped through his fingers. Her heart jumped into her throat, and she took off. Her boots were caked with mud, and it made running difficult. But nothing was going to stop her from getting to him.

He broke free from the angels and ran toward her. They collided at the edge of the battlefield, sinking into each other's arms. The embrace caused pain to ricochet through Liz's body, but she didn't care. He was in her arms again. He was safe.

Ryland buried his face in her wet hair. "Thank You, God."

Chammu'el and Aelaem left them and moved to check on those remaining in the field.

Liz melted into Ryland, gingerly wrapping her arms around his waist. When he flinched, she pulled back.

He flashed a crooked smile. "Just a scratch." Ryland leaned back to examine her, taking in the blood that coated her body. He frowned. The fear in his eyes plucked at her heart.

She shook her head. "I'm fine. What about you? How bad is it, really?"

"I've had worse. It'll heal in a few hours. That cut on your eye looks rough. Come on. I've got a kit in the truck." Ryland wrapped his arm around her, and they held each other up on the way to his truck.

As much as she hated to mention them, she had to know. "What about Markus and Kade?"

Ryland huffed. "Kade ran. Got a few shots in. Took off." He growled the words.

Liz wanted to ask why he was so ticked at Kade, but pain settled back in and stole any other thought. Her wounds pulsed with every heartbeat. Ryland pulled her closer to his side.

He looked at her mud-covered vehicle. "I'll get your Jeep tomorrow."

Liz fought to see out of her swelling eye. She touched it lightly.

When did that happen? And where was Arie? Worry balled in her stomach.

Ryland leaned her against the truck bed and fumbled with the door. His grunts told her he was hurting, too. Liz moved to help him when she heard a *thump* and a rustle behind her.

Her skin tingled. A tidal wave of pure evil hit her with impossible force.

"Liz, move!"

Before she could take a breath, she was picked up and heaved through the air.

Liz roused to find herself lying in the mud. Again. She tried to open her eyes. Blood seeped into them. She wiped it away and struggled to sit up. The world spun. An immense, dark form towered over her. A sour taste filled her mouth. A fog of filth clung to her skin. Markus. She looked for her sword. It lay several feet away. No way could she reach it in time.

A shadowy blur flew over her and plowed into Markus's midsection. They toppled to the ground. *Ryland!* Both of them scrambled to their feet.

Ryland lunged at Markus, blades flying. The clang of steel rang in her head so loudly, she thought her ears would bleed. If they weren't already.

Their blades locked together. Markus reared his head and brought it crashing into Ryland's skull. Ryland stumbled, then came at Markus again.

Ryland's blade grazed Markus's neck. Ryland ducked Markus's swing and brought his blades across the demon's thighs, slicing wide. Ryland lunged, swinging both swords for the kill.

He wasn't fast enough.

Markus landed a kick to Ryland's head, then sliced across Ryland's abdomen. Ryland staggered. Markus drove his sword into Ryland's side.

Liz started with the strike, grabbing her own midsection. "Ryland!" The agonized cry tore from her soul. She tried to pull herself up again but couldn't make her body cooperate. Tears slid down her face.

Markus laughed and kicked Ryland off the blade. Liz watched as Ryland sailed through the air and smashed into a tree. He slid down into a heap.

She cried out. "No! God, please, no!"

Markus stalked toward her. "Keep calling if you want. He's not going to answer." He kneeled. A depraved smile added to his menace. "The little warrior is alone and at my mercy."

Liz scooted back. Too much blood poured from the gash in her side. Searing pain sliced through her skull. Every nerve came alive with agony. She tried to pray, but Markus's words wormed their way in. Where was God? Where was Arie? Would God really bring them through the battle to have them die now?

She glanced at Ryland. He hadn't moved. Her heart broke at the thought that this could be his end. All because he had tried to save her. Despite her earlier choice, in that moment she knew she didn't want to be without him.

God, please, don't take him. Me. Take me instead.

The heat of fury filled her as she looked up at Markus. He tormented her, dragging his blade along her inner thigh. A shiver rattled her bones. It made sense now. He'd ordered the demons not to kill her because he wanted the job for himself. All she could hope at this point was for it to be quick. And that Ryland would recover. Liz squared her shoulders. She would not go down crying and sniveling.

"Ah, my beautiful, brave warrior." Markus mocked her.

Liz glared at him before turning away. "The big, scary demon bested the injured, defenseless woman. Ain't you somethin'?"

He grabbed her hair and jerked her head back. Liz sank her teeth into her lip. He didn't deserve the satisfaction of hearing her cries. She eased her hand toward her boot to reach her dagger. If she were going out, so was Markus.

Markus laughed again and batted her hand away. He extracted the blade himself. "Ever the little fighter. We would make a great team, darling." He released her and rose to his full height. He flung her dagger, and it stuck in the ground. "For now, you'll be my message. When you see Arie-Chayal, tell him…I win."

Liz didn't respond. He raised his blade. She kept her eyes locked on his. Her insides quivered. She glanced at Ryland's still form.

I love you. I'm so sorry. For everything.

Liz returned her gaze to Markus. She saw the fire of intent in his eyes.

It was over.

Markus brought the cold steel down fast and hard. It drove all the way through her, piercing the ground. A scream tore from her lips. Her world exploded in flame and torment as he gave the blade a quick twist.

Liz watched her life pump in bursts out of her and onto the ground. She grasped the sword but didn't have the strength to pull it out. Black seeped around the edges of the world. Markus's laugh sounded hollow.

Then there was nothing.

XIV
My Heartstrings Come Undone

Arie-Chayal landed on the deserted field while Markus's malicious laugh still echoed through the whispering pines. The angel scanned the area. His eyes fell on the two prone figures lying only feet from one another.

"No. Father, please no."

Arie-Chayal sprinted to Ryland, who was closer. Ryland's pulse beat strong, and the guardian could sense the man's body healing. Hesitant, not knowing what he might find, the angel moved to his charge. At the sight of Liz's mutilated body, the angel dropped his sword and fell to his knees in the mud.

His guardian's heart shattered as he examined her. The porcelain skin of her face was marred with splotches of purple, black, and blue. Lacerations and vicious bruises covered her fragile flesh.

"Oh, Elizabeth."

His gaze landed on the gaping wound in her thigh from the demon's blade. Blood flowed like a river, pooling beneath her. Arie pressed the tip of his wing over the brutal gash.

A tortured prayer left his lips as crystal tears formed. For a moment, he lost himself to his grief. He beseeched the throne of Heaven for a miracle.

It was not her time to go Home. He would have been informed. Surely. Tears fell without constraint as Arie pleaded with the Father.

Ryland stirred. A fierce roaring rattled his skull. It felt like someone had taken a sledgehammer to his bones. He held his head as he sat up, then blinked to clear the haze. A single thought pierced the fog.

Liz.

Where was she? Was she all right? Panic laced his blood and clogged his throat. He strained to see in the dark. He spotted a familiar form kneeling a few yards away. There was a body on the ground before the angel.

Motionless.

Terror like he'd never known pierced his chest, tearing the breath from his lungs. He rose and staggered toward the angel.

The angel moved aside, revealing the body to Ryland.

"Lizzy?" One strangled word made it past his constricted throat. "Oh, God!" Ryland moved to her, the dizziness and pain in his body forgotten.

He skidded to his knees beside her. Ryland's heart twisted. Liz was ghostly white. Arie lifted his wing. Ryland's stomach lurched at the sight of bone and torn muscle in the gaping hole in her thigh. He whipped off his belt and secured it above the injured area as tightly as he could. He eyed the blood-soaked ground. She'd lost so much. Ryland searched frantically for a pulse. He pressed harder, hoping against hope.

His heart flipped over when he felt the weak beat against his fingers. "She's still alive!"

"Yes. Barely. Lay your hand over her wound," Arie commanded. "Now pray. She is not healing as quickly as usual. We don't have much time." His voice cracked at the end.

Ryland reached down to the core of his faith and yanked hard, begging God to spare her. If he could offer himself in exchange for her, he would. His life for hers. She was worth the trade. He knew it wasn't rational. Certainly not the way God worked. But he'd give anything to keep her here with him.

Ryland cradled her head in his lap as he prayed. She felt so cold. If he lost her, it would leave a chasm in his soul. They were a part of each other. Always would be. He couldn't lose her. Not like this. She made the sun brighter and the air sweeter. Liz had to be in this world. If she weren't, he didn't want to be either.

Ryland settled beside her and pulled her upper body across his lap. He leaned down and kissed her forehead. Fear clawed at him like a wild animal. A cold void existed where her essence should've been. It chilled him to his soul. He couldn't feel anything from her.

"We've prayed, now let's go." Ryland shifted his legs beneath him and readied to carry Liz to the truck. "Why is she not healing?" He didn't even try to keep the hardened edge out of his voice. She should've started healing by now.

"There could be many reasons. It is not for us to question." Arie's voice was even and stern.

Ryland shook his head slowly. Ignoring the angel, he gently slid one arm under her back and the other around her legs. He positioned a hand over the gash. As he rose to his feet, he felt her warmth return. It spread outward, reaching into him. Whispers of thought and emotion touched his spirit, Liz's unique imprint etched in them.

Ryland glanced at Arie and saw a slow smile spread across the angel's face. At the same time, there was movement under Ryland's hand on her leg. He jerked it away as a jolt of electricity burned up his arm. Ryland eyed the wound. While not completely closed, the bone was no longer visible.

Ryland readjusted Liz in his arms. Knives gouged his body, reminding him of his own wounds. Fresh blood seeped down his back. He walked on. Liz needed help. He had no idea why she hadn't healed fully, or why she was still unconscious. *God, please...*

Arie morphed into his human form. He stopped Ryland and took Liz. Ryland didn't protest. He opened the passenger door, and Arie slipped in with Liz in his arms. The angel held her close as Ryland drove. They were both silent, praying and hoping.

Ryland slumped in a chair by Liz's bed. The doctors had worked on her for two hours. Now she was covered in bandages, along with a myriad of bruises. An IV in her wrist provided much-needed blood.

While they'd taken care of Liz, a nurse tried to usher him to the adjoining cubicle. He'd refused at first, not wanting Liz out of his sight. The nurse said she would leave the curtain open between them, so Ryland finally agreed.

When the nurses finished with both of them, Ryland pulled out his cell to call Liz's parents. He'd forgotten with all the activity. As he looked down, he noticed the blood coating him and his clothes. Not all of it his own. *Liz's blood.* His stomach heaved and his heart squeezed so violently, he was sure it would rupture from the pressure.

Ryland glanced at Liz. His hands shook and his vision clouded while he tried to dial. Nothing had ever shaken him like this. He was a rock. A warrior. A protector. Yet he'd failed to protect the most important person in his life.

"Hello?"

"Pastor Brantley, it's Ryland."

"What's wrong? You don't sound good, son."

He took a breath, and it turned into a wheeze. His ribs hadn't fully healed yet. "We were in an accident. Liz is in the hospital." He knew he'd have to come clean with Liz's dad. The man wouldn't buy the wreck story when he saw them, or their vehicles. *Later.*

"How bad is she? And what about you? Are you okay?"

"She's pretty beat up. Minor concussion and some cuts and bruises. They said she'll be okay. She hasn't woken up, though." Ryland caressed Liz's hand.

"Sit tight. We'll be right there."

Ryland watched Liz lie there, helpless and broken. There were two things in the world he wanted right now. Liz to wake up and demand to be let out of here, and to hunt down Markus. For the umpteenth time in the past few hours, he prayed. But his failure and his fear for Liz wouldn't turn him loose. His inability to protect her gnawed at him. The air closed in on him. His lungs compressed.

Ryland looked up at Arie, who stood guard on the other side of the bed, cloaked from anyone else's sight. "I need to get some air. Stay with her?"

"Of course." Arie nodded once.

Ryland trudged downstairs and out the front doors. He took a deep breath of the humid night air. Needles of fire stabbed his chest. The doctor had wanted to admit him for observation. He'd refused. The wounds were already partially healed. By morning, they would be just a memory. He sat on a bench to the side of the doors and leaned his head against the brick building. Ryland closed his eyes.

I should've never let her out of my sight.

Her being a soldier didn't lessen his protectiveness, or what he felt was his obligation. It ate at him that he'd failed her. He had more experience. She didn't even know everything about what she was—what *they* were. And he'd abandoned her. All for the chance to finally get a hold of Kade.

Never again.

A fresh wave of heartache overtook him. He shifted his focus and thoughts back to the battle. She'd taken out demons like a seasoned warrior. Pride welled up in him. She definitely learned fast. She was a natural.

"Where is she?"

Blake. Ryland stifled a growl.

Ryland stood slowly and turned. Face to face with Blake, he barely controlled his fury. The man stood before Ryland, confident and sure. Like he had every right to be there. Gritting his teeth and schooling his features, Ryland sized him up.

Blake had a couple of inches on him. Ryland was broader across the shoulders with a thicker build. Other than that, they were evenly matched. Both men were corded with muscle. But Ryland wondered if the guy had ever even been in a fight. He looked a little too polished.

Just a pretty boy wannabe. I could take him.

"Liz is resting. She's in rough shape, but they said she should be fine. Once she wakes up." Ryland angled his head. Suspicion whipped in his mind. "How did you know she was here?"

"Friend of mine is a nurse." Blake's gaze raked Ryland. "She said it was a wreck. I'm thinking that's not quite right. At least, I'm assuming from those blades you wore earlier." Blake smirked. "What kind of mess did you get her involved in?" His voice dropped, laced with threat. "Obviously, one you couldn't handle. If she'd been with me, she wouldn't be lying in a hospital bed."

Blake's words had the desired effect. Ryland ground his teeth. At this rate, he'd grind them to powder soon. Every muscle in his body tensed. Rage boiled under the surface and heated his skin. He barely reined it in.

"It was pouring rain, and she had a wreck. It happens. Just a bad night." He tried not to let his guilt show.

There was something in Blake's eyes Ryland couldn't identify. And again, he couldn't read his emotions. There wasn't a stinking thing coming from him.

"A real man wouldn't let his woman have a bad night." Blake flashed his teeth. "Oh. I forgot. She's not your woman anymore." He moved away as Ryland bristled. "I'll be taking over from here. You can run on home and lick your wounds."

Blake sauntered through the doors. Ryland clenched his fists until his short nails bit into flesh, drawing blood. It took all of his willpower to keep from going after Blake and throwing him into a wall.

Pretty face first.

Blake hadn't expected Elizabeth to look that bad. Her beautiful face looked like someone had taken a club to it. There were bandages everywhere, her skin so pale, they almost blended together.

The amount of discomfort and protectiveness he felt shocked him. He was experiencing things he couldn't quantify. Things he thought were impossible anymore. Blake tilted his head and watched her. Somehow, the woman had to have him under a spell.

He touched her hand. So cold. The gentle rise and fall of her chest and the sounds from machines the only indications she was alive. Blake's eyes narrowed when his thoughts focused on how much he wanted her to open her eyes so he could see the fire in them.

Yes, she'd certainly bewitched him.

His thoughts were interrupted when Liz's parents came in, followed by Ryland. Blake suppressed the desire to throw Ryland out the window. With a slight hesitation, Ryland introduced Blake to Elizabeth's parents. Blake moved toward the door, and they took his place at her bedside.

Blake and Ryland glared at each other.

Blake had planned on staying with her, being there when she awoke so he was the first person she saw. He couldn't do that now. Not with the three of them there. Things would be…awkward.

Blake noticed both men watching him with discerning eyes. He folded his arms and stood as far away from the group as he could get. Observing their interaction could prove informative.

Ryland filled Liz's parents in on what the doctor had said. He thought about sinking into the nearest chair. It'd been a long time since he'd been beaten up like this. Then he glanced at Blake and decided to forgo it. He wanted to pull the painkillers out of his pocket, but he couldn't give Blake a clue of how bad a shape he was in.

Liz's mom crossed the room and put her hand on Ryland's cheek. "You should get some rest, sweetheart."

Ryland shook his head. "I'm good." His eyes fell on Liz.

Mrs. Brantley gave him a sad smile and patted his cheek. She glanced at Blake and lowered her voice so only Ryland could hear. "I know how much you love her. Don't give up. Everything will happen in His time." She tilted her head. "You really should go home and get into bed. At least for a little while."

"Thank you for being concerned, but I'm not leaving her." He made a point to make eye contact with Blake. The man visibly snarled at Ryland.

Try it, pretty boy. I dare you.

Mrs. Brantley sighed. "Just as stubborn as she is. Well, go to the nurse's station and get us a couple of pillows and blankets. I'm not leaving either."

Ryland could feel Blake's eyes on him as he made his way out the door. Ryland laughed silently. Blake was fidgeting and scowling. Good. What was this guy hiding? He rolled the question around in his mind while he got the items Mrs. Brantley had requested.

When he returned, the nurse came with him to check Liz's dressings and IV. Blake was jumpier now than when Ryland had left. He wondered if Pastor Brantley had said something to him. Ryland grinned at the thought. Liz's dad didn't pull punches. Especially when it came to a man hanging around his daughter. Ryland should know.

Blake stepped up to the bed while the nurse switched bags on the pump. "If you will excuse me, I must be going." He planted a kiss on Liz's forehead, which drew a glare from Ryland, then nodded at the Brantleys.

Ryland eyeballed Blake as he stalked past and was rewarded with a cold stare. When Blake walked into the hall, the strange tension in the room went with him.

"I can't say I care for that fella." Pastor Brantley grunted.

"James!" Mrs. Brantley softly slapped his arm.

"Hey, you don't like him either." She frowned, and he smiled. "I just call 'em like I see 'em." He nodded toward Ryland. "What do you think?"

"Something's off about him, that's for sure."

Mrs. Brantley shook her head. "I think you two probably aren't the best judges of that."

Both men shrugged. It seemed Liz's dad had the same feeling Ryland did about Blake. They let the subject drop. The three of them spent the next hour catching up. Then Mrs. Brantley shooed her husband out of the room.

"It's late. You need your sleep." He protested, and she put her hands on her hips. "One of you boys is going to listen to me tonight. Move!"

"Fine. Fine." Pastor Brantley gave Ryland a look and a nod. "Take care of my girls."

"Will do." He'd do a better job of it this time around.

Pastor Brantley gave Liz a kiss on her uninjured cheek. He nodded to Ryland and kissed his wife before striding out to the nurses' station.

As the pastor left the room, Ryland addressed Mrs. Brantley. "I'm gonna take a quick walk and loosen up a little."

Ryland leaned over the bed and took Liz's chilled hand in his. He ran his fingers down the curls cascading over the pillow, then kissed her softly on the forehead. "I'll be back in a few minutes. I love you." He couldn't stop himself from saying it.

Heading into the hall, Ryland saw Pastor Brantley leave the nurses' station and started after him. He had to tell the man the truth. He'd never lied to Liz's dad before, and he couldn't let it stand. Even if it had been for a good reason.

Ryland took as deep a breath as he could manage and caught up with him. The pastor nodded but continued walking without saying a word. Ryland was glad. He needed a minute to get his thoughts together.

Hopefully Liz won't kill me for this when she wakes up.

The two men remained silent until they reached the courtyard in front of the hospital. Ryland searched for a way to begin, but the pastor spoke first.

"Well, this could've been worse. God was watching over you both."

He gestured at Ryland's bandaged arm.

"It was worse."

Pastor Brantley pointed to a bench. "Here, let's sit."

"I need to apologize. I lied to you earlier. There was a wreck, but that's not what caused her injuries." When Pastor Brantley said nothing, Ryland dove in. "The gash on her leg went to the bone. We prayed and, thankfully, she was healed. Partially." He took a shaky breath as the scene replayed itself in his mind. "We almost lost her."

"You said we prayed. Who is 'we'?"

It all poured out. Everything about their guardians, their gifts, what they'd faced tonight, and finally, the fact Liz was at the top of a demonic hit list. Ryland observed the pastor, waiting for a reaction.

"Well," the pastor sighed. "That's quite a tale. I was aware she had certain…abilities, but I never thought…" Pastor Brantley straightened. "God knows what He's doing. If He's called you both, He'll protect you and give you the strength to face what comes."

Ryland's jaw dropped. Liz had told her dad about what she could do? But as close as she and her dad were, it made sense. And he was a pastor. It was probably a little easier for him to accept than it would be for most people. Still, Ryland was shocked the man could speak in such a matter-of-fact manner about it. Maybe the preacher knew more than he was saying.

Ryland focused his senses and read Pastor Brantley. Determination and faith wafted from the man. There was no deception. Nothing indicated the pastor was hiding anything. His surprise and curiosity took a backseat as his mind came back to their situation.

Ryland ran a hand through his hair. "I'm sorry I didn't tell you the whole truth before. But, what we do, well, it has to be protected. Secret, for the most part."

"I understand. But we have to fight together. Just not the same way." Pastor Brantley smiled. "I'm glad you're home, son. She needs you. When you win her back, try to hang on to her this time, okay?" His eyes twinkled as he bumped Ryland's uninjured arm.

"That's the plan."

Some of the tension left Ryland's shoulders. At least her parents were on board. Though worry still squeezed his chest. Fear battered the faith he desperately clung to. His heart had been gouged out and was now lying in a bed upstairs.

He prayed silently and hoped those prayers would be answered. Soon.

XV
Hold On, Small One

This had to be the most uncomfortable chair in the history of the world. More akin to an ancient torture device than furniture.

Ryland had endured it most of the night. An acceptable consequence, though. He refused to be away from Liz any longer than necessary.

Around six a.m., he gave up trying to sleep and went to the cafeteria. He bought two cups of coffee and some donuts and headed back to Liz's room. Mrs. Brantley slept in the recliner, and he wasn't about to wake her. One of them should get some rest.

Even sleeping, he could sense her worry and also, her faith. What a lady. He'd thought of her as a mother since his own parents had died. Liz's parents had claimed him as part of the family. His younger brother, Nathan, as well. He appreciated it more than they knew.

Ryland took two donuts out of the bag. He set the remainder and one of the coffees on the table beside Mrs. Brantley. He stood by Liz's bed to eat his breakfast. He'd had enough sitting for a while.

Watching Liz had become his new job. He took comfort in the motion of her breathing. Shoving the last bite of his donut into his mouth, he twisted his fingers in the fiery curls spread across her pillow. Ryland wrapped her hand in his, praying the vigil wouldn't have to last much longer.

Mrs. Brantley stirred behind him. "Ryland, did you get any sleep?" She stood up to stretch.

"A little." He gestured to the table. "I brought coffee. Figured you'd need it. It should still be hot. There're donuts, too."

"How sweet of you. This chair was rock hard. I'm not sure I slept a full hour at a time." Mrs. Brantley tested the temperature of the liquid and took a sip. "Has there been any change?"

Ryland knocked back the last of his coffee and grimaced. "None."

"Maybe the doctor will have something new. He should be in anytime." She brushed Liz's hair from her face. The look of sorrow in Mrs. Brantley's eyes broke his heart.

As if he were responding to a cue, the doctor sauntered in. Unfortunately, he didn't have anything new for them.

"Her tests all look good, and there's no swelling in her brain. She *should* be awake." He shook his head. "All we can do is keep her comfortable and wait." The doctor shuffled out of the room, leaving two disheartened faces staring after him.

The nurse came in, so Ryland waited outside the door while she changed Liz's dressings. When the nurse finished, she found him in the hall and patted his shoulder before sending him back in. Ryland resumed his post and took Liz's hand. Mrs. Brantley stepped out to freshen up and make some calls.

Ryland talked to Liz, praying she could hear him. "You can scream at me, punch me, or hug me, I don't care. Just wake up." He gave a halfhearted laugh. "Maybe if I nag enough, you'll get ticked off and wake up to lay in to me."

He laughed again when he thought of how God must have a sense of humor to have put them together. They were both strong, passionate, stubborn people. But where she was ruled by emotion, he required a plan. Somehow, they'd always evened each other out. When they weren't butting heads. They could be explosive at times. Mostly they complemented one another. He grinned at his thoughts and kissed the long, tapered fingers laced through his.

Ryland pulled the blanket under her chin, then tucked it around her feet. *Her feet are always cold,* he thought absently. Gently lifting her head, he adjusted her pillows.

Ryland leaned forward and rested his forehead against their joined hands. He pleaded with Heaven for the woman he loved more than his own life.

The day dragged on. Shelley and Dylan stopped by. They tried to urge Ryland to get some rest, but he refused. He only left his post by the bed a couple of times. He had to be there when she woke up. Later in the day, Liz's mom went down to the cafeteria to get them supper. Ryland didn't feel like eating, but Mrs. Brantley had insisted.

Ryland rearranged his position in the chair and continued trying to stimulate a response from Liz. He stroked her hand. Her face. Her arms. He talked to her. He played with her hair. He even sang, though he couldn't carry a tune worth spit.

He was in the middle of telling her a monstrously bad joke, the only kind he was good at, when her hand twitched under his. He held his breath. "Liz?"

Hope flared to life. But moments passed, and her eyes remained closed. The spark of anticipation fizzled, and his broad shoulders sagged. He exhaled slowly and rested his head against the rail of the bed.

A few minutes later, he felt someone enter the room behind him. Someone who was a blank slate.

"Any change?" Blake's voice fell flat and cold.

"No." Ryland had no desire to speak to the man. And no way did he want him here.

Liz squeezed his hand. This time, there was no doubt. It wasn't his imagination.

"Lizzy?" He cupped her cheek in his hand.

Blake moved to the other side of the bed. Ryland shot Blake a glare as he grabbed Liz's other hand. Mrs. Brantley walked in, and Ryland waved her over.

"What is it? Did she wake up?"

Blake moved to the side as Liz's mom took his place next to her daughter.

"She moved her hand. See?" Ryland pointed to Liz. "She's moving! Come on, Liz. Come on, baby." Every cell in his body burst with excitement.

Liz shifted her body. Her eyelashes fluttered. Her right eye opened slightly, the left one still swollen shut.

Ryland's heart took flight. "Liz? Can you hear me?"

Her breathing sped up. Liz tilted her head toward him. Her lips parted, and she licked them. "Ryland?" Her voice was scratchy and low.

"I'm right here." He smoothed her hair and smiled at her.

"Mom?"

The woman moved closer. "I'm here, too, honey."

Blake cleared his throat. Ryland didn't look at him. Liz was awake, and she had called for him. He could sense her again. She filled the void that had swallowed his head and heart. Even though her feelings were jumbled, one thing stood out. It burned into him, charging his spirit.

When he looked into her eyes, her love for him resided there.

The faces hovering over Liz were blurry. Everything in her brain muddled, pieces and flashes she couldn't arrange. *Arie left me. Ryland tried to save me. Markus. Markus was there and he...* Liz shifted to look at her body, and a stabbing sensation ripped her breath away.

"Stay still, baby." Ryland settled her back onto the bed. "You've got a fractured sternum and some broken ribs. You shouldn't be moving around."

She heard Mom's voice. "I'll get the nurse."

"You stayed with me." It wasn't a question because somehow she knew Ryland hadn't left her side. At least, not for long. "But you were hurt." She lifted her hand to his face.

"Of course I stayed. Wild horses and all, right? And I'm fine." He gave her a grin and turned toward her fingers to kiss them.

A blurry form to her right made a strangled noise. "Blake?" Had he stayed too? And he and Ryland were both still in one piece?

"I'm here." Blake leaned in and squeezed her hand. He shot a look at Ryland she didn't understand, but her head hurt too bad to think about it.

Ryland scowled at Blake.

"Thank you. Both of you." Liz looked between them. "How long was I out?"

Ryland answered. "Overnight. And most of the day."

She turned to Blake. "How did you know—"

The nurse and Mom came in and cut off her question. The nurse gave Liz a pill and checked her over thoroughly. When the nurse left, three faces hovered over her bed again. A weird vibe permeated the room and gave her chills.

Mom finally broke the awkward silence. "I'm going to call your daddy and let him know you're awake." She patted Liz's hand and smiled. "I'll be right back."

"Okay."

Mom left, and the tension in the room ratcheted to intolerable levels. Liz didn't have the energy to analyze it. She felt like she'd been hit by a convoy of trucks. She scanned the room. Where was Arie? She couldn't even feel him. She'd have to ask Ryland later. After Blake left.

She closed her eyes. Liz wanted to be grateful for the men on either side of her, each showing his dedication. But having both of them in the same room was headache-inducing. The hostility was palpable. She really couldn't deal with their alpha male crap right now.

Liz opened her eyes and looked at the ceiling, choosing her words carefully. Which was difficult considering her head felt like it'd been through a meat grinder. "Look, guys, I appreciate you being here, but the pill's kicking in. Maybe y'all should—"

Blake interrupted her. "Absolutely. You need your rest. I have some work I need to deal with anyway." He smiled. "I'll be back later this evening. Maybe sneak in a cheeseburger?" Blake winked at her.

Liz tried to smile. Nope, that hurt. "Sounds good. Thank you."

Blake glanced at Ryland. "I know my girl."

Oh, for crying out loud.

Ryland grunted. Blake leaned in and kissed her lightly on the lips. Liz felt Ryland squeeze her hand. The anger boiling in him burned her. Awkward much?

"See you in a few hours. Rest well, darling." Blake walked toward the door. "Ryland, you coming?"

Liz saw Ryland's jaw tense. He kept his eyes on her. "You go ahead. I'm sure I'll catch up with you later."

The obvious double meaning of his words hung in the air. Liz would've rolled her eyes if they hadn't hurt. Blake sighed and glared at Ryland some more before striding into the hall.

Liz brought her gaze back to Ryland. The atmosphere in the room lightened as she looked into his eyes. Her last thought before she'd blacked out, when she'd looked over at Ryland and thought they were both dying, came back to her.

I love you.

Liz sighed. She couldn't handle all of this right now. Especially with a heavier issue weighing on her.

God was supposed to be with her. Where was He last night after the big battle? Where were the angels? They'd left her and Ryland, injured and weak, when they had to have known Markus would be back.

She looked away from Ryland. Her throat dried out, and her cheeks warmed. The fragility of her faith wasn't something she wanted him to see. His emotions punched her again. So much faith and hope. He loved her. But she didn't deserve him. She wasn't the same person anymore.

Mom walked back in, and Liz was grateful for the distraction. "I see Blake is gone." Liz wondered if she'd imagined the relief in Mom's eyes. "How are you feeling, sweetie?" She caressed her daughter's hand.

"Sore."

"Well, I'd guess so. Dad's on his way. I'm going to meet him downstairs. Are you hungry?"

"No, thanks. I don't think I'm quite ready for food."

Once Mom had gone, Liz and Ryland sat quietly. In the silence, all of the things in Liz's head and heart finally got the best of her. They spilled over onto her cheeks.

Ryland tenderly wiped her tears. "Hey. You're going to be fine. Just don't scare me like that again, okay?" He gave her a crooked grin.

"No, I'm just... It's nothing."

"What is it?" Concern creased his brow.

"I have a lot to think about, that's all." Liz couldn't ask him the question that tormented her. And she couldn't tell him how she felt. The tears flowed in earnest now. Trembling sobs shook her body, sending streaks of fire shooting through her. She was powerless against the painful storm that broke inside of her.

Ryland gingerly gathered her in his arms. He held her to him, whispering comforting words as the sobs wracked her. He knew her wounds weren't all physical. The feelings blasting from her hit him like a line drive. Turmoil. Utter turmoil. It tore into his heart.

Liz nestled her head on his shoulder. Ryland held her as tight as he could without hurting her. He poured all the love and support he could into her. Ryland emptied his heart and gave her all he had, hoping she could feel it, draw from it.

After a while, her tears were spent, and the sobs eased. Liz wiggled in his arms. A small cry escaped her lips and rent his heart. Ryland held her with one arm and pulled the blanket around her to stifle the shivers that made her tremble. If he could take her pain into himself, he'd do it in a second.

"Thank you," she whispered. Her eyelids fluttered.

"You're welcome." He brushed the back of his hand tenderly down her uninjured jaw. "You know you can talk to me. About anything."

"I know."

The medicine worked its magic. Her eyes drooped closed.

"Rest. I'll be here when you wake up." Ryland settled her on the pillow and tucked the blanket more securely around her.

"You don't have to—" The medication and exhaustion won, and she sank into oblivion.

Ryland watched her sleep. Her parents came in, and he gave his chair to Mrs. Brantley. Chammu'el appeared at Ryland's side. Though in human form, he was cloaked, hidden from everyone but Ryland. The angel jerked his head toward the door. Duty called. Ryland hesitated. When the angel motioned for him again, he said his goodbyes to Liz's parents, kissed Liz tenderly, and promised to return soon.

The air thickened as they walked into the hallway. The stench of evil choked Ryland. He scanned the corridor. Seeing nothing, he took one last look at Liz before he followed his guardian to whatever task awaited him.

Hopefully, the assignment would be hunting Markus and repaying him for what he'd done.

Markus watched from the shadows as Ryland and Chammu'el left. Several angels guarding the halls looked his way, yet none made a move. Curious. He was being allowed access to Elizabeth, even in her weakened state. His lips curled in his version of a smile. How he loved being able to work unimpeded.

This was more than work, though. Markus thoroughly enjoyed the havoc he created. And breathing nightmares to life in Elizabeth's unconscious mind was a special treat. The fear and uncertainty they fostered were taking root. Soon the resulting confusion would make her the perfect soft target.

Markus slipped into her room, noticing the sharp eyes of the pastor that immediately flitted in his direction. Ah, her father had sensed Markus's presence. When the man's gaze connected with Markus's eyes, he stilled for a moment. The pastor broke the connection, and Markus shrugged. A coincidence. If the man could see him, Markus doubted he would have simply picked back up the conversation with his wife.

The demon glided to the bed. He took in the bruised form lying before him. He may have put her there, yet he was surprised when he wasn't pleased about that fact. His master preferred her dead. His goal was gaining her allegiance. Gaining *her*. A brief flash of something he couldn't label slid through his being. Fear? Sadness? He wasn't sure. Those emotions were foreign to him. What he did know was he hadn't intended to kill her.

At least, not yet. If she died, it would not please him.

Markus erased the troubling thoughts and focused on his task. He laid a large hand on Elizabeth's head. He threaded his way into her mind, planting nightmares, sowing doubt, and covering it all with a thick layer of fear.

His job complete, he watched her sleep. Her brow furrowed. Her eyes began to move rapidly under her lids, letting him know he'd accomplished his goal. He wondered how long it would take before she broke.

A flash of light by the door and the accompanying wash of peace burned his flesh. He growled as he faced Arie. Well, so much for getting his fill of watching tonight.

Before Arie could speak or attack, Markus whisked away. He didn't need a confrontation with the angel right now. There were more important things to attend to. Markus had quite the surprise planned for Elizabeth. When he was finished, she would have no doubt to whom she belonged.

XVI
Lie Awake

"For crying out loud!"

It was impossible to get comfortable. Liz's head split. Her arm itched under the bandage. Her left eye and jaw were sore. The stitches on her leg felt like they'd rip open with the smallest movement. Not to mention, each breath felt like someone was playing whack-a-mole on her ribs. She pulled the well-worn afghan up and tucked it around herself.

Healing like normal people sucked.

Liz had insisted on going home, not to her parents' house. It was the safest move. Markus could attack while she was down. There was no way she was taking the chance of her parents getting caught in the crossfire.

"What?" Ryland called from the kitchen.

"Nothing. Just whining."

"Yeah, well, it's justified. At least for a little while." He buried his head in the fridge. "What do you want to drink so you can take your pill?"

"Coke. But I don't need a pill." The words were more of a grumble.

"You know the drill. Every six hours or you'll be even grumpier. That, I can't handle, princess." Ryland smiled as he knelt beside her. He handed her the medicine and the Coke. "Down the hatch."

"Bossy," Liz growled with just a hint of a smile. He'd taken to calling her princess the past few days and joking about how he was her trusty manservant.

"Someone's gotta keep you in line." He pointed at her drink. "Last Coke. I'll hit the store this afternoon."

Liz had tried several times to tell him he didn't have to do those things. He never listened, so she'd given up. Ryland watched as she swallowed the medication.

Liz stuck out her tongue at him. "There. Gone. Happy?"

A grin tugged his upper lip. "Absolutely. If you'd listen to me about everything, life would be a heck of a lot smoother." He tweaked her chin between his thumb and forefinger.

When their eyes met, the teasing mood vanished. It was replaced by a strange tension that grew thicker every day. An intensifying draw. Another wrinkle in the fabric of her life.

With his thumb, Ryland stroked the skin below the vicious cut on her eye. He stretched up and kissed the area with feather-soft lips. That small gesture completely undid her. Her belly flipped and dropped onto the floor.

The current running between them lit every nerve in her body. Emotion swirled like the mist rolling in over the hills. Her breathing quickened. She could see from the way his T-shirt strained over his chest, his had too.

Ryland pulled back and captured her gaze. He didn't move his hand. His eyes glistened. "I'm so sorry I let this happen to you."

Liz's brow furrowed, and she tilted her head. She placed her hand over his. "Ryland. None of this was your fault." Her heart wrenched. He shouldered an unnecessary burden.

The agony on his face stabbed her heart. "I never should've left you alone out there. I should've kept you—"

"Shh." Liz caressed his fingers. "It's done. We made it out." She sighed. Her chest ached, but not from broken ribs. "It's not your responsibility to keep me safe. I have to fight my own battles."

Ryland shook his head.

She placed two fingers over his lips, silencing him. "No more."

He'd never stop putting himself on the line for her. But now she realized she could never send him away. How could she utterly demolish someone's heart twice in one lifetime? Someone she now understood she loved more than breathing?

Ryland's eyes smoldered. He ran his fingers down the line of her jaw and across her bottom lip. Liz sucked in a breath. Every fiber of her being screamed for her to wrap herself around him and never let go. She wanted to fall into him and never resurface.

Leaving him before had been unbearable anguish. He'd offered everything she'd wanted, and she'd rejected it. It had left a hole in her heart no one else could fill. A hole that was quite possibly about to be carved out one more time.

This time, her heart wouldn't survive.

So she'd keep him close while she could. Fight with him. Watch his back like he watched hers. Then, for a little bit at least, she could have a part of him. Because once he knew the truth, it would all be over.

Maybe she could have one more kiss. One more moment with his arms around her, hearing his heartbeat.

She saw the ground rushing up to meet her as she fell.

No, she couldn't fall. She couldn't give him hope when there was none. Liz leaned back and took a deep breath. Hurt flared from him for an instant. Determination and patience followed. Ryland gave her a smile tinted with sadness and brushed her hair behind her ear.

She had to say something. Quick. Liz cleared her throat. "So, Chammu'el and Arie have kept you busy?"

"Yeah." Ryland didn't elaborate. He eased back onto the end of the couch closest to her. "Do you need anything else? I don't want you getting up if you don't have to."

"No, I'm good." She tried again. "What have you guys been up to while I've been down? Anything new?"

Ryland sighed. His reticence was obvious. He had to know if he didn't give her the information she wanted, she'd dig it up herself. "They're still in the same location. Just trying to figure out their next move."

See, that wasn't so hard. "Any leads?"

"A few." Ryland leaned back and extended his legs down the length of the couch. He tossed an arm above his head.

He closed his eyes and rubbed a calloused hand over his face. Worry lines etched around his eyes. His ruggedly handsome face hadn't seen a razor in at least three days. The dark stubble had taken on a life of its own. Liz was certain he'd barely slept. He looked older than his twenty-five years.

Ryland had been impossible to get rid of. He'd checked on her every morning, bringing her breakfast. Shelley and Mom took turns stopping by throughout the day while he was out. Then Ryland would come back in the late afternoon or early evening. After they had dinner and she was settled, he'd open his laptop and work until she was ready to crawl into bed. Then he'd pack up and head out.

Every morning he looked more worn than the day before. She knew he hunted for Markus every night. Ryland had let it slip that Markus had been jumping realms, making it difficult to track him.

In addition, the tension between Liz and Ryland was a tangible thing. She could feel him holding back, not doing or saying what he really wanted. His restraint was costing him.

For five days this had gone on.

Liz listened to Ryland's even breathing. She eyed his long form stretched out on her couch. Even sleeping, she could feel his love. His worry. His faith. *He's so sure of everything. I wish I could be.*

There was so much she didn't know and didn't understand. She hadn't had the chance to speak with Arie and ask all of her questions. He'd been absent since the battle. So had God.

No. Don't go there. Too easy to lose herself.

So Liz sat in silence, thinking, watching the other half of herself sleep peacefully. Trying to figure out how to tell him they could never be whole.

The soggy earth dragged her down in its clutches. Faces floated over her. Ryland, Arie, Markus. Ghostly images. Contorted. Cruel.

Ryland spoke. "You'll be the death of me."

Arie got in his jab. "I will never know why the Father chose you. You are too far gone to be of any use to us."

He disappeared, and she was alone with Markus. "See? They don't want you. They know what you are. Come. Join me, darling. We will revel in the darkness, together."

She slapped his hand away. "I'm nothing like you!"

"Then you will die." Markus raised his blade and drove it into her as the earth swallowed her whole.

Liz screamed and sat straight up in bed. Sweat rolled down her back. Her nightshirt clung to her. She checked the clock on her dresser. Seven. Well, at least she'd gotten two full hours that time. She climbed out of bed, refusing to think about the nightmare that plagued her.

Liz flicked on the bathroom light and started the shower. The spray soothed and refreshed her. She glanced down at the stitches in her thigh. The wound looked better than it had the day before.

When she emerged from the hot water, she felt better. At least mentally. Her body was a ball of pain. Why was she not healing faster? Liz sighed. It took her several minutes to dry and dress with all of her injuries. A shot of heated anger blasted through her.

Dressed in basketball shorts and a tank top, she grabbed her dagger and made her way to the living room. She went to the kitchen and started a pot of coffee. A granola bar was breakfast while she watched her coffee brew. When she'd polished off the bar, she grabbed a water bottle and downed her prescribed pills. Coffee in hand, she half-limped across the floor and settled herself in the recliner.

She was so tired of that freaking chair. And sitting. And doing nothing.

Liz reached for the remote and flipped for a while. Nothing caught her eye. She tossed the remote on the coffee table and spotted her Bible. A deep hurt washed through her. Promises flooded her mind.

I will never leave you nor forsake you.

I will uphold you with my righteous right hand.

The words didn't coincide with what had happened the other night. She'd faced the biggest fight of her life and had faced it mostly alone.

Darkness crept into the room even though the sun shone brightly through the blinds. Liz felt its frigid tendrils grasp for her. Her eyes darted around, expecting to find demons. There were none.

The darkness intertwined with the dread, fear, and rage in her heart. It formed them into physical things. They took shape and danced before her eyes. Terrifying questions waltzed with them.

Would she be left alone again, fighting to survive? Why did God abandon her when she was fighting for Him? Where was Arie? Wasn't his job to protect her?

She was kidding herself if she thought she could be a warrior, anyway. Shouldn't warriors have faith? Be strong even in the face of unspeakable evil? Her faith wavered after her first real battle. *Maybe I'm just not cut out for this.* She should just walk away.

For I am persuaded that neither death nor life, nor angels nor principalities nor powers, nor things present nor things to come, nor height nor depth, nor any other created thing, shall be able to separate us from the love of God which is in Christ Jesus our Lord.

The verse wound itself around the spinning darkness, slowing the dance. Liz wanted to grab for the promise. But doubt and fear resumed their ghoulish ballet, pushing hope to the background.

Someone knocked on the door and abruptly ended the performance in Liz's head.

"Hang on."

Liz used her good arm to propel herself out of the chair, hating that it took her this long to even get to her door. She should've unlocked it on her way to the kitchen. It was probably Ry on his morning rounds. She couldn't tell, though. Her senses had been out of whack since the battle. Rustling sounded on the other side of the door as she slid the chain and flipped the deadbolt.

Blake grinned down at her. "Delivery for Ms. Brantley."

Liz tilted her head as she eyed the flowers and the bag in his hands. "What are you doing here so early?"

It wasn't unusual for Blake to be there. He'd been by most days, always when Ryland was absent. Just never in the morning.

"Expecting someone else?" She didn't miss the slight edge to his voice. "I brought breakfast. Pancakes, bacon, and a cinnamon roll." He slid his eyebrows up and down.

Liz smiled. "Come in." She scanned the hallway and stepped back into the room.

Ryland was usually here by now. Had he finally given up? The thought hurt. Would he really disappear without a word? She doubted it.

When she moved toward the kitchen, Blake stopped her. "I've got it. You go get comfortable."

Her leg burned, so she didn't put up a fight. She returned to her chair and pulled her afghan around her. She shivered as she buried herself under the blanket. It was like there was frost in the air. The darkness that had surrounded her earlier hadn't lifted. She scanned the room again. Still demon-free. She frowned.

"Looks like you're getting around better." Blake pulled plates from the cabinet.

Boy, he sure was comfortable in her house. For some reason, the thought made her uneasy. Yet she had no problem with Ryland's muddy boots and grubby hands all over her kitchen. Interesting.

"Still sore, but it's getting easier." She watched him dish up the food from the take-out containers. "You didn't have to do that. I already had a granola bar."

Blake flashed her a brilliant smile as he sauntered over, loaded plates in hand. "You can't resist cinnamon rolls and bacon." He winked.

"How would you know?" Liz asked around a mouthful of bacon. "It's not like we've had breakfast together before." The unease in her belly grew.

"Who doesn't love bacon and cinnamon rolls?"

I'll give him that one.

Liz carved a piece off her cinnamon roll. "How's work going?"

"Great, actually. I think I'm about to wrap up the deal."

She felt a pang of disappointment, followed by relief. If he were leaving, that'd make it a lot easier to break it off with him. Whatever it was. Which is what she needed to do. There was no way things could work between them when her head and heart were full of Ryland. "I guess you'll be heading out of town before too long."

Blake set his fork down and held her eyes. "Soon. At least, that's the plan. Does that upset you?"

No. Yes. Kinda. Liz sighed. "Blake, I care about you. And I'm definitely…attracted to you." She cleared her throat. "I'm just not—"

He raised his hand to stop her. Blake scooted down the couch and covered her knee with his warm hand. "You could always come with me. We could give this a real shot." As her eyes went wide, he squeezed her knee. "Take some time to think it over. I've said it before, we could be great together."

"Blake, I—"

He pressed a finger to her lips. "Not yet." He leaned in and planted a light kiss where his finger had been. "Don't answer until you think about it."

Liz stood in a rush and grabbed their plates. She winced at the pinch in her leg. "I'm gonna put these in the sink. My pill is kicking in, and I could use a nap, especially with a full belly now." She rushed to the kitchen. Well, rushing for her. Her injuries voiced their displeasure.

A hint of disappointment passed through the air from him to her. Despite what she'd just said, he crossed the room and hauled her into his arms. Blake's eyes locked with hers, and she forgot what she'd been thinking. Liz couldn't move or even look away.

What was it about him? He looked at her, touched her, and she melted. Completely under his control.

Blake kissed her soundly as he tugged her closer. A charge went through her.

Liz broke the kiss. She backed out of his arms and gripped the counter to steady herself. Her breath came in sharp pants, and her heart pounded so fast she was sure he could hear it.

Blake's eyes were insanely dark. "You're right. You should rest." His smoky eyes and the way he reached to grasp her waist said rest was the last thing on his mind.

The air between them was so thick, Liz could hardly breathe. Finally, she was able to break eye contact and clear her head.

There was something not quite right here. They couldn't be alone anymore. She slipped out of his grip and walked toward the door. Not before she let her hand slide down his arm. Why did she do that? It was like she couldn't stop herself from touching him.

A voice whispered in her ear. One she hadn't heard in a while. One she'd rather forget. *Because you want him. You don't have to deny yourself. Let go.*

It shocked her out of her stupor. She could and would take control.

"Thank you for breakfast." Liz opened the door.

Blake followed. Instead of trying to stop her, he placed a hand at the small of her back. The heat from his hand scorched her through.

Blake kissed her cheek. "You're welcome." He stepped into the hall. "I'll check on you soon." With another wink, he was gone.

When Liz walked back into the room, the chill that had clung to the atmosphere was gone.

XVII
Never Alone

Pastor Brantley took a long drink of his sweet tea and braced himself for Liz's reaction.

"So, I had an interesting talk with Ryland."

"Really." He saw a flicker of interest in her otherwise blank stare.

Ryland was right. Something was wrong. She wasn't herself. *Lord, help me get her back on track.*

He took a deep breath. "Yep. He told me quite a story." The flicker in her eyes grew to a small flame. "I also met with your guardian, Arie, and another angel, Aelaem. They told me everything."

Liz's eyes blazed. Her face flushed, and he could see her jaw clench as she gritted her teeth. *And there's my Liz Whiz.*

"They had no right." Liz muttered the words.

"You should've told me yourself. It affects all of us. And you need to have more respect. For your guardian, and for Ryland." Liz's jaw hardened further, and he shook his head. "They're trying to help you, Liz. You're falling into a hole you won't be able to pull yourself out of on your own."

"I'm fine." She wouldn't look him in the eye.

Pastor Brantley let out a long exhale. "I don't know why *you* didn't tell me."

"Because I was handling it. You shouldn't have been dragged in to this." Liz shook her head and eased out of her chair to pace the room. "You don't understand how dangerous it is. It's why I left in the first place."

Pastor Brantley saw the shadow pass over her face. She still hadn't let go of the past. He rose and put his hands on her shoulders. "I understand more than you think. Lizzy, this is a war. The more soldiers, the better. Where two or three are gathered… Just because I'm not on the battlefield with you doesn't make me any less useful. We just fight in a different capacity."

Liz gave him a weak smile and stayed quiet. He wished he could say what he really wanted to say. To tell her everything. But she wasn't ready.

He also knew platitudes and trite words wouldn't help her. She had to work through this, just her and God. He pulled her into his arms and kissed the top of her head.

God, I give her to you, once again. Though his father's heart wanted to protect her himself, he knew she was in much better hands than his own.

Liz stood in the middle of the living room, staring at the dark TV. Now what?

She'd had a few visitors, and that was good. Then the weekly phone call from an acquaintance in Dallas had brightened her mood and hurt her heart at the same time. She didn't really want to think about that. So here she was, just her and an empty room.

Her need for revenge had her wanting to be out helping track Markus. Then again, she wasn't sure if she wanted to be involved in any of it anymore. Not that it mattered. The demons would still come after her. They always had before.

Her eyes landed on the cabinet in the corner. Liz pried the doors open. The box holding her katana sat open, the pristine blade on display. Ryland had probably cleaned it. She lifted it from the velvet and held it loosely, swinging it from side to side.

Immediately, the motion and feel of the blade in her hand brought the battle screaming back. She saw herself take down the monstrous demon, and a thrill of victory coursed through her. She remembered each enemy falling to her sword. The power from above that had surged in her blood. The strength far beyond her own. A tiny smile creased her lips.

Another scene swamped her vision, destroying her sense of accomplishment. Markus loomed above her, sword raised. Liz could feel the blade slice into her leg. Feel the fire of agony. The katana deserted her hand and clattered to the hardwood floor.

Liz retrieved the sword, shoved it in the box, and slammed it shut. She wanted to understand, yet none of this made any sense. Where was God? Why couldn't she feel Him? A thought struck her. Arie had said she'd be tested as her gifts grew. Her shoulders sagged as understanding weighed on her. If it were a test, she'd failed. Miserably.

"You have not failed, young one."

Liz whirled and came face to face with Arie. "Yes, I have." Liz flopped onto the recliner and lowered her head. She couldn't look him in the eye.

Arie knelt beside her. "Elizabeth, everyone questions. Especially when faced with trials." He cupped her chin. "I am sorry you are hurting."

Liz couldn't stop the tears from rolling down her nose. Questions spun in her mind.

"Where were you, Arie? We were hurt and exhausted and…" She rubbed her eyes with the back of her hand. "We were defenseless when Markus attacked."

His eyes glistened as he stroked her cheek. "Yet you both fought with great courage. We often do not understand the Father's plan. Yet we must have faith it will work for good."

"How is me being on death's door *good*?" Liz's breath came hard and fast. "And why is it taking me so long to heal? I thought that was part of the deal. It's been a week and…" Liz buried her face in her hands.

Arie sighed. "Healing is a gift. As with any gift, you can choose to receive it or reject it." She raised her head to protest, but he cut her off. "You may not have consciously rejected it, but you can block it. With doubt. With despair. You must have faith and open yourself completely. That is when you will receive the healing meant for you."

"Arie, I can't—I can't do this." Liz dissolved.

Arie gathered her to him, and she curled up against his chest like she used to do with her daddy when she was little. He whispered prayers and soothing words while the sobs wracked her body. Like hot steel cooled in water, her rage sizzled as it subsided. Liz let the doors of her heart fling wide. Finally, she captured some peace.

God hadn't forgotten her.

When the torrent eased, Arie released her. "I am your guardian, but I cannot fight your battles, and I cannot always be with you. You have to trust that even when He does not send me to your side, you are never alone. He is with you."

Liz grabbed a tissue and cleaned herself up. "I'll try."

Arie grinned. "That is all that is required." He sat on the couch and clasped his hands between his knees. Almost as if he were waiting. As if he knew what was coming.

They sat quietly for a few minutes as Liz worked up her nerve. There were some things she needed to ask—she just wasn't sure if she really wanted the answers.

"Arie, I have some questions."

"I will do my best to answer them."

"I've been feeling, well, everything. From everybody." She paused. "I feel what they feel. It's stronger from some people than others. With Ryland, it's overwhelming. Is this normal for...someone like me?" Could she sound any dumber?

"Some warriors are blessed with the gift of empathy, yes. It allows you to sense what others truly feel and need so you may minister to them specifically."

Liz had never really thought beyond battle. She had to pay more attention. "So, can I shut it off? Having everyone else in my brain all the time is…difficult."

"You can learn to control it, to reach further when you need to, or shield from others when necessary. This is one reason why I have stressed mastering control of your emotions. Otherwise, the combination of your feelings and those of others can overtake you and impair your ability to function."

"Hey, one more question." Liz adjusted herself in the chair. "You never did answer me about Ryland. Why is it so much stronger with him? Is he empathic, too?"

"Yes. He is." Arie's brow furrowed a bit. "Perhaps the sensations are stronger from him because of the emotional attachment you have with one another." He peered at her as though he'd asked a question.

Liz squirmed. Here was something else Ryland knew and hadn't told her. Her head pounded harder.

She rose and stood in front of Arie. "So, what's the plan? When do I get to go back to work? And what's been going on out there? Ryland never tells me anything."

"Ryland has been doing reconnaissance. We are trying to ascertain what Markus's next move might be. And you still require rest."

Liz pinched the bridge of her nose. "I may be sore, but I'm mostly healed, and I can help Ryland. I need to find Markus and—"

"Elizabeth, your gifts are not for seeking revenge. Markus will fall, in God's time." She thought she heard him sigh. "We will begin slowly. I do not want you to push yourself too hard so soon. Healing can take time. And patience." He gave her a grin and vanished.

Despite Arie's encouraging words and the modicum of peace she felt now, the cloud hanging over Liz wouldn't dissipate. She still had so much to work through. Not the least of which promised to be an unpleasant conversation with Blake. And she was worried about Ryland. It had been two days since she'd heard from him. If something were wrong, Arie would've told her. Right?

Liz picked up her phone and tried Ryland's number again.

No answer.

A sick feeling settled over her. *God, please, keep him safe.*

XVIII
That Changes Everything

"Where have you been?"

Liz grabbed Ryland and flung her arms around his neck.

Ryland threw his hands out and staggered from the force of her assault. "Hey, calm down. You're gonna break me in half." He chuckled and grabbed her waist.

Fire shot through Liz at his touch. She drew back as quickly as she'd thrown herself at him. She waved him inside as she collected herself.

"Why haven't you returned my calls or texts?" She stayed a safe distance from him.

Ryland ran a hand through his already-mussed hair. "I'm sorry. I've been busy." He gestured toward the kitchen. "Mmm. Coffee smells great. Can I talk you out of a cup? I've been out all night." He wandered into the kitchen without waiting for an answer. "You made cookies?" He snagged two from the cooling rack and shoved half of one in his mouth. "I guess you still make cookies when you're upset." Ryland grinned and winked at her.

Liz rolled her eyes. She brushed flour off her shirt. "Out all night doing what?"

She could feel guilt and anxiety crawl all over him. Ryland didn't say a word. He shuffled his feet and ran his hand through his hair again. Liz yanked a mug from the cabinet. She was really tired of secrets. Now that she knew he was okay, her anger flared to the surface as she poured the coffee. Liz shoved the drink at him, sloshing some of it onto the floor.

Ryland's eyes flew wide as a splash hit his hand. "Hey! That's hot." He grabbed a towel and wiped his hand and the mug. "What's going on? Why don't we go back to you throwing yourself at me?" He wiggled his eyebrows.

Liz stifled a scream and rolled her eyes. "I wasn't throwing myself at you. I was just glad you weren't dead." Liz stomped to the living room. "And why are you so…perky?"

He sauntered into the living room, and she stared at him as he sat in the recliner, cradling his coffee. "Is this about me not telling you what's going on out there?" He squeezed his temples with his thumb and forefinger. "I didn't want you stressing while you're trying to recover. It's being handled." Ryland took a huge gulp of coffee.

"What I need to know or not know is not for you to decide. Like this whole empathy thing." Liz flopped down on the couch.

Ryland didn't look surprised. He looked resigned, and she experienced something unexpected. His relief. "I wondered."

"Seriously? That all you've got?"

"What do you want me to say?" He set his mug on the side table and leaned forward. "Some of us have it, some don't. I had no way of knowing if you would. Or when it would kick in."

Liz glared. "You could've at least warned me."

"I know Arie told you what to expect."

"Kind of. He wasn't very clear." Liz sighed. "It feels like I never really know what's happening. Someone is always keeping something from me." She stood and paced, her main activity of late. "After everything that's happened, I didn't think you would do this to me again."

Ryland got to his feet slowly. "Liz, it wasn't my place to tell you. I was following—"

Liz raised her hand. "You're always following orders. That's perfect for you, isn't it?" Apparently she still had a lot to get out of her system. Being cooped up was not good for her temperament. And his being so flippant about things when she'd been worried sick wasn't helping.

"Liz." His tone should have been enough to stop her.

It wasn't.

"Blame everything on being the obedient soldier." Her mouth spouted vitriol of its own volition. "That way you can keep hiding things. Do whatever you want. Blame all your mistakes on the job." The bitter insinuation behind her words was harsher than she intended. She instantly regretted it.

Warning lit the air. Flashed in Ryland's eyes. She spun away, but he caught her arm.

At her gasp, his eyes narrowed. "Don't fight dirty. You're better than that."

His anger and hurt sparked in the air and sucked the oxygen from her. A hint of predator peeked out of his eyes, and she wasn't sure how to deal with it. An innate fear took flight in her stomach. She knew the second he felt it from her. Sorrow flashed through him and across his face. It was a razor to her heart. It wasn't him she was scared of. It wasn't even him she was really mad at.

Liz eased out of his grip and stepped back. She avoided his eyes. Her brain screamed for her to run. She knew deep down no matter how angry Ryland got, he'd never hurt her. Still, instinct had her moving out of range.

She sucked in a breath. "I'm sorry."

Ryland tried to stay calm. He knew she didn't really think that little of him, but her words cut. She was intent on her mission to push him away. Now she was terrified of him, too?

Ryland grabbed the back of his neck with both hands. "I've done the best I can with all of this. I've fought right beside you. Taken care of you while you recuperated. Watched your back. Yet you still don't believe me, and you sure don't trust me." He exhaled sharply and turned to the window. "I don't know what else I can do."

"I do trust you." She moved beside him and laid a hand on his arm. "I'm just trying to make sense of all this. I really am sorry about what I said. I didn't mean…"

Ryland glanced down at her. He saw his future every time he looked into her eyes. The amazing life they could have, the beautiful family they could create together. He also saw too much sadness and pain. It ripped at his heart.

He must have stood there too long, staring at her without speaking, because she pulled her hand away. Ryland grabbed it and tugged her back to him. The contact intensified the emotions churning around them. Everything she felt crashed into him, full force.

She did trust him, somewhat. But not nearly like he wanted her to. And it wasn't him she was scared of. It was herself. Her past. All he wanted to do at that moment was erase her fear.

Screw it. He'd wanted to get her back in his arms ever since she'd released him a little while ago.

Ryland slid one arm around her waist and one hand to the back of her neck. He drew her against him and held on tight as though she might vanish if he didn't. "That's all I needed to hear. For now."

Liz gripped the sides of his T-shirt, anchoring herself to him as she pressed her cheek to his heart. After a few minutes, he leaned back enough to see her face. Her eyes glistened. He looked deeper and repressed the grin that nipped his lips. Despite her arguments, her still holding him at arms' length, he saw the wall crumbling to dust as clear as he could see her beautiful face.

She picked up on what he was thinking. "Ry, I can't—"

"Don't." He pressed a finger to her lips. "No matter what you say, I'm not going anywhere." She opened her mouth, but he continued. "I know you need time, and I'll give it to you. In the meantime, we'll fight these demons. All of them."

Liz nodded. When she spoke, her voice was a whisper. "I can't make you any promises."

"I know." Ryland caressed her cheek. Her bruises had faded, and the cut above her eye was gone. He smiled. "Looks like you're finally healing."

She moved away. "Yeah. Getting there."

"That's great." Ryland shifted uncomfortably. There was one more thing they needed to discuss. "Lizzy, are you and Blake together?"

Liz bit the inside of her cheek. "No. Not really. I'm not sure." She got really serious about staring at the carpet. "No. We had a-a thing. It's over now."

His eyebrow jerked up. He couldn't stop the hope from creeping in. "So why is he here all the time?" Crap. He shouldn't have said that.

Liz's eyes narrowed. "How would you know that? Have you been watching my place?" Her fists balled at her sides.

Ryland held up his hands. "Not like you think. Arie's been here too. And Chammu'el. We've been taking turns keeping an eye on things."

He felt her anger abate. Slightly.

"I don't need bodyguards." She lifted her chin. "Or a babysitter."

Why did he love the defiant glint in her eyes? There was something wrong with him.

"It's not up to me." If he had his way, he'd never leave her side. He knew better than to say that out loud, though.

Liz sighed and looked at the clock. "You might wanna go." She avoided his eyes. "Blake's probably on his way."

Every muscle in his body constricted and he ground his teeth. Now it was his turn to clench his fists. "I thought you said—"

"He's coming to talk. I'm ending…whatever it is." She stole a glance at him and looked away again.

Ryland couldn't help the sheer joy bubbling inside of him. Liz caught his eye and crooked an eyebrow. He cleared his throat and headed for the door. "Well, ah, good luck."

Liz opened the door and leaned against the frame.

Ryland touched her cheek. Man, he wanted to kiss those lips. He pushed the thought down. She probably wouldn't be too receptive to that. Yet. "I'll check in later."

"Okay."

He placed a kiss on her forehead instead and stepped away as she shut the door. It wasn't much, but it was more than he'd had when he walked in. It was enough for now. She needed to heal inside as well as out. He'd wait—and help her all he could.

Ryland climbed into his truck and started it. That's when he realized he'd been whistling all the way outside.

"I'm glad you called, darling." Blake reached for her before she even got the door closed.

Liz ducked out of his reach. "We need to talk." Great way to start. That never put anyone on edge.

Blake's eyes darkened. "Oh?"

"Have a seat." All of a sudden, she had a strong urge to keep everything formal. Liz even thought maybe she should've taken a couple of iced teas out to the porch and met him there. Like an old-fashioned, proper Southern lady. She would've laughed at the thought if her stomach wasn't in her throat.

"Has something happened?" She could tell he was trying to stay cool, but by the way his eyes blazed and the stony look on his face, it took all he had.

Liz sat on the opposite end of the couch. "Shelley told me you paid my bills. Here you go." Liz handed him an envelope.

"That's not necessary." He waved her hand away. "It was my pleasure."

"I don't want to owe anyone anything." She laid it beside him.

Blake stiffened. "Liz, I want to take care of you. I saw something that needed to be done, and I did it." He scooted closer, and she stood.

"No. You stuck your nose in my personal business. I don't need you to take care of me."

Blake stalked toward her. "Where is this coming from? I thought you'd be happy." The slightest hint of anger wafted toward her, and she could've sworn the temperature in the room dropped ten degrees.

Liz edged around the coffee table. "I pay my own way." She crossed her arms and rubbed them. "Blake, we're not together. And we're not going to be." She took a deep breath. "I can't see you anymore."

The rage rolling through him slapped her in the face. She backed away, and he followed. Another chill scuttled up her spine. Her fight instinct tickled her limbs and the back of her neck.

"Is this about Ryland? He's probably trying to undermine me." Blake's arms and chest rippled as his muscles tightened. It made her uncomfortably aware of what a large and powerful man he was.

Liz had widened her stance before she realized what she'd done. "You need to calm down. This has nothing to do with Ryland." Okay, so it did. But that was none of his business.

As Blake eased closer to her, his face softened. "Elizabeth, I'm sorry. I didn't mean to get so angry. I...care about you." He acted like it pained him to say the words. "Please, stay with me."

"I'm not with you, Blake."

Blake reached for her again, and she flinched. He hesitated for a moment before locking her in his arms anyway. He lifted her chin gently and kissed her before she could react. Her lips responded and returned the kiss without her permission. The next moment, Liz broke away. He didn't release her. He took her face in his hands and forced her to look into his eyes. Again, they were almost black.

He lowered his face within an inch of hers. "You know we're perfect together. We're so much alike. Don't throw away what we could have."

Liz's head spun. The room spun. A strange feeling sprouted in her chest. Warmth and cold swirling together, like warm air trying to chase the frostiness away. It invited her closer to him.

"No." Liz dragged her mind back to reality and maneuvered out of his reach. She ran to the door and flung it open. "Please, just go,

Blake."

Blake's eyes ignited again. She pressed her back against the wall.

He touched her jaw with his fingertips. "I will respect your wishes. Think about what I said. Just know I can't wait forever." He kissed her on the cheek and was gone.

Liz shut the door and locked it. Her knees wobbled, and she collapsed against the wood. The room warmed again. She didn't. The coldness had taken over. A hollowness she didn't understand consumed her.

The sun dipped behind the hills and cast shadows across the living room. Darkness crawled into the corners. Instead of turning on a light, she fell onto the couch and let the blackness take over. She'd done what she needed to do.

And she'd never felt more alone.

XIX
Paradise: What About Us?

Liz sat straight up in bed, the scream lingering in her throat. Seeing the tan-colored walls of her bedroom brought her back to reality. *I'd like to start one day waking up to my alarm like a normal person.* She untangled herself from the red-and-black checkered covers and began her morning ritual.

Her stitches had come out a few days ago, and the latest round of x-rays showed her ribs and sternum were fully healed. Despite the fact it had been merely two weeks since the battle, it seemed like it had been months. She was beyond ready to get back to training. The scaled-down workouts she'd been doing weren't cutting it.

Liz pulled on an old pair of breakaway pants and a snug tank top and laced her athletic shoes. Once she'd yanked her curls into a ponytail, she strapped her dagger under her pant leg.

She downed a breakfast shake in record time, grabbed a water bottle, and made a beeline out the door. The drive to the barn gave her a chance to think about the past week.

Since her conversation with Blake, she hadn't seen or heard from him. Liz was glad he wasn't hounding her, but his complete absence left her unsettled. She couldn't help wondering if he were up to something.

Her thoughts drifted to Ryland. He'd given her the space she'd asked for and wasn't pressuring her, intentionally. But she could feel his hope, his desire, and it tore her apart. Having to tamp down those things in herself was a full-time job.

After Ryland and Blake had left, she'd sat alone in the dark for hours. Ryland again dominated her thoughts. He was so focused, had so much faith. Liz knew she could never match him. Never be good enough. They made a great team on the battlefield, but that's as far as it could go.

If she gave in, he'd soon learn she wasn't what he thought. That she wasn't what he needed. She and her ramshackle past would bulldoze through his life, plowing over everything. She was poison, and she couldn't let him be a victim.

Liz thought about the moment it had all snapped into place. *I'm not like everybody else, and I never will be.* It was a truth she couldn't avoid. She understood now. Their lives didn't leave room for anything other than their calling. Everything else shifted their focus off the mission.

She was destined to be alone. A servant and a warrior.

If that realization wasn't enough to convince her, the fact that every time she'd fallen in love, it had ended in disaster, was plenty to do the job.

As she sped down the highway and the wind whipped her hair, a strange calm settled over her. This wouldn't be easy. She had to work with Ryland for the foreseeable future. She had to be logical. Use her head, not her heart.

Liz rounded the corner, and the barn loomed in front of her. Her stomach filled with bouncing balls.

First test.

Ryland leaned against his truck, talking to Chammu'el and Arie. When he spotted her, he waved, and a disturbingly perfect grin lifted his beautifully carved cheekbones. When Liz didn't return the wave or the smile, confusion and worry shot from him like a laser. A frown replaced his smile.

Liz closed her eyes and took several slow, deep breaths. *In for five, out for five.* Arie had been working with her on her empathic abilities. He'd taught her how to restrict the flow or reach deeper, whichever a situation called for. He also showed her how to shield her emotions more effectively, and she was getting pretty good at it.

Except when she got mad.

Once she was calm, Liz imagined a dome covering her emotions, encasing them in protective glass. When Liz had completed her task, Ryland's head snapped in her direction. Realization crept across his features, followed by agitation. She may not be able to block him completely yet, but it was a start.

Her hands trembled, and her heart thudded in her ears. Liz had no intention of being cruel, yet she was prepared to do what she had to. She had to stick with her plan. No matter how he affected her.

Liz snagged her equipment from the backseat and launched out of the Jeep.

The second Liz didn't return his smile, Ryland knew something had changed. Her emotions were daggers, slicing into him. His breath caught from the assault.

Suddenly, it all stopped. The spot in his heart where he usually felt her was void.

His temper flared as he understood what she'd done. Man, that woman tried his patience. He wanted to march over and demand she remove the block, even knowing he didn't have the right. Not yet.

Cold and emptiness hollowed him out. He'd gotten used to feeling her. It was as though she were with him all the time. When she was hurt and unconscious, he'd felt like half a person. The same sensation filled him once more.

Ryland followed her into the barn and watched as she unloaded her gear. She strapped on her sword, fastened cuffs to her wrists, and slid small throwing blades into them. He moved into her range. Liz ignored him. When she was satisfied, she picked up a crossbow and held it to her shoulder. She stared down the length of it.

Ryland nudged her elbow. "Hey, you all right?"

"Peachy." Liz didn't take her eyes off the bow.

At least her sarcasm was still intact.

"You don't seem 'peachy.'" Way too calm. And way too quiet.

Liz scooped up three bolts for the crossbow. She barely looked at him and proceeded toward Arie. "It's work time. Gotta get back in shape. There's a demon I need to get rid of."

Ryland slipped in front of her, blocking her path. "Nope. We're not doing this. I told you we'd fight this together. We can't do that if you shut me out."

Liz's face was devoid of expression. He reached further, trying to decipher what she was feeling. Her emotions were just out of his grasp.

She slung the strap of the bow over her shoulder and crossed her arms. "And I told you I couldn't make any promises. Don't you get it? This is it. We fight, we hunt. That's our life. Everything else is for all the normal people." She sidestepped him, and he blocked her again. He saw a brief flash of anger before she closed it off. "Your forcing the issue won't change anything. It's pointless to want what we can't have."

Ryland couldn't decide whether to growl or laugh. "So our life isn't perfect. Whose is? We see the worst in this world, and we fight it. That should give us even more reason to hang on to the good. To have each other to come home to at the end of those hellish days." He leveled his stare at her.

Okay. A little too far. He wanted to punch the beam beside him until it snapped. *Stupid. That's good, scare her away.*

Surprise engraved itself on Liz's face. Finally, some emotion. She took several deep breaths and shifted from foot to foot. It gave him hope he'd actually gotten through to her. Until she opened her mouth and erased that hope in one swift blow.

"That's a nice thought, but it's not reality. We have to stay focused on the job. We can't do that when we're distracted by each other. I can't keep my head in the game if I'm constantly worried about you. That's just how it is."

She slid past him, but he grabbed her wrist. He couldn't let her leave it at that.

"Elizabeth, this is not a job. It's not a game. It's a calling. It's our life."

She jerked her arm away.

He wished she'd look at him. "Just because we're warriors doesn't mean we can't have the rest of what life can offer. We're still human."

For several seconds, she didn't speak. When she finally looked at him, the pain in her eyes speared his chest. She shrugged. "Maybe you can. Not me. I can't have both."

This time, when Liz moved away, he grabbed her shoulders and spun her around.

Enough. She wasn't hearing him, or she wasn't understanding. Fine. She would. She wanted to act like a brat throwing a hissy fit? Fine. She'd get treated like one. Throwing her over his knee and busting her butt crossed his mind. Probably wasn't the best idea. So he settled for second best. He'd give her a time out and cool her off.

Surprise flashed in her eyes and blasted through her wobbly shield. He quickly slid the crossbow from her grasp and tossed it on the ground. Liz sputtered and leaned over to pick it up. Before she reached it, Ryland ducked and tossed her over his shoulder.

"Are you kidding me?" she screamed. "Put me down, you jackass!"

He heard her slap a hand over her mouth before he laughed. "You need to learn a little lesson." He tightened his arms around her legs to restrict her kicks. Her punches to his back kept flying. "And you should watch your mouth."

Ryland tossed a glance at Arie and Chammu'el on his way outside. They stood with their arms folded, watching. Amusement hitched their lips, and the slight approval he caught in their eyes let him know they wouldn't interfere.

"Ryland David Vaughn, I swear, I will beat you to a bloody pulp if you don't put me down right now." Liz ground the words through gritted teeth. Her shield was in tatters now. Rage pelted him. She was out of control.

He could help with that.

"No. You won't. You're gonna learn to act like a grown woman instead of a sulking little brat." He intentionally laced his voice with steel. A part of him was laughing at what he was about to do. The rest of him knew he was running out of options and time. If he couldn't help her, she'd implode.

Liz's assault eased slightly.

Ryland reached his destination. He swung her down into his arms and secured her in front of him, confining her arms. "Are you gonna talk about this like an adult?"

His eyes gave no quarter. He made sure of it. He loved her. There was no way he was playing Switzerland and watching her go down in flames. He was all in, and they'd fight both of their demons together.

"Sure."

Yeah. She was lying. "Wrong answer."

Her eyes narrowed. He heaved her through the air. She landed in the pond with a loud splash, screaming, limbs flapping.

Under any other circumstances, he would've laughed. Instead, he crossed his arms as she got her feet under her and leaped out of the water. Liz shoved her dripping hair out of her eyes as she approached. Less than a foot of space remained between them as she stared him down. Silently.

Ryland poked the bear, needing her to say it. To make sure she remembered he wasn't the one who'd hurt her so badly. He wasn't the one who'd killed so much of her joy. "You're not going to yell? Tell me I could've drowned you, or you could've cracked your skull? Not gonna throw another fit and bust me in the mouth?"

A question flashed in her eyes. Shock charged the wind between them. "No. You wouldn't hurt me." It felt like the admission cost her.

Something in him ached that trust was so foreign to her now.

As if a switch had been flipped, the shock evaporated, and her brows dipped low. For about two seconds, he thought she just might punch him. But it wasn't rage in her eyes. Confusion and fear rode her hard. Not from what had just happened. No, these were buried ghosts still clanging around in the attic, rattling their chains.

Horrors he hadn't been there to protect her from.

The truth seeped into her eyes as they morphed from blue to green. She was terrified because he saw her. The real her. A fragile, delicate woman locked inside, who wanted to be held but instead kept getting crushed.

"Lizzy." Ryland gentled his voice. He reached out and brushed away the hair in her eyes. He caressed her soft, damp cheek. "Please. Talk to me."

When Liz finally opened her mouth, what came out wasn't what he wanted to hear. "I'm sorry. I can't do this." She whipped around him and darted for the barn.

Ryland let out a long exhale. He guessed it was better than her denying there was a problem. Or wanting to take his head off. Time. She needed time. There were things she had to let go of, things she had to face, before she could give him more. He closed his eyes and whispered a prayer before following her.

When he walked inside, Liz stood with Arie, speaking softly. When she grabbed a small, square hay bale and headed out the back door, Arie glanced at Ryland. Ryland could see the worry etched in his eyes. Arie tilted his head, asking a silent question. Ryland shrugged. Arie shook his head and followed his charge outside.

Chammu'el clapped Ryland's back on his way out. "Looks like you need to work out some frustration." The angel walked ahead.

Ryland followed, unable to tear his thoughts from Liz. She was in the middle of the field, setting up targets. Her face was so expressionless, it could've been carved out of stone. Fear slithered across his skin. The last time she'd looked like that, he'd lost her. He wouldn't let it happen again. He knew they could have their mission and a life together. Ryland was nowhere near ready to give up.

Chammu'el motioned him over.

Ryland forced his mind to clear. He had to focus if he was going to engage an angel who moved like the wind. Chammu'el was one of the fastest beings he'd ever encountered.

"Begin!"

Ryland drew his blades and charged his guardian.

The next evening, Hank pulled Liz into a crushing bear hug. "There she is!" He loosened his hold. "Sorry. I got so excited I forgot you may still be hurtin'. How are ya, Lizzy girl?"

Liz smiled and patted his arm. "Good as new."

"I'll be. You must have the constitution of a mule! I always knew you was a tough one, though." He gave her another wide grin.

Julie wedged between them and wrapped Liz in a quick hug. "It's good to have you back. And not just because I'm dead-dog tired from workin' doubles." She winked and went back to rolling silverware.

The bell on the door rang, and a family walked in and picked a booth.

Liz tied on her apron and washed her hands. Finally. Back to normal. She greeted her customers and set about getting their order.

She scanned the busy dining room and was reminded again of Arie's words and her primary mission. Liz was especially drawn to those who had demons attached to them. Bound by evil, no idea it was happening. It was her job to defeat the demons and guide these people to the One who could save them.

As she worked, her thoughts once again landed on Ryland. Oh, she was still ticked he'd had the nerve to throw her in the pond. Probably because deep down Liz knew she deserved it. Truth is, she wanted him to be right. Wanted to believe they could have something other than a life of war.

Liz watched the families enjoying their supper, and sadness settled over her. The desire to have what they had filled her. She wondered what it would've been like if she could've been Ryland's wife. The amazing children she and Ryland could've created. Her hand involuntarily fluttered to her abdomen. Regret wedged itself in and twisted.

Liz moved around the diner, refilling empty drinks.

Her call required her full attention. She had to stay strong. The mission required sacrifice. Liz's gaze swept over the customers again. For them, it was worth it.

For once, she could do something right. Be a part of something bigger. After all she'd done, she should be grateful she had the chance.

This was her penance, and she needed to give herself to it completely.

XX
Fire and Ice

The hair on the back of Liz's neck rankled. Her palms sweat as she twisted them in her lap. She squirmed in the pew. She tried to pay attention. Really. But she hadn't heard a word Dad said.

Liz slung her arm over the back of the pew. With the new position, she could see Ryland out of the corner of her eye, sitting three rows behind her. A lazy grin spread across his face when their eyes met. She tried to ignore it as Dad started the closing prayer. It'd been a week since he'd tossed her in the pond. Even though she'd told him countless times to back off, he hadn't given up.

As they filed out of the pews, Ryland slid out the back door. Liz rolled her eyes and moved to meet Shelley, who bounced up the aisle toward her. Liz quickly scanned the crowd. Thankfully, Blake had been MIA from church for the past two weeks. One less thing to deal with.

The perky little blonde embraced Liz with a smile. "Hey, chick. You look like you're feeling better."

Liz smiled in return. "Definitely."

"Awesome. So…" Shelley glanced at Ryland's back as he stood outside on the front steps. "What's up with you and the men in your life? Did you get it all straightened out?"

Liz swallowed hard. Shelley wouldn't drop it until she told her what had happened. "I paid Blake back and told him we couldn't see each other anymore."

"That had to be rough. Probably for the best." Shelley glanced at Ryland again.

"Yeah." Dad motioned he was headed out, and Liz nodded. She moved for the door, and Shelley followed.

"Liz, he loves you."

"I know. But I have enough crazy in my life."

Shelley gave her a questioning look and tilted her head. "Like what?"

Liz closed her eyes, took a breath, and popped them back open. "Work and stuff. I can't worry about someone else right now. Timing's off."

Shelley let it drop for now. The women walked out onto the steps. Ryland had disappeared. Liz didn't like the mixture of relief and disappointment swirling around in her.

Dad approached them and extended a hand to Shelley. "Here's the keys. Just lock up when you're done." He dropped them into Shelley's hand. "We'll try to save some dinner for you, but I ain't makin' no promises." He slid his arm around Mom and headed for the car.

Liz eyed Shelley. "What do you need the keys for?"

"Oh, some of the girls from youth group are working on things for the fundraiser. You know, the one for the mission trip next spring break? So I volunteered to stay and help."

"Ah, well, better get done quick. Dad wasn't kidding about the food." They both laughed.

The women said their goodbyes, and Shelley went back inside. Liz headed for her Jeep. Her mood took another roller coaster ride when she saw Ryland leaning against the driver's door. Though she couldn't say she was surprised.

She'd known she wouldn't be able to avoid him today. He'd been invited to the house this afternoon. Dad had called a prayer meeting in light of everything going on. A traveling evangelist named Duncan McLevoy and a friend of Dad's, Pastor Anders, were invited as well.

Liz squared her shoulders and tightened the lid on her emotions. One of Ryland's eyebrows shot up. Thankfully he chose not to mention the fact she'd just slammed her mental shields down so hard she could practically hear the impact.

"So, what's your mom making for dinner?"

The question threw her off. "Um, spaghetti."

"Sweet. I love her spaghetti."

Liz snorted. "You'd eat anything that didn't bite you first." She found herself laughing at his excitement. Maybe they could actually be friends, not just coworkers. Even as she thought it, she doubted it.

He slid out of her way and opened the door for her. She shook her head at his mischievous grin. She settled herself in and shoved the keys into the ignition. "What do you think you're doing?"

Ryland climbed into the passenger's side. "Hitching a ride. It was nice out, so I walked this morning. Figured you wouldn't mind giving me a lift." Ryland buckled his seatbelt and kicked his seat back. A grin played at the corners of his lips.

A sudden desire to kiss those lips welled inside, and she felt heat creep up her neck. No man should have lips that full. Or such dangerously long eyelashes. She forced her gaze elsewhere. He gave her a funny look, which changed to a smoldering one. Great. He probably knew exactly what she was thinking.

Fellow soldiers. That's all.

Oh, Lord, he looked and smelled so good. Her cheeks were on fire. Ryland chuckled.

She needed to keep it together for the fifteen-minute drive.

With him.

Alone.

Liz stole another look. Ryland grinned from ear to ear. His dominating presence filled the Jeep. She couldn't stop looking at him. She'd have to make this the shortest trip home on record.

Liz dragged her eyes away from the object of her obsession and started the engine. "Hang on."

"Huh?"

She tore out of the parking lot, drawing curious stares from members of the congregation still hanging around. Ryland grabbed the dash with one hand and the roll bar with the other. Liz stomped on the accelerator. She'd give him good reason to never get in her vehicle again. She laughed as she relished the control.

The rest of the ride was fairly quiet. Liz tried to make him fear for his life, and Ryland stayed occupied with hanging on. He occasionally uttered a "Look out!" or "Take it easy!" or "Woman, you're nuts!" She smiled, pleased with herself. She didn't slow down, and he didn't relax until she reached her parents' driveway.

"Hey, you lived to tell—" Liz was stopped by a jolt to her system. Electricity charged her skin. Warmth balled in her chest and radiated outward. She glanced at Ryland. His eyes were as wide as hers probably were, and goosebumps trailed up and down his arms.

A strange calm filled the Jeep. Unbelievable joy and peace. Liz eased down the driveway, both of them silent and scanning the woods. When they rounded the bend and the trees opened up, Liz drew in a sharp breath, and Ryland let out an awed, "Oh wow." Liz stopped in the middle of the drive.

It was like looking into the sun. Painfully bright lights illuminated the area, obscuring the house from view. She could just make out shapes amidst the glow. When some of the brightness receded, Liz gasped.

Freakishly tall creatures. Enormous wings. Flaming swords. Some with faces like lions. Majestic and regal, displaying the glory of the King to whom they belonged. The ring of angels wrapped around the house, wings touching. Two rows deep, they were staggered, forming an impenetrable wall of power.

It was the most magnificent thing she had ever seen. It filled her heart and soul with delight and even a bit of pride.

"The Lord's power is quite a sight to behold, is it not?"

Liz and Ryland both jumped, jarred from their trance.

Liz was the first to respond. "Arie! You scared us to death!" She wrenched herself around to see the angel who filled the backseat.

With both Ryland and Arie inside, her big vehicle suddenly seemed small.

"Obviously not. You are still speaking."

Was that actually a joke? Liz glanced at Ryland and saw the glint in his eyes.

In an instant, Arie was back to business. "Rarely do humans have the chance to see such a glorious sight."

Liz continued staring. "I'm guessing they're here because of the meeting, so there aren't any interruptions?"

"Precisely."

"Too bad we can't have them around—" Her words cut off as heaviness drove the joy out of her spirit. When the back of her neck lit up this time, it wasn't peaceful. An invisible, malicious fist gripped her airway and squeezed. The air thickened with the stench of evil.

Liz, Arie, and Ryland swiveled their heads toward the woods at their left. Markus, Kade, and about twenty ferocious-looking demons glared back at them. Liz could feel Markus's rage like it was swimming in her stomach, trying to infect her.

So, wall-o-angel wasn't exactly in his plan, huh?

Markus shouted something to Kade and the others in a language Liz didn't know. The demons vanished. Kade spoke to Markus, then followed them.

Markus flashed a sadistic smile. A malicious whisper invaded her mind. *I will have you.*

He captured her eyes with his. Somehow, Markus tore away the barrier shielding her emotions. Defying all logic, their minds merged. Vileness impaled her. Nausea caused her stomach to heave. Her head spun wildly, filled with whispers. Images of things she never wanted to see, or even knew existed, infected her mind and tried to seep into her soul. Pure, unadulterated evil no one could fathom in their wildest imagination.

Before she could even understand what had happened, he was gone.

Liz shivered uncontrollably. She had a fierce urge to scrub out her brain with steel wool and bleach. Markus was a bacteria. He'd gotten into her bloodstream and infected every cell. She sat motionless. He'd paralyzed her with his darkness.

Or woke up whatever is in me. Liz wondered if he had connected with something inside of her. Some darkness festering in the depths. Her mind flashed back. Years ago, she'd opened a door. Curiosity and rebellion had gotten the best of her, and she'd taken a bite of forbidden fruit. Now, the seed remained buried deep, in a place she hadn't wanted dug up.

Markus had found it and latched on, coaxing it to grow.

Ryland peeled her hand off the gearshift. "Liz, look at me." His voice was stern as he cradled her cheek in his hand.

Arie rested his hand on her shoulder. Slowly, the fog began to lift. Liz looked at Ryland. His hand tightened around hers. His eyes widened. He looked like someone had knocked the wind out of him. Whatever Markus had done had touched him, through her. She was sure of it. Liz gripped Ryland's hand and hung on.

While Ryland rode out the wave, Liz used what breath she still had to speak to Arie. "He sent those demons to attack whoever is still on their way here."

She knew this with a certainty. Apparently, Markus hadn't considered how much she would see and retain once he opened the gateway.

Arie gave her a strange look but didn't question her. "We are prepared. They will be protected. Have faith, young one." Arie squeezed her shoulder. "Are you recovered?"

Liz nodded. "I'll be okay." *I hope.*

"I've got her." Ryland resurfaced from the flood quicker than she had.

"Very well." Arie shot out of the Jeep in a streak of light.

"Let's get to the house." Ryland ran his knuckles down her jaw. "I need to get you inside that wall of angels where I know Markus can't get to you." Liz saw the flame of rage in him, felt the heat flare through his fingers. "The first chance I get, I'm going to give him a slow, excruciating ride back to Hell."

Liz shook at the vehemence and fury exuding from Ryland. She'd never seen this feral look in his eyes or thought him capable of such extreme wrath. Now, it was coming alive because of her. *I was right. Poison.*

"Ryland..."

"Liz, he violated you." Ryland ground his teeth so hard, she thought they'd break off. "I can't let it stand. I won't."

Liz was struck again by his unshakable love for her. His protectiveness. She shifted the Jeep into gear and continued down the drive toward the wall of angels.

Maybe once behind their fortifying presence, she wouldn't be able to feel Markus still creeping around in her head.

XXI
Into the Darkness

Liz and Ryland stood wide-eyed in front of the shining brigade.

As they moved closer, the angels parted. The peace flowing from them was like a balm to her assailed mind and soul. Once she and Ryland moved through the line, it closed behind them with a flourish. Wind whipped. Armor clinked. Boots stomped. The sounds of a well-oiled force, moving in perfect synchronization.

Liz slipped off her heels and carried them to her old room while Ryland sat with Dad. She swapped her dress for the cargo pants, T-shirt, and boots she'd brought with her. When she was finished, she walked back into the living room.

"Where's Mom?"

"Garlic bread. She forgot it. Told me to tell you to stir the sauce when you got here."

Momentary panic seized her. *Arie said they'd be protected.* Liz forced her shoulders to relax.

"Okay." *Lord, keep them safe.* Liz moved toward the kitchen and straight for the bubbling pot.

As she stirred, Ryland came up behind her. Liz thought he was going to put his arms around her, and she tensed. Instead, he stepped to the side and grabbed a loaf of bread. Liz felt a little pang of disappointment.

But she'd made her choice. Now she had to deal with it. She berated herself as he reached past her and dipped a slice of bread into the sauce.

"Really?" She laughed.

He popped the bread into his mouth. "I'm a growing boy. I require sustenance."

Liz smacked his hand when he reached for more. "Enough. It's about ready anyway."

"You're mean." He gave her a crooked smile and tweaked her ear.

She brushed him off and started the water for pasta. A warm feeling blossomed in her chest. Ryland's presence and silly antics were what she needed to help erase the memory of Markus. A shiver coursed through Liz at the thought, and Ryland raised an eyebrow. He leaned over and kissed her cheek. He pulled back, lightly touching the spot where his lips had been.

"Lizzy, we'll get him. I promise."

Liz nodded. Her stomach was in the throes of a hissy fit. Whether she wanted to admit it or not, he was breaking down her carefully constructed walls.

The sound of car doors closing drew her to the kitchen window. Mom, Dylan, Duncan McLevoy, Pastor Anders, and a few people she recognized from church were milling in the yard on their way to the porch.

"Thank God they made it. If they could see what's in front of them..." Watching the heavenly guard part again was as magnificent as the first time, and Liz's breath caught.

Ryland eased toward the window. "I know. This is one of the times I love knowing what's out there." He smiled. "Didn't know Mac was gonna be here. Good."

"Mac?"

"Yeah, Duncan McLevoy." Ryland let the curtain drop. "We've worked together before."

Liz wanted to ask what kind of work. His heat against her back stole her question. Her heart flipped as Ryland's hip brushed hers. She felt a reaction skitter through him as well and smiled.

She went to the stove and stirred the sauce again, even though it didn't really need it. Ryland sneaked another piece of bread from the bag and reached around her to dip it in the pot. Her pulse accelerated to dangerous levels.

Liz slapped at his hand again. "Stop that!" She tried to laugh off the nerves wreaking havoc in her.

He gave her a fake pout before people poured into the kitchen. Mom shooed the men out. Liz breathed a sigh of relief. In a matter of minutes, the food was ready, the guys had dropped the extra leaves into the table, Dad had said grace, and plates were being filled.

Liz was uncomfortably conscious of Ryland's knee grazing hers in the close quarters. It shot bolts of electricity through her leg and up her spine. Every time she glanced at him, he gave her his infernal grin. The one that did weird things to her. She passed the basket of bread to Ryland, and his fingers brushed hers. They lingered longer than necessary. She shot him a look and got a cock-eyed smile in return.

The man was incorrigible.

Dylan whispered in her ear, snapping her out of her thoughts. "Have you heard from Shelley? I keep getting voicemail, and she won't answer my texts." His brows knit together. "She should've been here by now."

Liz pulled her phone out of her pocket. "No. Nothing. She probably got to talking and lost track of time. I'm sure she'll be here soon."

Ryland leaned in and lowered his voice. "Everything all right?"

Liz grimaced. "He's worried. Shelley's running late, and he can't get a hold of her."

"Should we run back to the church and check?"

"Maybe. But Arie said everyone would be protected." Even as she said the words, a weird feeling descended on her. Something was off.

Ryland raised an eyebrow. She waved him back to his food. Liz closed her eyes and brought a shield down over her emotions. When she looked up, Ryland narrowed his eyes. Liz shrugged. She had to admit part of the reason she'd done it was because it got under his skin. Liz showed teeth in a satisfied smile.

After dinner, Liz took a spot by the window so she could keep an eye on what was going on outside. She wanted to know the moment when—if—Markus returned. Ryland broke away from his conversation with Mac and took position at another window.

As Dad addressed everyone, Liz skimmed the room. Dylan was missing. That strange feeling churned in her stomach again. She saw him pacing in the kitchen, phone to his ear. Panic swirled around him. Liz left her post to check on him.

His eyes were wild, and a frown had engraved itself on his face. "I still haven't heard from her. I'm going to head over there and see if she's all right." He started to move for the back door, but Liz caught his arm.

Something in her spirit warned her Shelley's delay wasn't due to anything Dylan could deal with. "Stay. Ryland and I will go."

"No, it's fine. I've got it."

Urgency pinched her heart, and she tightened her hold on his arm. "Dylan, I'm sure it's nothing. We'll be there and back with Shelley before you know it. Besides, I'm sure Dad needs you here." She tried to calm the storm raging inside of him the best she could, all the while dealing with a growing hurricane herself.

"Okay. But you call me if there's anything wrong, all right?"

"We will."

The two of them walked back to the living room. Ryland motioned her over. There was a hard look on his face, and his brow was creased. The clang of steel and shouts filtered in from the front yard. The storm within kicked up another category. Dad started praying, and Ryland pulled back the curtain a few inches so he and Liz could see out.

Markus had sent a small force against the angelic army. The demons fought like rabid beasts, but they weren't faring well. Light flashed and flame billowed as the heavenly warriors hit their targets with precision. The demons never stood a chance. Why would he sacrifice his soldiers? She looked at Ryland, the question in her eyes. He stayed silent, flexing his jaw, certain knowledge in his eyes.

Distraction. Markus had sent them to keep everyone occupied.

Her heart raced, and she whispered in Ryland's ear. "We've gotta get to Shelley."

Ryland nodded. As he dropped the curtain, something drew her gaze. She grabbed the drapes and pulled it back again.

Markus.

He stood well away from the battle, a sadistic grin plastered on his lips. He bored into her eyes with his. Liz tried to fight it, to throw up a mental wall and keep him out. Searing pain met her attempt. Darkness fell like heavy dew in her brain. Once again, pictures flashed and sounds gonged. Earlier they were disjointed and nonsensical. Now they were like a movie in her head.

Shelley! Liz swallowed the catch in her throat. She saw her friend as if Shelley were right in front of her. She'd pulled her car to the side of the road and was running away from it, demons on her trail. They caught her. She screamed, the sound rattling through Liz's bones.

Liz shook violently. Ryland turned her away from the window. He grasped her chin and brought her eyes to his. The vision shut off. Liz trembled, and beads of sweat sprouted on her forehead. Her legs barely held her up. Thankfully everyone else still had their eyes closed in prayer. Except Dad. He watched them with anger and concern warring on his face.

"Liz, look at me," Ryland whispered hoarsely. "Let me in."

Liz met his eyes. She didn't know what he could do, but without hesitation, she popped the lid on her emotions, opening her mind to him. Peace poured from him as he prayed through clenched teeth. He never broke eye contact. Liz began to feel grounded, anchored.

"How?" she croaked.

He rubbed her arm. "We'll talk about it later."

"Ry, I saw what's happening. Or what could happen."

"Are you all right?" A vein in his neck looked ready to burst.

"I'm fine. Let's go."

Liz looked around, not seeing Dad where he had been a minute ago. She found him in the kitchen, circling the island as he prayed.

"We have to go take care of something." She focused on evening out her voice. "We'll be back soon."

"I know. I felt it too." Dad patted her back. "Go. We'll give you backup from our end." Something in his voice told her he'd rather be going with them. Weird.

Dad kissed her forehead and nodded at Ryland. Ryland yanked her keys off the small table by the door, and Liz followed him out.

The skirmish outside was over before they got to the Jeep. One of the angels nodded at them as they jumped into the vehicle and tore down the driveway.

"Up by the bend, right before you start coming back into town." Liz barely got the words past the catch in her throat.

"This isn't your fault."

He really needed to stop reading her so well. "Markus is going after her because of me." Liz bit out the words.

Ryland glanced at the backseat, ignoring her remark. "What do you have back there?"

"I've got my sword and my bag. I've been carrying them everywhere since…" Liz let the sentence trail off and dug in the backseat.

She pulled out a set of short blades and her own sword and laid them across her lap.

Ryland's eyes left the road for a moment and settled on hers. "That'll work." He gestured at the blades.

"Shouldn't our guardians be here?"

"They'll be here if we need them."

Liz marveled at his confidence. "Yeah. Let's hope we don't."

Silence fell as they flew along. Nervous energy filled the vehicle. Liz's body thrummed with the need for action and the desire to keep Shelley safe.

Liz pointed when they rounded a corner. "Look! There's her car."

The car sat in the exact spot as in the vision Markus had injected into her brain. The car sat at an odd angle as if she'd slid off the road instead of purposely guiding it to the shoulder.

Shelley was nowhere to be seen.

Ryland slowed and pulled behind the compact. He grabbed the double-pronged blades from her lap, and she reached for the handle of her sword. They jumped out, each taking a different side. She'd have to think of some way to explain their weapons to Shelley. If they found her.

"Shelley?" Liz headed around the front of the car as Ryland took the back.

Shelley popped up from behind the passenger side. "Oh, thank the Lord!" Her hands were covered in grease, and some of her knuckles were bloody.

Liz rushed toward her and pulled her into a hug. "What happened?"

Shelley gestured at the wheel. "My tire blew, and I couldn't get a signal to call anybody." She wiped her brow with the back of her hand, smearing grease on her flawless skin. "I tried to do it the way Dylan showed me, but I can't get the stupid nut thingies off."

"I'll get it." Ryland bent down in front of the offending tire and laid the blades he held beside him.

Shelley's eyebrows went flying into her hairline as she looked from Ryland to Liz. "Um, Liz, why does he have two big, honkin' knives? And why do you have a sword?"

Liz glanced at Ryland. He shrugged, smirked, and went to work on the tire.

"Well, I had my stuff in the Jeep from martial arts class. When we couldn't get a hold of you, we thought you were in trouble, so we grabbed these just in case." At least it wasn't technically a lie.

Ryland chuckled, and Liz kicked his shin.

"Okay." Shelley scrunched her nose.

Liz checked to see if she had signal on her cell. No bars. She shoved the phone back into her pocket and leaned against the car. She and Shelley chatted, Liz constantly keeping watch, until Ryland stood and tossed the flat tire into the trunk.

Ryland wiped his hands on his pants. "You're all good."

"Oh, thank you!" Shelley gave him a quick hug. "Are you guys heading back?"

"Yeah, we'll be right there." Liz stopped as the air rushed out of her. She bent forward, grasping at her chest.

"Are you okay?" Shelley rushed to her side.

Ryland laid a hand on Liz's shoulder. Liz glanced at him out of the corner of her eye. His clenched jaw and sharp eyes said he felt it, too. He rubbed her back. "She'll be fine." He gave Shelley a smile. "She hasn't been feeling so great today. You go on, and we'll catch up."

"If you're sure," Shelley looked uncertain as Liz rose.

Liz nodded, unable to speak.

Shelley relented and climbed into her car. As she sped away, Liz grabbed her head. Knives jabbed at her brain. Her skin felt like someone beat her with a cactus, and her limbs grew weak. A deep chill settled into her blood.

"Can you get to the Jeep?" Ryland had an arm around her shoulders and another around her waist, holding her up. "I need to get you out of here. You're too weak right now."

Liz stopped him with a wave of her hand. Her eyes swept the tree line. They locked on to the source of the cold. "There. He's there." Ryland's gaze followed her shaky finger.

Markus emerged from the forest, Kade at his side, two other large demons at their backs. His obscene smile sent a shiver up her spine. A second later, flame leaped into her brain. Liz slipped out of Ryland's arms and sank to her knees. She saw Markus's delighted face and Ryland's panicked one before oily darkness dragged her under.

XXII
Darkest Part

Ryland crouched at Liz's side and took her face in his hands. "Block him! You can do it. Focus."

If she blocked Markus, it would keep Ryland out too. He didn't want to lose the connection with her, especially now. But they had to keep Markus out of her head. First, he had to give her enough strength to reinforce her shield.

Liz shook her head. "I can't. He's too strong." She cringed, and her entire body tensed. A desperate prayer ripped from her lips. "God, please. Help me!"

"Yes, you can. You have to stay open long enough to take what you need from me, then lock down." Ryland caught her gaze with his. He should've gone over this with her before now.

"I don't know how to do that!" Tears rolled down her cheeks.

Her anguish ripped at his heart. He pulled her close to him as he kept an eye on Markus and Kade. They hadn't moved. They watched him and Liz with amusement clear on their grotesque faces. Ryland dragged her behind the car to give them some cover.

"You can feel me there, right?" She nodded, and he brushed her tears away. "Okay, open up so I can give you what you need. Reach out and grab what you feel coming from me. Use it to help put up a barrier. Make it your own." He hoped it made sense to her. "Shut off the flow and put up the shield."

Red-hot rage tore through him and exploded down his limbs as he glanced at the demons again. He reined it in, guarding her from it. She didn't need that right now. Ryland held her tight and pushed whatever strength he had through their link, hoping it would be enough.

He desperately wanted to give her more. But their connection was limited. She continued to keep her heart partially closed to him, and now it was affecting more than their personal relationship.

As he felt her tentatively siphoning strength, a question tickled his brain. It was strange the demon hadn't attacked her this way until today. Or had Markus done this before, and Liz hadn't told him? Judging from her reaction, he didn't think so. How was Markus doing this? Demons typically had to possess someone to have that much power over them.

He could feel the evil invading their link. Foreboding swam in his mind. He reached deep, trying to breach the places she'd walled off. Dark, veiled areas of her heart she hid from everyone. So much he couldn't get to—didn't know.

She had to take what he gave and make it a part of her, let it in deep. Yet she was still shutting him out.

He couldn't shake the feeling Liz knew why this was happening. He could feel it there, beyond what he had access to.

What was she guarding so fiercely? What was she keeping from him?

Markus's evil speared Liz's brain. She had a sense of falling back into the pit, the sucking black hole she'd barely gotten out of. She fought it, did what Ryland said. She tried not to think about how deep she'd let Ryland in, how much he may have seen and felt. She hadn't exposed everything. He'd still seen too much, though. Unlocking anything more was not an option.

Those places had to stay hidden. Especially from him.

Visualizing herself taking his strength and adding it to her own, she built a wall against Markus's onslaught. Liz continued to pray as she did it. In her mind, she saw a giant hand reach down and add bricks to the wall. *What...?* The strength she'd used flowed back into her and Ryland, with more added to it. As the barrier was fortified, she could feel Markus shrinking back, withdrawing the tentacles he'd extended into her.

"Thank you." Liz breathed the words, both to God and Ryland.

"Wasn't all me." Ryland's voice filled with awe.

"You helped." She gave him a quick smile.

Ryland tilted his head toward her. "You good?" There was something in his eyes, whether uncertainty or fear, she couldn't tell.

Had he seen everything? Surely if he had seen the blackness inside of her, he would've pushed her away instantly. All she'd done, all the things that twisted her into something ugly. She couldn't let him see any of it.

"I'm good." Liz pointed at the demons. "That doesn't look so good."

Markus's eyes blazed as he yelled commands in the same language he'd used earlier. Kade and the other demons started forward.

Ryland picked up his blades as they stood. "Stay away from Markus and Kade." There was an edge to his voice that sent shivers down Liz's spine. He locked his eyes on hers. "I mean it. Do what I say this time. No matter what happens, you stay away from them. Promise me."

Liz nodded as she picked up her sword. "I promise." She knew she was weak, and there was no way she could take on Markus or Kade right now. She reached down and pulled her dagger from its sheath.

The demons crossed the small field and closed in. Liz and Ryland stood shoulder to shoulder, weapons raised and ready. Liz wondered again where their guardians were. She pushed away the doubt. They weren't alone. If they needed help, He'd send it. As the demons drew closer, the urge to fight settled over her like a mist, energizing and fortifying her.

Ryland gave her a nod. "Go."

At his quiet words, they lunged forward to meet their enemies, hopefully taking them by surprise at the sudden offensive move. Liz dropped her shoulder and plowed into the first demon in her path as she saw Ryland slice at Kade out of the corner of her eye. Kade grunted and stumbled. Markus vanished.

Lovely.

She smashed the handle of her dagger into her opponent's temple. He staggered, swinging his blade wildly. It slashed her right forearm. Liz yanked the arm to her chest.

The demon tackled her to the ground. Her sword tumbled from her hand. His weight trapped her, cutting off her air. The monster ground two hard punches to her ribs. It felt like her bones were exploding. Liz drew back her right fist and aimed at his face. He caught it and twisted, slamming it to the ground above her head. She bit back a cry as the motion further opened the gash and pulled at her bruised ribs.

She shook her head clear and remembered she still had her dagger in the other hand. Liz curled to the left and pulled the blade back. She drove it into his flank, withdrew it, and drove it in again, just between the ribs. The demon let out a howl and released her arm.

Liz drew up her knees and shoved, flipping him off her. She rolled to grab her sword and scrambled to her feet. Before he could lift his own blade, she'd driven hers through his throat. A strange gurgling sound and black ooze emanated from the wound.

She whirled and ducked a swing from the next demon. Hmm. A female. She'd never seen that before. Liz skidded to her knees. She slashed, catching the demon across the tops of her thighs. The creature sank to the ground with a disturbing cry.

Liz leaped to her feet. She glanced around but didn't see Markus. Ryland and Kade were engaged in what she could only label a death match about twenty feet away. Both covered in black ooze and crimson blood, they sliced and hacked with unreal speed. Kicks and punches flew furiously, pummeling without mercy.

Ryland was magnificent. He moved like an ancient warrior, lithe, elegant, and deadly. Her admiration took a backseat as Ryland fell, Kade's blade jammed into his thigh.

Her heart jumped into her throat. A red haze fell over her eyes. Liz moved forward, then stopped, remembering her promise. It took all the willpower she had. When Kade yanked his sword away, Ryland pushed to his knees and swept the demon's leg with his good one. He must be ok —

The thought got cut off by a blow to the back of her head. Stars danced in front of Liz's eyes. She fell facedown in the dirt. Her whole body went rigid.

"Liz, come on, baby! Get up! I can't —" There was a loud grunt and a *thump*.

Liz managed to flop to her back. The demon stood over her, legs covered in black tar. Shoving the pain away, Liz raised her foot and planted her boot as hard as possible between the demon's legs, crunching bone.

Ha. Works on girls, too. The demon bent her legs inward and let out a series of groans. Liz slid out from under the creature and crawled to her feet. Her head spun, and she grabbed it with one hand. The she-devil charged.

Their blades collided midair. Liz parried, jabbed, and blocked for all she was worth. She tied up the demon's blade between her own dagger and sword. The demon pushed back. Liz returned the shove, landing them in a stalemate, neither moving.

The demon growled and hissed. "I'm going to —"

"Shut up, skank." Liz reared back and head-butted the demon in the nose.

She was certain her eyes were coming out the back of her head. A loud snapping sound was followed by a grating howl and a spray of black ooze. The demon staggered. She yelled and lunged at Liz. Liz side-stepped, drawing her blade along the creature's abdomen.

Finally, her opponent fell to her knees.

"This time, you're gonna stay down." Liz dropped her dagger and took her sword in both hands. She buried it in the demon's neck, twisting with all she had.

"Excellent work, darling."

Liz's skin crawled. Her muscles tensed to the point of snapping. Face to face with Markus, the haze that enveloped her earlier intensified. Rage built inside of her until it was a living thing, seeking control.

"I'm not your darling." Liz gritted out the response and met his eyes. Fear and dread were the furthest things from her mind. There was only the need for revenge. She could taste it.

"You could be."

Liz snorted. "Well, if you can't beat 'em, try and get 'em to join you, right?"

"Not quite." Markus stepped closer. His presence enveloped her. "You could be who you truly are. You could release what is locked inside, what you cannot show anyone else." He nodded toward Ryland, who was still tangled with Kade. "You know he could never understand. Once he sees the real you, what you've done, what you're capable of, he'll cast you aside."

"That's not true. He loves me." Liz wasn't sure why she'd blurted that. Maybe because Markus had given voice to her private fears. She wanted to yank the knowledge away from him, to refuse his knowing her that well.

"He doesn't deserve the faith you put in him." Markus smiled, a grotesque sight. "War is here. You should reconsider whose side you've chosen. Though, I'm thinking you're not entirely certain of your choice yourself."

"Why would I choose the losing side?" Liz tried to put all of her faith and conviction into her words. Her heart filled with fear and doubt. Which fed the pull Markus had on her. Fed their strange connection.

His eyes bored into hers, and she could feel him try to break through again. When he hit the wall, he gave a violent push, then retreated slightly. He didn't go away. She could feel him tapping against the bricks. Looking for weaknesses. "We'll see. As for Ryland, he loves who he thinks you are. Who he wants you to be." Markus leaned in, and she could feel his offensive breath on her cheek. "Why are you defending him when you know it to be true?"

"Get away from her!" Ryland's yell rent the air.

Liz choked on her answer.

Markus smiled. "I know you better than he ever will, my love."

One word snapped her out of her trance. "You don't even know what love is." Liz backed away from him. Before he could respond, she sliced her sword across his abdomen. "You should never let your guard down."

Markus stepped back, surprise leaping into his eyes. He grinned, wiped his clawed hand across the ooze coming from his wound, and licked a finger. "Such a hot temper. I could teach you how to really put it to use."

Liz gritted her teeth and raised her sword again.

"Not yet." Markus wagged a finger at her. He waved his hand toward where Ryland and Kade fought, and Kade disappeared.

Liz tilted her head, thankful Kade was gone, but knowing Markus had a reason. "What do you really want, Markus?"

"Ryland has a few axes to grind with Kade, and he might win. I can't afford to lose my lieutenant. Just yet." Markus's grin widened. "What I wanted was you. Here. And I have it."

Liz's brow quirked. "What do you mean? And what axes?" When he laughed, she shook her head. "I'm so going to enjoy ending you."

"Not today, darling Elizabeth." Markus widened the gap between them. "And you will have to ask your guard dog about his…secrets." He clucked his tongue.

Ryland made it to her side, and she gave him a quick glance. Her thoughts focused on Markus's words. *Secrets?*

Ryland gripped his blades and made a move toward Markus.

"Not so fast, wonder boy." Markus spread his wings and focused on Liz. "As much as I hate to leave you, I must."

"Yeah, I'm all broken up about it." Liz smirked. Her anger at Markus had driven out her fear. And apparently shut off the little filter in her brain. "So that's all you wanted? To taunt me? Come on, Markus. Can't you do any better?"

"Oh, I have, trust me." Markus laughed. "I've accomplished all I set out to do today." He winked before they heard a *whoosh*, and he was gone.

Ryland's eyes blazed, and his jaw was set like stone. Added to his bloody appearance and the knives dripping with black ooze in his hands, he looked even more the ancient warrior, about to tear down the world. He dropped the blades next to the sword that had slipped from her hand.

Suddenly, everything Markus had said rained down on her and soaked into her soul. His words shook her to her core. Her rage drained away, leaving her weak.

"Liz?" Ryland shook her gently.

Liz hadn't even felt his calloused hands on her arms. "Yeah?" She brought her eyes to his and saw the fear that had impaled her.

"Are you all right? Answer me." His voice was nearing frantic.

"I'm…okay." Liz pushed at the fog. "He was just trying to mess with my head."

"Looks like he did a pretty good job." Ryland ground his teeth together, and his hands grasped her arms tightly. He eased up when he saw her wince. "Sorry. I'll get him, Liz." He grazed her cheek with his fingertips. "I'd do anything for you."

"I know." His words lanced her heart. "That's what I'm afraid of."

He obviously knew more than she ever meant for him to, yet he remained by her side. He fought with her, for her. And even though she was terrified, his light touched that within her own soul, pulling her away from the dark.

He was too good for her.

Ryland didn't say anything, just pulled her to him. He held her for a few moments before setting her away. "We need to get you patched up."

"You don't look so hot yourself." Her eyes took in the bruise on his jaw. The lacerations on his arm and his torso. The hole in his left leg.

"Yeah, I guess so." He shrugged. "We'll get these wounds taken care of, then run by my place and your apartment so we can change before we go back to your parents'."

Liz nodded and followed him to the Jeep.

They were silent while they took turns bandaging each other up. Most of their injuries had already started to heal. When they were done, they climbed in and took off toward his house. Liz laid back in the seat, letting the wind blow her hair around her face. Ryland's phone rang, shattering the quiet.

Ryland grabbed the phone from the cup holder. "Hello? Hey, Pastor Brantley, we're on our way—"

Bricks landed with a *thud* in the pit of Liz's gut when Ryland's face dropped. The bevy of emotion swirling from him held nothing good.

"We'll be right there." He dropped the phone and gripped her knee as if he were bracing her for whatever he was about to say. Liz held her breath. Ryland's grip strengthened. The Jeep lurched forward as he stepped on the accelerator.

"Ryland, what's going on?" Panic surged in her belly as deep sadness barreled at her from him.

Ryland sighed. When he looked up again, his eyes were clear and focused. Now, rage pulsed between them.

"The church is on fire."

XXIII
Farewell

Tongues of fire lapped at the walls of the church, ravaging the house of worship Dad had lovingly built so many years ago.

Firefighters and their equipment cluttered the yard and the parking lot, doing the best they could to extinguish the blaze. It was obvious when they did quench the flames, the building would be a total loss.

Liz and Ryland jumped out of the Jeep before the dust of their arrival had settled. Liz ran to her parents. They stood in front of a firetruck, clinging to one another as if they let go, they'd be lost to the wind. She and Ryland took turns embracing them, giving what peace they could.

Their world was ablaze, ashes raining down on their heads. No one could tear their eyes away from the carnage. No one said a word. Not even about Liz and Ryland being injured. They hadn't given their bandages a second glance.

Ryland stood beside Liz and wrapped an arm around her waist. She laid her head on his shoulder. If he hadn't been there, she would've hit the ground. Her body trembled. Her stomach pitched. The acrid air invaded her nostrils and clung to her skin.

The four of them, and everyone else who had been at the house, stood in a loose huddle. They watched the flames leap higher, licking and devouring. The group jumped in unison when the roof collapsed, sending a shower of sparks heavenward. Ryland enclosed Liz in his arms and shielded her face. He stepped back, urging her to a safer distance.

Liz numbly complied.

A deep shiver ripped through Liz's body despite the intense heat emanating from the inferno. She latched on to Ryland's arms, desperate to be grounded. If she didn't anchor herself to him, she was sure she would fly away on the back of a beast named horror.

Liz raised her head for a moment as a warm sensation spread through her. Arie, Chammu'el, and a few other angels appeared on the fringes of the small crowd, just on the edge of the forest that surrounded the grounds. Arie nodded. Liz took another glance at the blazing church. The sight caused her to bury her face back in Ryland's shoulder.

Misery descended like a cloud. Fingers of despair clawed at them. Devastating emotion exuded from everyone around her and seeped into every pore she owned. She'd forgotten to put her shields in place. Now, it was impossible. The torrent was overpowering, coming hard and fast, and there was no way to stop it.

Liz winced as the flow kept coming. Pounding her relentlessly. Drilling into her brain. Tears clouded her vision. The utter heartache radiating from each person present settled on her skin and burrowed inside. It stung as it wormed its way in.

Please, God, take the pain away. Liz glanced at her parents. *They shouldn't be suffering like this. It's not right. Please.*

Ryland tilted her chin up and whispered to her. "Don't fight against it. Imagine you're shutting off a valve. Ride out the wave and close the valve as it comes through." He rubbed his hand up and down her back.

"I'll try."

She felt Ryland reinforcing her, but he'd been sapped as well. He'd given her too much earlier. Given her strength he needed. The thought sliced her heart.

Liz untangled herself from Ryland, amid his quiet protest, and sank to the ground. She pulled her knees in and rested her head on them. She rubbed her temples, attempting to ease the massive headache fracturing her skull. Her ribs caved under the weight and the thick smoke permeating the air. Every breath was a challenge.

Thick like molasses, time inched forward, having no meaning. Scattered shouts, the blast of water, crackling flames, groaning lumber, and soul-rending sobs formed a cacophonous symphony. It pounced on her, void of mercy.

Ryland crouched at her side. She basked in the waves of concern and love. Sensed the power emanating from him, a power he wore so lightly and comfortably. Felt the strength he gave. Liz struggled, refusing to consume any more of him. He'd done more than he should. She fought against him, focusing on blocking him.

"Let me do this. You can't take much more." His voice was soft, laced with firm command. The command melted into pleading. "Please, Liz. I can't let you sit here in agony when I can do something about it."

"I can't let you drain yourself for me. I'll keep praying, and I'll be fine."

A tear leaked out of the corner of her eye. She whimpered. *Pull it together, Brantley. You can handle this.* Liz wondered if she could as the flow of emotion inched toward flood stage.

"When God sends an answer, you don't turn it away because it doesn't come how you wanted it to. I'm here, and I can help. I'll do whatever I have to to keep you safe." The steel was back. "Now's not the time to be stubborn. If you don't let me in, you'll overload."

Ryland cupped her face with his hands. She opened her eyes. His fierce love for her rushed to the forefront of the tidal wave. Even though she tried to stop it, her feelings for him sprang through the surf, answering his heart's call to her own. She couldn't hold it back. Terror ripped into her as she sensed what was happening.

The wall was breached. Her soul was laid bare.

Ryland's eyes widened. For a moment, his control wavered. Liz felt his heart leap.

"Ry, no—"

Whatever she was about to say got jarred off her lips by snapping, cracking, and more groaning. The church fell in on itself with a mighty crash. Sparks, ash, and smoke plumed into the sky. A collective wail sounded from the onlookers.

And the next wave of emotion hit.

Savage.

Merciless.

Devastating.

Liz collapsed against Ryland like her bones had turned to soup. His arms closed around her like a vise. She could barely stop the urge to vomit as nausea and dizziness hit her. A second before her head folded in on itself, Ryland rushed in. He'd been poised and ready. He stemmed the flow to a trickle. The intensity of the ache lessened. This time, with her walls obliterated, he'd been able to connect fully and help her shield from everyone else.

A strong, warm hand rested on the back of her neck, and a thumb massaged the knot forming there. Liz surrendered to his touch. He murmured soothingly in her ear. She slowly became more aware of what was going on around her. Voices and noises swirled on the wind, then faded. Fire engines pulled away. Liz kept her head down and squeezed her eyes shut, refusing to look at the charred remains.

The fog was lifting from her mind. The pain from the earlier assault, all but gone. It left her with the sensation she'd been through a blender. She worked her head side to side as Ryland's hand rested at the base of her neck. Summoning her courage, she opened her eyes.

She wished she'd kept them closed.

Ryland helped Liz to her feet. The look of abject horror on her face and the utter despair gushing out of her were a painful jab. He saw her waver and wrapped her in his arms.

Liz looked away from the gruesome sight. Ryland desperately wished he could take the ache from her. He held her close while she trembled and cried. Every sob tore through him. But she needed to let it out. She had to start the healing process. Judging from the impact of her internal demons crashing into him when she'd opened up, there was a lot of healing to be done.

He was grateful he'd been able to help her. Glad she'd let him in. He berated himself for not preparing her on the way here for what could happen. Helping train her, helping her fight, were the main reasons he was here. He should've done better by her. Especially after what Markus had done.

The mere thought of him made Ryland's blood boil. There was no doubt in his mind who was responsible for the fire. Ryland knew this was only the beginning. The demon would unleash as much terror and destruction on them as possible. That wasn't even taking into account what he was sure Kade had planned.

Ryland kissed the top of Liz's head as the sobs quieted. With everything that had happened today, he feared it might be too much for Liz. Would she take off again? Ryland tried to quell the worrisome thoughts. She'd grown so much in the past few months. She could handle this. And he'd be right there with her.

When her tremors stopped and her tears were spent, Liz peered at him through puffy eyes. Ryland brushed away a strand of hair stuck to the wetness on her cheek, noticing the dried blood at her hairline.

"We missed a spot." He pulled her hair back so he could get a good look. Seeing the cut wasn't deep, he placed a light kiss there and let her hair fall back over it.

Liz shivered, then eased out of his arms. She kept a tight hold on him.

Pastor Brantley's quiet, strained voice drew Ryland's attention. His eyes were on Liz. "I'm going to take your mama home. We could both use some rest." He dragged a trembling hand over his face.

Mrs. Brantley clung to her husband's side, her face drawn and eyes downcast.

Ryland tightened his grip on Liz as she balled his T-shirt in her fists. "I'll see Liz home."

"I appreciate it." The pastor looked over his two girls. "I don't think any of us should be alone right now." He straightened his back, and Ryland could feel him reining in his own feelings. "God has a plan, even in the midst of what we think is chaos. He'll bring us through."

"Yes, sir." Ryland agreed. But a small piece of him wondered what good could come of this tragedy.

Pastor Brantley leaned forward and whispered in Ryland's ear. "Be on your guard. We both know he's not done yet. Keep her close and keep her safe."

"I will."

Ryland had a million questions rolling around in his head as he watched the man lead his wife to the car. From the words of warning to the emotions coursing from him, Ryland got the feeling James Brantley knew more than he was letting on. But the answers would have to wait.

The rest of the crowd broke up. All of them stopped to offer words of comfort to Liz. She didn't say a word, simply nodded and woodenly returned a hug or handshake. When they were all gone, she moved from Ryland's side and stepped closer to the destruction.

It was as though the events of the day had sucked the life from her. She barely even blinked. Her anguish bled into him as if someone had sliced her open. He had to get her out of here.

"Lizzy, we need to go." Ryland gently touched her elbow.

She didn't respond.

"Come on. Let's get you home." He rubbed her arms, trying to stimulate some sort of reaction.

Liz nodded. He put his hand on her back and pointed her toward the Jeep. She reached out and grabbed his shirt again, hanging on to it like a life preserver. Ryland helped her climb into the vehicle. When he walked to the driver's side and looked up at the scorched remains, a familiar tingle set up in his spine. A surge of fire raced through his veins. Ryland darted his gaze to the tree line.

Markus eyed the destruction and smiled triumphantly.

Ryland shot a glance at Liz. She stared straight ahead, seemingly oblivious. He turned back toward Markus. Ryland had the overwhelming urge to separate the demon's head from his body and punt it down the road. The fact Liz needed him helped him rein it in.

Ryland leveled his eyes at the demon, projecting a promise of retribution. He was certain his message had been received since he saw Markus's grin fade before the demon vanished.

Kade paced the dusty garage, kicking a slow-moving imp out of his way. He'd had Ryland right where he wanted him. Then Markus had sent him away so he could play his games with the woman. Now here he was, waiting for orders when he should've been gutting the fledgling hunter.

For several years now, Ryland had proved to be more than a nuisance, dogging Kade at every step. Several times, Kade had been so close to the killing blow. Then angels would swoop in, or some other stroke of luck would save the kid. Depriving Kade of the victory that, however small, was rightly his. He wasn't used to losing a fight. Especially not to an inferior.

Seething fury splashed from him in brutal waves, staggering the imps in the corner and garnering him irritated glances from the other soldiers scattered around the building, though they dared not say anything.

Screw them. All of them. Soon, they'd obey *him*. Or be sent to the pit in bite-sized pieces.

The current object of his rage landed outside and sauntered in, looking pleased with himself. Markus enjoyed toying with his prey too much. It distracted from the goal and gave an opportunity for the tables to be turned too easily. Better to eradicate the problem as viciously and brutally as possible. Kade let a smirk erupt. Let Markus play. He would fail, and Kade would step in. Much sooner than his commander expected.

Markus homed in on Kade. "Report."

"The humans were successful in setting the blaze, which I'm sure you knew." Kade snorted. "Though, it was pointless. There was no one in the building."

Markus's eyes flashed, and he stepped toward Kade. "Your opinion is neither necessary nor wanted. You are here simply to carry out my orders." He leaned within a couple of inches of Kade's face and lowered his voice. "You will do well to remember your position." Markus stepped back. "And our next move. Is everything in place?"

"Things are being arranged per your *orders*." Kade growled the last word. Feigning submission to this weak excuse of a demon grated on him.

"Excellent." Markus walked away, and Kade quelled the urge to follow him and rip his shriveled heart out of his throat.

The rest of the brigade present scattered, and Kade wrapped his talons around a passing imp. The creature's eyes bulged in terror as Kade lifted it into the air. It squealed, clawing at Kade's hand, kicking furiously.

Kade squeezed slowly, increasing pressure in small increments. He reveled in the hideous sounds the creature made, the terror he inflicted. With a hollow snap and a sickening sound of suction, the imp's head separated from his gnarled body and dropped to the ground. It rolled, coming to rest against an old tire. Kade tossed the body after it. The two demons beside the door took a step back as he stalked by.

He walked outside and surveyed the landscape. He actually liked it here. They didn't parade their depravity in the open as much in the country. No, these people did their best to cover their wretchedness, the worst of them even showing up at church on Sunday. They thought they could slide past his notice, cover their sins. Which was good for him. He'd never been one for easy prey.

He craved the challenge, the thrill of a good hunt.

This was where he would prove himself to Lucifer. Markus was making it too simple, gift-wrapping the ammunition. Ammunition he would use to bring Markus down and usurp his command.

Kade took a deep breath. He'd waited long enough. He was mostly responsible for them being so close to victory, so close to such a rich harvest. Kade was the one who made the needed moves, set things in motion. And he would be the one to collect the rewards. Markus would not swoop in, take the credit, and savor his spoils.

Yes. It was time.

First order of business: Ryland Vaughn had to die.

XXIV
Distance

I hate Markus.

Like a needle stuck on a record, it played in Liz's brain *ad nauseam*.

Liz followed Ryland down the hall to her apartment, clutching his hand. Her head pounded, and her body ached.

A sense of loss bit into her with sharp teeth. Memories of the fire and how Markus had violated her mind brought a shiver. She worried she might lose her lunch. The beginnings of a volcanic eruption bubbled to the surface. Red-hot lava ready to infuse her veins and spread until it seeped from every pore.

Ryland skidded to a stop. "Liz, we'll get him. I promise." He squeezed her hand. "Just try to stay calm."

Liz took several deep breaths and prayed silently, trying to stem the tide.

She wanted to go after Markus. But she was too weak, and besides, Arie and Ryland wouldn't let her try it now anyway. She mumbled under her breath, drawing a sideways glance from Ryland.

Ryland unlocked the door. His hand rested on the small of her back as he guided her inside. Liz let him lead her to the couch. She leaned her head back, exhaling and coughing the remains of the smoke.

Ryland crouched in front of her, removed her boots, and scooted them under the coffee table.

Liz lifted her head. "You don't have to do this."

He raised her pant leg and unfastened the sheath. "Hush."

After setting the dagger beside her boots, Ryland grabbed her ankles and swiveled her body to put her feet on the couch. Liz let him, too mentally exhausted and too sore to protest. He grabbed the afghan from the chair and tucked it around her. The acrid odor of ash clung to both of them, a fresh burst of it hitting her with his movement.

Ryland knelt on the floor and ran his knuckles along her jaw. Liz leaned in to his touch. As their eyes locked, the incredible sadness and weariness in him tore at her. Before she thought about what she was doing, Liz lowered her head to his shoulder, trying to give him what comfort she could. Trying to replace what she'd depleted from him.

Ryland snaked his arms around her. He absently played with her hair as they sat in silence, each drawing comfort from the other. Liz heard his heart drumming rhythmically under her cheek. Their pulses pounded together.

They were a strong team. That was undeniable. It also scared her to death. Was she capable of giving him the unbridled trust it would take to truly be together? The trust she knew he had earned? And could he accept everything about her? All of her secrets?

Ryland pulled back and ran his thumbs across her cheeks. "You rest. I'll be right back."

Liz stared at him as a momentary panic seized her. She didn't want to be alone. To be without him.

"I'm just going to the kitchen."

The amount of relief she felt at the statement was ridiculous. She didn't want him to leave, yet his being there compounded her conflict. She knew she needed him. The knowledge both infuriated and delighted her.

Ryland foraged in the cabinets. She laughed quietly as he opened each one and shuffled items around, grunting, clearly perplexed. Soon, he'd collected a wet rag, first aid kit, ibuprofen, and a large glass of milk.

Her humor faded as she watched him. Even with his large, rock-solid frame, Ryland moved like a tiger on the prowl. Graceful, with a barely contained wildness. Muscles rippled under his shirt. Liz drank him in from head to toe. Her heart pounded against her ribs, and the butterflies in her belly took flight. His rough exterior, his beautiful heart and soul, his unshakeable faith, their shared mission, and the strange and powerful bond between them, all made him incredibly difficult to resist.

Ryland was perfect for her.

They weren't even a couple, and he was completely focused on taking care of her. He was always there, no matter how hard she tried to push him away. Ryland was her rock, the one person who understood her better than anyone else. When she hurt, he hurt. When she laughed, he laughed. When she fought, he fought by her side.

He opened the cabinet above the stove. "Bingo, baby! I knew I still had a stash in here somewhere." Ryland pulled out a bag of Oreos as if it were precious cargo.

She flushed when he caught her staring. He grinned, and she quickly averted her gaze. "When did you hide those here?"

"After you got home from the hospital." He set the cookies on the tray with the rest of his loot and brought it into the living room. "I knew if you got a hold of 'em, I'd never get any. So I hid them." He set the tray on the coffee table and plopped down beside it. "Now, let me see that cut."

Liz slid her feet to the floor and scooted to the edge of the couch, so they were knee to knee. A buzz of electricity shot through her.

Ryland picked up the wet rag and brushed her hair to the side. He carefully wiped the area around the cut. She flinched. He paused for a second, then proceeded to clean the blood away and cover it with a bandage.

Ryland dropped the rag on the tray and picked up the milk and ibuprofen. Liz took them without argument. She kept her eyes lowered. His intense gaze made her nervous. Liz reached past him to put the glass on the table. Her arm brushed his and sent another jolt through her system.

Liz eased back on the couch and pulled the afghan around her. She drew her knees in and her feet underneath her backside. Ryland grabbed the milk and the bag of cookies and made himself comfortable on the cushion beside her. Like that was the one spot in the world he belonged.

Ryland ripped open the bag and dug out a cookie. He dipped it in the milk and let it soak for a bit, then shoved the whole thing in his mouth. The process was repeated half a dozen times in less than two minutes.

Liz didn't hold back a laugh. "Hungry?"

"Haven't eaten since lunch and it's"—he looked at his watch—"after nine. Like I said, I'm a growing boy." He dunked another cookie.

Her mischievous streak flared to life. Liz snatched the glass from him. She giggled when his bottom lip protruded in a pout.

He reached for the bag as she slid it off his lap, but his attempt was futile. "You're mean."

"Am not." Liz fished out an Oreo and made a show of dunking it and slowly taking small bites. "Man cannot live by Oreos alone," she joked. She grabbed another cookie and continued her taunting.

"Wouldn't it be great if he could? And if his woman wasn't a greedy cookie hog?"

The room went quiet as his words hung in the air. A weird tension whipped into the space. Ryland met her eyes and held them. Emotions crackled and sparked between them. Liz looked down and shoved a cookie into her mouth so she wouldn't have to speak.

Ryland cleared his throat and shifted in his seat. "How about some sandwiches?"

Liz nodded mutely, and he headed to the kitchen. She could hear him rummaging in the fridge.

When he'd called her *his*, a warm, happy feeling had bubbled up inside of her. She couldn't help it. The thought both elated and terrified her. But her path was set. She needed to give herself to her call completely, right? There wouldn't be anything left for him. Though she tried to convince herself, a voice inside told her she was wrong.

"Hey, you've got hamburger patties in the freezer. How about some burgers?"

"Oh, you don't have to do that. Bologna is fine." Her voice sounded too breathy.

"Eh, I don't mind. Won't take long."

"Okay." Liz didn't know what else to say and didn't trust her voice.

She put the cookies and milk on the table and reached for her Bible. She might as well read while he was occupied. Plus, it would take her mind off him and the strange energy between them.

Liz rifled through the pages. She came upon Ecclesiastes chapter four. As she read, verses nine and ten claimed her notice.

Two are better than one, because they have a good reward for their labor. For if they fall, one will lift up his companion. But woe to him who is alone when he falls, for he has no one to help him up.

She had people and angels around her to pick her up when she fell, so she wasn't sure why this verse had caught her attention. Liz pushed past the sensation she was missing something and hunted for another passage to read.

It is not good that man should be alone. Liz had no idea why the words popped into her head. She steered clear of Genesis. The pages fluttered open at Song of Solomon.

Nope! Definitely not that!

She paused at Proverbs next.

Who can find a virtuous wife? For her worth is far above rubies.

Liz squinted and chewed the inside of her cheek. Maybe reading wasn't the best idea. She certainly wouldn't call herself virtuous. She had to work on that. The wife part, she skipped over. She thumbed through to the New Testament.

Liz's gaze floated to the kitchen where Ryland pulled burgers out of the skillet and lay them on a paper towel-covered plate.

She went back to the Bible. The next page she landed on was First Corinthians chapter seven. Liz made an unladylike sound in the back of her throat and shut the book with a hard snap. She didn't like being told she was wrong, and she got the distinct feeling that was what had just happened. Her skin heated until she thought her head might blow off.

There's no way she would've made it through today without Ryland. Many other days, the same held true. He was always there, praying, fighting, and pulling her butt out of the fire. How could they ever have a normal relationship, though, with what they were called to do?

What is normal? It's whatever you make it. What's right for you both, not everyone else.

Liz squirmed in her seat. Ryland returned, carrying a bag of chips and a plate stacked with cheeseburgers. He grinned, and everything she'd just read scrolled through her mind. She couldn't help but laugh.

Ryland cocked an eyebrow as he picked up the paper plates he'd set down. He piled two burgers and some chips on one. He set it down beside her. "What's so funny? You finally lose it?" He hurried into the kitchen, then back with two cans of Coke.

"Maybe. Laughing about something I read." *And arguing with a Book about a man. Perfectly sane, right?*

Liz turned on the TV and found a *Friends* marathon. Funny was safe. They ate and laughed, occasionally commenting on the show. Liz soon found herself completely relaxed. By the time they'd finished their dinner, it kind of seemed like the events from earlier in the day were a bad dream.

They cleaned up the mess together and reclaimed their spots on the couch. Liz pulled her feet up beside her and leaned against the couch's arm. Ryland stretched out next to her, his socked feet slung up on the coffee table. He reached for the afghan they'd balled up at the other end while they ate and tossed it at her. He laughed as it caught her in the face.

"Gee, thanks." She shook her head as she spread it out.

Ryland pulled half over his legs and threw his arms across the back of the couch. As if on instinct, she nestled her feet against his knee, partially hiding them underneath. In what seemed an unconscious gesture, Ryland rubbed her feet absently. His eyes never left the television. His touch spread a soothing warmth through her.

This is how it could be. How it should be. The idea popped into her head unbidden. Liz shoved the thought aside and snuggled closer. She was going to enjoy this, right here and now, and not worry about the future.

Ryland wasn't paying attention to the show. He was too busy watching Liz. Despite the upsetting day, they'd had a nice evening. He wished every day would end like that.

It did his heart good to see her shoulders weren't as tense, and some of the despair had left her eyes. When he'd first gotten her home, he'd wondered if he was going to be able to keep her out of the black hole she crawled toward. First Markus's violation, then the emotional tsunami at the church. He'd helped her all he could, fighting the wave and teaching her how to deal with it. He wished he could take her pain from her as easily.

Liz looked over and smiled. She wiggled her feet under his knee, and he tickled the bottoms. Liz giggled. *I love that sound.* Ryland's eyes didn't leave her face.

Liz yanked the elastic band out of her ponytail and laid her head on the arm of the couch. Her curly hair formed a wild waterfall over the side. He grinned and squeezed her feet, keeping his hands busy so he wouldn't reach over and run his fingers through her hair.

As Ryland continued watching, Liz's eyelids drooped. Eventually her breathing evened out. He sat, enjoying the peace on her face. Finally, he reached for the remote and shut off the TV. Ryland slid out from under the blanket, careful not to disturb her. He grabbed his boots and sat in the recliner to lace them up.

Moving quietly, Ryland wrapped his hands around her calves and stretched out her legs. He tucked the blanket around her until he was satisfied she wouldn't get a chill. He left the small lamp on the side table on, not wanting her to wake up in total darkness. After jotting a quick note on the tablet by the lamp, he knelt next to her head.

Ryland stroked her hair. He ran his thumb across her brow and down her face. The light kiss he grazed across her cheek only made him want more.

"I love you, Elizabeth," he whispered before he slipped out the door.

XXV
Revelations

I love you, Elizabeth.

Liz was sure she'd heard Ryland whisper it in her ear the other night. The words had penetrated her sleep-addled brain and cut straight to her heart. He hadn't expected an answer. Still, she'd wanted to say it back.

She unlocked the door to her apartment and dragged herself in after spending the day working on cleanup at the church. She crossed the living room, peeling her soot-and-ash-covered clothes off on the way to the shower.

Ryland never mentioned what had happened that night a week ago. They hadn't had much chance to talk anyway. Any extra time was spent cleaning up the church. And no one said much on those days. Picking through the remains of their house of worship was an agony too intense.

He never pressed her about their relationship. Never gave any indication he expected something from her. He simply helped her with her training and fought by her side in the ever-increasing number of skirmishes.

Markus wasn't letting up, hitting them from all sides.

The hot water from the shower was like balm. Liz let it wash away the clouds in her mind. When she stepped out, her body felt refreshed, even if her spirit was still beat up. It had been a long day. She'd worked the breakfast shift at the diner, then had gone straight to the church. What was left of it.

In spite of her fatigue, she was restless. She couldn't stand the thought of sitting alone in front of the TV again. The pistol on her nightstand caught her eye. A little target practice was just what she needed. Liz dressed quickly, grabbed her gear, and headed out the door.

She was about to back out of the parking lot when headlights flashed, and a familiar sports car pulled beside her. Liz rolled her eyes and exhaled a sharp breath. She had hoped he'd given up. Well, it wouldn't be the first time she was totally off about a guy.

Blake climbed out of his car, and Liz jumped out of the Jeep. She wanted to get this over with quickly. She had to remind him they were never going to happen, and then get out of there as fast as she could.

Cold fingers touched Liz's spine, tapping her with their chill. Her senses kicked in to overdrive as she scanned the woods behind the apartment and the parking lot. Nothing. The chill wouldn't relent. Liz shook her head and rubbed her arms through her sweatshirt. A tingle pricked the back of her neck. The thought that the chill could be connected to Blake tickled her mind. She toyed with the idea but rejected it as her overactive imagination fueled by stress.

"Where you headed? Not leaving town again, are you?" Blake cocked his head to the side and studied her.

"No." Liz narrowed her eyes. "I have some things to do." A cool breeze danced across her skin. She glanced around. Still nothing. "Why would you think I was leaving?"

"You've had a run of bad luck, and I thought maybe you'd had enough. Seems like the universe is baying for your blood." He shrugged. Blake appeared nonchalant, but Liz sensed a rigid undertone.

Liz crossed her arms. "Why are you here? I have some place I need to be, so if this isn't important..." His new attitude wasn't sitting well with her. She backed up, but he grabbed her arm.

"I can't let you keep doing this."

"Keep doing what?"

Liz tried to pull free. He tightened his grip. A feminine fear pinged its way through her system.

"Putting yourself in harm's way for someone else's war. This isn't your battle. If you keep this up, you'll die." Blake's face softened a bit, and he released her.

Shock zipped up Liz's spine. He couldn't know.

"What do you mean? What war?"

There was a flicker in his eyes she couldn't interpret. She couldn't feel any emotion coming from him.

"I shouldn't have put it like that. I just mean you keep holding to this faith, this God of yours, and He's done nothing to protect you. Yet you keep taking unnecessary risks."

The chill around her increased. What risks? What was he talking about? There was no way he could know what was really going on. Was there? Liz opened the vehicle door and put it between her and Blake. "You may have turned your back on God. I won't. I have to believe everything's happening for a reason, and He'll protect me."

It had taken her a while to come to that realization. As she spoke the words out loud for the first time, she knew it as truth.

"God." Blake spat the word. His vehemence made her muscles tick. "Where was He when you were almost killed? And why did He let your father's church burn to the ground? It's idiotic to trust a God who lets those things happen to people."

Liz faltered. He'd vocalized everything she'd agonized over. She took a deep breath. Her faith had to hold, no matter what.

"Blake, that doesn't make me an idiot. It means I have faith. God can use anything for good. To teach us, make us stronger, whatever. It took me a while to understand that."

Blake's expression held no clues for her. Liz couldn't get a good read on him. She thought she sensed regret, along with a frightening rage he worked to conceal.

Blake grabbed her hand and placed his other hand on her waist. Her stomach dropped as he pulled her to him.

"Come with me," he whispered. "Leave all this." Liz softened as he caressed the side of her face. "We could have an amazing life. We could go anywhere—do anything. Please say yes."

His gaze held hers and, for a moment, Liz was enraptured. He cared for her. It was evident in his eyes, as was his desire. She should pull away. An invisible something restrained her. Whatever it was pooled in her belly and reached out to him, yearning to say yes.

Liz blinked. Reality rushed in, and the spell was broken. She remembered who she was, what her mission was. She didn't, couldn't love Blake. Not like he wanted her to. Someone else owned her heart and always would. This ended now.

Liz slid her hand out from under his and pushed him back. "No." She stepped away when he reached for her. "I can't. I care about you, but not in the same way you seem to feel about me. I'm sorry. You need to leave now. And please, don't contact me again, Blake."

Liz moved to climb into the Jeep. Blake struck like lightning. He yanked her hard, slamming her against the vehicle. The gun at her waist bit into her lower back. She tried to catch her breath. He didn't give her the chance. He caged her between his arms and pressed his body to hers.

Fear snaked through her blood, freezing her in place. Memories flashed through her mind at warp speed. Blond hair. Brown eyes glowing with rage. Screaming. The flash of a knife. The smell of diesel fuel. Panic gripped her.

She wouldn't be a victim. Not again.

Liz's breath came in short gasps. She squirmed and shoved at him to no avail. How was he so strong? It was as if her fear was negating her own strength. Liz forced her mind to focus. He'd have to ease up eventually, and she'd have her chance. She would wait. Having somewhat of a plan calmed her breathing, and her heart stopped thrashing quite so wildly.

Blake moved his mouth to her ear. "It's Ryland, isn't it? You're still in love with that sorry excuse for a man who abandoned you and lied to you," he hissed.

No way had she told him those things about Ryland. "Blake, let me go. Now," she breathed out between gritted teeth as the chill deepened. Prickles raced up her back, and the sense of danger enveloped her.

Blake ignored her demand. "He can never give you what I can. You'll see. You made the wrong choice. It's going to get you killed, and this time, I won't save you."

The implication crawled up her spine, bringing a surge of adrenaline.

Liz shoved him. She twisted to the side and body-checked him as hard as she could. It gave her the room she needed. Liz moved her hand under her sweatshirt, resting it on the grip of the gun as she backed into the open car door. "Right or wrong, it's my choice. Now leave, Blake. Don't come back. Or we *will* have a problem."

Before he could grab her again or say a word, she jumped in, slamming and locking the door. The old engine roared to life, and she threw it in reverse. Liz backed out and floored it, spraying gravel and dust.

Shivers wracked her body. His words and actions would've been impossible to believe had she not experienced them. Gone was the man who'd helped take care of her when she was injured. He'd held her. Caressed her. Kissed her so tenderly. How could she not have seen it? *Fool me once... Never again.*

Liz stepped on the accelerator and glanced in the rearview mirror.

At least it was over. Hopefully he'd leave town, and this would all be a bad memory to add to the others.

Blake watched her tear out of the parking lot and dodged flying gravel. He dusted himself off and returned to the car. A muscle in his jaw ticked as he slammed the door.

Well. That wasn't what he'd expected. He'd never been rebuffed by a woman before. He always knew what they wanted, what they needed. Which was exactly what he offered. Being rejected by

Elizabeth stung. Surprising. Also infuriating, given everything he'd put on the line to claim her.

She didn't *want* to want him, but she did anyway. Deep down, she knew they belonged together. She just wasn't ready to admit it yet. Eventually, she would.

He laughed. She would, or she'd regret it.

The late evening sun glinted off the metal roof of the barn and showered the field in brilliant golds and pinks as it sank toward the hills. Liz smiled when she noticed the big, black Dodge Ram parked off to the side. She'd never been more thankful Ryland was here. Her encounter with Blake had her rattled. Before anything else, Ryland was her best friend. And she could really use a friend about now.

Liz gathered her small bag with ammo and ear plugs in it and hopped out. She didn't plan on bringing up what had happened with Blake. But she had a hard time keeping her barricades up around Ryland, and there was a good chance he'd end up pulling it out of her. He always could get her to admit things she didn't want to.

She hated that.

Liz heard the release of a crossbow mechanism. A *whoosh*. A *thunk*, and the sound of tearing paper. She quickly muffled her emotions the best she could and headed around the back of the barn.

She rounded the corner, and Ryland raised his head from the crossbow. "What happened?"

Crap. He's fast.

"Ran into Blake." Liz tossed her bag down and walked over to where Ryland had piled a stack of targets. She grabbed two and headed down the field.

"And?" He picked up the stapler and followed her.

"'And' nothing. He's leaving town soon."

Liz held the paper target to one of the frames Ryland had

constructed. The hill behind provided the perfect backstop for a shooting range. He stapled the target and moved to the next frame. Liz didn't miss the grin tugging at the corners of his mouth. She shot him a look.

He cleared his throat. "Are you okay?"

"One less thing to deal with."

They finished hanging the last target and walked back across the field. Liz caught him watching her. His face distinctly said, *There's more to that story, and you're gonna tell me.* She shook her head and grinned. When she turned around, she yelped and jumped back into Ryland.

"Arie!" Her hand flew to her chest. "For cryin' out loud!"

The angel stood with a serene look on his face, unaffected by her shouting. "Training on varied weapons, I see. Excellent."

"Yeah. I wanted to get a little more familiar with this." She pulled the pistol from its holster. "I'll probably take a few shots with the crossbow too, if there's enough daylight left. And if Ry doesn't mind sharing."

"Not a bit." Ryland grinned and dropped the stapler.

"Continue. I will merely observe." Arie clasped his hands in front of him.

Liz shook her head as she slid by him. *What an odd duck. But, gotta love him.*

An hour later, they'd spent a hundred rounds of ammo and twenty bolts each. The sun dipped behind the pines, and the moon peeked above the opposite horizon.

Arie watched as they packed up and retrieved the now-shredded targets. "Your aim with the crossbow is improving greatly."

"About time." Ryland snorted. "At least now I don't have to worry about her accidentally taking out my eye." He poked her in the ribs.

Liz stuck out her tongue. Arie actually smiled. The crossbow had been her nemesis. It was so bad, even Arie had cracked a few jokes about it. She smiled, feeling more relaxed than she had in weeks. Coming out here had been a great idea.

"Thanks." She slid the gun back into its holster and picked up her bag.

Liz and Ryland followed Arie to the front of the barn, Ryland continuing to torment her on the way. They rounded the corner, and she ran into Arie's back.

"Hey, what's—" Liz's words fell from her lips when she looked past the angel.

Blake leaned against the hood of his car, arms folded and a smirk on his face. She felt Ryland stiffen before he slipped in front of her.

"You have no right to be here." Arie's tone was frozen steel. Hard. Cold. Deadly.

Blake flashed an eerie grin. "According to whom? I'm free to go and do as I please. I don't live by your code or under the thumb of your God."

Liz's mouth fell open. She heard Ryland's knuckles pop and his teeth grind. She pushed her way around Ryland and Arie. They both made noises in protest, which she ignored. This was going to stop. Right here, right now.

"Blake, you shouldn't be here. I told you, it's over. Just let it go." Liz moved closer to Blake, shaking off Arie's hand. A familiar fire ignited in her belly. The one that usually ended in an exploding, volcanic mess. She'd had enough of this garbage. "Leave. Now."

Blake actually chuckled. Liz started for him. Arie grabbed her arm again, and this time, he wasn't gentle about it. She had no choice other than to move where he placed her, behind him and Ryland. Liz glared at Arie. He spoke before she could.

"Elizabeth, explain." Arie jerked his head toward the intruder.

Liz crossed her arms. "This is Blake." Again, she stepped out from behind the shield they'd formed in front of her. "He is—was—my friend."

Blake laughed. A twisted sound she hadn't heard from him before, shooting shivers through her bones. Fear wrapped around her like a blanket. All of her blood rushed to her head. The air swirling around her developed teeth.

"He is not what you think, child," Arie said tenderly, his voice thick with sadness.

"I don't understand." Liz looked at Ryland, afraid of what she'd find in his eyes because of what vibrated off him. She saw and felt the progression as everything clicked into place in Ryland's mind.

Disbelief.

Understanding.

Rage.

Deadly intent.

"Yes, you do." Arie kept one eye on Blake as he spoke. "You can feel it. Have felt it."

"No." Liz's head spun. "No way. I would've known." Liz's feet itched to run. She didn't want to believe what Arie said. The truth burrowed into her spirit as it bombarded her senses. "You're wrong."

"No. I am not." Arie glared at Blake with scorching eyes. "Once my brother, now he is my enemy."

This couldn't be real. It had to be another nightmare. Liz shoved past Ryland and Arie, despite their objections. She walked within three feet of Blake and looked him in the eyes. They were coal black, rimmed in red. Flame licked his pupils.

It was no nightmare—at least, not the unconscious kind.

Wave after wave of nausea shredded through her. Warnings she'd dismissed flashed across her mind. The times she'd felt something was off. The chill following him in and out of a room. The near-painful shock every time they touched. The feeling in her gut she'd ignored.

The corners of Blake's lips edged upward. His smile dripped with venom and unadulterated evil. Ice latched onto her spine and shattered her bones when he spoke.

"Allow me to properly introduce myself, darling." Blake bowed ceremoniously, his eyes never leaving hers. "I am Markus. Captain of the battalion of Begoriel, of the legions of Lucifer. At your service."

XXVI
Angels

Liz stared blankly at Markus as he bowed. Betrayal twisted like a knife. It carved out a portion of her heart and crushed it as if it were dry leaves. All of her mental and emotional defenses crumbled in a steaming pile at her feet.

Liz doubled over and let loose the bile burning the back of her throat. The world tilted and jerked on its axis. Two steel arms clasped around her, dragging her away from the vile traitor. Ryland settled Liz between himself and Arie as Markus's laugh echoed across the field. The sadistic sound turned her blood to ice, the shards cutting on their path.

The last couple of months flashed through her head. The day at the lake. He wasn't in the right place at the right time. He'd sent the demons in the first place. He'd been in her home. Around her family. The night she cooked dinner for him played like a movie reel. *Oh God, I almost... Oh God!* She doubled over again. Anything remaining in her stomach was about to make an appearance. Ryland's arms tightened as he bent with her.

Markus advanced a step. "Has something made you ill, darling?"

She'd hated it when Blake called her *darling*. Now she knew why. How did she not catch it? A desperate urge to rip out his throat charged her muscles. Liz lunged for him, but Ryland held her back.

Ryland speared Markus with his gaze. "I should've taken care of you the first chance I had." He released Liz and reached for the handles of his blades. "Let's rectify that."

"Ryland. Stop." Liz straightened and grabbed his arm.

The spinning slowed. Her stomach settled. Another force took charge. It filled her lungs, pervaded her veins, and permeated every tissue in her being. She tasted it on her tongue. Bitter and potent. Its red haze draped her eyes. She could see the cloud forming above her, around her.

Pure, focused rage.

Ryland stalked closer to Markus. The fury she felt whipping through Ryland would've terrified her if hers hadn't exceeded it. Every muscle in Ryland's body bunched, ready to pounce.

Markus sneered. "You need to control your guard dog, darling. He's pulling at his leash."

Liz gripped Ryland's arm tighter, barely restraining him. A strange heat generated around the two of them. So intense it felt as though her skin was on fire. Out of the corner of her eye, she saw Arie give a warning glance and shake his head once.

Liz felt Ryland immediately cool down, as if he'd been doused with a bucket of water. She could sense him trying to calm her as well. Her shields flew up, dislodging his attempts to reach inside. Liz refused to fan away the hazy cloud. She clutched at it like a favorite teddy bear. Her muscles tensed. Her shoulders drew back. She dropped into a fighting stance.

Liz leveled her hate-filled gaze on Markus. Without a second thought, she reached for the dagger at her calf. As she stood, she yanked her handgun from its holster. She held the knife in her left hand and aimed the gun at Markus with her right.

The demon laughed. "That will not vanquish me."

"No. But it'll sure hurt. And it'll weaken you. Then I'll send you to Hell. In so many pieces they'll never get you put back together." Liz barely recognized her own voice.

"Liz, stop. Right now." Ryland's words were harsh and commanding. When he gripped her shoulders, she didn't even flinch, maintaining focus on Markus. Ryland's next words were softer, if only slightly. "This isn't the time. Or the way. As much as I wish it were."

Liz shrugged him off and evaded his attempt to recapture her by stomping toward Markus. She didn't have to see Ryland's face to feel the sadness and fear whisper from him. An urge to run back to him threaded through her.

She lowered her weapons a few inches. She'd wanted to change so badly. But it seemed everything conspired against her efforts.

Arie caught her eye, pleading without words. Liz could hear the whispers in her mind. She didn't have to face this alone. There was nothing to prove. She was loved and worthy of being protected, defended. But she had to let them in, had to let them stand with her.

Liz let her arms drop to her sides and inched back toward Ryland.

Ryland reached for her. "Lizzy, forget him for now. Give me your hand." He beckoned her to him.

Markus spoke in a hushed, seductive tone. "You can have everything you want. No rules. No orders. No more pretending. No more hiding."

Markus's gaze lured her. For a few brief seconds, Liz was transfixed. A mist settled over her mind. She heard Ryland and Arie calling to her but couldn't understand what they were saying. All of her focus was held hostage by Markus.

"We would be unstoppable." Markus extended a hand to her. "Come with me. Be free." His eyes softened as the red laced through the black.

She heard his next words clearly in her mind. He promised freedom. A place where she truly belonged, without judgment. A life devoid of constant battles.

Her weapons slid to the ground. He smiled and curled his fingers inward, motioning her to him. Liz trembled as she watched herself reach out to him, as if outside her own body looking on. She extended her hand toward him, caught up in the wave of promises. Those swirling red depths begged her to fall into them.

Arie watched the scene taking place in front of him with his hand on the hilt of his sword. His heart wrung itself dry. He knew Markus whispered to her, offering things he had no intention or power to give. Arie also knew what the demon offered was exactly what Elizabeth craved.

Arie was helpless to intervene. The Master had ordered him to stay his hand. The choice had to be hers and hers alone. He restrained Ryland. The tortured look in the young man's eyes flayed him.

Elizabeth had to close the door she had opened. He had to have faith she would.

Ryland's chest nearly cracked open from the furious pounding of his heart. He couldn't get air to his lungs. He was powerless. Reduced to a spectator as the woman he loved was seduced by evil incarnate.

When Liz's hand inched toward Markus's, a faraway look in her eye, fear and panic clenched down on his spine so hard he thought his legs would buckle.

"Liz, you can do this. You're strong. Fight."

As Ryland watched her move toward the edge, he sank to his knees. He was inches away from losing her forever.

Liz glanced down at her hand. It would be so easy to give in. To give up and stop fighting. To let Markus take her. But something was missing. His words didn't ring true. A tiny beam of light cut through the fog in her brain.

Markus's eyes narrowed. His pleading intensified.

The light expanded. One strand at a time, the web Markus had spun unraveled. True promises swirled in her thoughts from the One she fought for. She let the truths expand, pushing Markus out.

Liz slowly lowered her hand and edged backward. The fog lifted.

A glance behind her revealed a serious Arie, with a glint of joy in his eyes. To her right, Ryland rose from his knees, his relief and pride rushing through her like a fast-moving summer storm. A few strides had them both beside her.

Liz leveled a hard stare at Markus. Heat still simmered in her belly. Thankfully, not the all-consuming conflagration it had been. "I will *never* choose you."

The red of Markus's eyes morphed to fire. "You're an idiot. A soon-to-be-dead idiot."

Markus dove for her, and Arie disappeared. Ryland slung his arm around her midsection and yanked her back, shielding her with his body. An explosion of light and flame erupted in the air as Markus crashed into an invisible wall. The force tossed him like a rag doll, up and over his car. He smashed into a towering pine. The tree uprooted from the impact. He landed with a sickening *thump*.

Markus slowly pushed to his feet. His metallic eyes cut through the gathering dusk and latched on to Liz and Ryland. Markus let out a thunderous bellow. He worked his neck side to side, then began to morph into his demonic form.

Charred skin consumed Markus's body like tar come to life, creeping and oozing its way from foot to head. As his true flesh emerged, height and weight were added. The khakis and button-up shirt he'd worn as Blake ruptured at the seams. Ebony wings sprang from his back. Armor encased his legs, torso, and finally, his arms. What once was a beautiful façade was now usurped by his authentic, hellish form.

Liz preferred dealing with this incarnation. It was easier. It was honest. She rolled her shoulders, loosening herself up for the attack she was certain was imminent. Ryland pulled his blades and readied his stance. Her own weapons were still lying on the ground where she'd dropped them. Right in Markus's path.

Markus stomped toward them with his sword drawn, murder in his eyes.

Here we go.

Liz dove for the dagger and gun.

"Liz, get back here!" Ryland shouted.

Liz skidded across the grass on her knees, stopping right in front of her goal. She scooped up the weapons and popped up. Markus was closing fast. Her heart leapfrogged into her mouth. She sincerely hoped that divine wall of protection was still active. She lowered her stance and waited. Ryland leaped to her side.

As Markus made it to the spot where the barrier had been, two colossal angels appeared with flaming swords, raised and ready. They stood directly in front of Liz and Ryland, blocking Markus's access. Arie and Chammu'el focused the wrath of Heaven on Markus.

Arie's words resounded across the valley. "This is protected ground. By the order of the King of Kings, you may go no farther."

A rumble resonated from Markus. It set Liz's skin to crawling.

He leered at her between the guardians. His ferocious glare seared into her soul. "Fatal error, darling," Markus hissed. "I will have what I want." He vanished, a foul, demonic odor lingering after him.

Arie and Chammu'el sheathed their swords and moved toward her and Ryland. She barely noticed. Liz stood stock-still. His words were an icy blade, slicing to her core. She'd just painted an even bigger bull's-eye on her back.

The magnitude of what she'd almost done pelted her. Sent shockwaves through her spirit. Liz thought she'd known what being tempted was. She had no idea the powerful sway evil could exert.

She had been seconds from saying yes to Markus.

Her legs became jelly. Spots clouded her vision. Nausea waylaid her again with a vengeance.

God, please, forgive me!

The earth rose up to meet her.

XXVII
Of These Chains

All Liz saw was blackness and stars.

She blinked several times, trying to clear her vision. A familiar, angelic face hovered into view. Tears clouded her eyes as she grabbed for his robe.

"Arie, I'm so sorry!" The tears overflowed. Guilt choked her.

Her guardian's eyes softened. "Oh, child, you have nothing to be sorry for. You should rejoice! A victory was claimed here tonight." Arie caressed her cheek with the back of his hand.

"I was so close to saying yes. I was weak." Liz shook her head.

Arie's arm wrapped around her shoulders, and he helped her sit up. "Hush, now." He chuckled, and Liz raised an eyebrow. "Even Christ was tempted. What makes you think you are so special you could avoid it?" His eyes twinkled.

A smile crossed Liz's face without her permission at his attempt at a joke.

"Do not let Markus win now by giving in to doubt and guilt. Remain strong. Claim your victory and move on."

Arie stood beside her and lifted her to her feet. Her eyes were drawn to Ryland, standing behind Arie.

He saw everything.

Arie's voice jolted her. "We will meet in the morning. Markus will be more determined than ever, and we must prepare. Rest well, young ones." Then he stepped into thin air.

Ryland cleared his throat.

Liz couldn't face him. He was so strong, so faithful. He would've never let things go that far. He reached for her hand, but Liz pulled back. He deserved more than she could give. He deserved someone equally strong and faithful at his side.

He needed to let her go.

Liz bottled everything up and corked it. She did her best to keep her face blank. A strange sense of calm settled over her. She raised her eyes to Ryland's.

A slow crack slid down the surface of her resolve at the love in his eyes.

The second Liz's eyes met his, Ryland felt a hitch in his heart. He'd been so proud of her for the way she'd stood up to Markus. But the intense emotion flowing from her, and the way she'd so quickly cut it off, had him worried.

Liz's face could've been carved from marble. Cold and unreadable. She held her head high, shoulders square. Without a word, she glided past him.

Ryland silently observed Liz as she gathered her things and tossed them into the Jeep. She never looked his way or acknowledged his presence. He didn't try to snuff out the anger. She must've picked up on it. For a moment, her face betrayed her shock. Then she clamped it down.

Just when he thought they were getting somewhere. Ryland shook his head as she walked over to lock the barn doors. Job done, Liz sauntered back to the vehicle, still without a word.

He'd had enough.

Ryland stepped forward and grabbed the door as she opened it. His voice came out harsher than he intended.

"Why are you doing this?"

Liz sighed heavily. "Doing what, Ryland?" She finally met his eyes. "All I'm trying to do is get home and go to bed. I've had kind of a rough night."

Her sarcasm was met with narrowed eyes and a wave of irritation. She wasn't trying to aggravate him, she just knew if she didn't get out of here soon, he'd have her doubting her decision. That, she couldn't have.

"You know exactly what I'm talking about. Us. This insane dance."

Ryland moved in and his manly, woodsy scent filled her senses. It curled around her and made her belly flop. Every part of her wanted to reach out to him. Her heart screamed for his. But she couldn't let it happen. One day, he'd be grateful he'd dodged the bullet.

"There is no dance. I told you I couldn't make any promises. It'd be pointless anyway." Liz stopped, not ready to divulge her newly forming plan. "Thank you for taking care of me and for being my friend. But it has to end there. I just can't give you what you want." *Or what you need.*

Ryland stared at her for what seemed like forever. A spark lit up his eyes. "You're gonna leave, aren't you? When this thing with Markus is over, you're taking off." He stepped closer, and Liz sucked in a breath at the vehemence in his voice.

"Ryland, let go of my door. Let me go."

Both of them knew she wasn't talking about just tonight. Liz's control was slipping. The longer she stayed this close to him, the more she was in danger of opening Pandora's Box and letting everything tumble out.

"No."

Ryland's complete dismissal of her command irked Liz. She gritted her teeth and tried to jerk the door from his hand. It didn't budge.

"Ryland."

"I'm not letting you shut me out, and I'm certainly not letting you leave."

"You can't stop me."

"You'll never get past this if you keep ignoring it. You're not going to run. Look what happened last time." His voice dropped low. "Neither one of us could survive that again."

Words tumbled out before she could stop them, tinged with the anger she hadn't realized she still held. "Yeah, I remember exactly what happened. I made mistakes. You made things worse. I left, and you hunted me down. And when you found me, all you did was tell me I was wrong and expect me to blindly trust you. You only threw out a proposal to get me to fall in line." She was out of air by the time she finished, lungs burning and tears pricking her eyes.

Whoa. Where did that come from?

Liz could've sworn there was actual fire in Ryland's eyes. The heat coming off him in waves was frightening. She climbed into the Jeep, knowing she'd gone too far.

Halfway in, Ryland pulled her back out and slammed the door. Liz gulped.

Fear crept up her spine. In her heart, she knew Ryland would never hurt her. The knowledge didn't stop the panic from pinging around in her gut. She let her anger take over. It was so much better than fear.

"Everything I've done, everything I've said, was either to keep you out of trouble or to keep your little reckless, ungrateful butt alive."

Ryland's jaw clenched tight, and his lips pressed into a thin line. She expected smoke to roll out of his ears. Liz clamped her lips shut, scared speechless. If it was a reaction she'd wanted, she had it now. She mentally braced herself, uncertainty making her skin tingle.

"I know all of this has been hard for you. It hasn't been gravy for me either. Frankly, I'm sick of your crap. You say you forgive me, then you hold it against me." Ryland advanced, and Liz backed into the Jeep. "Now here you are trying to run again. This time, I'm not gonna make it easy for you."

Ryland's face looked pained. She was glad her shields were holding so far. He took a deep breath and ran his hand through his hair, leaving it sticking out in all directions.

His eyes locked with hers again. "You know what I think? I think in some messed-up way, you think you're protecting me. Taking the high road. Truth is, you're just scared to death."

"Ryland, stop. You don't know anything." Fury gurgled in her throat. The bitter taste hung in the back of her mouth. She was about to blow.

The anguish in her voice cut him to the bone. It was unavoidable, though. The truth hurt, and Ryland was nowhere near finished. He'd fire until he was out of rounds. Every time he'd get close and it seemed like they were making headway, she'd drive a wedge between them.

He was done with the games.

Even if he couldn't have her, there was no way he was letting her keep suffering when he could do something about it. She had to get rid of whatever was eating her alive. Ryland knew he had to blow her carefully-constructed delusions to bits to have any hope of setting her free.

He just hoped she wouldn't hate him for it.

Liz saw Ryland take a deep breath, like he was about to jump the cliff into dark water. A shiver ran up her spine.

His eyes held hers, allowing no escape. "I know a lot more than you think."

Liz gritted her teeth, afraid to speak because the words that climbed up to hang on her lips were things she'd regret for the rest of her life. She clenched her fists and tried to calculate if she could shove him back far enough to give her time to get away.

Ryland didn't give her time to think. "You can't stop running. It's how you cope. Yeah, you've stopped fighting your call, but you don't really want it. That's why you fell for Blake."

Liz's blood reached the boiling point. She stood as straight as she could and narrowed her eyes. "I don't know what—"

He held up a hand to stop her. "You thought he wasn't involved in all of this, and that made him safe. A place for you to hide and pretend none of this is real. With me, you can't hide. You have to face it. Be honest with yourself for once."

The top of her head was about two seconds from blowing off. Her rage at his words jumped over her emotional blockade, knocking it down with the motion. He was right. And she didn't like it.

Her heart slammed violently against her ribcage. The rage inside of her reached out to the anger spilling from Ryland and pulled it in, feeding off it. She barely reined in the desire to lash out with her fists. He was the last person she wanted to hurt, but Liz needed an outlet, someone or something to blame for the turmoil inside.

Ryland was the closest target.

"Shut up! You have no idea what I want, or why I do the things I do."

Liz tried to open the door again and escape. Ryland planted a hand on each side of her. He had her caged between his mountain of a body and two steel bars.

"Don't I?" Ryland leaned in. His warm breath tickled her cheek. His voice was hushed with a stony edge. "No one knows you like I do. No one could ever love you like I do." His lips were millimeters from hers. "So you can run all you want, but you'll never love anyone like you love me. And you know it."

He was pushing all of her buttons. She had to get away.

She'd fought off Markus, why couldn't she get Ryland out of her head? Liz already knew the answer. Ryland was everything Markus wasn't. Loving, protective, tender, and good. The hold he had on her reached the very depths of her soul. His having that kind of power over her infuriated her even more.

Liz tried to push him back. Even with her enhanced strength, his own abilities and his sheer size made it a futile effort. She swiveled her head, looking for another route. She tried to turn and climb over the door through the open window.

Ryland thwarted the attempt with ease, grabbing her waist and tugging her back down. This time he squeezed his arms against hers, pressed his leg against her knees, and pinned her in place. Once again, she was trapped between the Jeep and his rock-solid frame. He wasn't hurting her, but she wasn't going anywhere.

Liz went nuclear. She fought him until her breath came in ragged gasps. He neutralized her with minimal effort. "Let. Me. Go."

"No."

Liz went limp for a moment. Bingo. He loosened his grip. She took her opportunity. Ryland was quicker and slung an arm around her midsection, holding her tight. Face to face. She closed her eyes to keep from looking into his.

Ryland held her firmly in one arm and brought the other hand to her cheek. Her nerves were already lit up like a Christmas tree. His touching her face so tenderly made it worse. He tilted her jaw and lifted her eyes to his.

"I'm trying to help you." Ryland stroked her cheekbone with his thumb. "But you have to let me. There are chains that have you all bound up, and you're just adding to them. You're gonna self-destruct if you don't get a hold of yourself. And I can't lose you again." His voice cracked.

His love and worry stole her oxygen. The world froze as they locked gazes. His heart was in his eyes. His affection for her went beyond what she had words to explain. It flowed through their connection like balm. Her heart answered. It scrambled and clawed to get out, longing to bind with his.

Liz was losing the energy to fight him. She was battling on all fronts. She was barely hanging on to her sanity. Even her prayers felt cold and detached. The peace she'd clutched so tightly was slipping through her fingers. She'd get it back. But she couldn't let him fall with her until she did.

He had to stop trying to save her.

"I don't need your help." Liz took a ragged breath, lowered her gaze, and ripped her own heart out. "You lost me a long time ago, Ry."

His hurt bit into her. Razor-sharp teeth sank into her battered heart and shook it side to side, like a dog with a rope toy. The air thickened. Tears threatened. She refused to blink, knowing as soon as she did, they would overflow, and she'd be helpless to stop the flood.

She knew sometimes the break couldn't be avoided. Sometimes, a person had to be shattered into pieces to be put back together the right way. Yet she was going to fight it as long as she could. Liz never wanted to be shattered like that again.

Ryland swallowed hard. "I don't believe that. And neither do you."

Why can't he just let go? Even as she thought it, she knew it didn't matter. They could both walk away and never look back. But they'd still be connected. They'd always be a part of each other.

Liz went toppling over the edge she'd been hovering on.

Liz pushed, shoved, and twisted, trying again to move the mountain that was Ryland. Years of pent-up anguish and fear burst free. Relentless, they showed no mercy as they clawed and ripped their way out of the splintered boxes she'd kept them locked in.

Ryland absorbed her blows. He held her tighter with each flurry. He quietly bore it, letting her fight herself and take it out on him. Liz's strength faded with each blow until she sagged against him. Her breaking point laughed at her in the rearview mirror.

Tears ran in rivulets down her cheeks. Her legs gave out, and she sank to the ground. Ryland stayed with her. He crouched as she knelt, his strong, solid body sheltering her. Shielding her from the world. Liz let her exhausted head drop against his shoulder as she drenched his shirt. The steady thump of his heart pounded in her ear.

"That's it, baby. Let it go. You don't need it anymore." Love and understanding flowed from his soul, a slow yet powerful river. It submerged her. Drenching every cell. Quenching the fire that consumed her.

Liz sucked in air, attempting to fill the lungs that felt like they'd been punched empty. Ryland's roughened hands were velvet as they stroked her back while he crooned in her ear. Some words were prayers. Some were for her. Most she couldn't make out over the blood rushing in her ears. Liz didn't need to understand his words. His voice soothed the beast roaring within her.

Understanding rippled through her. She'd accepted her call, yet never fully surrendered. The anger she'd held close, the agony from her past she'd clung to, the need to find "normal," all blocked her submission. The remaining pieces of the wall she'd built came crashing down.

It all snapped into place.

She and Ryland would never have a "normal" existence. And that was okay. Yes, they had to focus, to devote themselves to the mission. But they could also be devoted to one another. They were better together. Where one was weak, the other was strong.

I get it, God. I give. No more running, and no holding back.

Ryland wove his fingers into her hair and cradled her head. Liz knew he'd sensed the change. She could hear his smile in his whispered prayers. She could feel his joy and love, coating her like honey. Sweet and rich. There in the dirt, safely enfolded in Ryland's arms, Liz waved a white flag. The prisoners she'd kept shackled were released. The chains, broken.

Except the one that bound her heart to the man who held her.

XXVIII
Taking Life

Liz's cheeks hurt from the smile she couldn't erase. It was the kind of smile that hadn't shown up for quite some time, and she reveled in it. She cranked up the stereo, relishing the breeze whipping her hair and the sun warming her skin.

Even with the threat of Markus hanging over them, Liz felt almost serene. Truly giving up her coveted control was a unique freedom. One that could only come from faith and pure trust. Foreign concepts Liz was slowly learning to embrace. Over the past week, she'd spent a lot of time in prayer, training harder than she ever had. She'd never felt this centered. This strong. This peaceful.

Liz pulled up beside the barn, a cloud of dust swirling as she bounced to a stop. Ryland leaned against his truck, wearing a broad grin. Neither her elation nor her smile faded. Liz knew the moment the burst streaming from her heart hit Ryland. His smile got impossibly bright, as if he'd swallowed the sun.

No more running. No more fear.

Well, mostly.

As Ryland opened the door for her, a twinge of worry raced up her spine. Old fears tried to rear their heads. Liz squashed them right back down. She wasn't falling anymore. Ryland waited for her, and she was about to reach up and grab the hand he extended. She was going to climb that mountain with him, knowing in her soul the view would be more spectacular than she could fathom.

Ryland leaned on the door as Liz climbed out. "Someone's in a good mood."

"Hmm. Maybe." Liz couldn't resist giving him a little wink. Nervous energy coursed through her veins. She reached into the backseat and withdrew her duffle bag.

Ryland laughed. "Is this temporary, or is my girl back?"

Liz's stopped cold in her tracks. Her heart skipped a beat. Or two. Ryland's eyes widened slightly, and she felt apprehension skitter under his skin. His words hung in the air. Finally, one corner of Liz's mouth sneaked upward.

"Maybe." She edged around him, throwing him a mischievous look over her shoulder.

Liz laughed as a wave infused with surprise and pleasure wrapped around her. She fairly hopped toward the barn. Ryland caught up and strode beside her.

Inside, Arie, Chammu'el, Hadriel, and Aelaem waited for them. When they walked in the door, all four angelic heads lifted. Hadriel caught Liz's eye and winked. Arie and Chammu'el smiled and nodded. Aelaem charged them, a grin splitting his ethereal face.

Liz jumped back and smacked into Ryland as Aelaem grabbed her by the shoulders. A breath later, her head was pressed into Aelaem's ribcage, and her lungs were being squeezed in a monstrous bear hug.

"It is good to see you well, young one!" the angel boomed.

Liz muttered an incoherent reply, her face smashed flat.

Aelaem held her at arm's length. "Sorry about that." If an angel could look sheepish, he nailed it.

Liz grinned. "It's good to be well."

"In every way, it seems." He gave her a knowing look that glowed with joy.

"Absolutely."

Aelaem tossed an arm around both her and Ryland and led them toward the group. "Today, we get to liven things up a bit."

Liz shook her head and cocked an eyebrow. Seeing the stern warrior so jubilant was a new experience. Everyone gathered in a circle.

Liz blurted out the main question pecking at her mind. "So, what's the plan? When do we go after Markus?"

"We cannot be hasty," Arie admonished. "We must take into consideration the humans surrounding him. It is possible some of them are innocent." He glanced first at Ryland, then at Liz. Knowing the question before she spoke, he continued. "I do not know who or why. But if you attack simply for revenge, they may be caught in the middle. You must do everything in your power to keep them from being casualties of the war they have been pulled into. But, as I have said before, if they attack…"

Ryland nodded, acceptance and resignation written all over his face. Liz's shiny mood dimmed. She shivered, and Ryland's hand rested on her back, rubbing soothing circles.

The thought she may have to hurt another person was a knife to the gut. She couldn't relive those days. The brutal fights. The fury she'd unleashed on innocent targets. Before the black cloud could descend fully, she shook it off. *I'm not her anymore.* Ryland's thumb rubbed the center of her neck and drew her back to the present.

After their prayer, Liz headed out the back door with Hadriel and Arie. Ryland stayed inside to work with Chammu'el and Aelaem. *Lucky dog. It'd be nice to have those huge beams that hold up the barn to hide behind.* Arie was more than aggressive in his training techniques. Liz found it difficult, if not impossible, to dodge his strikes and charges in the open.

Not that the demons would take it easy, or that she'd always have cover. Liz sighed and withdrew her katana from the sheath at her side. Still, couldn't they at least use practice swords for this? Shaking her head, Liz faced the two angels.

Arie drew his blade. "Today, we work on defending against multiple attackers." He tipped his head toward Hadriel. "Demons have no honor. They do not fight fair. We must adapt and be ready for their unorthodox methods."

Liz nodded. "Evil fights dirty. Got it."

Liz tightened her grip on her sword.

She didn't have a chance to fully register the movement as Arie spun and brought his massive broadsword across his body. Pure instinct had her raising her own to block. The clang of steel on steel rang out in the valley and echoed in the trees. The force reverberated up her arms.

"Very good, young one."

A blur to her right announced Hadriel's move. Liz swayed to avoid the strike and brought her sword across the angel's body. The steel whistled through the air, inches from Hadriel's midsection. Hadriel grinned and advanced again.

Liz dodged and caught a flash in the corner of her eye. Arie. Liz threw her blade out to block Hadriel, dropped to the ground, and rolled out of the danger zone between the two angels. Leaping to her feet, she shifted her weight to her right foot and lunged sideways. Arie's blade sliced through the air near Liz's shoulder.

Liz ducked and swung for his back, barely missing as the angel laughed. When she rose, she froze. A razor tip of steel pierced the back of her neck. Arie and Hadriel were in front of her, watching with humor lighting their eyes. Liz lunged forward and whirled around with all the speed she had, sword at the ready. A well-built, dark-haired giant stood in front of her.

"You should watch your back, *katan ehad*." Sidriel lowered his blade. One eyebrow rose, and the corner of his mouth twitched. His denim-blue eyes sparkled.

"What does that mean? Whatever you called me?" Liz dropped her sword to her side.

"Little one."

Liz rubbed the back of her neck. When she looked down, there was a trace of fresh blood on her hand. "Cheater," she grumbled.

"What is it you humans say?" Sidriel tilted his head, and a smirk played at his lips. "All is fair in love and war."

Liz grunted. Of course she'd get stuck with the sarcastic angel.

Hadriel stood beside her now and bumped Liz's shoulder with her own. "Don't worry. You will learn or die." The white-headed angel grinned and winked at Liz.

Wow, everyone's a comedian today. Liz wrinkled her nose at Hadriel, causing the angel to laugh out loud.

Apparently, Arie was done with jokes. "Again." He moved closer, stalking like a tiger. "Use all of your senses, trust your instincts, and stay attuned to the Father. He will guide you. If you listen carefully, He will show you things you cannot see on your own. Close your eyes."

Liz did as ordered. She held her sword in front of her. Okay. She was listening. She focused. Everything around her became clearer. The wind in the pines. A hawk squawking in the distance. Grunts and the sound of clanging metal from inside the barn drifting on the breeze.

The almost inaudible crunch of a boot on dry grass behind her.

Liz opened her eyes and spun. Her blade collided with Sidriel's. She twisted the swords three times before breaking the contact and swinging. Sidriel forced the strike upward and thrust. She arched backward, and a tingle skittered down her back.

Behind you.

Sending a sidekick to Sidriel's stomach, Liz twisted and ducked low. Still crouched, she swung her right foot out and swept Hadriel's legs out from underneath her.

Arie and Sidriel teamed up and charged, blades high in the air. Liz dropped to her knees between them and palmed the flat edge of her katana with her free hand. She extended her arms upward, blocking the twin steel strikes. The impact spread an ache through her arms and torso.

Okay, so it was no-holds-barred kind of day.

The angels kept coming, full bore, for another half-hour. When they finally stopped, Liz sucked air into her tortured lungs. Her arms felt like they were about to fall off, but the rush as she parried their blows and struck back was awesome. A slow grin spread across her lips.

Liz shook her head in amazement at how much more effective she was when she really opened herself up, listening to the Voice from above and drawing on all of her senses. There was still plenty to work on, and she had a few cuts and bruises to show for her efforts. Still, she was proud of what she'd been able to do.

Arie clapped her shoulder. "You did well."

Liz beamed at the compliment. Hadriel gave her a fist bump and a smile as she walked past her. Liz raised an eyebrow. These angels surprised her every day.

Sidriel drew up beside Liz. "Good work. You might live through this." He winked.

"Uh-huh." Liz laughed at his deadpan voice.

She looked up to see Ryland leaning against the door of the barn. His smile and the pride radiating from him warmed her and sent tingles zinging into her belly.

Hadriel and Sidriel left, and Arie and Chammu'el probably wouldn't be far behind. Soon, she and Ryland would be alone. Excitement and terror barreled through her like a freight train. Anticipation and nervousness blared from Ryland like music from a loudspeaker. He'd given her space this past week. She'd had enough space now. Apparently, so had he.

Dark thoughts crept in, seeking purchase in her anxiety.

Once he knows the truth, he won't want you. You're damaged.

She pushed her worries down. She'd never know if she didn't take the chance. He was worth the risk.

"Be on your guard." Arie broke in to her thoughts. He stepped up on one side, Chammu'el on the other.

Liz and Ryland tore their gazes from each other. Something in Arie's voice made Liz pause. Trepidation sneaked up on her.

The normally silent Chammu'el chimed in. "Only engage the enemy if necessary. Now is not the time for hunting." He gave each of them a pointed stare.

Liz felt something else in the air. There was more they weren't saying. She glanced at Ryland as the same confusion and concern poured from him. "Did something happen?" Her light mood began to fade.

"Two young women were kidnapped not far from here." Arie's sorrow was written on his angelic features. "And the body of another was found. I was made aware of this only moments ago. There is reason to believe Markus is responsible."

Liz sucked in a breath as Ryland's arm came around her. "How do you know it was him?"

"There are things I am not at liberty to tell you. You must have faith all will be revealed when it is necessary."

Ryland found words first. "What do we need to do?"

"Pray, rest, and wait. There is nothing else you can do at this time. It won't be long before Markus makes his next move, whatever that may be. We hope to intercept him first." Arie laid a hand on each of them.

The two angels nodded and faded from sight.

Liz huffed out a breath. So much for her good mood.

XXIX
Arms

Ryland saw Liz swallow hard. For a second, he wondered if she could handle any more bad news.

He took her hand and squeezed it. "If he did this, we'll get him. And we'll get those girls back home where they belong."

Liz nodded and squeezed back. The faith he felt from her warmed him from the inside out.

Ryland jerked his chin toward the barn, and they walked inside. Silently, they gathered their belongings and headed for the door. He had to find some way to get her out of the gloom settling over them both.

"How about some lunch?" He checked his watch. "Well, I guess now an early supper. Looks like we got a little carried away today."

Liz's response was a whisper. "Sure."

Did he sound too cheerful, given what they'd just learned? "I've got a couple of steaks at the house I can toss on the grill." He closed the big doors and secured them with the padlock. Ryland faced her with a hopeful grin.

"You want to cook for me?" A playful glint sparkled in her eyes and lightened his spirit. "You're not exactly the world's greatest cook." Her laugh wrapped around his heart and squeezed.

Ryland raised an eyebrow and cracked a grin. "Hey, pot. Kettle here. And I'm getting better." He tried to look offended. "I made you burgers!" He tossed his gear into the bed of the truck. "Besides, you gotta eat. Give a guy a chance."

Liz threw her bag into the Jeep and gripped the side as if she needed help remaining on her feet. Ryland knew he hadn't read her wrong, so what was going on? *Fix it.*

He lowered his voice. "It's been a long week, and we could both use some down time. Especially now." Ryland inched toward her. "I'd really like to spend time with you. If you want. And if you're ready."

Ryland waited, shoving his hands into his pockets to keep from touching her. He wanted to reach out and smooth away her nerves. Give her whatever reassurance she needed. But he didn't want to spook her.

Liz's answering smile wrecked him. The three words she spoke exploded in his ears, sending excitement traveling down his spine.

"Supper sounds great."

Liz had expected to be nervous. Yet she moved calmly around Ryland's kitchen, putting together a salad while he fired up the grill on the back porch. He had a beautiful home. It'd come to him when his parents had passed.

If she'd stayed, would they have been married by now? Would this have been her kitchen? Would they have a baby on the way? The last thought came out of nowhere. Liz didn't want to feel the things it reminded her of.

She turned her focus to chopping lettuce.

"I have some green beans in there your mom gave me from her garden."

Liz jumped at the sound of Ryland's voice, banging her head on the cabinet. Her face flushed. *It's not like he can hear my thoughts. Good grief.*

"You okay there?" He grinned and brushed her forehead with his knuckles.

"Right as rain." She smiled back, hoping he didn't notice her burning cheeks.

"I'll throw the beans on the grill with the steaks." Ryland reached around her and sneaked a carrot.

"Hands off." Liz smacked his hand. "This is for dinner."

"Seriously, you've gotta stop being so mean." He gave a mock pout and dug in the fridge for the beans.

They maneuvered around the room, getting supper together and bantering back and forth. Occasionally they'd bump into one another. Each time, Ryland would grin, and Liz would flush, heat generating from the point of contact. She grabbed the salad bowl and plates and escaped to the porch.

After setting her armload on the table, Liz walked to the edge of the steps. She leaned on the rail, closed her eyes, and tilted her head back. The impending evening washed over her. The air full of pine and cedar. The crickets chirping. A coyote in the distance. A night off was just what she needed, and she intended to enjoy it. It didn't hurt she was spending it with the hottest, sweetest guy on the planet.

For a moment, she felt guilty. Here they were, together, having a good time, and people were hurting. Arie had said it was being handled. There was nothing for them to do right now. So they should take advantage of every bit of good they could get, right?

She shoved away the morbid thoughts and decided to get the most out of the time they had. Her cheeks raised in a grin. Liz turned and tried not to stare as Ryland's back rippled under his T-shirt with the slight movement of flipping the steaks. Prickly heat crept into her cheeks again. She tore her eyes away as he laid down the tongs and pulled out a chair.

She needed to get a grip. Made difficult by the fact the man was so fine she was about to break into a sweat. A bubble of laughter escaped her.

"My favorite sound." Ryland tipped his chair back on two legs.

"What's that?" Liz plopped down opposite him. She needed the table between them.

"Your laugh. It makes it feel like all's right in the world." His eyes darkened. "You're even more beautiful when you smile."

Liz's heart rolled over, and her breath hitched a ride. "Thank you," she whispered.

Ryland beamed. He scooped up their plates and loaded them with food. After he said a quick prayer, they dug in, though Liz wasn't as hungry now. Psychotic butterflies had taken flight in her belly and bounced around with fervor.

What am I doing? He deserves better than me.

Keeping the thoughts at bay was more difficult than she'd assumed. She forced herself to focus on the present. *I'm not who I was.* She shut the negative ideas off at the source and shoved them into a box.

Ryland inhaled his food as if he'd never eat again. When he'd finished, he sat and watched her. Liz shifted and concentrated on her plate. His direct, assessing gaze warmed her face. Liz popped in her last bite and jumped up, grabbing their dirty dishes and running for the kitchen.

Ryland followed. As they washed the dishes, they kept bumping elbows. Sparks went flying up her arms and straight to her heart. When they dried the last plate, she darted back out to the porch.

What was wrong with her? It's not like she'd never been around men before. But with Ryland, it was different. Special. With him, Liz felt innocent again. Like there'd never been anyone else in her life. Oh, how she wished that were true.

Liz shivered and hugged her arms to herself. The October evening was a little cool for her taste. Still, after the long summer of heat and humidity, it was a welcome break.

Ryland draped a small blanket over her shoulders. "Thought you might need this." He sat on the swing. "You never did like it when it dropped below sixty." He laughed and patted the seat next to him.

Liz pulled the blanket around her and sat. Her stomach bounced to her throat and back. There were several inches between them, but she could feel the heat rolling off him. All she could think about was snuggling in to his side. Nerves kept her where she was.

They swung in silence. Ryland reached for a knife and stone and started sharpening, a contented look on his face. Liz pulled up her feet and watched the sun slowly slide toward the hills.

They rocked and chatted. No tension, no expectations. They were able to just be. Liz couldn't remember feeling that way around any other man. They were acting like her parents. She smiled as she thought of them, probably doing something similar this very minute. Mom talking on and on about her flowers and garden, Dad reading his paper and giving the occasional, "Mm-hmm."

Yep, like an old married couple. Liz didn't hold back her nervous giggle. The idea they could be like that someday was appealing.

Ryland tilted his head as he peered at her, a twinkle in his eye. "What's got you tickled?"

"Nothin'." Liz wasn't sure she wanted to mention the M-word. No matter how great it sounded. "Just happy. I needed this. Thank you."

"Anytime." The way he said it sounded like, *I'd love to do this every day.*

Liz cleared her throat and unfolded her legs to stand.

Ryland rose with her. "You leaving?" His eyes said he didn't care for that.

"Yeah, I need a bath and sleep." Liz stretched, and a yawn popped out. "Maybe more than I thought."

Ryland moved closer, carefully, as if gauging her response. "I'm glad you came." His fingers grazed the side of her face and brushed a strand of hair off her forehead.

Liz held her breath. Time suspended. Unspoken words filled his eyes. Things it wasn't time to say yet. They mirrored the words she'd hidden in her heart. She reined them in and could tell Ryland was doing the same. His jaw tightened with the effort, and his hand trembled on her skin. Emotion swirled around and through them, both of them knowing, feeling, yet unable to speak it.

In the back of her mind, Liz began to wonder if they should be doing this. It was the worst possible time to start something. The doubts slipped from her lips. "Ry, I'm not sure if we should…I mean, there's so much going on right now." Her now-glistening eyes held his. "I want us to have a chance, and if we do this now…" Liz rubbed her hands down her face and moved to the railing, leaning against it.

"There'll never be a perfect time. We'll take one demon down, and another will rise in its place. There'll always be a fight. That's our life on this earth." He ran a finger down her shoulder and took her hand, interlacing their fingers. "We have to grab on to every piece of happiness we can. If we stop living, evil wins. If we only focus on what we're fighting against, we forget what we're fighting for."

"I understand that. But maybe we should wait until Markus is out of the picture." A tremor wobbled Liz's voice. "How can we focus on our jobs if we're wrapped up in each other?"

Ryland bristled. "First, it's not a job. We don't punch a time clock. This is who we are. Second, it's not going to be easy. Nothing worth having ever is. We do our best. We put God first, then us, and everything else next. It's that simple."

"Is it really?"

"Yes."

Liz desperately wanted to believe him. She tilted her head. "Let's say you're right—"

"I am."

She smiled. "Okay, smarty pants." Liz sobered. "There's more to it. There are things you don't know. A lot happened while I was gone, and not much of it good. You may not feel the same about me once you know."

Ryland cupped her face in his hands. Such intense love and understanding poured from him. It shot through her and collided head-on with her doubts.

"Nothing will change how I feel about you. The past changed you, but it doesn't define you. We'll work through it together, when you're ready." He tapped her chin with his thumbs. "God brought us back together for a reason. I'm not arguing with Him."

"You don't understand—"

"Just hush and trust me, woman."

Ryland's lips crashed down on hers. Liz slid her hands up to link behind his neck. She laid open to him all she was, all she had. An audible click reverberated through their joining.

This. This was love. This was home.

His mouth moved over hers, taking control. Firm yet gentle. His kiss demanded everything and gave nothing less in return. His hand moved to her waist and tugged her to him. Emotions ignited in a frenzy, showering sparks on them. Clinging to him with trembling hands, Liz leaned in to him, lost in the sway.

She felt Ryland's restraint. Even with the passion that whipped through them, he was conscious of her in every way. He held her delicately, determination flooding him. He needed her to know he would protect her. In no way would he cause her harm. She was safe. She was cherished. Though she had no idea how she knew that.

Ryland broke the kiss for a moment. Liz felt breathless and dizzy. She gazed at him through misty eyes. The love in his crawled into her chest and wrapped around her heart. Ryland smiled and moved in again. He feathered light kisses on her lips, her cheek, and her jaw. His grip on her nape tightened, and he pressed her head in to his shoulder.

His warm breath tickled her ear. "Lizzy, we'll take this at your pace. Whatever you need." Liz nodded. He gave her a kiss so soft she wanted to weep.

A happy shiver coursed through her.

"This time, I'm not letting you go." The world lit up as he smiled at her. "You're mine."

Normally, such a possessive statement would've sent her into a fit. Not this time. Liz had no problem being his.

"Well, Ryland Vaughn, here's to an interesting adventure."

Ryland lifted her off her feet and kissed her soundly.

Maybe things would work out after all.

Markus watched from a distance, perched in a tree. They couldn't see or sense him as he watched their every move on the porch. Rage roiled within him. Yet again, he'd rained down catastrophe, and it had done nothing except move them closer together. Exactly where he didn't need them.

The two of them joined would be a powerful weapon. And at the worst possible time for his side. The final battle breathed down their necks. Lucifer constantly pushed his army to move farther, faster than ever before. Time was running out. Markus growled, causing the wildlife in the area to scatter.

There was one avenue left open to him to ensure Ryland and Elizabeth never fulfilled the potential between them. One thing that would put a halt to the major threat to his army and his plans and leave Elizabeth broken. Primed for him to swallow up.

Markus smiled as he leered at Elizabeth. He followed as she flew down the highway, keeping back so she wouldn't sense him. As he flew, a new plan for her wound through his twisted mind. This time, it wouldn't fail.

XXX
Bring It On Home

Two large hands clasped Liz's ankles, wrapping them in an iron grip. The hands tugged, yanking her and the rolling board she lay on out from under the Jeep with unbelievable speed.

Liz sprang to her feet. She slid her right foot back and aimed a roundhouse for the midsection of the titan imposing on her personal space. Her opponent stumbled and laughed. She dropped her shoulder and plowed into him. Those massive hands clamped around her waist and flipped her over. Her legs flailed in the air as she let out a yelp.

A mere second later, her back hit the soft grass, and a grunt escaped her even though her landing had been gentle and controlled. Before she could respond, one hand held both of her wrists above her head. A torso made of steel leaned across hers. The other hand manacled her knees, pinning her to the ground.

"No fair." Liz breathed as she struggled. "I couldn't see you coming. And you weigh a ton. Get off me." She arched and drove her hips into his side in an attempt to toss him off.

Ryland laughed again but didn't let her go. He rose and moved his hand to the other side of her hip, effectively trapping her. "Gotta stay on your toes, baby." Hazel eyes twinkled. "Besides, you knew I was there."

Liz thought about the tingles that had stung her skin the moment before he'd grabbed her ankles. She grinned. "Whatever. Still a cheap shot." She pushed herself to a seated position.

"Uh-huh. Worked, though." He leaned in another inch and grazed his lips over hers.

"Quit trying to distract me."

"Never." He gave her another quick kiss. "I thought I told you I'd be over this afternoon to work on the Jeep." Ryland raised an eyebrow. "So why did I find you under it and all greasy?" He yanked at her tank top where a splotch of oil marred the name of a band.

"Got bored. So I went ahead and changed the oil. I still have to put the new starter in."

"I'll take care of it. Besides, have you ever even worked on one before?"

"No. Can't be too hard, though. You can do it."

He narrowed his eyes, but his smile kept him from looking menacing. "Ouch. Hurt me why don't ya?"

"That can be arranged."

"Woman, you are asking for a taming." He tweaked her chin.

"Oh, and you think you can tame me?" Liz snorted and tried to scoot out from under his arm.

Ryland caught her with a hand on her waist and drew her back to him. "I'm definitely gonna give it a try." He flashed a crooked smile before swooping in.

He planted a kiss on her that sent her head spinning. Their merging emotions forced the breath from her lungs. Her body temperature soared. Desire uncurled deep within and spread along her limbs. Their combined want and passion pushed all thought from her mind.

Ryland broke the kiss. His ragged breath told her he'd been affected as much as she had. "That's probably enough."

Liz nodded too many times. "Yeah. I'm...I'm good."

"For now." Ryland's eyes darkened.

"Excuse me?" Liz sputtered as a vise tightened on her ribcage. *Surely he's not...* Worry wound through her stomach. This time, she was going to do things right. She'd thought that's what he wanted too.

A full-blown grin creased his face, and she could tell he bit back a laugh. "One of these days you're gonna marry me. Then all bets are off."

Relief combined with a whole different kind of panic set up under her skin. *Not yet. Please, don't ask me yet.* Liz wanted to be his wife. To spend forever being his. But there was still so much she hadn't told him.

And when she did, she might lose him.

Liz didn't block her emotions quick enough.

Ryland leaned back. His brow wrinkled. Concern and the faintest hint of hurt shot through their link. He cupped her face. "Relax. I'm not asking right now. But we should talk about it, Liz. And about you blocking me."

Liz slid back and jumped to her feet. "Let's just get this done, okay? I have to be able to get to work tomorrow, and if we get in there and it's not the starter, I don't—"

"Hey, hey. Calm down." Ryland stood and took her by the shoulders. "I didn't mean to scare you." He rubbed her biceps with his thumbs. "We don't have to talk now. Let's get this done and get some lunch." He placed a kiss on her forehead.

"Okay."

"Lizzy, I won't rush you. But I already told you, I'm not letting you go." He brushed her jaw with his knuckle. "I'm in this. I'm with you. All the way."

Without another word, Ryland took her hand and led her to his truck.

Three hours later, Liz and Ryland were stretched out on a blanket beside the river, enjoying a fast food picnic.

"So you got that scar from a demon-possessed woman in Omaha?" Liz hitched an eyebrow and shoved a French fry into her mouth.

"Yep." Ryland tossed his burger wrapper into the bag and leaned back on his elbows. The scent of the river mingled with his aftershave and tickled her nose. "Kade had that girl four kinds of messed up, and had for a while. It took me and Mac and a local pastor two days to get his claws out of her." He winced. "Put up a heck of a fight."

"Ah. So that's the kind of work you and Mac did together. I thought maybe he was a computer geek like you."

"Nope. And I'm not a geek. Just good at what I do." He narrowed his eyes and tried to look put out. "Next question."

Liz chewed the inside of her cheek. "And that's your history with Kade?"

"Part of it, yeah. The rest is a whole other story."

"Okay." She could accept that. There were things she didn't want to get into either.

"Your turn." Ryland rolled to his side and looked up at her expectantly.

Liz froze. This was it. The moment she'd dreaded since they'd gotten back together.

Her instinct was to find an escape route. She swallowed and avoided looking at him.

Ryland reached up and touched her chin. His eyes were serious. "You heard the gory details of my time without you. Now it's your turn."

Liz shifted uncomfortably. She crossed her legs in the grass and let out a long sigh. She looked out over the water. She couldn't avoid it any longer.

Ryland had opened up and given her a glimpse of the last few years of his life. Some stories were interesting, and some she'd rather not have heard. At times it was all she could do to keep her jealousy and temper in check.

His description of the few months he'd given up fighting and his faith were what one might expect, and the hardest part to hear. Liz gritted her teeth, knowing she had no right to be angry. Hearing he'd hooked up with a couple of women during that time had just about cut her in half. If she felt that way about his story, how would he respond when she laid all of her crap on the line?

"Are you sure? You won't like what I have to say."

Ryland took a deep breath. "I'm sure I won't. But we need to get it out so we can move past it all."

Liz agreed. They couldn't move forward until they'd dealt with the past. All she could do was take a deep breath, lay it out for him, and pray he could handle it.

She opened her mouth to start her sordid tale, but a loud screech sounded in the trees. As Liz and Ryland both jumped to their feet, five demons stepped into the clearing.

This wasn't exactly what she had in mind when she'd been looking for a way out of this conversation.

Ryland turned back to the demons advancing slowly. *So much for a quiet afternoon.*

"Truck." Ryland barked the command. They needed to get themselves armed before the demons engaged. There was no outrunning them.

Liz hustled to the truck. Ryland flung open the door. He was glad he'd left his bag in the backseat. Getting the toolbox open fast enough would've taken a miracle. No sooner had he tossed Liz a long sword and grabbed his own blades, the monsters were on them.

Ryland shoved Liz out of the way of the first strike and ducked, thrusting upward. The demon gave an unholy howl. Out of the corner of his eye, he saw Liz engage two more. His thought about how proud he was of her got cut off by a blade tearing into his side. He retaliated, not bothering to check the injury. Nothing vital was hit as far as he could tell. He swiftly dragged his blades across the throat of his enemy. The two remaining demons descended.

The demons unleashed a flurry of blows. He dodged one, got clipped by another. These demons weren't playing around. They were going for a quick kill.

Though thoroughly engaged in the fight, he kept his senses wide open, waiting for Kade or Markus to show up. Surely they wouldn't miss out on trying to off him. Especially Kade.

He got lucky, and one opponent left himself open. Ryland swooped in, capitalizing on its weakness, and shredded the creature's abdomen. The thing dropped to the ground. Then his buddy unloaded on him. Ryland eventually got him down as well. He buried one blade through the demon's shoulder, pinning his sword arm to the ground. The demon swung with its other arm and bucked, trying to dislodge Ryland.

He speared his other blade straight into the demon's chest and twisted. As his enemy went limp, Ryland leaped to his feet and looked toward Liz's last position.

One demon lay on the shore, thick fog already encompassing him. Liz was farther down the beach. She looked like something out of a movie. Elegant and inhumanly fast, she swung and parried. A grin creased Ryland's face. Apparently the demon didn't recognize he was being drawn in.

Liz feigned weakness and dropped back. The demon rushed in. A ghost of a smile graced Liz's lips as she waited. When the demon lunged, she knocked his sword to the side and swooped in behind him, her blade instantly to his throat. Without hesitation, she brought her arm across. The demon's head tumbled to the ground, followed by his body.

Ryland moved toward her as she bent over and braced her hands on her knees. "You all right?"

Liz drew in a deep breath and straightened. "Yeah." She glanced at the demon now encased in the black mist. A grin tipped her lips. "Guess that training the other day came in handy."

Ryland smiled and shook his head while he looked her over for wounds. A shallow slice across her thigh. A busted up cheek. A gouge on her shoulder. He breathed a sigh of relief, knowing they would heal quickly. His girl had given the demons a run for their money.

Ryland draped his arm around her shoulders. Neither said a word as they gathered the remains of their interrupted lunch. Once back at the truck, Ryland pulled out his ever-present first aid kit and tended Liz's wounds. She did the same for him. Most were already starting to heal. Her soft touch soothed him, spreading warmth into his skin. She didn't say a word the entire time.

Ryland knew they were both trying to get their heads straight after the battle, but there was more to this silence. Liz had been about to drop her past on him before the interruption. Now, he wondered if she'd clam up. He hoped not. The sooner they got everything out in the open, the better.

He helped her into the truck, then retrieved a clean shirt from his bag before crawling into the driver's seat. On the way back to her place, they talked briefly about the fight. Mostly things were quiet. Not uncomfortable, just loaded.

When they reached her apartment, he was almost surprised when Liz asked him in. Did she want to get this over with, too? Ryland nodded and followed her. She shed her boots and ran to her room to change. She returned quickly and headed straight to the kitchen. After grabbing a bag of Oreos and two glasses of milk, she plopped on the floor beside the coffee table. He dropped down beside her.

She ate three cookies before she finally spoke. "I guess we should continue our conversation."

Ryland noticed her hand shaking as she dipped a cookie into the milk. He gave her a questioning look. "We don't have to do this right now."

"No, I'm good. If I don't get it out now…" Her voice drifted off.

The sudden urge to tell her to forget it bubbled up in his brain. But she'd heard all of his dirt. The things he was most ashamed of. If this were going to work, he had to let her get hers out too.

Finally, she spoke in a soft voice. She avoided his gaze. Then she dove in. "When I got to Dallas, I didn't have a lot of cash. None really. So I picked up bartending jobs here and there. Some pretty, um, interesting places." She swallowed hard, and her cheeks colored blood red.

Ryland held his tongue. He knew this part. Of course, she had no idea. The place he'd tracked her—he'd rather forget. It'd broken his heart when the trail led there. Still did.

Liz glanced at him, then away. "Places that had…entertainment, you know? That's where the money was. Unfortunately, the demons, too. Most ignored me. When they did attack, thankfully I was always by myself." She blew out a sharp breath. "Usually, I just poured drinks, waited tables. But, sometimes…they'd be short on dancers and I'd…" Her voice trailed off, and she looked like she'd rather disappear. "I needed the money, and at that time, I didn't really care how I got it."

"It's okay, you don't have to say more. I know." As soon as the words left his mouth, he bit his lip.

Liz's back went ramrod straight. She met his eyes, and he didn't like the wariness in them. "What do you mean?"

Ryland sighed. "I had to work a little to find you. I didn't just call motels, then show up on your doorstep. I ended up in some other spots, too. Following your trail."

Liz sucked in a breath. "You didn't—did you…see?" Terror and shame coursed through the air between them.

He grabbed her hands in his. "No. I dug around and found out where you worked, then I…" Ryland made a face, not sure how she'd take the next part. "I waited outside until your shift was over and followed you."

Liz's eyebrows hit her hairline. She made a strange noise, then shook her head. At least she didn't look like she was going to hit him.

"You're not mad I followed you?"

"No. I was mad you found me. Back then." She gave an anemic smile.

Okay, that was out of the way. Knowing he needed to keep her talking so she didn't retreat into herself, he urged her on. "What happened when I left? Where did you go?" A slight change in direction should help. He hoped.

Liz pulled her hands from his and clasped them in her lap. "I tried to put as much distance between us as I could. In every way." She avoided his eyes again.

Ryland had a feeling what she was going to say. Her shame grew and seeped into him. He stayed silent, steeling himself and nodding for her to continue.

"I hitched a ride with a guy. Ended up staying with him for a couple of months. Then I dumped him and hopped a bus farther west." She rushed on, as if she stopped, she'd never get started again. "I got jobs waiting tables. Just restaurants." Liz watched him for a second. Seeing his encouraging half-smile, she went on. "Anyway, I thought if I could find someone else, maybe I could, you know, forget." She ducked her head.

Ryland rubbed his hand down her arm, then entwined their fingers.

She took a gulp of air and dove back in. "There were, um, a lot. Of guys. I just—I didn't want to be alone." Liz picked at the carpet.

He tried to control the anger blasting through him at the thought of anyone else touching her. It was the past. She was his now. Nothing else mattered.

Liz shifted her position, breaking their contact. "I met this guy." She flicked a glance at him before looking away again. "He was a fight promoter. Underground, MMA fights. I'd fought a couple of times in a local show. He was there one night. He approached me and offered a partnership. I ended up moving in with him. Things were good for a while, I guess. With my extra abilities, I won every match. He never knew I basically cheated. Didn't care."

"All right." He didn't want to press, but he had the feeling she was building up to something.

She spit the words out at break-neck speed. "We weren't making a lot yet, so he still worked at a repair shop. On big rigs. He hated it and wanted to go bigger with the fight thing. I was done. I couldn't keep doing it. It wasn't right."

Tears slid down her cheeks. Ryland held his breath as the agony that slid through her hit him. Liz held up a hand when he started to cut in and tell her to stop.

"I came to the shop late one night, bags packed. I told him I was leaving, and he went nuts. He'd never been mad like that before and had never tried to hurt me. I'd seen the demons around him. They didn't attack so I ignored them. Maybe if I hadn't, he wouldn't have..."

A sob shook her, and Ryland crept forward. He didn't want to scare her. The extreme emotions whipping around them sliced into him. He cradled her hands in his.

Liz seemed to gain strength from the contact. "He hit me from behind as I was walking out. It all happened so fast. He was on me, and before I could even think, he—" She choked on the words.

He didn't need to hear more. "Shh. You don't have to say it." Ryland pulled her to him, slowly, to give her the option to refuse. He wasn't sure what else to do.

Liz broke as she collapsed into his arms. Ryland held her. Stroked her hair. Murmured comforting words with no meaning.

He was angry at the people who'd used her. Furious he hadn't been there for her. Devastated at what she'd been through. If he ever ran into the man who'd put his hands on her, Ryland worried whether he'd be able to keep from killing him. He discarded the thought and focused on Liz.

Pride welled in him. She'd been strong enough to survive it. Finally clawed her way out. Smart enough to realize she couldn't make it alone. More than that, he was humbled she trusted him enough to let him in. She'd even kept her emotions open. Ryland knew that cost her.

If it were possible, he loved her even more.

"If you don't want, I mean, I understand if you can't..." Liz let the words hang in the air.

Ryland moved her back a bit so he could look at her. He smiled as he brushed away the moisture on her cheeks. Her eyes and the link they shared filled with confusion and hope. How could she ever think any of this would make him want her less? Love her with any less intensity?

"I do want, and I can."

"What?"

Facing Liz with one leg to each side of her hips, he pulled her toward him again, her legs still crossed. Shock fluttered over her features.

Ryland kissed her temple. "I can deal with it, and I still want you."

The relief and overwhelming gratefulness coming from her hit him like a Mack truck. He leaned forward again until his lips pressed against her forehead. Then he pulled back, lifting her chin until their eyes met.

Liz babbled through her tears. "I thought you'd think I was trash. I never..."

"Hush. Don't say that." Ryland cupped her face in both hands. "We've both changed." He wiped her fresh tears with his thumbs. "But we move forward from here and make a new life. This, right here"—he drew an invisible circle around them—"this is all we need. You, me, and God. Nothing can shake that."

"We're still good?" Her voice was so soft it nearly broke him.

"Yeah. We're good."

They'd both have to work through what had been said tonight. But they were solid. He gave her a smile. She squealed when he palmed her waist and twisted her around. Ryland pulled her back against his chest.

Settling his arms around her, he kissed the top of her head. "You're stuck with me."

Liz laughed. "Really?"

"Yep." Ryland's voice went serious again. "From now on, no more secrets. Everything out in the open. You can tell me anything." He narrowed his gaze. "And no more emotional shields. We stay open. No hiding."

"All right. No shields, no secrets."

For a second, Ryland thought he felt a flutter of guilt from her.

He had to be sure she understood. "We trust each other completely. That's how this is gonna work."

"Okay." Liz nodded and smiled.

Ryland leaned her back, dipped his head, and brought his lips down on hers, sealing their agreement with a kiss. He poured all the love he had into it. Liz melted into him. His gut reacted like hungry raccoons had been set free in there. She'd always had that effect on him. The one person who could drive him crazy and test all of his limits.

God, I love her. They made a great team, as evidenced by the fight earlier. Thank God she finally understood. Yeah, it bugged him she hadn't said she loved him yet, like he'd told her. But she would someday, and he would wait. They were together, and that was what mattered.

He just had to hang on to her.

XXXI
Freight Train

"Lucifer will not be pleased." Kade had the audacity to laugh about it. "That attack was pointless. You should have sent me in and let me kill them both." Kade laughed again. "Look at you. You keep letting opportunities pass. But go ahead. You're just making it easier for me to take your command."

Markus didn't bother looking at his second as the demon crept up beside him.

Screw Lucifer.

A sneer curled Markus's upper lip as he remained silent, thinking about the scene he'd watched earlier at the river. Before he'd sent his soldiers in. He tilted his head to the side. Ridiculous. She gave herself to Ryland yet had thrown all Markus had offered back in his face? Oh, she'd soon learn she'd made the wrong choice.

They were becoming a formidable team. Taking on five of his best warriors with relative ease. He'd hoped at least they'd have been injured enough to slow them down. Regardless, the two of them had tasted a reminder. This wasn't over.

Markus finally faced Kade, his voice boding no argument. "They were getting too comfortable. I needed to make sure they knew we weren't going away. Don't worry, you'll get to spill his blood soon enough." Markus stretched to his full height as he stared Kade down. There was no way he was telling Kade his plan to have Ryland killed had failed. And that he'd sent someone else to do it just so Kade wouldn't have the satisfaction. "Put the rest of the plan into motion. Immediately."

Kade bowed. "As you wish."

Markus didn't miss the smirk and air of defiance Kade telegraphed before he disappeared. The idiot didn't even realize his mission was the backup plan.

Markus's thoughts turned back to Elizabeth and Ryland and the way they'd smiled and returned to life as normal after the fight. They acted as if they weren't at all concerned about the danger and death churning in the ether around them.

Soon they would be. But by then, it would be too late.

"Hey! Not yours." Liz slapped Ryland's hands away from the slice of pecan pie. She wiped down the counter around him. Scanning the diner, she checked her other table. "You have a problem with stealing food, you know. You should see someone about that."

Ryland leaned over the counter. "Hey! I'm a—"

"Yeah, yeah. You're a growing boy. Bless your little pea-pickin' heart."

"So hurry up and give me a piece of that. I'm dying of starvation over here, woman."

Liz laughed as she cut another piece. The permanent smile she'd been wearing the past few weeks widened. "You just had a huge plate of chicken and dumplings. With potatoes." She shook her head as she handed him the plate.

Ryland flashed her a satisfied grin and slid back to his booth while Liz delivered pie and fresh coffee to her only table. When she was done, she walked toward him, thinking about how things had changed between them since their "bones out of the closet" conversation. Liz had never imagined it would feel so good to have someone to share the burden with. *Trust.* The thought wove its way through her mind as she leaned against the booth where Ryland sat.

Ryland glanced at her and tapped his fork against her arm before digging in again. He demolished the pie in a few bites. He pushed the plate back and put a hand on his stomach. "You're not trying to fatten me up for the kill, are you?"

Those twinkling hazel eyes melted her into a puddle.

"Not yet."

Ryland shook his head. "Promises, promises." He twisted in the seat to face her. "Your dad says they're about ready to start the rebuild."

"Yeah." Liz worked her neck side to side to release the knots forming. "His buddy Dale came by with the backhoe yesterday and dug the foundation. They were gonna pour the concrete today, but the rain last night put it off a day or so."

Liz smiled when she thought about how the community had come together and thrown a few fundraising events. Along with three anonymous donations, they had more than enough to rebuild.

Liz held up her finger for him to wait a minute and went to the register to ring out her customers. As they walked out the door, she returned to Ryland and slid into the booth across from him.

Ryland took a swig of his sweet tea. "Hopefully things will stay fairly quiet, and we can get it built with no interruptions."

Liz nodded. They shared a silent acknowledgement. *The peace won't last.* Even though Arie had reported an increase in numbers in the demonic force in the area, attacks had been few and far between since they'd been jumped by the river. And there was no word on the missing girls. That didn't bode well. Arie and Chammu'el had stepped up their training even further, and angelic numbers had also increased. Oh yeah. Trouble was brewing.

Liz and Ryland had discussed the heaviness and anticipation in the air. While they remained alert, they went about their lives. Living as close to normal as they could. It was a new concept for Liz, but she was following Ryland's lead. She just hoped they were ready for whatever else Markus might throw at them.

The mere thought of his name stiffened her spine, and icy fingers poked her abdomen.

Ryland waved a hand in front of her face. "Hello, earth to Liz. Where'd you go?" Worry tinged his eyes, and she knew he'd felt the wash of fear from her.

Liz swatted at his hand, and he took hold of it. "Sorry, just thinking. You say something?" She squeezed his hand before she stood.

"Yeah, what time are we heading to your mom's? She's making Mexican chicken casserole tonight, and I am not missing that."

"Good grief, all you think about is food." Liz shook her head and laughed.

He gave her a pathetic excuse for a pout and shrugged. "So, what time?"

"Six. But I get out of here in a little bit and thought we might take the four-wheelers out." Liz picked up his plate. "There's some really good mud from the rain."

"Sure you want to get all muddy, princess?" He winked at her.

She stuck out her tongue at him and went behind the counter. As she reached for the full bus tub, an icy, dark cloud descended on the diner. Liz glanced at Ryland. He sat bolt upright, and she could feel his senses sharpen and reach out. Their eyes met, and they both swiveled toward the door.

Five men walked in. They looked a little rough around the edges. Nothing that would normally cause her any alarm. What did draw her attention was the inky cloud hovering around them. One of them stood well over six feet, and when his eyes met Liz's, they were black as coal.

She sucked in a breath. *Possessed*.

She could feel it ooze from his pores. The evil stifled the oxygen in the room. Gloom settled over the place like a wet blanket over a bonfire. The men sat at a table on the far side of the diner. The cloud dissipated, and several demons materialized.

Liz felt Ryland at her side. "You're not waiting on them." His order came through gritted teeth.

Liz bristled. Her emotional shields instinctively dropped into place. Apparently they needed to have a conversation. He weaved his hand through hers and squeezed. The action carried a silent cue to drop the wall between them. Liz sighed and gave in, bringing the barrier down.

That was a battle for another day.

When her shield dropped, she immediately wished she'd kept it up. Evil, hate, a strong desire to cause pain, and so many other negative emotions and desires collided in her brain, they squeezed the breath out of her lungs. She took a step back, fighting for control.

"Julie's about to leave. Better me than her, anyway." Liz pulled her hand from his and eased behind the counter to get her pad and pen she'd left lying on the counter.

Ryland's sound of displeasure resounded in her ears. She ignored it.

Walking slowly, she sent up silent prayers. *Thank God there are no other customers here.* Liz let calm slide into her veins. Hopefully they didn't know what or who she was. This was the first time she'd encountered a real possession, and she had no idea how much information the demon might feed the man, or how any of that even worked.

A quick look to her right told her what she already knew. Ryland was laser-focused on her every move. Her senses went into overdrive, and her entire body vibrated. Every noise amplified. Every nerve ending, hyper-sensitive.

Focus. Stay calm. Be ready to strike if necessary.

Liz shoved down the anxiety. Her smile was a little too bright. "What can I get for you boys?"

The big one spoke with a voice that sounded like a shovel dragging across gravel. "Coffee all around. Nothing else." He looked her in the eyes.

He knows.

The others were oblivious, making crude remarks she tuned out.

"Be right back." Her smile never wavered.

Liz slid behind the counter and pulled out a tray. She set five mugs on it. When she picked up the coffee pot, her shaky hands resulted in hot coffee splashing on her. She hissed and mopped it up.

Ryland appeared at her side. "Get anything?"

"Nothing good." A shiver worked its way through her bones. "The big one is possessed and knows who I am." She set the pot back on the burner and scooped up a handful of creamer.

Liz picked up the tray and returned to their table. She delivered their drinks without incident and moved away quickly. She retrieved a tray of silverware to roll and headed for Ryland's booth. It was something to keep her hands busy, which she desperately needed.

An eerie silence settled over the room, the only noise the muffled sound of Hank's radio in the kitchen. "Bad Moon Rising" floated through the door. Liz nearly laughed at the irony. Ryland threw his leg across the seat and angled for a better view, his eyes rarely leaving the group in the back.

The men didn't stay long. The big one tossed some bills on the table and ambled toward the door. Two of the demons taunted Ryland and Liz as they passed their booth. The demons got in their faces, spewing vitriol in a strange language. Liz wanted to rip into them, but she continued with her work. A glance told her Ryland was about to combust. Every muscle taut, he clenched a roll of silverware until it bent in half.

The creatures knew Liz and Ryland couldn't really respond to them in public. Even so, they soon gave up their game and vanished.

"That was…interesting." Ryland tried to straighten out the ruined silver.

"Maybe they just wanted us to know they're watching."

Her gut told her Markus was up to something. He always was. The feeling of dread intensified as she rose and carried the rolls of flatware to the wait station.

"You gonna be okay for a bit?" Ryland followed and reached for her hand.

"Yeah." Liz nodded, smoothing her emotions so he wouldn't worry. "I've got a couple of things to take care of, but I'll be back to pick you up in a little bit." He tucked a wayward strand of hair behind her ear. "Just watch yourself. If I can get back sooner, I will."

An eerie weight settled in Liz's heart. "You be careful too. I've got a bad feeling." She couldn't live with herself if she didn't warn him.

There's no way I can lose him now.

"I will. Stop worrying. You'll get wrinkles." Ryland flashed her a grin, even though she knew he felt exactly what she did.

Ryland pulled her close and gave her a light, playful kiss. He tugged her ponytail before he stepped back. "See you in a bit." He headed out the door.

Liz cleaned the "table-o-evil" before moving on to cutting lemons for the dinner shift. A few minutes into her work, pain tore through the back of her skull. The knife slipped, and she sliced the tip of her finger. As she dropped the blade, a strange wave of dizziness swept over her. She doubled over. Liz gripped the counter, barely able to stand.

She took deep breaths and regained her balance. The next instant, it felt as though a dagger slipped between her ribs. Liz gasped and grabbed her side. Another hit rammed her abdomen, a kick with an invisible steel-toed boot. A strike to one kidney. Followed by a jab to the other.

Ryland.

She had no idea how or why this was happening. Horror sliced into her as another blow to the head sent her reeling.

Liz tried desperately to catch her breath and stay on her feet.

Julie emerged from the kitchen and ran to her side. "Hey, are you all right?" The waitress put an arm around Liz to help steady her.

"Not sure. I feel sick." Liz didn't know what else to say, but she could barely get those words out. She had to get to Ryland. She looked at Julie and plastered on a smile. "I need some air. I'm gonna head outside for a minute."

The girl didn't look convinced. "Okay." Julie sighed. "It's raining, so take my umbrella. It's by the door. I'll keep an eye on the dining room. I don't mind staying a few extra minutes."

Liz tried to focus. The crippling pain slowed her down. Forgetting the umbrella, she emerged from the diner into pouring rain and frantically searched the parking lot. Ryland was nowhere to be seen.

She spied his truck on the edge of the lot. Liz ran to it, fighting to stay upright with the swirling in her head. The truck was empty, and the toolbox was open. Peeking inside, Liz saw his favorite double blades were missing. A tremble quaked through her. She reached in and grabbed one of his handguns, then closed the lid. She pulled her dagger out from under her khaki work cargos. With the gun in one hand and the knife in the other, she glanced around again to make sure she was alone.

A roar split the air. A series of grunts and growls followed. The noises came from behind the diner, near the woods.

Ryland.

A burning sensation assaulted the back of her calves. She ignored it, melted herself to the building, and slinked around the side. Water poured from the ancient gutter directly into her eyes. She squinted and wiped it away. More grunts and the sound of flesh hitting flesh assailed her ears. Her heart jumped into her throat. Liz was almost to the corner when she heard a tortured groan and a sickening crack. Shattering bone. Her heart fell to her shoes.

The voice was Ryland's.

She whipped around the corner. The men and demons from the diner were scattered in a haphazard circle. They held an array of knives, bats, and pipes. Evil thickened the atmosphere. Deadly intent and sadistic satisfaction crashed into her in wretched waves. Liz fought a gag.

Two of the group shifted, and she saw Ryland in the center of the circle. He was barely keeping himself upright on his knees. His handsome face was almost unrecognizable. He looked as though he'd been coated in blood. As soon as the rain washed it away, it was replaced with fresh red.

"Ryland!" His name ripped from her throat.

"Liz. Run!" Somehow, out of a destroyed chest, he forced a warning.

Liz ignored the command. Her entire body shook. Adrenaline shot through her as if a dam had broken. She had to get to Ryland. She charged.

A loud crack shattered the day.

Ryland's body jerked. His eyes widened slightly. A wave of terror for her shot into Liz's heart from him, along with agony she'd never known.

Ryland fell to the ground.

An inhuman scream filled the valley. Liz vaguely registered it came from her. The men and demons scattered as she came running. Sneers and laughter assaulted her ears as they shuffled out of her way.

Liz hit her knees beside Ryland. His face was torn and bruised. His shirt, shredded. Black bruises and vicious gashes covered his torso. His ripped and bloody hands still held one sword, the other on the ground nearby. A gaping hole lay open in his upper chest, the end result of the bullet that had detonated into him.

Liz pressed her hands to the gunshot wound and leaned on it. "Hank! Julie! Ryland, baby, come on. Stay with me. God, please! Arie! Chammu'el, where are you?"

Snickers and outright laughter sounded at her agonized wails and pleas. She wondered vaguely why they weren't attacking. Liz pressed harder as blood spurted from the wound. It covered her hands. A hard rain pelted them mercilessly, washing the blood into the ground and swirling it in a puddle underneath them. The flow from his chest continued, covering her hands again.

"Please, Ry, hang on. Somebody help!"

Liz looked around, past the morbid onlookers, hoping someone had heard above the thunder crashing above. Seeing the back door still closed, she lowered her head and prayed, the plea tearing from her soul. She continued to keep pressure on the wound as she pleaded with Ryland and God.

Blind fear and agony squeezed her bones and ground them to dust. A deathly chill cascaded over her body. Liz swallowed hard and slowly moved a hand to his throat. Nothing.

Methodically, she moved her hand to the other side. Then both wrists. No pulse.

Liz reexamined every pulse point. She tilted his chin, blew in two breaths, and placed her hands over his heart, compressing with all she had. Crimson life pulsed from the hole. She repeated the entire process over and over, not knowing what else to do. A frustrated scream escaped her lips.

She aimed her frustration at the crowd around her. "What is wrong with you?" The tirade fell on deaf ears. Liz focused again on Ryland. "No. You're not doing this. You are not leaving me, Ryland David Vaughn! You promised!"

She felt for a pulse one last time. Her heart shattered. The pieces dug into her soul, ripping irreparable holes. Unbearable pain destroyed everything. It left her hollow in its wake.

Liz leaned over and whispered in Ryland's ear. "I haven't even told you I love you yet. Please, don't go." She raised her eyes to the sky. "God, please, take me. Not him. Take me."

The heavens remained silent as they wept.

The dormant volcano inside exploded in a seismic rush. Searing lava boiled out of her core and twisted its way into her system. It filled every crevice, whirling in her heart and mind, demolishing whatever remained in its path as the tremors shook her soul.

Liz smoothed Ryland's wet hair from his battered face and kissed him lightly. She ran a gentle thumb over his swollen lips, then planted a kiss there. She feathered a delicate hand over his bruised cheek. Her tears mingled with the rain and dropped onto his broken body.

Slowly, she picked up her weapons and rose to her feet. Liz looked down at her hands. As she saw the very essence of him clinging to her, diluted by the rain, the eruption inside intensified.

The tears ceased. An unnatural calm filtered along her skin. Sank into her marrow.

Liz lifted her hooded gaze to the men and demons around her. A mist settled over her eyes.

All she saw was red.

XXXII
Army of Me

The veil descended over Liz's eyes and mind with a vengeance.

She embraced it. Relished the intensified nature of the new beast that raged within her. Fury surged in her veins, searing its way into every nook and cranny. Her mind held one jagged, crystal thought.

Retribution.

Liz straightened one vertebra at a time. She deliberately made eye contact with each man and demon surrounding her. Rage. Cruelty. Delight at the agony they'd caused. It surrounded them. Permeated them. Pulsed from them. Riding the need to create more chaos, Liz closed her eyes, opened herself up, and let it fuel the fire within.

She would bring the chaos they desired, riding on the back of vengeance.

When she opened her eyes again, the desire to mete out justice had consumed her.

The demons smiled, satisfaction and amusement flickering in their yellow eyes. As she leveled a look of pure destruction at them, their expressions changed. Fear swept across their faces. One even trembled. They quickly vanished.

Good. Tell your master I'm coming for him.

Liz focused on the human leader, standing a few feet from her. His black eyes stared her down. A sneer curled his lips. He twisted the metal pipe in his hand. The next second, he lunged.

She deftly slid away from the blow and brought a crushing strike to the base of his skull with the butt of the gun. The man sank to his knees. Liz threw a roundhouse to the side of his head. Another man rushed her. Liz dropped, blocking the crowbar he wielded with her knife handle. She rolled to her back and landed a solid kick to his groin.

Liz leaped to her feet in time for a fist to come from nowhere and graze her temple. She didn't allow the hit to register. She slammed an elbow into his jaw. A loud crack rent the evening air right before he hit the mud.

The fourth grabbed her wrist from behind as she lunged for the second attacker, who had regained his footing. A punch landed to her side, right over her liver. The gun fell from her hand. Liz let out a grunt as pain carved her abdomen. The rain allowed her to slide from his grip. Wrangling his neck, she pulled his torso into her knee. Liz smashed the handle of her dagger into his temple. He tumbled to the ground, unconscious.

Two down, two to go.

She retrieved her gun and whirled around. The rage gripped her tighter, fueled by gut-wrenching agony. The man with the broken jaw clawed to his feet. Liz sliced across his midsection, controlling the depth. She was going for pain, not death.

Death was too good for them.

The big one had made it back to his feet and tackled her from the side. They went rolling, and the knife fell from her grasp. Liz landed on her back with the leader's weight pinning her in the mud.

She jerked her head to the side as a fist pounded into the ground. Liz pushed, using her body to flip him to his back. She pounced and rained down furious punches with vicious strength and speed. He stopped fighting back, his head lolling to the side.

Sight faded into a tunnel as Liz continued to pummel him. Tears cascaded down her cheeks, taking over for the rain. She floated above her body, watching herself rain down judgment. She refused to let her eyes roam to where Ryland lay. Lifeless.

The last man standing attacked from behind and yanked her up.

The blade of her dagger glinted, and she lunged for it. The man stepped on the blade and steel crashed down across her shoulders. She threw a brutal kick to his knee as she fell, the audible snap letting her know she'd hit the mark.

Liz snatched the blade and rolled to her feet. Her badly bruised shoulders and battered midsection screamed. She promptly ignored them, her mission forcing all other thoughts away.

The man lunged and she swung, catching his forearm and filleting it cleanly. He pulled the arm to his body and blasted a wild punch toward her with the other. She ducked and whirled behind him, landing a punch to his kidney. He gasped as he fell and attempted to crawl away. Liz went after him.

She was nowhere near finished.

The next second, the world flipped upside down, and she flew through the air. Her back met the ground. The impact punched her lungs empty. The vibration rattled her body, and pain burst through her like white-hot lightning. Liz lay motionless for a few seconds. Dragging in a breath, she struggled to her feet. The vapor in her mind slowly began to clear.

"No more!"

The roar shook the ground and jostled her bones. Arie's voice filled the valley. He stood over her in human form, eyes glowing with a preternatural light, an eerie luminescence writhing on his skin. Heat emanated from him. His anger was a living thing. Targeted at her.

Sadness rode the back of his righteous fury as he surveyed the area. His focus landed on her hands. "What have you done?"

Liz lifted the shaky appendages to take a look. They hid under layers of blood not her own.

Awareness ripped into Liz with merciless talons. The haze lifted completely. Liz glanced at the bodies scattered around her. Some moaning and moving sluggishly. Some still.

How did I do that? Most of it, she didn't even remember.

They were people, not demons. She'd used all the strength in her, all the power bestowed on her by Heaven, to deliver punishment she'd decided they deserved.

"Oh, God. Oh, my God! What did I do?" She turned a tortured gaze on Arie.

Hot tears burned her eyes. Liz's head was crushed under the grip of an unseen vise. A bitter, vile taste rose in her mouth. The fury drained from her body, leaving her weak and trembling. An agonized prayer for forgiveness wrenched from her lips. The thing she'd worked so hard to control, the thing she thought she'd let go of, had commandeered her entire person.

She hadn't even tried to fight it.

Her shoulders slumped. Sobs wracked her body. She fell to her knees, her legs no longer having the strength to hold her up. Liz glanced to where Ryland's body lay. Grief impaled her. Everything inside shattered, the pieces cutting her to ribbons with brutal reality.

Arie knelt beside Ryland, his large hands covering Ryland's bloodied chest. Arie's lips moved. Liz couldn't hear the words. None of it mattered anyway. Ryland was gone. Unless Arie was praying for him to be raised like Lazarus, there was no point.

Liz clawed her way to her feet. A slight relief blew over her when three of the men rose to their knees, dazed but alive. The leader lay prone, exactly how she'd left him. The weight in her soul crushed her. She moved toward him. Needing to feel a pulse. Needing him to still be alive. Not for him, but for her.

The back door flew open, and Hank burst out. He surveyed the scene before focusing on Liz. "Are you all right? What happened?" Panic laced his voice as his eyes ran over her.

Liz was barely able to form an answer. "They attacked Ryland. He's—" She choked. "Call 911." Her voice sounded scratchy. Not her own.

"Oh my God, is he okay?" The big man lunged for Ryland.

Arie didn't move, and Hank didn't appear to notice him.

Liz moved to pull Hank back. "Go call. Now. Before these guys get away." She couldn't tell him Ry was gone. The words wouldn't form.

Julie now stood on the back steps.

Hank yelled in Julie's direction. "Call an ambulance. Now." Hank spared a glance for the mostly incapacitated attackers. Then dropped down and started CPR on Ryland.

The fact he didn't question what she'd done, or how, wasn't lost on Liz.

Arie stood and walked toward the tree line, even though he was apparently cloaked from Hank's view. Liz moved away as well and left Hank to his fruitless labor, ignoring his calls for her help. Ryland was gone. There was a gaping hole inside of her. The place where she usually felt him. Nothing she or Hank could do was going to put Ryland's essence back where it belonged.

She wandered to the leader of the group and tentatively reached a hand for his wrist. A pulse pushed back against her fingers, strong and regular. She sighed a thankful breath and glanced at the others. The rest of the men huddled together, trying to get each other moving. Liz heard sirens in the distance and knew they wouldn't get far if they did run. Oddly, it brought her little satisfaction.

She looked back at Hank working on Ryland. She felt nothing. Liz had been reduced to a cold shell. Her heart had been dug out and now lay on the ground. Bruised, bloody, and non-functioning.

Arie stalked in her direction. His eyes held no sympathy. Gave no quarter.

"They ambushed him?" Arie motioned toward the humans. He raised his chin and sniffed the air. "And they weren't alone."

Liz nodded numbly. "Markus is a coward. Sent humans to do his dirty work, knowing Ry would hold back." She gritted her teeth. "He shouldn't have died like this. It's not right."

Fresh tears flooded her, and she avoided Arie's eyes. She didn't blame God. She blamed Markus. As anger besieged her again, Liz tamped it down with what little strength she had left. Never again.

"And you took it upon yourself to mete out vengeance." Arie's voice carried a lethal tone.

Right before her eyes, he morphed into his true form. The ominous, ancient warrior with fire in his eyes. His entire being radiated heat and flame. The sword on his hip, steel and conflagration. Never before had she seen this magnitude of majesty and power.

This was the Seraphim.

Liz's entire body trembled, and she stepped back, tripping in her haste. Heaven's fury poured out in a violent tidal wave. It stole her voice and all thought. She continued backing away from Arie, farther into the woods.

Arie's voice sounded foreign to her ears. Sadness tempered the steel as the timbre lowered. Liz felt the warning in every cell of her being.

"I suggest you search your heart. The Father has seen fit to bestow grace, and I recommend you not abuse it. Your perceived control is an illusion, Elizabeth. As has been demonstrated here."

He paused, and Liz nodded. Fear kept her lips pressed together.

"I have business." Arie was gone, and she was too terrified to even wonder why he was leaving.

"Liz?" Hank's pained cry shredded what was left of her heart. He ran to her and grabbed her arm. "I don't think…I mean, I can't…" He ran a hand down his face. "Honey, he's gone."

Liz stared. She allowed Hank to pull her back to the last place she wanted to be. She dropped to her knees beside Ryland. He was no longer there. Agony ate her alive, leaving her hollow.

Sirens grew louder in the distance.

Liz ran her hand gently across Ryland's swollen face. Her lips pressed a kiss to his forehead. Grief consumed her again, and she let it seep down her face as she bent over him. Her mind numb, she laid her cheek over his heart. She needed to be close to his warmth before it was gone forever.

Hank ran around the corner, officers and EMTs right behind him. The paramedics moved her aside and set to work. Hank stepped back and put an arm around a pale Julie. Liz stepped away.

Their work was pointless.

The paramedics' hands flew in constant motion as they worked. They thought they could still save him? She saw one of them shake his head. Maybe not. They loaded him onto a gurney, and she moved to follow as they headed to the ambulance. A hand on her arm stopped her.

"Liz Brantley?" the officer asked. She nodded.

A new kind of fear tore through her. Would she be in trouble? Or would they see it as self-defense? Would they even believe she'd inflicted the damage on the four assailants? She glanced around for Hank. He and Julie were being led back into the diner by an officer. Hank gave a nod and a sad smile before going inside.

"I'm going to need you to answer some questions. I understand the victim is your boyfriend. He was attacked?" She nodded as he jotted notes. "Those four jumped him, I take it?" He pointed to the group now surrounded by officers.

"Yes."

"And you jumped in to help?" The incredulity in his voice was almost an insult.

"I tried…"

The officer shook his head and narrowed his eyes. "Well, we've been looking for most of these boys anyway." He eyed her like he was still trying to figure things out. "Did you, uh, have a weapon?"

"Yes. A knife and—"

"Sarge? We need you for a minute," one of the other officers yelled.

"Well, looks like those fellas will be fine, I wish I could say the same for…" Sympathy filled his kind eyes. "I'll be back with a few more questions, but I think it's pretty clear-cut here. We'll get 'em locked up, and you won't have to worry about 'em, hopefully. Hang on." He smiled and walked to his men.

Liz nodded again. A violent flurry of emotion attacked her brain. Everyone around her was worked up. Added to the hurricane inside of her, the sensations pushed her to the breaking point. She grabbed her head and doubled over.

In the midst of the mental melee, ice wrapped itself around Liz's body. Evil tickled her senses, instigating a whole other riot in her head.

The air thickened. Twigs snapped behind her. Before she could fully stand, blinding pain smashed the back of her skull. Lights flashed behind her eyes. The world exploded in Technicolor.

The agony subsided as she slipped into darkness.

XXXIII
A Red Sun Rises

Markus's roar echoed through the massive garage.

Kade refused to defer to the enraged demon. Instead, he raised his chin, throwing down an unspoken challenge to his commander. Markus was currently at a disadvantage, having remained in his weaker, human form. Even if he hadn't been, Kade knew he could take him. Kade's strength had been growing, as had his following, right under the commander's nose. The moron hadn't even noticed.

Kade raised his voice. "I saw an opportunity. I took it." A sneer curled his lips.

An opportunity to better my own position.

"She was not to be touched. Your job was to kill Ryland." Markus stepped closer until they were nose to nose. "I would've thought getting revenge would have sufficed for you today. Did you even confirm the kill?"

Kade growled under his breath. "There's no way he survived." He'd seen Ryland's bloody mess of a body. The men Kade had chosen had done a fine job. He would've done it himself, but honestly, as long as the man was dead and out of his business, Kade couldn't care less who got the honor. He had bigger things to worry about.

"So no. Idiot!" Markus glanced at the woman bound in the corner. "Now half of Heaven will be breathing down our necks, even more determined than they were." He eyed Kade again. "All because you failed to follow orders."

Every muscle in Kade's substantial body tensed as he watched Markus kneel beside the woman. Kade quirked an eyebrow as Markus brushed the hair from her face.

Curious.

The commander grasped the woman's neck. Seconds later, he jerked his fingers away. Markus focused swirling red eyes on Kade as he stood.

Markus raised his hand, showing blood from the back of the woman's head. "I told you she wasn't to be harmed, yet I find this." Steam rolled off Markus's head, and the putrid smell of brimstone permeated the air.

Kade inhaled the familiar, homey aroma and pulled back his shoulders. Once again, he kept his gaze level, denying Markus the deference he demanded. Before Kade could react, Markus's fist flew through the air and connected with his jaw. Kade stumbled back.

Take the shots while you can, Markus. Things are about to change.

The commander was weak, and for centuries had a reputation for going soft when it came to his marks. Kade never made that mistake. He got what he wanted, what he needed, and left them with nothing. If he let them live at all.

"I did what was necessary. What you lack the spine to do." Kade rose to his full demonic height and extended his ebony wings. "You've lost sight of who we are and what we do. The human warriors were to be exterminated. Not—"

Kade's words were cut off by another blow from Markus. Kade flew several feet in the air and crashed in a rustle of leathery feathers and clang of metal. Markus was on him in a heartbeat, yanking him up by the breastplate.

"Enough! I am demon. I am Markus!" Markus morphed into his true form, and Kade laughed, black ooze dripping from his mouth. "I will eliminate them, and I will have victory. However, you will not be here to see it." Markus released Kade with a vicious shove. "You are relieved of your position. If you're lucky, you'll be reassigned. If not, you'll be banished to the pit for your insolence. Leave my sight!"

The building quaked and rocked. Dust shook loose from the rusty ceiling. The imps to Kade's right twittered and cowered.

Kade wiped the black tar from his lip with a grin. "As you wish. But know this. Lucifer will know how you have failed him. Your command will be mine. And I will personally see to your punishment." Kade laughed and edged toward the door.

"Leave before I disembowel you and have the imps cart your carcass away."

"Certainly, *my lord*." Kade spread his wings and took flight. He buzzed Markus's head as he swept away, his laugh rippling through the metal building.

Markus would regret this. Kade would have command, and he would make sure Markus suffered horribly. All in due time.

Markus sneered as he watched Kade fly away. If he'd been thinking straight, he would've gutted him as he passed over. The fact Kade had spoken the truth added sparks to the powder keg about to erupt inside of him. He worked his neck side to side as he donned his human meat suit again. It would work better than his demonic form for what he had in mind. His head jerked to the chattering imps cowering by an old lift.

"Be gone!" His command sent waves through the concrete floor.

When they didn't move fast enough, he pulled a knife from his belt and threw it with expert precision. The blade sank into the throat of the closest imp. The others scattered in a flurry. The body dissolved into the mist, and Markus was left alone with his prisoners. He spared a glance for the wide-eyed, whining girls in the corner opposite his prize. They were a part of another plan altogether. Too bad the human in charge of the girls had gotten himself arrested. He'd deal with that later. That particular plan didn't include Elizabeth, and he needed to focus on her right now.

Markus knelt beside Elizabeth. He surveyed her with curious eyes as she lay in a heap on the dusty floor. He had hoped he wouldn't have to kill her. Now, it was almost assured he would. He tilted his head as he watched her easy breathing. She entranced him. Elizabeth was destined for things she could never imagine, for power she couldn't conceive. Making her all the more attractive. Markus reached and smoothed his fingers along her brow and across her cheek.

I envy Arie-Chayal.

The angel had everything Markus desired. Arie-Chayal was still in the Father's grace, he had heavenly beauty and power, he wouldn't soon be banished to the pit for all eternity, and he was the guardian for this captivating creature.

Markus could've still had it all. Not relegated to being a desecrated, tormented being. His withered heart saddened as he thought of all he'd given up to follow Lucifer so long ago. The question that had dogged him for millennia tortured him more at this moment than ever before.

He banished the thought. There was nothing for it. He'd made his decision. His fate was sealed. Even though he fought a losing battle, he couldn't bring himself to back down. He was evil, his mission to corrupt and control. He would do so until the end.

Elizabeth stirred. Since she was here, he may as well take advantage. He couldn't release her. To send her back was unwise at best. Suicidal at worst. He had one more chance to sway her. With Ryland dead, Markus would make sure her despair would be her undoing. Oh yes, he'd received report of the havoc she'd wreaked in her rage. He would use it to prove to her there was evil in her. That she belonged with him.

Kade may not have been so wrong in taking her, after all.

Elizabeth's eyes fluttered open, and she struggled to sit up. When she focused on his face, panic flew across her features. It was soon replaced with fire. She fought against her restraints. He chuckled when she tried to stand. Liz slid back down the wall, hands flying up to hold her head. A cloud formed around her, dark and ominous.

Yes. Feel it. Become it.

Markus willed the fire to consume her. So much rage. So much anguish. Magnificent. His lips curled into a smile as she ceased her struggle. Markus leaned close to her soft skin.

"I'm pleased you've graced me with your presence, darling. We have much to discuss."

James Brantley covered the waiting room with prayer as he wore a trail in front of a row of chairs. He'd been at it for over three hours. That's how long they'd had Ryland in surgery. When they'd brought him in, they'd barely been able to maintain his weak heartbeat. The doctor had told them to prepare themselves. James had called Nathan to let him know about his brother. But even after several tries, there was no answer. He left a message, hoping Nathan would get it in time.

He glanced at his wife, who busied herself knitting as they waited. Her lips moved in silent prayers. She brought a smile to his face despite the situation. Teresa looked up with dark, tired eyes, and blessed him with a grin filled with encouragement.

Hank sat in the corner, finally quiet after apologizing more times than James could count for not watching out for Liz better. The poor man blamed himself for letting her get taken. The police assumed she'd been kidnapped by other members of the group who'd attacked Ryland. James knew there was someone else behind it. Someone the cops would never touch. Some *thing*.

The urge to go after his daughter welled inside again, and he forcefully pushed it down. *She's in God's hands.* He knew there was a plan, and her rescue was already in motion. The battle was upon them, and his warrior's heart surged. He hoped he'd get to be a part of it and have a hand in taking Markus down.

For now, he was needed here. The young man they loved like a son wouldn't wake up alone.

If he woke up at all.

James sighed. The fervency of his prayers increased. As they did, peace settled. He felt a familiar presence at his side. An encouraging touch on his shoulder. James patted the spot as thankfulness swirled in his chest.

Arie arrived in the waiting room to see Aelaem comforting his charge. Arie joined his spirit with Aelaem's to channel peace into the weary heart of the man of God. Arie moved to Teresa Brantley. Her protector, Levia, stepped aside, and Arie wrapped his velvety wings around the woman. He let the peace of Heaven flow through him to her, and joy flushed him as her face spread in a knowing smile. She couldn't see him, but she could feel him.

Arie turned toward Hadriel, who held Hank in the corner. At his nod, she moved to join him, as did Aelaem and Levia.

"Remain with them at all times." He motioned to the pastor and his wife. "We have four stationed in the operating room." Arie saw the question in their eyes before it was asked. "There is a guard stationed in the area where Elizabeth is being held, but we have been ordered not to intervene as of yet."

Their nods of acceptance were absolute. No one thought to question the order. They accepted the will of the Father without hesitation or doubt.

The angels left their captain's side and surrounded their charges, flaming swords drawn. Arie was about to take his leave when an urgent order rang out from above. In the blink of an eye, he was in the operating room at Chammu'el's side. His heart fell as he took in the scene. He raised his chin and reached to assist the surgeons alongside his brother.

Father, thy will be done.

XXXIV
Disaster

Liz awoke to the noxious odor of diesel fuel lingering in the air. She coughed, fighting back the dizziness from her screaming head. She opened her eyes, deliberately looking past the form to her left.

Lifts, random steel barrels, rusting parts. With a start, the knowledge of where she was sank in. The closed-down auto shop not far from the barn. She was certain because she'd been inside once with Dad, long ago.

Black memories stained her thoughts. It was a place similar to this where Alex had ensured she'd never forget him. Where decisions were made and things were done that had changed her life forever.

She moved her gaze to the demon. Seeing Blake's face hovering over her made Liz's stomach lurch. She tried to stand and ended up sliding back down, sheer agony splitting her skull. Nausea shoved the contents of her stomach into her throat. The ribbon of anger Liz had coiled tightly after coming unhinged earlier was rapidly coming unraveled. She strained to rein it in. She couldn't let herself fall back into that black hole. But guilt and grief taxed her tenuous control.

Ryland was dead. She'd been taken and stashed in a place akin to what lived in her nightmares.

Liz straightened her spine. She wasn't going to let Alex or Markus win. Even if she died in the fight, her soul would never fall. It belonged to Someone else now. She locked her defenses in place and shoved the hurt in a box. Silent prayers rumbled from her heart.

Muffled sounds on the other side of the room caught her ear. *It sounds like...* Liz craned her head to see around Markus. She sucked in a sharp breath, and the dizziness in her head intensified.

Two teenaged girls huddled in the corner. Dirty, trembling, clinging to each other. They had to be the ones who'd gone missing. They met her eyes, the sadness and hopelessness in theirs tearing at her soul. Markus followed her gaze and smiled, the sight chilling her.

Liz forced herself to think. She checked them over for external wounds the best she could from her position. They appeared to be intact, as far as she could tell. At least physically. But what could Markus possibly want with them? She tried not to think about that right now. She had to keep a clear head and find a way out. Which she would do as soon as she got those dang ropes off.

God, now would be a great time for some help!

After several minutes of twisting and yanking, she'd only succeeded in gouging bleeding grooves into her wrists. Liz stilled and settled for trying to set Markus on fire with a look. Or at least, delve into his brain and wreak some havoc. It was worth a shot.

Markus's eyelids lowered to half-mast. Blinding agony ripped through her head. Rancid images impaled her brain as he forced himself in. Liz's hands instinctively flew up to guard herself, struggling to expel him. As suddenly as it began, it was over. His presence receded. She sucked in air and dropped her head to her knees.

Markus snickered. "Darling, never try to play mind games with a master." He rearranged his position so she was trapped between his crouched legs and the wall. He blocked the girls from her line of vision.

A deep chill set into her marrow. "Don't call me darling. And stay out of my head."

"But you requested my assistance. Remember? What luck I was already keeping my eye on you." His voice slithered over her skin in a seductive rhythm. "You're special. You don't even realize your potential. I could show you."

What was he talking about? She'd never asked him for help. She thought back, and truth threw her eyes wide.

Yes, she had. She'd invited him in.

The past slapped her in the face. She saw herself surrounded by candles and books. She felt the evil that suffused the room. Heard the mysterious voice murmur he could help. That he could make the things she saw fade into nothing. Liz had believed since God had cursed her, there was no way He'd help her. In her desperation, she'd called to the other side.

Now she knew. It had been Markus who'd answered her traitorous call.

The words Ryland had spoken when she'd told him about her dabbling came flooding back. *Shut the door. Banish him from your mind.* He'd said in order to do it, she had to completely surrender to God.

Liz thought she had.

Clarity came in a rush. She hadn't let go of the past. She'd preserved pieces of it, hanging on to the guilt and fear. They propped the door open. Now the worst parts were walking through, and they had razors for teeth.

Markus ran a finger from her shoulder to her wrist. His heated hands burned her flesh, even as invisible frigid fingers shimmied up her spine. Liz jerked. Being trapped in a corner, she was unable to avoid his touch. He pinched her chin between his thumb and forefinger. Liz fought, and he clamped down harder. She shot him her best defiant glare.

When their gazes connected, her mouth went dry. His eyes were an inferno, the center red, darkening into black. The flame called to her. All thought scampered out of her mind like mice running from a tomcat.

His whisper tickled her ears. "No one knows the real you but me. If anyone else saw the darkness in your soul, they'd desert you." Markus cupped her jaw in his heated palm, and Liz barely denied the urge to lean in to it. "With me, you would never be alone."

She wasn't alone now. Was she? Her God, He was here with her. Wasn't He? *But Ryland is gone.* One more thing she couldn't have. One more piece of her heart mutilated beyond recognition. Doubt muddled Liz's brain. She was caught in a vortex begging to carry her away from the light. That light in the corner of her mind, urging her to fight.

She was so tired of fighting.

Markus's voice, silky as melted chocolate, sang a sweet song to her fatigued spirit. "We are the same. The fallen. Outcasts. Where do those like us belong, except together?"

Markus cradled her face in his hands. His fingers worked their way down her throat. Across her collarbones. Down her arms. Smooth. Languid. Sparks danced on her skin. A flame ignited. Want sprang to life, begging her to reach out to him. To take what he offered. To enjoy her fill.

Wait. She didn't want him. This feeling wasn't real.

Fight!

A voice pried into the edges of her mind. It rode the light, gaining power.

Resist the devil and he will flee from you.

Liz's head drooped. Her shoulders sagged. *So tired.*

Markus placed a hand over her heart. "You can't resist. You want this. Say it. Renounce your former life and begin a new one. Stop giving and take what's yours. What you deserve."

The thought gutted her. Liz could never deny Him. He'd saved her. Given her mercy and grace she didn't deserve. And then there was Ryland. She couldn't, wouldn't, spit on his memory by embracing everything he'd fought against. What if Markus was right, though? Did she have the power to resist? No, not her own. But she had access to a greater Power. If she could only tap in to it.

The fog lifted.

The Lord is their strength, and He is the saving refuge of His anointed.

Liz clung to the words emanating from the light. She yanked her head from Markus's grasp and shoved his palm away. Resistance blossomed.

She leveled her fierce gaze on an astonished Markus. "You're wrong. I can resist. Just needed a little help." Liz pushed herself upright, the dizziness waning. "You were right about one thing, though. There is darkness in me. I may fight it every day. But I'll never fight alone." Strength flowed through her weary body.

She wasn't just fighting to free herself. Now she had others to fight for. Liz glanced at the girls, staring at what was happening with wide eyes. She gave them what she hoped was an encouraging smile. Then she turned back to their captor.

Markus narrowed his eyes, and Liz saw recognition flash. The knowledge he'd lost his hold on her.

Forever.

The door into her mind and spirit slammed shut to him. The sound reverberated off the metal walls.

He rose to his feet and glared. His jaw worked, and every muscle he had rippled and tensed. "You had your opportunity. No more chances."

A new vigor revived her stubborn, sarcastic spirit. "Look who's talking. You ran out of chances a long time ago. At least I still have choices." A smirk shaped her lips.

Markus roared. The sound shook the ground and rattled the metal building. A building that brought back memories that no longer held sway over her. The ties were broken. The wounds would heal.

He seized her bound wrists and yanked her around. Liz's head snapped back and smacked the concrete, sending shards slashing through her wounded skull. The girls yelped. Liz heard them shuffle but couldn't see what they were doing. Probably trying to hide. Markus dragged her across the floor toward an interior door. Fear tickled the back of her neck.

Liz tried to pull her feet under her. Markus moved too quickly. Her back raked over a section of grates. Her T-shirt shredded as the metal ripped into her flesh. She ground her teeth. A vision of Ryland gritting his teeth flitted through her head.

I will not cry.

Prayers tore from her lips, loud and feverish. Markus laughed. It spurred her on. Markus had something planned for her she may not survive. Fine. She wouldn't go out alone. And she'd do what she could to free those girls first. With her last breath if she had to.

The thought numbed the pain in her mind, shoving the fear down and bringing clarity. If she were going down, she wouldn't make it easy on him. She'd tear the place down with Markus in it.

Markus grabbed the doorknob, then froze. "What do you want?" he barked.

Liz craned her neck to see who he was speaking to. The imposing demon had entered so silently, Liz hadn't even know he was there. The new addition spoke in that strange language she'd heard them use before. Liz saw the girls looking at Markus like he'd lost his mind.

Oh, yeah. They can't see the demons. Must think he's talking to himself.

As Markus responded to the demon in the same, odd language, an idea sparked. This could be her chance.

She was mostly hidden from the other demon behind Markus and a crate. A plan formed in her mind. Carefully, moving an inch at a time, she pulled her legs into a crouch. Her lacerated back screamed its disagreement. Liz held her arms as still as possible to not alert Markus to her movement. The underling demon lowered his head and closed his eyes as Markus berated him.

Markus switched back to English. "If they want a fight, we will oblige. Tonight the ground will be watered with the blood of angels."

"Yes, my lord." The demon bowed and disappeared.

Now or never.

Liz jumped. She rammed her shoulder into the arm gripping her and drove a short snap kick to Markus's knee. He stumbled and grunted, releasing her. Liz slammed her joined hands into his temple, then bolted toward the girls. Her head pounded, and the open skin on her back pulled and stung with each step.

They were already on their feet, having seen what she was doing. She motioned for them to move, and they took off running ahead of her, straight for the back door.

Please let it be unlocked. And no guards.

Right as she reached the door the girls thankfully had just run through, steel arms clamped around her middle and flung her feet into the air. She kicked and writhed. His grip tightened, shutting off her air supply. Without a thought to the already searing pain in her head, she flung it back. He tilted, and she smacked his shoulder instead.

Markus grinned. "Nice try." He hauled her across his body. One arm locked around her midsection to restrain her upper body, and one wrapped around her legs. "I'm nowhere near finished with you."

His laugh dragged icy fingers through her veins. He whipped around and headed back the other way. The ache in Liz's head was excruciating, and her back was on fire where his arm raked the gashes. Warmth trickled down to her tailbone. A ringing set up between her ears, and her vision blurred. At least those girls had gotten away. She hoped.

God, please. I don't think I have a lot of time here.

Or maybe she did. Which might be worse. A ticked-off demon with a grudge and a point to prove was not a recipe for fun. Panic electrified her muscles. Liz jerked wildly as Markus kicked open the door, imbedding the knob into the sheetrock behind it.

Somebody had to be coming for her. She had to stall. Get him talking. He loved to hear himself talk.

Markus tossed her into a chair. Her entire body protested at the impact. The rough fabric abraded her wounds, opening them further. She couldn't stop the strangled noise clawing up from her throat.

Markus reached behind her and grabbed several bungee cords. "Can't have you trying to escape again."

The tears won.

Markus wrapped the cords around her shoulders, midsection, and feet, binding her tightly to the chair. He straightened and shook out his arms before stretching his neck side to side. The face she had once thought so beautiful twisted with malice and intent.

He touched a heated finger to her lips, and Liz wrenched away. "It didn't have to be this way. You made this choice. Now there are consequences."

His hand clamped on her jaw, squeezing with such force she

thought the bones would shatter. He traced a finger from her lips, down the center of her chest, all the way to her belly button. A disgusted shiver wracked her. Followed closely by a blistering shot of terror.

Markus laughed, low and menacing. "Ah, so many options. So much time." He settled both hands on the arms of the chair and leaned close, his hot breath feathering across her skin. "By the end of this night, I'll know every secret you have."

Please, no. God, please. Markus's words, the promise contained in them, dropped an iron ball into her gut. Abject horror curdled her blood.

Markus rummaged in an old toolbox. Liz thrashed against her bonds. Adrenaline surged. She fought and prayed, willing strength to her muscles. He laid something on the cluttered desk and leisurely rolled up the sleeves of his expensive-looking silk shirt. Picking up the object and twirling it in his hand, he grinned.

A retractable knife with a razor-thin blade.

It glinted in the waning light peeking through the broken blinds. As he moved in, Liz mentally checked out and switched into survival mode. This was a battle, and she would win. Whatever it took.

Markus leaned over her, his red-rimmed eyes looking strange in Blake's face. "What do you say? Ready to find out who Elizabeth Brantley really is?"

Bring. It. On.

XXXV
Lift Up Your Face

The doors to the operating room flew open, and a bevy of doctors burst out. James Brantley's head snapped up. Each face displayed a different expression, and he couldn't get a clear read on any of them. A hard knot settled in the pit of his stomach.

James touched his wife's hand, and they both rose as the group came to a stop in front of them. He took a deep breath and prepared himself. He put his arm around Teresa's shoulders and drew her close. The doctors continued to chat among themselves, so James cleared his throat.

"How is he?" He struggled to keep his voice even.

The lead surgeon was the first to speak. "I've never seen anything like it. Amazing. Simply amazing." The doctor shook his head. "It's a miracle!"

The other doctors started in again. Everyone talked at once. The Brantleys stared open-mouthed at the group.

James lifted his hand. "Wait a minute. What miracle?"

The surgeon's head swiveled from side to side. "His internal injuries were extensive. His spleen had ruptured, and his liver was perforated. And his heart, well…" Awe filled the man's words. "As we worked, the field kept filling with blood, and we were about to call it." He rubbed his temples.

Another doctor broke in. "When we suctioned and had a visual of the area again, the sutures were gone, and the organs were repaired.

As if the injury had never happened. An honest-to-God miracle." The man's awe shone on his face.

James stared, a slow grin spreading across his cheeks. He glanced at his wife. Tears rolled down her face. *Thank you, Lord.*

James's smile broadened, and he wiped away a tear with the back of his hand. "Can we see him?"

"Certainly." The other doctors filtered away, shaking their heads as the lead surgeon grinned. "He should be coming out of the anesthesia. I'll walk you back." The doctor led the way, uttering "Amazing" the whole way. "Right in there." He pointed at the room and walked away, still shaking his head.

They entered recovery to see Ryland sitting up and sipping a cup of water. He was pale, bruised, and swollen, but a smile spread across his face. It slowly faded as he looked behind them.

"Where's Liz?" Ryland's voice cracked, and a frown tugged his lips down.

James cleared his throat. "She was taken." The words stuck in his throat.

Ryland's jaw flexed, and his brow furrowed. He tossed back the blanket and threw his legs over the side of the bed. The pastor placed a hand on Ryland's shoulder. James knew instantly there was no way he'd be able to stop him.

Truth be told, he had no intention of trying.

Ryland had no doubt who was to blame.

Markus.

Rage clawed at him with steel fingers. *I'll tear him apart.* Never in his life had he hated a thing so much. Even Kade. He had to get Liz back. Now. A new thought laid him raw. It was his fault Markus had the chance to grab her.

He'd known the minute he'd walked out of the diner something was wrong. He should've never left her. They could've come up with a plan together. Instead, he'd decided to handle it himself, hoping to protect her.

After checking Ryland over from head to toe and nodding to her husband, Mrs. Brantley gave Ryland a hug and left the two men alone. Ryland glanced at Chammu'el, standing guard in the corner. With a glance, the angel let him know he'd back Ryland's play. Ryland caught the pastor's eye and saw the recognition he needed.

Everyone was on board.

Ryland eased his legs to the floor. He swayed, thankful for the arm Pastor Brantley tossed around his shoulders. It didn't take Ryland long to get solid. Without a word, he grabbed the clothes the pastor handed him and slid them on, followed by his boots. Ryland forced himself not to think about what Markus might be putting Liz through. His heart called to hers to hang on and fight.

I'm sending that thing back to Hell, tonight. God, give me speed and strength. Keep her safe.

"What's the plan?" Pastor Brantley asked.

"Markus moved their operation to an abandoned shop out on 25. I'm assuming that's where he'll have her." Ryland winced at the discomfort in his still-healing body. "We'll gear up and head over there."

The thought crossed his mind it was the worst place in the world for her to be. Those ghosts still haunted her. That building could make them corporeal. He prayed she'd stay strong until he could get to her.

Ryland ignored the nurse yelling at him as they strode down the hall, Arie appearing on one side, Chammu'el on the other. The group stopped by the waiting room to grab Mrs. Brantley and scooted out the door before the nurse could catch them.

Arie leaned over and whispered in Ryland's ear as they crossed the parking lot.

Ryland lowered his voice so only the pastor could hear. "The angels are ready and waiting on us. If you're in this."

The pastor nodded. "I'm not sitting this one out." The man's tone boded no argument.

"Absolutely." Ryland knew even suggesting he stay behind would be pointless. "You can keep guard." He frowned, the idea of giving orders to the man foreign to him. "I mean, there might be a few humans to deal with." The pastor gave him an odd look, and Ryland tried to qualify it. "You can't fight what you can't see, sir."

James Brantley grinned as he put his wife in the car and shut the door. He rounded on Ryland and clapped his shoulder. "Son, trust me, I can fight." He opened the driver's door and leaned over the car. "There are a few things we need to discuss."

"Are you going to actually do something, or just talk me to death?"

Liz let her old defenses slip into place. She knew she shouldn't be antagonizing him. Yet the words popped out of their own volition.

Markus grinned and stopped twirling the blade. "Playing the tough girl until the end, I see. By all means, let's begin."

He dropped to his knees in front of her. Markus tilted his head, and his eyes roamed her body, sending a shiver through her. He reached for her arm and held it in an iron grip as she fought to pull away. He struck in a flash. The steel slid across her skin like it was butter.

The cords held her in place. She bit her lip and stifled a cry. Markus smiled, eyes shining with wicked light. He plunged in again.

Liz had no idea how long it went on. Each cut, each hit, compounded her agony. She bit her lip until it bled. She squeezed her eyes shut and sent her mind elsewhere. She was determined not to break. A weak laugh trickled from Liz's lips. Maybe she was losing her mind. Blood pooled underneath the rickety chair, the puddle expanding with every drop from her torn body.

Liz let her gaze fall to her red-crusted arms and the shredded denim covering her legs. The last round of cuts closed, and the flow ceased. Traces of blood remained, but the wounds healed. She marveled once again over the miracle of the instant healing. But she could still feel the pain. She closed her eyes and waited for it to ebb. After a few seconds' reprieve, it began again, instigated by Markus's sadistic ministrations. Liz struggled to stay conscious, to stay alert for any opportunity to break free.

I appreciate the healing, God. Could we skip the slashing part?

Markus peered at her through narrowed eyes, not hiding his displeasure that she hadn't broken. She ignored each verbal jab or gave a flippant response of her own. Every time he asked her if she'd had enough and was ready to change her decision, she laughed in his face. He swung across her abdomen, anger lighting his face.

Liz flinched. Ah, didn't like his handiwork disappearing, did he?

Liz hadn't felt anything this time. She looked down. A thin, red line formed through the slice in her shirt. *Okay...* As she watched, the cut sealed.

Slowly, she lifted her head to see Markus fuming. Smoke wafted from his skin. *Whoa.* That was new. Liz flashed him a toothy grin. She even winked. What was wrong with her? *Don't poke the beast, idiot.*

With a low roar, Markus swiped again. Over and over he slashed and gouged. Liz felt only pressure. No more pain. Every time, the cuts sealed immediately. Life-giving fluid remained where it belonged, not adding to the puddle on the floor.

Liz didn't even try to stop the laugh rumbling out of her belly. Tears, now of joy, fell freely. How could she ever doubt now? She had no idea why she'd felt the cuts earlier and not now. Maybe it was a test. She didn't know, and she didn't care. All she knew was God had shown up.

Sulfuric-smelling smoke now filled the room, stinging her eyes. She couldn't usually sense emotion from demons, or angels for that matter, unless it was extremely powerful. This time, she was bombarded with a wall of fury from Markus.

Liz gave another smile, cracking her abused lip open further. "No weapon formed, remember? Got any other bright ideas?"

Markus bellowed. He brought the back of his fist down, crashing into the side of her face. The chair sailed across the small room, smacking the other wall and landing on its side. Her jaw felt like it'd been shattered with a hammer, and the taste of iron filled her mouth again.

Don't get cocky. Got it.

Liz had to stay focused. She had to be more careful. Her attitude was about to bite off more than a mouthful.

Especially when she was tied to a stinking chair.

"Laugh while you can." Markus glided across the floor. He jerked the chair upright and set it down so hard, her teeth rattled and her brain clunked against her battered skull. "You'll beg for me to end you soon." He shook his head. "Such a waste."

He shocked her by gripping her hair and slamming his lips down to kiss her. Bile rose in her mouth. The kiss she had once craved now sent revulsion swirling through her veins. He pulled away with a smile and kicked the chair back against the wall.

Liz turned her head and spat. "That's the last time—"

Liz's lungs compressed. The darkness in the room intensified. Ice crawled its way up her back, ending in a collection of tingles at her neck. Evil became a tangible thing, clawing at her flesh.

Mist floated into the room, darker than the haze generated by Markus's rage. The acrid odor choked her, sending Liz into a spasm of strangled coughing. She glanced at Markus. The coal black had dominated his eyes, a glowing red pupil pinpointing the center.

His smile made her stomach drop. "My army is here. I'm afraid you've run out of time."

Liz worked down the lump in her throat. She breathed deep, trying to ignore the stench and instead draw in peace. Her chin shot up in a show of defiance.

God, uh, now would be a great time to send in the troops.

Markus's gaze never left hers. His body began to change. *Finally.* She would never have admitted it, but Markus torturing her while he looked like Blake made it worse. She welcomed his demon form.

Darkness deepened, seeping into every corner. Markus's true skin claimed its territory, the structure of that beautiful face still evident under the ruined covering.

"Taking human form stifles my abilities." Markus stretched, his wings spanning the room. "Now I can demonstrate real power."

Liz gasped as he reached out with clawed hands, grabbed the chair, and pulled her toward him.

"You think losing your precious Ryland was bad? You haven't seen terrible. I will destroy everything you love while you watch, and after, you will die. Painfully." He tossed her back again. "We'll see how powerful your God is."

The mention of Ryland filled her eyes. She blinked away the heartache. Liz stared Markus down, putting all the power she possessed into her voice. "My guess is you'll be seeing His power any minute now."

Markus leaped at her. He dragged his vicious claw across her midsection. She screamed as the talons sliced her skin, unable to hold it back this time. Four deep, red grooves pooled, stretching from one side to the other. Liz closed her eyes, praying hard and out loud. Yeah. She'd felt that one.

Stay strong. Just a little longer. Liz pulled up courage from her toes. God had a plan. She just had to hold out. She plastered another smile on her face. Deep down, she knew this was not going to be her end.

"You're more foolish than I thought." Markus gave a chilling laugh. "Your God has abandoned you. It's over." His eyes darkened further. "Wipe that stupid grin off your face."

A swift blow landed to her cheek, snapping her head back and swiveling the chair in circles. She knew she must look insane with her smile firmly in place and blood trickling from her mouth. She didn't care. He wasn't going to win, no matter what happened here.

Liz had another smart-aleck comment all ready when a warm tingle started in her toes and coiled up her body. It gained vigor as it flowed. The warmth permeated the room, chasing away the heaviness of evil. Exhilaration and pure joy flooded her system. Invisible, brilliant power encased her. Markus was forced to take a staggering step back as light effervesced around her.

Liz could sense them. Hundreds of angels. Maybe more, for all she knew. They encircled the evil beyond these walls. Strength surged in her blood. She could feel her guardian and the others—visualize their stoic faces, ready for battle.

Markus's brow furrowed. Fire flashed in his eyes. She could've sworn she saw fear skitter across his face and crawl over his flesh.

Liz raised an eyebrow, her grin impossibly bright.

"I think the cavalry just arrived."

XXXVI
Worlds Collide

The near-liquid, heavy air made breathing difficult. Buzzing filled Ryland's ears, right before sharp stings pricked his skin. Just what they needed. Mosquitos the size of birds. Ryland remained motionless. His sole focus was getting to Liz and taking out Markus.

Ryland glanced at James Brantley, crouched by his side. He marveled again at the big pastor's gliding movements as they'd crept through the woods. Even with his hulking frame, Ryland had stealth in spades and could sneak in undetected with the best of them. James Brantley put him to shame. The man moved like a ghost.

He'd always thought the pastor moved like a soldier. Hadn't known why. Ryland knew he'd never been in the military. Now he understood.

Liz was going to flip.

"Four guards out front. Human," James whispered.

"Fewer than I expected." Ryland's shoulders didn't relax.

The exterior lights on the building and a large dome suspended on a pole lit the area nicely, giving them a good visual as night fell. His eyes slid over the structure. Then a scream rent the silent air, and Ryland almost leaped out of position. James's hand on his shoulder held him back. James shook his head once.

"Lizzy," Ryland hissed.

"I know, son. Just hang tight."

"Minimize your contact with the humans." Arie moved behind the two men without a sound. "Put them down quickly and as gently as possible."

Like any of this was gonna go gently. Ryland kept his snort to himself. Both men nodded. Ryland did a quick weapons check. He noticed Pastor Brantley did the same.

The pastor had a dagger strapped to each leg, a holster with a .40 caliber pistol on his belt and two additional clips, a k-bar military knife on the other side, and twin katanas slung over his back. Ryland was similarly armed—he just hadn't expected it from his companion.

Every muscle in Ryland's body twitched, burning for action. He could feel Liz's fear and her agony. But those feelings weren't in control of her. Courage, determination, and defiance struck him hardest. A small grin tugged at his lips. *That's my girl.*

"Arie, when will we—"

The atmosphere thickened. A mist crawled along the ground. Weight, invasive and dark, slammed into Ryland's midsection. The nape of his neck prickled with sweltering heat. The stench of sulfur overwhelmed the earthy scent of the forest.

The demonic army had arrived.

They began to appear, scattered around the men who remained oblivious out front. Behind the building, hellish creatures dotted the space and extended into the trees. Soldiers were positioned on both sides of the garage, surrounding the area.

"A few more than I expected." Ryland wasn't afraid. Maybe a little nervous. He'd never faced this many at once before.

"I'm thinking we'll have a little help. Even up the score." James grinned, his eyes sparkling.

Ryland nodded, marveling at this side of Liz's dad he'd never seen. As they crouched and waited, Ryland couldn't keep his ire from building. The idea Markus had put his hands on Liz made his insides boil. He could feel the pain in her body as if it were his own. There were wounds everywhere. She'd been tortured.

It would take all he had not to do the same to Markus.

Yet Ryland was certain to the core of his being God wasn't going to take her from him. Not today. He let the knowledge seep in and temper the rage wanting to explode and wreak havoc.

Maybe he could help her, reassure her. Arie had said she thought he was dead. Could he use their connection to let her know he was still with her? He motioned for Arie. After a quick whisper and a nod from the angel, Ryland relaxed and closed his eyes.

Before he could put his plan into motion, a strange sensation crawled up his spine. Power swirled. Peace and light joined forces and mixed in a rapturous duo, brightening the night. Strength flowed through his veins. His body felt charged, like lightning could shoot out his fingertips.

Ryland looked up, as did James, and they both caught their breath. The sky lit up, and warriors descended. Seraphim floated to earth in all their flaming, heavenly glory. Eyes and swords blazed in blinding brilliance. They landed with a grace and litheness he had no clue existed. The forces of darkness had no choice. They had to step back.

A desperate need to fight blanketed him. A consuming desire to destroy Hell's minions took over. Every muscle in Ryland's body coiled tight, ready to strike. Lights flared behind the men. Arie and Chammu'el moved behind James and Ryland, now in full heavenly form.

Heaven's legion was primed for battle.

Ryland tightened his grip on the sword in his hand. Liz's sword. He focused on reaching her. He concentrated on letting her feel him. Arie seemed to think it would work. His thoughts homed in on Liz. Ryland put everything he had into connecting with her. Recognition flared through their link. Disbelief. Finally, acceptance and pure joy. The love and sheer elation pumping into him filled his heart to overflowing.

Ryland turned his attention back to the battlefield. Now it was time to get his arms around her. His focus narrowed to the imminent fight. The warrior took control, awakening within him with power and fortitude. All other thought shoved to the back of his mind.

Arie sounded a battle cry that shook the earth. The clash of steel and flesh echoed through the trees as the heavenly force engaged. James nodded at Ryland. They charged full-bore toward the warehouse with Arie and Chammu'el at their sides.

A thunderous roar exploded from Markus to coincide with the detonation of emotion within Liz. The combination set her brain on fire. *Oh God, it's too much.* She tried to free her hands to grab her head, but the cords wouldn't give. Rage and violent intent were the first to hit. At first she thought it came from Markus, until she realized it was directed *at* him. Someone near planned on ripping him to shreds.

Markus growled. "Sit tight. I'll be back for you." He crashed through the window and into the chaos.

Liz tried to clear her head. The agony in her skull stole her concentration. If she could calm the flow, she could think. The rage quieted. Worry followed, soon replaced with focus and love. An awe-inspiring love infused the depths of her heart and pervaded the turmoil in her mind. The soul behind it connected with hers.

Not possible.

Ryland?

Liz closed her eyes and centered her thoughts, reaching out. She had no idea if it would work, but she had to know. Her heart fluttered, and her stomach pitched as she sorted through the sensations scrambling for attention.

The battle outside began with the deafening clash of metal and ferocious war cries. She picked up everything swirling in the air around her. Liz sorted through each emotion, each consciousness. *Angel. Demon.* Until she found the essence she hunted for. Her pulse seized.

Ryland. But, she'd watched him die.

Liz sucked in a breath. Her heart started back up with a lurch. Not knowing how, or even caring, she knew he was making her aware of his presence. His battle rage filtered through, infecting her. Her limbs tingled with the need to fight. Liz struggled against her bonds. The cords raked over the open wounds.

Liz jerked and pulled. Her movements sent the chair careening into a wall. Unable to kick or reach to stop herself, she smacked the drywall. She yelled when knives tore into her head and along her body. The chair landed at an awkward angle, propped against a crate.

Great. Any other brilliant ideas, Einstein?

Liz sensed Ryland getting closer. A sudden spear of agony carved down her back. It wasn't hers. *God, he's been hit!* She couldn't even form full prayers anymore. She winced at the sharp sting. It faded. Liz breathed her thanks, wondering how she'd felt his wounds. Again.

A question for later.

She returned her attention to getting out of her predicament. The bungee cords around her had slid up and loosened in her flight across the room. Ignoring the agony, she worked her arms until the cords slipped farther up. Finally, she was able to work them above her shoulders and wriggle out from under them.

Liz reached for the bonds on her legs. She unhooked them and tossed the cords aside. She sprang from the seat and immediately grabbed the wall as the world spun. Once she righted herself, she searched for the knife Markus had used to free her hands. Not finding it, she headed out of the office and hoped they'd left a weapon lying around.

Liz flattened her body against the wall and peeked out. Good and evil were zinging around every which way, and it was hard to tell who was where. Seeing the building was empty, Liz eased out, hugging the wall as she headed for the back door. She wondered again if the girls had made it out. She'd done all she could for them, so hopefully they were safe.

She'd almost made it when the door blew off its hinges and sailed into the garage. Liz ducked behind a stack of metal shelving. The makeshift shelter was quickly abandoned when a rush of love and sheer desperation blasted into her.

Liz rounded the corner and flung herself at Ryland. His battle-hardened features softened as he crushed her to him. The pain the action caused was secondary. She didn't care. A tear sneaked down her cheek, and she bit back the rising sob. It wasn't the time to fall apart.

Ryland's voice was hoarse. "How bad are you hurt?" He took in the smeared, streaked blood decorating her tattered clothes.

"I'm fine. Now. I thought you'd... How did you...?" Words hung up in her throat.

"We'll talk about that later. We need to fight now. Can you do that?"

Ryland didn't let her answer. He favored her lips with a quick kiss. He reached for his dagger and sliced through the ropes binding her hands. He grabbed her wrists and kissed them both, his eyes never leaving hers. The sound of a throat clearing brought them back. Arie stood right behind Ryland. Liz launched herself into his arms.

The angel patted her back. "Are you well? Can you fight?"

"Yeah." Fire shot through her to her toes. "I can fight."

Ryland retrieved the sword he'd thrown down and placed it in her hand. Liz had never been so happy to see a weapon. She was more than ready to use it, dizziness or not.

Liz followed the man and the angel to the door. "The two girls were here. I gave them a chance to run, and they went out the door, but then—Markus! Did you see Markus? He jumped out the window when the battle started."

Ryland's head swiveled at break-neck speed. "Were they all right?"

"Seemed to be. I'm not sure. I'm not even sure why he took them."

"They were retrieved." Arie broke into the conversation. "The girls made it to the highway, and a kind couple happened by." His eyes glinted, and she didn't have to wonder who the "couple" really were. "They are on their way to their respective homes."

Liz's heart eased, then sped up again. "But, Markus. Have you seen him?"

"No, I haven't. Not yet." Ryland ground out the words.

Blades at the ready, Liz sandwiched between Arie and Ryland, they moved out.

Light streaked across the night as Seraphim darted through the darkness. Liz held her breath, so amazing was the sight. Black and white vapor trails collided in the sky, then crashed to the ground. Flaming swords swung with the fury of Heaven, cleaving demons in two. Battle cries, groans, and the clash of weapons and armor echoed across the valley in a surreal scene.

Ryland snapped her out of her state of awe. "We need to get up front and check on your dad. Something tells me he's fine, though."

"What is my dad doing here?" Liz raised an eyebrow. Leave it to Dad to fly into the middle of a war to get her. "Wait. What makes you think he's fine?"

Ryland coughed and sliced through an imp before turning back to her. "I'll let him answer that."

They ducked to avoid the top half of a demon before it thudded into the side of the building. Sidriel appeared at their side. He nodded, grinned, and jumped back into the madness. His blade dripped black. He looked as though he were having the time of his life.

Liz, Ryland, and Arie cut a path toward the front. With every swing, Liz felt stronger, power surging around and through her. A demon took aim at Ryland's head from behind.

"Duck!"

Ryland crouched. She used his back as a springboard, swinging her sword with all she had. The demon stared with eyes wide before sliding to the ground. In two pieces.

"Thanks." Ryland yanked his blades from another body.

"Anytime."

The battle lessened as they moved, the majority of forces concentrated behind the building and farther off in the valley. Liz's chest heaved. She could feel herself still healing. She wasn't one hundred percent yet.

The threesome rounded the corner, and the breath flew right out of Liz's mouth as it dropped open. Her eyes went wide, and her sword hung, limp, by her side.

In the center of scattered, downed human guards and several black, smoky piles stood Aelaem and Dad. Dad wandered among the men, speaking to them or praying over them, tying up the conscious first. Others stay as they lay, obviously having put up quite a fight and paying for it. She had no doubt they were still alive, though.

When the angel and the elder warrior looked up at the trio staring at them, they grinned ear to ear. Dad ran to Liz and scooped her up. She woodenly returned the hug, reality not quite computing. Dad. Fighting demons. With Aelaem. Dumbstruck, she stared up at her father.

"Are you okay?" Dad's brow furrowed as he took her in.

"Yeah. Good. I'm…good." The truth rained down on her hazy brain. "Why didn't you tell me?" Liz squeaked out.

"Well, I don't usually do this anymore." He laughed. "I'm retired, you could say."

Liz pointed at the carnage behind him as the humans groaned and tried to get up. "I don't think you understand retirement."

"Guess not." Dad shrugged. "You had to find your own path. I had my call—you had yours. So I just tried to point you in the right direction."

"And I didn't listen." Liz shook her head, and the twinge of betrayal she'd felt when she'd found out about Ryland reared its head. She squashed it. "This is…a lot." Liz ducked, a black wing sailing over them and the luminescent white one on its tail. "Uh, maybe we should talk about this later."

Ryland and Dad nodded, Arie and Aelaem having already left their sides to rejoin the fighting.

"Let's find Markus." Ryland's face became stone, and Liz felt him clamp down on all emotion.

"I know he's still here." Liz shivered. "I can feel him."

"He's probably—"

Chammu'el crashed down in front of them, tangled with a ball of blackness. He raised his sword, and with two swipes made quick work of the demon. He sauntered over to them with a wide smile. It was apparent this angel lived for battle.

"Markus is around back, near the tree line." Chammu'el spread his wings. "The Lord prevail!" He launched skyward.

Dad grinned again, Ryland shook his head, and Liz stared. Fear crept up her spine as she felt Markus draw near. The back of her neck tingled. He was looking for her. How she knew was beyond her. Yet there was no doubt in her mind. She'd find him first. This ended tonight.

Dad blocked an incoming blade, slicing across the demon's middle. A sharp kick displaced the creature's knee. Dad swung true, sending his sword straight through and out the creature's back. The demon fell to the ground as Dad removed the blade.

Dad glanced up at them, and he pulled his knife. "I'll meet you two back there. Go with God." Dad tore off into the trees after a running demon.

"He seems to be in his element." Ryland laughed.

"Uh-huh." Liz raised her sword and readied her stance for the two demons coming at them.

Her limbs trembled, and she swallowed hard. She couldn't shake the fear in her belly. But the fear quickly morphed into anger. Deep breaths. She couldn't let the rage take control ever again. Anger had no place here. Neither did fear.

"Don't worry." Ryland stalked forward, Liz on his right flank. "I'm right here with you. We'll do this together."

Liz nodded as they closed in on the demons. "You're in my head again."

"Yeah."

"We need to have a conversation when this is over." Liz moved wide right while Ryland edged to the left.

"We will." Ryland settled into position. "Ready?"

"Ready."

XXXVII
The Brave Ones

A curved, rusty blade careened through the sticky air, intent on taking Liz's head. She ducked as it skimmed her hair. Liz stayed low and sank her sword into the demon's liver. If they even had livers.

"You good?" Ryland yelled. He landed with a grunt, a flailing demon on top of him.

"Better than you right now."

Ryland kicked up and propelled the creature over his head. He flipped backward, landed on top, and pinned the creature with both blades. Ryland bobbed his eyebrows at her and aimed for the demon lumbering up behind him.

Liz took off in his direction. Scaly arms cinched around her from behind. She mule-kicked back and shoved off. Liz swung her sword as she whirled, but the momentum threw her off. The demon lunged for her. A second later, a beam of fire sliced through the demon. A brilliant, ethereal Hadriel stood next to the fallen enemy. The angel nodded and swept away in a blur of light and flame.

"Thanks!" Liz yelled to her back.

Liz slid to the left to avoid getting kabobbed. The blade snagged her shirt, grazing her side. She hissed and took the demon's legs out from under it with her sword.

"Need help?" Ryland shouted as he kicked to one side, and then the other, knocking both attackers back several steps.

"Nah. Got it." Liz was now the one doing the skewering.

When the immediate threats had been dispatched, Liz and Ryland worked their way down the side of the building. They battled as one, back to back. When they were parted, they returned to position quickly. Nothing separated them for long.

Liz couldn't help her smile, even in the midst of battle. The two of them fought as a cohesive unit. Ryland urged Liz forward and reined her in when necessary. She did the same for him. He gave her a grin before stepping away to dispatch another demon.

When it looked like they'd be overwhelmed, an angel would appear. The warriors would slash through the disfigured bodies of their former brethren with heavenly fire. When the threat was largely contained, the angels would leave, a pile of demonic pieces sinking into the mist behind them.

Gotta love that kind of backup.

Finally, Liz and Ryland reached the back of the garage. The angels had done a magnificent job of thinning out the demons. The fight was nearly over. Liz grinned. If Lucifer and his army had thought her hometown was an easy target, they had another thing coming. Soon, Markus's thrall would be broken, and, hopefully, they could squash whatever he had cooking that involved those girls. If he ever showed himself.

"Can you still sense him?" Ryland tossed the question over his shoulder.

"Yeah." Liz kicked out and sent a demon flying into a flaming blade.

"I have yet to see Kade or sense him. Anything?" Ryland crisscrossed his blades, sending a charred head to the ground.

"No. Markus banished him. I think. I was kinda out of it." Liz's stomach clenched. "He's close."

"I've got your back, babe. Stay focused." Ryland moved to where she could feel his heat behind her.

What was Markus waiting for? Within seconds, Liz had her answer.

The first wave smashed into her. She gasped. The darkness clasped razor-like fingers around her, battering at her mental barriers, trying to annihilate them.

"Liz?" Ryland reached for her.

"Ry, I need—"

A second wave of attack ripped the words from her tongue as Ryland was attacked from behind. Liz's head exploded internally, a haze settling after the blast. She stumbled, nearly walking into a sword. Liz slid to the left and raised her blade too slowly to block the next attempt. Arie swooped in, taking the demon down with movements too fast to track.

God, help me. Tears stung the backs of her eyes. The barriers she'd erected against Markus were holding for the most part, but he was battering them for all he was worth. She rested her hands on her knees as she doubled over. Arie's hand encompassed her shoulder.

"Resist, Elizabeth." His voice was an anchor. "Greater is He who is in you."

Markus's voice rang in her ears. *You cannot resist me. You're not strong enough.*

Ryland rushed back to her side. His concern poured into her overloaded brain. "Are you hit?"

"It's Markus. He's trying to get in my head again." She coughed. "I closed the door, like you said. He's trying anyway." Liz grabbed her head.

Her shield wavered, pieces of the wall shattering under the brutality and intensity of the attack. Markus's hate and evil trickled in. This was more powerful, more invasive than any of his previous attempts. Vile images flittered across her mind.

Ryland's eyes narrowed as he stood in front of her. "Okay. Come on, Liz. We've done this before. Get your shield back up right now."

Liz closed her eyes and focused. She could feel Markus there, pounding his way in little by little. A prayer soothed her mind as it made its way upward.

You're weak, exhausted. You've already lost. Markus's voice assaulted her mind. But the sound was fading.

The pain eased as Liz concentrated on her favorite verse. *Fear not, for I am with you; be not dismayed, for I am your God.* Over and over she repeated it. She felt power rolling into her from Ryland. She used it to shore up the wall. The assault abated into nothingness.

"That's it, baby." Ryland's hand rested on the back of her neck.

Arie touched her head and took off. This particular battle was over. Liz could swear she heard Markus's rage-filled scream echo in her mind. A smile tugged at her lips. At Ryland's questioning look, she nodded.

When her mind cleared, Liz and Ryland resumed their back-to-back positions. Liz scanned the quieting field. Where was Dad? As soon as she thought it, she saw him at the wood's edge. He polished off one of the remaining demons, waved to Liz, and headed toward Aelaem. He looked — happy.

There were few demons left. The rest had either been taken out or had run. Liz let her shoulders relax. Her limbs were dead weight, her head throbbed, and she sported new cuts and bruises all over her body. They stung like the dickens. Liz leaned against Ryland's back as they maintained position. Waiting.

She twisted her head toward Ryland. "Any sign of Kade?"

"Saw him. I didn't want to leave you." Ryland's next words came out cold and precise. "I'll find him. Eventually."

What was he not telling her? Bad blood obviously flowed between Ryland and Kade. More than just being on opposing sides. And more than Kade's possession of someone Ryland didn't even know.

The sudden quiet brought a tingle of fear to her skin. Markus was still out there. Liz pushed the unease from her being, choosing to have faith. Choosing to trust.

"Good girl." Ryland's voice brought her out of her head.

"Felt that, huh?"

"Yeah. I feel everything when you leave yourself open. Just focus. Listen, and He'll tell us what's next."

"That easy?"

"Yep."

Liz closed her eyes, reaching out with her mind and spirit. The distant sounds of clanging blades, howls from the enemy, and shouts of praise signaled a battle won. The lingering smell of sulfur and ash mingled with something sweeter, like roses and honey, and the pine from the forest.

Heavy steps crushed leaves and twigs, breaking into the now-calm clearing. An acrid odor floated on the breeze. Familiar and unwelcome.

"He's here."

The steadiness of her voice amazed Liz. She was no longer the scared, angry little girl who always ran instead of facing whatever came. She was a warrior. Not perfect, not the most powerful, but a warrior nonetheless.

It was time for the fight of her life.

Ryland moved to her side. They faced Markus as a united front. A flare of fury for everything he'd done spiked in her blood, and she shoved it down. She readjusted her grip on her sword and widened her stance.

Liz saw Ryland's muscles flex, ready for action. The little vein on his forehead pulsed. Various wounds and bruises decorated his tanned skin. Liz laid a hand on his arm. Electricity carrying a surge of pure power from above shot between them. It charged their damaged bodies for one more fight. A calm control blanketed them both.

Markus stopped about twenty feet in front of them. "I see you're both still alive. I should remedy that." His voice was laced with venom and something else. Fear?

"So you're gonna talk my ear off again. Lovely."

Ryland's elbow bumped her side, and he sent her a sharp look.

Yeah. Not the time. "Sorry," Liz whispered. Calm. Focus. She had to stay centered.

"Markus, you're late. Your army's already been sent to Hell." Ryland's icy smile gave Liz chills. "I'd be happy to help you join them." He twirled his blades.

Markus laughed, and Ryland shot her a wink. They'd practiced this a million times. Liz slid to Markus's right while Ryland circled to the left.

Markus's eyes swung in her direction. "Won't work."

Markus speared Ryland with his gaze, then lunged for Liz. His blade sliced a thin layer of skin from her shoulder. He rushed her again. Ryland swooped behind him and caught him on the back, both blades carving downward.

Markus howled. He whirled, and his sword landed with a crash between Ryland's as they crossed. Every muscle in Ryland's upper body flexed to hold the block as Markus advanced. Markus surged forward with a Herculean push. The two went flying, landing with a crash, denting the ground.

Liz didn't hesitate. She ran forward and plunged her sword into Markus's back. Markus twisted to face Liz and leveled those red and black eyes on her, full of fury, shaking her to her core. He leaped, and the dance began in earnest. Each time Markus focused on one, the other would draw him away, trying to maneuver for the blow that would put him down.

Time stilled.

Parry. Strike. Block. Lunge. Swing.

While they inflicted a substantial amount of damage, Markus kept coming. And they were not unscathed. Liz's body was on fire. Her grip slipped on her blade as her arms grew weaker and covered with blood. White-hot pain flashed on the backs of her eyes. Ryland didn't look much better than she felt. Their hurt coalesced, swirling together and slowly weakening them.

They were wearing down. A fleeting thought asked, where were their guardians? The next thought told her this was her and Ryland's fight, and they had Someone much greater than the angels at their side.

Liz fell to her knees as Ryland engaged Markus. She gulped in air and prayed for an end to this fight. Preferably with them winning. No. They couldn't lose this one. Even if they had to fight through their weakness, even if they weren't getting a recharge from Heaven, they'd fight with everything they did have. Markus was not going to be around to carry out whatever disgusting plans he had.

Renewed fervor surged through her. Determination. They would use whatever they had left to take him down. The spark in her grew brighter. She saw it pass through Ryland as well. His eyes blazed as he sprang forward.

Ryland swung his blades, digging into Markus's thick hide. The momentum of the powerful move threw his body to the right, and Markus landed a blow to Ryland's head with a spiked sword handle as he sailed by. A sickening crack rent the air.

"Ryland!"

Markus brought the steel across Ryland's abdomen. He kicked Ryland with such force, he flew several feet through the air, landing facedown in a cloud of dust.

Liz raced forward. Markus blocked her blade. She spun and brought it back down with every ounce of strength she had, slicing into his dominant arm. Markus's sword clattered to the ground. He stumbled back, clutching at his shoulder to stop the flow of black fluid.

Ryland pushed himself up, and Liz looked him over to ensure he really was okay. Relief rushed through her, but the glance cost her. She'd only looked away for a second before flipping around to land the final blow to Markus.

By the time Liz's eyes met Markus's, it was too late.

XXXVIII
A Demon's Fate

"Lizzy!"

Liz shifted, but not far enough. The dagger slid into her flesh on her left side, angled up toward her lung. She looked up into Markus's black depths, inches from her face. Shock sucked the oxygen from her. Markus smiled cruelly, and evil curled around Liz like liquid smoke. A flurry of noise and movement swirled around her. Markus was ripped away and flung through the air.

Liz glanced down where the blade had invaded her. A large hand covered the wound in her abdomen as Ryland's warmth wrapped around her. *So warm. Like a blanket.* Liz felt his fear and pain. Strangely, not her own. Her consciousness clouded over, and her body floated into numbness as precious blood coated Ryland's fingers.

She met his wide eyes and smiled. His lips moved. There was no sound. He lowered her to the ground gently. Liz's head rolled to the side, and she saw Arie and Chammu'el battling with Markus and Kade.

Liz smiled at Ryland. "Don't worry. It doesn't hurt."

At her quiet words, Ryland froze. His eyes glazed. He suddenly sprang back into motion, ripping his tattered T-shirt over his head. He raised her arms and threaded it around her, tying it over the gushing wound. Liz pushed herself up. Ryland held her down. She looked into a face covered in deep red.

"You're hurt." Did she say that out loud?

"I'm fine. Just rest."

Liz nodded, and Ryland prayed. Out of the corner of her eye, she saw Kade. He sent a razor-sharp gaze full of malevolent promise at Ryland before leading Chammu'el on a chase into the woods.

Arie and Markus were nowhere to be seen now.

Liz tried to get up again but found herself clamped against Ryland in an iron grip.

"Stay. Down. You're hurt. Let them handle this." His firm voice came out so rough, it startled her.

"I can't...sit here."

"Yes, you can, and you will." Ryland's face was set. Hard. "For once, you're going to listen to me."

A loud crash reverberated through the ground. Arie and Markus had landed not far from Liz and Ryland. Their swords locked together in a test of will. Angel and demon, once brothers, exchanging a death glare. Liz slid her arms around Ryland's torso and hung on tight as her vision clouded. Chammu'el emerged from the woods, shaking his head when he caught Ryland's gaze.

Kade had escaped. She felt Ryland stiffen.

Markus shot upward, Arie on his heels. They were out of sight in seconds.

Liz could feel the gash in her side begin to stitch together, though she knew it would take a while. The cut was deep. The numbness lifted, as did the clouds in her head. She untangled herself from Ryland. He started, and she feared he might argue as she worked her way to her knees. Apparently deciding not to fight her, he rose to his feet and pulled her up with him.

"Come on. We should get you checked out."

"But Markus..."

"No. Arie will get him. My only concern right now is you." Even though he said the words with conviction, Liz could tell part of him still yearned to get a hold of Markus.

Liz didn't have the energy to argue. She lifted her chin in a silent protest. Ryland raised an eyebrow as defiance swept through her. He sighed and put his arms around her, careful of her wound.

Chammu'el sauntered over to them. "The victory is the Lord's!" His tone was jubilant. He nodded to Ryland. "Go. Tend to your wounds and rest. We will finish here." The guardian placed one hand on Liz's shoulder, and the other on Ryland's. "You did well."

"Kade?" Ryland's question came through gritted teeth.

Chammu'el shook his head, then walked toward his brothers who remained on the field.

James Brantley bounded from the woods. His smile faded as he took in Liz. He ran to her side.

"I'm fine, Dad. Really."

He hugged her gingerly. "Markus?"

"Arie's taking care of it," Ryland answered. "We're gonna go get bandaged up."

Liz grabbed Dad's sleeve. "Dad, thank you. For fighting, for coming to get me, everything. I don't know how we would've done it all without you."

"Hopefully you'll never have to find out." Dad kissed Liz's cheek. He sobered. "I'm going to find Aelaem, then make an anonymous call to the police. I checked out the warehouse and the office." His voice wavered, sadness and horror infusing his words. "There's evidence of a trafficking ring. Between that and what I got some of the fellas trussed up out front to tell me, it's not just here." Dad nodded toward Ryland. "That fella who led the attack on you has been working with at least one other person in Texas and Louisiana. Markus offered to fund them and help secure, ah, the girls." He blew out a sharp breath, sorrow filling every word. "I just never imagined we'd have to deal with this here. It's hard to believe people could be this evil, even without a demon's influence."

A jagged pain speared Liz's chest. There was no telling what unbelievable suffering those two girls had been spared. "What about the girls? Surely they'll talk to the police when their parents report they were found."

Dad nodded. "Aelaem and Hadriel were the ones who got them

home, and he said they were scared and exhausted, but both were already hollering to sic the cops on the men who took them. Said they'd never forget their faces. Between them and what we found, there's no way these guys are getting away with this."

"Hopefully this will stop this part of the ring." Ryland tightened his grip on Liz. "I just wish there was something we could do about the rest of it. I've been involved in a couple of rescues before." Ryland sighed. "What these victims go through is more horrible than any decent person could imagine. And most people don't even realize things like this can happen anywhere, not just overseas."

Liz held Ryland tighter. "We'll do what we can. Tonight was a good start."

Dad sheathed his sword. "That it was. All right, I'm gonna make that call. I suggest we all clear out before the police get here."

Liz and Ryland assured him they were leaving and made him promise to check in later. Liz pulled him into a hug before he took off.

"I'm gonna grab my blades. You okay for a minute?" Ryland held her shoulders gently as concern brightened his eyes.

"Yeah. Just hurry. I'm past ready to get out of here." Liz had had enough of this place.

As Ryland strode toward the edge of the clearing, she reached down to pick up her blade. The wound in her side pinched, and she wrapped both arms around her waist, sword dangling from her hand.

The *whoosh* of wings and a solid *thump* sounded behind her. The flood of evil hit her a second later. She didn't have a chance to turn before a massive arm snaked around her throat. Her eyes shifted to the right. Ryland had returned, but now a long, narrow blade pressed against his neck. A trickle of blood dripped from the tip.

"One move, and this blade severs his spine, and I snap your neck." Markus's hiss blew into her ear.

Ryland blinked once, slowly, telling her to hold.

"What difference does it make?" Liz choked out. "You're just gonna kill us anyway."

"Smart girl."

Markus kissed her cheek. She cringed. Ryland blasted her with a ball of rage. She winced and threw him a sharp look. His eyes instantly apologized.

Markus's gaze shot to Ryland. "Stay, dog." Then he returned his focus to Liz. "I'm going to miss you, darling. We had such an interesting time together." He clenched her tighter, and Liz fought a wave of nausea. "What a shame."

Liz swept the area with her eyes and reached out with her mind. Dad was still around front. Arie and Chammu'el were nowhere to be seen. Any other angels were aiding their wounded or finishing off remaining demons. Too far away.

They were screwed.

For a moment, Liz stood paralyzed. Doubt once again attempted to seed itself in her mind and poke holes in her faith. Her knees twitched, ready to give out any second. This couldn't be how it ended. Could it?

Be strong and courageous. Do not be afraid, for I am with you.

Liz pulled the words into her spirit, clinging to hope. Markus spoke. She wasn't listening. As she let her faith soothe her, clarity arrived.

Her sword was still in her hand.

She tossed a glance at Ryland. He quickly looked at her hands and blinked twice. Liz worked the blade around in her fingers slowly, careful not to alert Markus. Her head swam and her limbs tingled, both with nervousness and power. Markus's grip tightened.

Liz closed her eyes and said a prayer. Quiet calm expanded inside of her, followed by a shot of adrenaline. In a feverish burst of speed, she slid a fraction to the right and stretched her arms in front of her. The blade grazed her left side as she plunged it back and into Markus's midsection. She withdrew and stabbed again. At the same time, Ryland jumped back, slapping Markus's blade away.

The chokehold on Liz's neck loosened. She whirled. Markus stumbled back, and she mirrored his steps, her blade still buried in his midsection. Liz drove the steel in as far as she could. Disbelief and fury swirled in Markus's black eyes as he watched the blade.

Movement to her left caught her eye. Ryland and Markus shot their eyes in the same direction. All three of them froze. It was Kade. He stood not far from the tree line. Watching. He gave a wicked grin and clapped twice. Then he disappeared, leaving Markus to his fate.

Ryland twitched as he watched the retreating form. She knew he wanted to go after him. He recovered and slid behind Markus in one fluid motion. Ryland crossed his blades as he stepped in. Liz withdrew her sword and leaped back.

Ryland ripped his blades through Markus's thick neck.

Markus's head rolled in the dust at his feet. His body soon followed. Finality rode the sounds of ruffling feathers and jangling armor as the formerly magnificent fallen angel thundered to the ground.

Dust flew.

The earth bellowed.

Liz and Ryland remained still, gazes locked on the surreal sight at their feet.

A shadowy mist rose from the depths. It wound around their legs as it covered the body. The fog thickened. Sulfur and the scent of brimstone filled their nostrils and coated their throats. Liz and Ryland stepped back, coughing and sputtering. A high-pitched wail pierced their ears. Then the pit sucked in Markus.

No evidence remained.

For now, at least, Markus was gone.

Liz stared at the spot where he'd been, half-expecting him to spring from the earth.

Exhaustion established itself firmly in her limbs, and Liz trembled. Her hand couldn't clutch her sword any longer, and it clattered to the dirt. Her wounds screamed. She looked down at her torn clothes. Blood and ooze coated fabric and skin. Liz's shoulders sagged.

The battle had been won. But victory, in the physical and beyond, had come at a great cost. Paid in blood and tears. Pieces of herself. But the pieces that remained were all she needed. They reformed into something new. Something stronger. She was becoming whole. Fully reborn.

A warm, familiar hand caressed her arm. Liz met Ryland's eyes. She knew the love and pride there matched her own. Everything he felt joined with the symphony inside of her in a perfect harmony. The line blurred where one ended and the other began.

One look burned an imprint on each of their souls. Commitment. Strong and true. Trust in each other. Trust in their God. All they felt, all they'd been through, all they'd fought together, stitched their hearts and spirits into a beautiful patchwork. The warmth of it wrapped around them. Solidifying what they would become. Together.

Liz didn't fight the tears. Ryland pulled her into his arms, cradling her against the heart she adored. She slid her arms around him, hanging on with everything she had. She would never let go again.

The breeze carried the lingering scent of battle to her nose. The tears gained momentum. Her body and spirit had had enough. She'd reached the end of her strength. As her legs gave out, Ryland held tight. They sank to their knees in the dirt.

Liz lifted her chin, and Ryland brushed her lips with his. A simple kiss, yet bursting with so much. She laid her head on his shoulder. He held her as the tears fell. Absorbing every hurt. Every shiver. Every sob. She felt his pain as well, his exhaustion. Liz strengthened her hold on him. They each took from the other and gave just as much in return. Infusing each other with peace. With love.

When the torrent subsided, Ryland took her face in both hands and peered deep into her eyes. Deeper than anyone had been before. Than anyone else would ever be allowed.

"Marry me."

It wasn't a question. It wasn't an order. A simple statement. As if it had already been decided.

Liz's heart screeched to a stop. When it started back up, the organ fought against her ribs, trying to reach him. A warm, peaceful swell washed through her, starting in her toes and spreading upward. She heard the click. Destiny and providence colliding with acceptance and trust. The world paused to listen. Craning its ear. Hushing its inhabitants.

He wiped her tears with his thumb. "You're crazy, and beautiful, and stubborn, and strong. You're a force of nature. And I want to ride the storm with you every day, every night." Ryland's eyes touched her soul. He saw it all, felt it all. Yet he didn't shy away, didn't flinch. He delved deeper.

Liz's breath caught in her throat.

Ryland's eyes glistened. "I love you with all I am. I need you by my side. Always. Please, say you will."

The smile that lifted her cheeks was pure joy. No fear. Only love. Only trust.

"I love you too, so much. Yes. Absolutely, yes."

Ryland's grin could be seen from space. He brought his mouth to hers. The kiss stormed through her in a series of hurricanes. The battle weariness faded as they sealed their promise. He tugged her back to him, and she knew he'd never let her go.

He whispered in her ear. "We have company."

Liz's head snapped up. "Dad!" They leaned on each other as they pushed to their feet.

Dad smiled. The sparkle in his eyes rivaled the glow of the moon. He walked over and patted Ryland's back, avoiding his injuries. "'Bout time, boy."

"Sure was." Ryland grinned and kissed Liz's forehead.

Arie and Chammu'el stepped out of the shadows. Wide smiles dominated their faces. Arie nodded his approval. She would've sworn she saw a knowing twinkle in his eye before he and Chammu'el tilted their heads and shot toward the stars.

Liz had stood tall, waged war on her demons, and won. She was in the arms of the man she loved, and in the hands of a magnificent Commander. Their enemies had been taken down, and the hometown she loved freed from Markus's dark oppression. Two women saved tonight, and who knew how many more spared from the evil these men and demons had planned. A wide grin plastered itself across her face.

Ryland tightened his arm around her waist. Dad went ahead of them, walking around the garage with a smile on his face, humming a song. Liz leaned against Ryland to whisper one more time she loved him. She hadn't gotten the words out when a flash at the corner of the building caught her eye.

Vicious, oppressive evil smacked her between the eyes a second later.

XXXIX
Mended Souls

It all played out before Liz in slow motion, though in reality, it was merely seconds.

Kade stepped out of the shadows in front of Dad. Dad skidded to a halt. He reached for the sheathed blade at his hip. Ryland took off running toward them, roaring.

Neither one of them were fast enough.

Liz made eye contact with Kade. Saw the glint of malevolent excitement in his eyes. The length of burnished steel in Kade's hand flashed in the moonlight. Dad's blade was halfway out of its sheath. Ryland was still several feet away. Kade grinned and lunged forward. He buried his sword to the hilt through Dad's chest.

A feral scream ripped from Liz's lips. She jumped forward, but her muscles gave out. Ryland slid to a halt. Shock detonated along their link.

Kade removed his sword and stepped back. His malevolent and pleased gaze locked onto Liz as she and Ryland stared, stunned into paralysis. "Now, you're all in." He glanced at Ryland. "Both of you." He extended his wings and lifted off the ground. "Be prepared. You're about to see how a true demon conducts business."

Hovering above them, his gravelly laughter chilled Liz's heart. A black streak announced his departure.

Liz's mind and body kicked in to gear the same time Ryland's did. Dad faced them as they rushed toward him, disbelief glazing his eyes.

He glanced down at the wound leaking precious crimson, then crashed to his knees.

"Daddy!" Liz collapsed in the dirt beside him.

"Stay with him. I'll call for help and get the kit." Ryland threw the words over his shoulder on his way around the building.

Liz wrapped her arms around her father and eased him to the ground. She slapped her hand over the wound, desperate to stop the blood flow.

"Liz Whiz, it's okay." Dad's voice was weak and strained. She felt his resignation resonate in her chest.

Panic tore through Liz. "It's not okay. You—you're hurt bad, Daddy."

He laid his hand over hers and patted. "Liz, it's time. Time to go… home."

Ryland landed on his knees in a cloud of dust, ripping open the first aid kit. "No. It's not time. You'll be fine. I called the ambulance, and they're on their way." He moved Liz's hand and placed several gauze pads over the gaping hole. Ryland flashed a falsely cheerful grin. "Though I don't know how we're gonna explain this one."

Dad chuckled. It sounded more like a gurgle. Red tinged his lips. "Listen. Job…done here. Your time." He reached for both of their hands and brought them together over his chest. "Keep fighting. Together." His gaze landed on Liz. "Take care of"—he coughed, struggling—"Mama. Don't let her cry…too long." His smile was anemic yet true.

"No, Daddy, you can't go." Liz choked on the words. Tears created tracks in the blood and grime on her face. She felt Ryland's grief before he squashed it for her. All he broadcasted was support and love. She laid a hand on Dad's shoulder and forced a smile. "You still have things to do. Who's gonna marry us if you're not here? Or walk me down the aisle?"

Dad's grin was just as boyish as ever. "Mac. He agreed…take the church." Dad tried to clear his throat. It ended in a horrific cough again.

"What do you mean?" Ryland couldn't hide the crack in his voice. "Talked...him earlier. Had a"—he sputtered—"feeling."

Liz didn't get a chance to protest. Aelaem, Arie, and Chammu'el were suddenly surrounding them.

Aelaem bent toward Dad, who she now knew was his charge. "You've fought well, my friend. It's time to go home to your reward."

"No!" Liz pushed Aelaem to the side, and he let her. "No. We just have to pray. He'll heal, right? That's part of the deal. We heal fast. I did. Look at Ry—he was dead! God brought him back. He can do that. He won't let—" Her babbling came to a halt when she realized everyone was staring at her. She shook her head. "No. You can't take him."

"Lizzy." Ryland was at her side, his arms around her as he shot her dad a look of understanding.

She continued shaking her head, unable to speak anymore. First, she'd lost Ry, or thought she had, now Dad? No. This wasn't happening. She wouldn't let it.

Dad took her hand again. The light in his eyes faded as he spoke. But his voice strengthened, one more time. "Elizabeth, God has a plan. I've fulfilled...my part. Ryland's right. Let me go...home."

"I can't."

The emotion from everyone present poured into her. Her shield had long ago been left in tatters. Combined with the riot inside, it formed a deafening cacophony. Cracks formed in her heart. They filled with sorrow. Liz wanted to rage against it. Fight the angels, if need be, to keep him here.

Ryland squeezed her to his side. Liz met her father's eyes. His light was fading. Sadness and joy both swirled in his unfocused gaze. She felt Arie move behind her and settle his wings around her and Ryland.

Unwanted understanding filtered through her anguish.

Though her heart shattered with every beat, Liz knew she couldn't keep him here. Her spirit whispered there was a season for everything. A time to be born and a time to die. How odd her complete rebirth, culminating in her breaking her ties to the dark and trusting completely, had happened the same night Dad would be reborn into the light.

The realization didn't stop the tears. Or the pain. She knew, though, she could handle this. She could let him go. She could go on. No bitterness. No blame.

Dad took Ryland's and Liz's hands in his again. "Love well. Fight hard. Never forget…why we fight." His words were breathy, his voice weakening further.

Liz leaned down and kissed his cheek. She threw her arms around him and swallowed the sobs threatening. Her weeping couldn't be his last sight of her. Liz sat up and wiped her eyes. She flashed the brightest smile she could muster.

"I love you, Daddy."

"I love you, Liz Whiz." His countenance radiated peace, despite his injuries. He glanced at Ryland. "Take care…my girls. Love you…son."

"I will, sir. Thank you. For everything." Ryland's voice broke, and he cleared his throat. "I love you, too."

Dad looked up into the stars and smiled. "Goin' home, kids."

The last breath left his body soundlessly as four unknown angels descended.

The quartet stepped to Dad's still form. They didn't acknowledge the others present. The angels reached down and retrieved Dad's soul. It was him, but different. A shimmering, glowing version of the man she once knew. Dad glanced down at them once, a smile she'd never seen before on his face. As the group rose toward the heavens, Liz leaned against Ryland for strength. She tilted her head back to watch until they slipped out of sight.

Wrapped in Ryland's arms, Arie and Chammu'el's wings cradling them, Liz knew she would survive.

She would make Dad proud.

The casket sat at the altar, forcing Liz to believe it was real.

Daddy's body lay there, in front of a pulpit that wasn't his. One he'd stood behind a few times before. Pastor Anders occupied the spot now. Words came out of his mouth, and Liz was sure they were eloquent, but she didn't understand them. They were a jumble, falling on her grief-stricken ears with no more impact than a light breeze.

Ryland's arm tightened around her as fresh tears coursed down her face, dripping off her nose. She'd given up trying to stop them. As she brushed them away, Liz's mind wandered back, trying to make sense of it all.

Not long after the angels had taken his soul, the ambulance had come. Ryland had made up a mostly-true story for the cops who'd arrived shortly after. Something about how they'd been driving by, had seen activity around the abandoned building, and had stopped to check it out. How they'd found Liz, who'd helped the other girls escape. How there'd been a fight, but Dad's attacker had gotten away.

When they'd questioned Liz, she'd said she didn't remember much of anything.

Ryland had described Kade's human form, leaving out his name. It had been relatively easy to get them to think that was all there was to it. Especially since the girls who'd escaped were at the police station, giving their statements. An officer warned Ryland to call 911 next time instead of intervening, then told Ryland and Liz he might have more questions. He'd suggested they get checked out by the EMTs. They'd both declined. Then the officers had given their sympathies, shown their relief Liz had been found, and turned their attention to the men tied up on the ground.

Liz floated out of her memories for a moment. Pastor Anders stopped talking, and Dylan started singing a song. She knew it was one of Dad's favorites but couldn't remember the name right now. Her brain kept swimming back to that night.

Liz and Ryland had watched the paramedics load Dad into the ambulance. As they had driven away, she'd clung to Ryland with what pitiful strength she'd had left. She barely remembered Ryland helping her into the truck. Or driving to Mom's. Or telling her what had happened. She only had a vague recollection of falling onto the couch afterward and Ryland covering her up.

The next few days had floated past in a haze of tears, soul-crushing pain, well-wishing visitors, and helping Mom make arrangements. Ryland had stayed by her side, sleeping on the couch at Mom's while Liz retreated to her old room. Angels were constantly present, and the peace they brought soothed her. At least a little. Some days, she was afraid the ache would never go away. That it would just swallow her whole. Then Arie would whisper to her, or Ryland would hold her, and the agony would fade a bit.

Now as she sat at Dad's homegoing service, it rushed in on her again. Liz curled against Ryland, reaching to her other side to cling to Mom's hand. Dylan finished the song. Pastor Anders said a few more words. Then it was over. Everyone stood.

Ryland gave her a quick hug and kiss. "I'll be right back." He moved into the aisle and toward the front, joining the other pallbearers.

Liz focused on him as they passed, not on what they carried. Ryland was quickly at her side again as promised and ushering her outside and into a car. The rest was a blur. Ryland gone for another few minutes to complete his task, then back with her. Sitting in the wind she knew was cold but didn't feel. More words spoken. A prayer. Then they were standing again.

The next thing Liz knew, only she and Ryland were left, staring down at the coffin sitting on the contraption that would lower it into the ground.

Liz finally came to herself and looked around. Panic shot through her. "Where's Mom?"

Ryland moved behind her and wrapped his arms around her stomach. "She's fine. Your aunt took her back to the house. The ladies have dinner waiting there for us all."

"Okay." Liz's head bobbed absently. Mom was okay. Well, she would be. Mom was strong. Liz couldn't help wondering if she could conjure up strength like that. Or at least enough to make it through all of this.

"Let me take you home, baby girl. You haven't eaten all day." Ryland's worry seeped into her, even though she could tell he was trying to hold it back.

Again, Liz nodded. There was no more reason to stay here. Her daddy was gone.

But as Ryland lifted her into the truck, a comforting thought finally broke through her haze. Daddy was Home. No more fighting. No more pain. No more impossible choices. If only things could be that amazing, that easy, on earth.

Liz looked over at Ryland as he settled in his seat. He gave her a smile before leaning toward her. He kissed her, feather light, caressing her cheek with his roughened thumb. Love shot through her, pure and true. It lightened her heavy heart. He gave her another quick kiss on the nose before putting the truck in gear. Liz glanced out the window as glorious wings caught her eye. Their guardians stood smiling. She returned the sentiment, and this time, it was true.

Maybe everything really would be all right.

Paint-splattered jeans, Ryland's flannel shirt and jacket, work gloves balled up at the end of her fingers, and a ridiculous bright orange sock hat.

Liz looked like she'd fallen into a yard sale and had crawled through the other side.

And she'd never looked more beautiful.

Ryland watched as she tugged the hat down and shivered. He laughed and shook his head. His woman did not like the cold.

Liz ranted as she tried to tie on a work apron, complete with dangling hammer and tape measure clipped to the side. Ryland took pity and tied it for her.

Liz huffed. "It's not supposed to be frigid in October."

Mac yelled from the roof of the church. "Quit your belly achin'. Get busy workin' and you won't be cold." He chuckled.

Liz stuck out her tongue, and the man laughed. Ryland was relieved to see Liz's lighter side peeking out again. It had been a couple of weeks since they'd had her dad's homegoing service. While she'd grieved and been unusually quiet, she'd shown a strength he'd known all along was inside of her. He couldn't be more proud to make her his wife one day. He only wished James could be there to see it.

As he looked around at the members of the congregation and their new pastor, Mac, working so hard on building the new church, he knew they'd be all right. It would take time, but all of their souls were mending from the loss.

Ryland sauntered toward Liz. He tossed an empty water jug at her. She caught it with ease and chucked it back at him. He grinned, deciding to do a little tormenting of his own. If she wanted to play, they'd play.

"Why don't you make your pretty little self useful and get me some water instead of standing here whining?"

Liz shoved at him. "I'm plenty useful. Now get your own water." She scooped up a handful of nails from the box, deposited them in her apron pocket, and shimmied up the ladder to join Mac on the roof.

Ryland gave a lopsided grin. He let his eyes roam over the site and all they'd accomplished. The new church rose like a beacon in the field and would be ready for services in another month or so. Half the town had been there, working to see it finished. Pastor Brantley would've been proud.

He walked over to the open tailgate of his truck. He refilled his bottle at the large cooler and took a long swig. His gaze rested on Liz, working side by side with Mac. He was glad his best friend and his fiancé got along so well. She sat easily on the peak and laid shingles effortlessly, as though she'd been doing it all her life. But he knew she wasn't one hundred percent yet. Concern fluttered through him. She caught his eye and raised an eyebrow, then refocused on her task.

Busted. She did not like being babied.

But Ryland had no intention of letting her overdo things. When he'd insisted she slow down to give her body and mind time to heal, she'd fought him. Hard. He'd put his foot down, and she eventually gave in. Why did the most stubborn woman in the world have to be the one who owned his heart? Ryland smiled. He would move Heaven and earth to keep her safe and happy, and he wouldn't let anyone stand in the way of that goal.

Not even her.

"Hey," Liz yelled from the roof. "We need another bundle of shingles up here when you're done lollygaggin'." Her voice echoed, followed by several scattered laughs.

"Oh, yes ma'am!" Ryland gave a mock salute and headed for the pallet stacked high with shingles. He picked up a bundle and tossed it over his shoulder.

"Come on, slowpoke." Liz stood over the ladder, rolling her eyes and grinning.

"Calm down, woman. I'm comin'."

Liz wrinkled her nose and held the top of the ladder secure while he tossed the bundle onto the decking. "Bossy." Liz stuck out her pouty lip.

"Pushy." Ryland winked at her.

Liz leaned over and planted a kiss on his lips. The sweetness of it skittered through him, nearly making him lose his grip.

"If y'all are about done with all that, I'd like to get this roof done before supper." Mac gave them a grin.

They laughed, and Ryland climbed back down. He tried to calm his racing heart, which seemed intent on cracking right through his sternum. The woman did things to him even he didn't fully understand. He loved and wanted her with a ferocity that sometimes scared him.

She owns me.

XL
Untraveled Road

Lightning bugs flitted through Liz's stomach like someone had injected them with caffeine.

She glanced around the beautiful restaurant, then let her eyes rest on the man in front of her. Ryland had seen her through some of the roughest times of her life, especially the last few weeks. She'd been able to keep it together and begin healing. Due mostly to him.

Liz almost protested when he grabbed the rather sizable check and slid a card into the folder. She knew he wouldn't budge, so no point in trying. It still felt odd letting someone take care of her, no matter the situation. He insisted, though.

She went back to her perusal of the dining room. The steakhouse sat on a cliff overlooking the river. They were seated in front of a huge picture window showcasing the water churning over the lock. A massive fireplace dominated the far wall. The fire crackled and the lights were dim, lending a romantic feel to the room. There were few other customers, which meant fewer uninvited guests. The only supernatural creatures present were a couple of angels.

That suited her fine.

Liz watched the river while Ryland polished off his dessert. She'd inhaled her own chocolate torte minutes ago. Now they sat with steaming mugs of cocoa in front of them. He appeared so calm on the outside, but she could feel his anxiety.

How odd. Ryland was a rock. The unshakeable warrior. Yet

tonight, he fidgeted in his seat like a teenager on a first date. Liz tried to hide her grin. Because along with his unusual case of the jitters, a steady stream of love had blasted her way all evening.

Liz cleared her throat and broke the silence. "Did you hear Shelley and Dylan are pregnant?" She had no idea why she brought it up. Other than his nerves were seeping into hers.

"Yeah. He told me and Mac the other day while we were working." Ryland grinned. "He's just a little excited. I would be too." His eyes glinted as he watched her.

Liz kept her composure. This was exactly why she shouldn't have brought it up. Man, she was stupid. Maybe he'd overlook the anxiety and momentary sadness pulsing through her. Chalk it up to normal nerves. After all, she was still young.

An odd look zipped across his face, and she felt his momentary confusion. Thankfully, Ryland didn't push. He took a sip from his mug, his eyes connecting with hers over the rim. The hazel pools softened as they drank her in. She could get lost in there. He had a pull on her not even Markus's seduction could rival. Ryland's power reached the very fiber of her being. He set the mug down and reached for her hand. Ryland flipped it over, palm up, and traced circles with his thumb. A surge of electricity shot through Liz.

"Are you enjoying yourself?" He never broke the stare and continued to caress her hand.

Warmth washed through her. Lately, everything she felt from him was deeper, more potent than before. Arie had said the connection would intensify as their bond strengthened. Especially after they were married. The thought both frightened and elated her.

"Absolutely. Thank you."

Ryland grinned, and satisfaction slammed into Liz. "I'm glad." He raised her hand to his lips and kissed her palm. "Have I told you today that I love you?"

"Once, I think." She scrunched her brow. "I could stand to hear it again, though."

He leaned in, and the air around them charged. "I love you, Lizzy."

His husky words sent shivers down her spine.

"I love you, too," she breathed.

Liz reached over with her other hand and ran her finger down his square jaw. She wished the table weren't between them, and they didn't have an audience.

Ryland stood and tugged her up. "Let's get out of here and go for a walk."

He'd read her mind. Again.

Liz grabbed her purse, and Ryland slid her jacket over her shoulders. With his hand at the small of her back, he led her from the restaurant. A charge zoomed up her spine from his hand, making her entire body come alive.

When they got outside, he led her down the path along the river. The chilly air made her skin tingle, but she didn't care. His warm hand wrapped around hers, and his heat at her side made it more than bearable. The crickets set up their symphony. Light shimmered across the water from the full moon. It was perfect.

They hadn't said a word for several minutes when Ryland finally broke the comfortable silence. "You know you're my life, right?"

His words were quiet, and they shot straight to the depths of her heart. It was the sweetest thing anyone had ever said to her.

Liz nodded. "I feel the same."

Ryland stopped and took both of her hands in his. His impressive frame dominated her vision. Her favorite sight. The look he gave her smoldered, burning right into her. His eyes never leaving hers, he released one hand and reached into his pocket.

He dropped to one knee.

The lightning bugs in her stomach went into overdrive. Liz sucked in a quick breath. The earth spun off its axis. His smile lit up her world.

"I know I already technically proposed, but I wanted to do it right. The way you deserve." The light in his eyes became flame. Burning for her.

Liz tried to breathe. Her lungs refused to cooperate. Ryland opened the box and held it on his palm. A delicate diamond ring lay nestled in the velvet. Liz looked from the ring to Ryland, and her eyes filled.

"I want to build a life with you. I want to face whatever battles come, side by side. I want to love you, curl up with you every night, and wake up with you in my arms every morning. I want to give you all I am, and I want all of you."

He removed the ring and tossed the box to the ground. A small laugh bubbled up inside of Liz. Ryland took her shaky left hand. He squeezed it and slid the ring on.

"Elizabeth Diane Brantley, will you be my wife?"

Liz looked at the man she treasured more than her own life. Then a strange thing happened. Her hands steadied. Her breath slowed. Her pulse glided into a mild rhythm. But her heartbeat wasn't performing solo. Another heart sang with it in flawless harmony.

Strong and sure.

She laughed. The happiness wouldn't be contained. "You're supposed to wait for my answer before you put the ring on."

Ryland's rich laugh blended with hers. "I wanted to lock you in." He bobbed his eyebrows.

She laughed harder. "Then yes. I'll marry you." Liz thought she might explode from the combined dynamite of their emotions.

Ryland jumped to his feet. The world tilted again as he scooped her up and swung her around until she was dizzy. When he set her down, he drew her in so tight she feared for her ribs. She was right where she was meant to be.

Their lips met in the most explosive kiss she'd ever had the pleasure of being a part of. Ryland wrapped his fingers around Liz's nape. As she melted into him, he tangled them in her hair, tilted her head to the side, and dove deeper. He caught the sigh that rose from her heart. She traced her hands from his chest, down to wrap around his waist. Liz savored every second.

He tasted like chocolate and forever. Home.

Liz thought she would liquefy into a puddle as his passion burned through her, and hers accelerated the blaze. Embers flew on the air between them. When he finally pulled back, they were both gasping for breath.

"You make me the most blessed man breathing."

Liz knew it was the other way around.

Ryland leaned his forehead against hers. The chilly night around them filled with a sparkling fog from their ragged breaths.

When she finally found the words, she whispered in his ear. "You never gave up on me." Liz touched his cheek. "I'm the blessed one."

Ryland grazed his strong fingers up and down her back. Liz rested her ear over his heart, listening to its song. Her favorite melody. After all they'd been through, she needed to hear it every day.

They stayed still, just holding each other, until a flash of light to their left interrupted them. Arie and Chammu'el moved toward them, smiles on their faces.

Arie patted Ryland on the back. "Congratulations. Again." Arie smiled, and Chammu'el nodded. Then Arie's face slid back into business mode. "I apologize for the timing, but we must move. Markus's demons are wreaking havoc tonight, under orders. They have a new leader."

Ryland's smile faded. "Kade."

Liz never knew one word could be so loaded.

"Yes. I fear he has even more devious and terrible plans than Markus. He has already begun to put them in place."

Ryland sighed, then looked at Liz. "Are you ready?"

Courage soared within her. Determination. His eyes twinkled, and she knew he felt it. Oh, yeah. She was ready. She nodded and squeezed his hand.

"Let's gear up, then." He planted a kiss on her forehead and steered her toward the truck.

Arie walked alongside them for a moment. "Meet at the barn. One-half of your hours." Then he and Chammu'el vanished.

Liz laughed. He was learning.

As they headed toward yet another fight, Liz eyed the man at her side.

Life wouldn't be perfect. Kade was starting a reign of mayhem, and they were in his crosshairs. Both she and Ryland wanted retribution for what Kade had done. Ryland still hadn't fully explained his past with the demon, and Liz had her own secret. Something that would affect the rest of their lives.

For the first time, none of those things sent fear careening through her blood. They had their God, their guardians, family, and each other. It was more than Liz ever imagined she'd get to have. She still didn't feel worthy of it all.

But she would cherish it.

Liz looked across the seat, into the eyes of her future husband, as they prepared to run into battle. Her partner. Her friend. Her fellow warrior. Her everything. Ryland was her home.

And there was no other place she wanted to be.

THE END

Do not miss Liz and Ryland in

Reconciliation

Book Two of the Reluctant Warrior Chronicles.

Coming Soon from L2L2 Publishing.

Author's Note

Dear Readers,

Thank you for taking the time to read The Reluctant Warrior Chronicles. My desire is not only will you be entertained, but you will also find hope and learn to release your fears and scarred past to Him, as the characters in this story are learning. There are some extremely difficult topics dealt with in this series, and I attempt to show the characters' journeys toward the redemption and healing waiting for them through Christ.

One other note. In Ephesians 6, it says our weapons are not against flesh and blood, but spirits, principalities, and powers. I believe that. I also believe these spirits can and do affect the physical world. That being said, this is a work of fiction. I have asked the question, "What if?" What if there were some who were given physical gifts from Heaven, in order to battle against the enemy in this realm? To fight not only spiritual, but flesh and blood battles? I am not attempting to reinterpret Scripture. I am taking creative license in creating a world around a question. I am taking internal and spiritual battles and making them corporeal. My hope is this illustration will provide greater insight into the evil we all face, and the importance of maintaining our faith and our relationship in Christ, so we may fight the good fight.

Thank you,
Amy Brock McNew

Musical Inspiration

Scan the codes on the next page to listen to Amy Brock McNew's chapter playlist or watch *Rebirth's* book trailer. Enjoy!

Chapter 1 "By Your Side" Tenth Avenue North
Chapter 2 "Desperate" Fireflight
Chapter 3 "Make a Move" Incubus
Chapter 4 "Rebirthing" Skillet
Chapter 5 "Like a Machine" Thousand Foot Krutch
Chapter 6 "Welcome to the Freak Show" The Protest
Chapter 7 "Perfect Storm" Alana Lee
Chapter 8 "Chasing Twisters" Delta Rae
Chapter 9 "Blow Me Away" Breaking Benjamin
Chapter 10 "Made of Stone" Evanescence
Chapter 11 "Familiar Taste of Poison" Halestorm
Chapter 12 "Heavy Rain" Main Theme from Heavy Rain Soundtrack
Chapter 13 "Game On" Disciple
Chapter 14 "My Heartstrings Come Undone" Demon Hunter
Chapter 15 "Hold On, Small One" Loftland (DJ Swoon Remix)
Chapter 16 "Lie Awake" Alison Krauss and Union Station
Chapter 17 "Never Alone" Barlow Girl
Chapter 18 "That Changes Everything" 12 Stones
Chapter 19 "Paradise (What About Us?)" Within Temptation, Feat. Tarja

Chapter 20 "Fire and Ice" City of the Fallen
Chapter 21 "Into the Darkness" The Phantoms
Chapter 22 "Darkest Part" Red
Chapter 23 "Farewell" Apocalyptica
Chapter 24 "Distance" Christina Perri, Feat. Jason Mraz
Chapter 25 "Revelations" Assassins Creed Revelations Main Theme
Chapter 26 "Angels" Within Temptation
Chapter 27 "Of These Chains" Red
Chapter 28 "Taking Life" We As Human
Chapter 29 "Arms" Christina Perri
Chapter 30 "Bring It On Home" Little Big Town
Chapter 31 "Freight Train" Sara Jackson-Holman
Chapter 32 "Army of Me" Bjork
Chapter 33 "A Red Sun Rises" City of the Fallen
Chapter 34 "Disaster" In The Verse
Chapter 35 "Lift Up Your Face" Third Day
Chapter 36 "Worlds Collide" 12 Stones
Chapter 37 "The Brave Ones" Shine Bright
Chapter 38 "A Demon's Fate" Within Temptation
Chapter 39 "Mended Souls" Casey Hurt
Chapter 40 "Untraveled Road" Thousand Foot Krutch

Scan the first code to listen to Amy's playlist on YouTube, the second to watch *Rebirth's* book trailer:

Acknowledgements

As I sit down to write this, I find myself overwhelmed. In a few short months, *Rebirth*, my first novel, will be in the hands of readers everywhere. Maybe then it will finally sink in that this is real! For now, I'll try to thank everyone who's had a hand in this book.

First of all, God. Seriously, He must have a great sense of humor to deal with me. For so long, I fought with Him over this story. Much of it is inspired by events in my own life, so putting it out there for all to see is nerve-wracking to say the least. I didn't want to write it. I was ashamed of what I'd done, of choices I'd made, of who I was. But I realized I'm not that person anymore. This is a story of redemption. Of rebirth. This is a story of victory, and someone needs to hear this. To know they're not alone. So, after a lot of huffing and puffing and hissy fits, I sat down and started writing. And something amazing happened. I found healing as I filled those empty pages with words. Things I wasn't even aware I still held on to, I was able to let go. I cried. I laughed. I prayed. Now, my story is in His hands, and hopefully, the hands of those who need it.

Throughout this journey, I've met some awesome people in addition to those tried and true family and friends who stood by my side, pushed me along, and sometimes even dragged me through.

My irreplaceable husband, Brian. You are my rock, my strength, my balance, and my sanity. You've been at my side the entire way; supporting me; helping work out some, shall we say, interesting, scenes; cooking for me and the kids so we didn't have takeout every night. I couldn't ask for a better partner in all of this and life in general. No way would this book exist if not for you. I love you, baby. All my life.

My kids. Y'all are crazy and wonderful and amazing. Y'all are my reason. Your support means everything to me. I love you more than chocolate.

To my baby sister by blood, Amanda, and my big sister by providence, Angie. You two. (I'm shaking my head here.) You saw *Rebirth* when it was an utterly disgusting, warbled mess of a first draft. And you still loved it. You helped me with plot problems and character names. You yelled at me when I needed it. You kicked me in the seat of the pants. One took me to the beach, the other took me for days of pampering. You both answered calls and texts at odd hours with some crazy woman on the other end muttering about something stupid a fictional character did that had her in a tizzy. You are both amazing and there is no way I could make it without you. You two are my lifeline. "There were never such devoted sisters…"

My Aunt Vickie. You're more a second mom than an aunt. You're partly responsible for the insanity that is The Reluctant Warrior Chronicles. After all, you taught me my ABC's. I will never forget that. Also, please come help me conquer that fudge recipe. I have more books to write and I'm gonna need the chocolate.

Lindsay Franklin. What can I say, chica? You taught me so much. You helped mold and rework *Rebirth*, and me, into what we are today. We won a contest and we're published. How cool is that? I never could've done it without you. I hired an editor and found a friend. I'm forever grateful. Oh, and bacon cheeseburgers rule all.

Ah, the insane posse that is Realm Makers. So much awesome in one group. Late night word sprints. Conversations that, if overheard by sane people, would probably get us tossed in the loony bin. Walking into a conference room and all of us proclaiming, "Yea! Second breakfast!" Through freak outs and celebrations, meltdowns and desperate pleas for help, you guys have been there. You've given me help, encouragement, brought me awesome news, cheered me up, and commiserated with me. Josh H., Liberty, Ralene, Ben, Colette, Pam, Brittany, Heather, Avily, Kat, Rosalie, and so many others, you guys rock the most. You are my tribe, and I love y'all.

And Michele, my friend and now publisher. You are as excited about all this as I am! Thank you for loving my story, for believing in it so passionately. Thank you for giving me the means to get it out there. Your friendship and your faith in me and my writing means more than I can say. Unleash the giggles. We did it!

There are simply too many people who have blessed me and helped me along this journey to be able to list them all here. But you know who you are. My circle and my heart are full of some of the most amazing people to ever walk the planet. Thank you. I love you all.

And to my readers, I look forward to meeting you. It's impossible to put into words how much I appreciate the fact that you took the time to read my work. This story is my heart on the page, my guts on the page, and I wrote it for you. Whoever you are, wherever you are, know that you are not alone. There is someone who has been through the battle you're facing. They fought, just like you're fighting now, and they conquered. No matter how dark it gets, there is always light. There is always a way out of whatever pit you find yourself in. All you have to do is reach out. There is Someone waiting for you, reaching for you, from the other side.

About the Author

Meet **Amy Brock McNew**. Author. Fighter. Musician. Former nurse and martial artist. This wife and mom is a lover of music, chocolate, the beach, and cherry vanilla Coke. Her home is a zoo, filled with teenagers—both hers and those she seems to collect—and animals of all kinds. Strangely enough, her kids are the ones who have to tell her to turn the music down.

Amy and her Taekwondo-instructor husband are constantly acting like overgrown kids—and loving every minute of it. She longs for the day when her husband retires so she can write her adventures of love and war on a back porch overlooking the ocean. In flip flops.

Visit **AmyBrockMcNew.com** to learn more about her.

Reviews

Did you like this book? Authors treasure reviews! (And read them over and over and over...) If you enjoyed this book, would you consider leaving a review on Amazon, Barnes & Noble, Goodreads, or perhaps even your personal blog? Thank you so much!

More from L2L2 Publishing

If you enjoyed Rebirth, you may also enjoy:

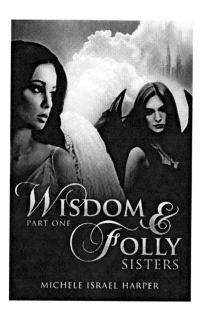

Wisdom. She may have crafted the worlds by the Maker's design, she may have been by His side since the beginning, but her heart aches. Her sister is gone. Defected, to a group of rebels who loathe their Creator with every fiber in their beings, who plot His downfall. Her new assignment? Fight them. Defeat them. But how can she fight her sister, when all she wants to do is bring her home? Folly. Fury seethes within her. Jealous of the attention the Maker lavished on her sister, she turned to a new master and became his favorite. Or so she thought. Determined to prove herself, to become invaluable, she realizes destroying her sister just may be the key to Lucifer's heart. Her plan? Engage Wisdom. Distract her, defeat her. If only there wasn't the minor detail she wasn't counting on. Missing her sister.

More from L2L2 Publishing

If you enjoyed Rebirth, you may also enjoy:

Wisdom. She is furious. Her sister has destroyed countless of the Maker's creatures and shows no sign of remorse. Or of stopping. She knows Folly's end is near and cannot wait to staunch her sister's wrath. Forever. Now if only her heart believed her. Folly. Her hatred wanes with each passing day. What's the point? Her defeat has been promised, and its surety strengthens with each step of time's cruel march. Can nothing change her path? Why did she leave heaven's bliss for such a cruel taskmaster? But Wisdom has orders to thwart her sister. Folly's orders are the same. And both are determined to win.

More from L2L2 Publishing

If you enjoyed Rebirth, you may also enjoy:

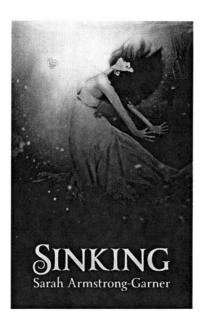

Jocelyn washes up on the shore of eighteenth century Ireland, alone, naked, and missing all of her memories. Taken in by a lonely old woman full of plots and schemes for the lovely yet enigmatic creature, Jocelyn knows only one thing. She longs for the sea with every ounce of her being. Yet it tried to kill her. Aidan Boyd loves two things. His ship and the sea. When Jocelyn is thrust upon his vessel in the midst of his superstitious crew, he finds himself intoxicated by her—willing to give up everything for her. He soon finds he cannot live without her. But something holds Jocelyn back. The whisper of another's love. The embrace of water. Does she belong to this world? Or could Jocelyn possibly be from the sea?

More from L2L2 Publishing

If you enjoyed Rebirth, you may also enjoy:

Candace Marshall hates zombies. As in, loathes, abhors, detests—you get the idea. She also refuses to watch horror movies. You can imagine her complete and utter joy when her boyfriend surprises her with advanced screening tickets to the latest gruesome zombie flick. Annoyance flares into horror as the movie comes to life, and Candace finds herself surrounded by real-life, honest-to-goodness zombies. She learns how to shoot and scream with the best of them and surprises herself with—courage? But, just when Candace thinks it can't get worse than zombies, it does. Don't miss this lighthearted adventure, Book One of the Candace Marshall Chronicles.

CPSIA information can be obtained
at www.ICGtesting.com
Printed in the USA
FFOW02n0134260517
36001FF